EDWIN BLACK

format c:

Brookline Books

Library of Congress Cataloging-in-Publication Data
Black, Edwin.
Format C / Edwin Black.
p.   cm.
ISBN 1-57129-078-8
PS3552.L323F67   1999
813' .54--dc21   99-19611
CIP

1 3 5 7 9 10 8 6 4 2

Published by BROOKLINE BOOKS
P.O. Box 1047
Cambridge, Massachusetts 02238

Printed in the United States of America
Set in Baskerville
Designed by Elizabeth Black

ACKNOWLEDGMENTS

Humble thanks is given to my learned *hevre,* Ariel L. Szczupak and Bradley Kliewer–two of the best minds occupying that sizzling triangle between man's consciousness, God's message and cyberspace. Eternal gratefulness is expressed to powerful compatriots Malcolm Brown, Pat Connolly, Bill Davis, Alice Lucan, David Pordy, Lynne Rabinoff, Lori Stuart and Jane Wesman, who have reached across space to touch, to share, and to endow. Visionary courage is recognized in Milt Budoff, who saw the horizon and fearlessly sped with excitement to the other side. Special insight is acknowledged in Eddie Benaim, Margaret Dutcher, John Kalter, Barbara Opall, and many others who waved, smiled and helped as I raced by. Blessings are recited for the energized companionship of awesome composers and musicians John Barry, The Gipsy Kings, Jerry Goldsmith, Ofra Haza, James Horner, Tangerine Dream, John Williams and most especially Hans Zimmer–all of whom came to the rescue when the day was dark and the sheet was white; oh, I hear them now. Salutes are offered to Susan Anastasi and Mark LaFlaur for their insight and excellence. Embraces are proffered to my manuscript readers all over the world who helped me understand their fears and joys, and how shocking the journey would be.

Unrepayable debt is confessed to Miriam Bass and my mentor Edward T. Chase, who each extended their hand and held high the candle.

A promise is partially kept to my parents, Harry and Ethel Black, whom you shall meet as Moishe and Rivke. An explanation is conveyed to my sister Leikhah, who has now discovered much of what she already knew. And pride is felt because the third writer in the family, my teenage daughter Rachel, has learned that an author's duty is to endure and share.

A word will have to be invented to describe the appreciation I have for my wife, Elizabeth, a brilliant writer, who labored, edited, and inspired every minute of every hour during this perilous journey. An earth without air, an ocean without water, a life without soul, just as barren would be my existence without her.

CONTENTS

PART ONE

THE OS WAR

1

DAN LEVIN

Thin and young, maybe twenty, he looked as if he was ready to play a soccer match. He lifted his cap a bit, exposing straw blond hair, joked with his friends, and even shoved one playfully.

Suddenly, almost routinely, he pulled down on the brim, and savagely screamed, *"Schnell! Schnell!"* Eighteen naked and bony Jews ran from the long staging line just over the muddy ridge. There they stood, at the slimed, fecal-filled edge of the pit, holding pained knuckles over their genitals in a pathetic attempt at modesty. With all the bravado of a dart thrower at a *biergarten,* the young German flipped his thumb against the safety at the left rear of the Luger, and then pressed the barrel deep into the temple of the closest Jew. His friend at the opposite end of the group did likewise.

The piteous faces of the victims told all. Obediently waiting to be executed, these eighteen, and endless eighteens just like them, were no longer men with lives to lead. Each of them had simply given up and now walked willingly to the ultimate slaughter of the Holocaust, the open-air killing pit, which in a universe of unspeakable, humiliating deaths was the saddest. At the pit, operated by specially-commissioned *Einsatzgruppen* commandos, there was no ruse, no fraudulent shower head, no crowded room of helpless gasping victims unable to escape, no pretense of official execution recorded with sadistic if exacting documentation. Here, there was just a long line of passive men who had abandoned all possibility of resistance, stepping as instructed to the brink—not now . . . yes now . . . not now . . . yes now . . . waiting for a bullet to slump them vanquished into the lye-seasoned ditch.

Fer vas nicht? In a moment, they would leave the sad, bloodied earth to become powerful memories that would live on eternally, cry forth for revenge and inspire generations. No Nazi could shoot that away.

The young German raised his eyebrows as a signal. Two unison gunshots. Seventeen men fell lifelessly into the pit, each brain pierced by the force of a single determined bullet fired from either end. As the shoveling *Sonderkommandos* frantically scooped soft earth over their bleeding brethren, they looked up and saw one man in the middle still standing, still waiting for a projectile to decide everything forever. Weeping uncontrollably, one hand still covering his genitals, one hand draped over his eyes, bitter herbs in his tears, this last of the eighteen shook like a candle about to flicker out and wondered. When?

Disappointed and inconvenienced, the two soldiers swaggered toward the quivering Jew. "My name is Chaim," he murmured with the determination to die whispering his name in the ears of his executioners. "Chaim, my name is Chaim." No one heard him. Instead, the two youthful Nazis demonstratively argued about which one would devote an extra bullet to the man's brain. Finally, they laughed and agreed. Both placed their guns on either side of Chaim's head, recoiled their faces from the expected splatter, pressed in on the trigger and then . . .

Dan draped his hands over his sweating face, screamed silently, squeezed tears from his eyes, reached for the TV remote and clicked off the History Channel.

Hyperventilating in the silence, Dan finally opened his eyes, focused and recomposed himself. After a moment, he shook it all off, wiped his eyes and sniffling nose, calmly picked up the shot glass he wanted to throw at the television, combed his fingers through short gray hair above a closely cropped salt and pepper beard and mustache, and then acted as though nothing had happened. Nothing ever happened whenever this happened. But it never stopped happening.

He looked at the 20-inch flat screen LCD monitor through still moist eyes and spoke a command: "DSL Connect Web." Then, "Nas." Nasdaq.com loaded. Dan looked at the increase, 19.3 points up.

He spoke again: "DJ." Dow Jones loaded: up 44.9 points.

Though still weakened, he continued the voice commands: "Quicken silent password." A portfolio downloaded onto the screen. It read: "Daniel Levin, Chicago IL, Consolidated Portfolio." A dozen graphs representing Nasdaq, New York Stock Exchange, AMEX, bonds, treasury notes, money market accounts, overseas investment funds, and commodity holdings layered into sharpness.

"Accounts." One by one, they appeared: investment, savings, checking, IRA, money market, and bond accounts, each with an icon representing the financial institution. At the bottom of the screen, a tally zipped in from the left:

"$2,456,760 YTD Gain . . . Annualized 23%."

He looked away unimpressed.

Dan picked past bottles of Glenkinchie, Talisker, Lagavulin, Dalwhinnie, Timnavulin, and Laphroaig, grabbing instead for the tall, mysterious, gold-embossed black bottle of 18-year Glenfiddich, a rare single blend sold nowhere in America, purchased from an out-of-the-way scotch connoisseur shop tucked into a quaint Covent Garden alley, a bottle he would have never considered owning because, as a scotch snob, Glenfiddich was too commercial. But this bottle was something different, and now among his favorites, not for daily tastes before bed but for those special moments when he needed to chase away the salty aftertaste of tears and sweat. He poured a short shot and touched the vaporous surface to his lips and tongue, just enough to enthrall his nostrils with transferred memories of the peaty, fog-filled glens that yielded the "waters of life" sacred to scotch devotees, and just enough to confirm that one's relationship with scotch is so intensely personal and idiosyncratic, it can never be understood by a nonbeliever.

Flopping into his chair, Dan grabbed for his remote and pressed number 5 on his CD player. The platter began rotating: first, Leonard Bernstein's *Jeremiah Symphony,* then the film score to *Last of the Mohicans,* then Phillip Glass' *Canyon,* then *Le Parc* by Tangerine Dream. Finally, the fifth disc, Hans Zimmer's *Black Rain,* slid beneath the laser. He pressed the skip button ahead to the "Black Rain Suite," the hot, defining movie composition in Zimmer's career.

The console phone's ringing couldn't be heard over the soundtrack's loud syncopations, but Dan saw the light blink on line 4. The private line.

He paused the CD, but the music continued in his head.

It was her.

"What are you doing?" he asked in a flat voice. "Sure. I'm right near Northwestern . . . A ride home? Sure . . . Okay, pick you up in fifteen, twenty minutes . . . I'm doing nothing . . . Fifteen, twenty minutes."

Dan put down the scotch. He almost never drank more than a tablespoon at a time. So he wasted more shots than he drank. But it didn't matter. Just a taste was fine.

Still wearing his Bill Blass wing collar tuxedo shirt, unbuttoned at the top, and plain black slacks, Dan flew down the living room steps, exited from the rear patio, and pulled open the doors of his red Honda Del Sol parked behind the townhouse. The day's rain had temporarily taken a breath. When Chicago's sky was clear and blue, it was irresistible.

He pressed down both latches on the chest-high detachable Del Sol roof. Swinging the finely balanced lightweight canopy almost straight up, he looked with satisfaction at his black-interiored convertible, the one sculpted so arrogantly for style that Honda's designers wouldn't even build in a proper coffee holder. The crappy coffeeholder bothered Dan. But it didn't matter. The rest of the design was fine. He lugged the upright roof to its under-trunk rack, slid it into place and latched. The roof stowed and stable, Dan slammed the trunk lid down, then the passenger door, and then dropped butt-first and ergonomically correct into the low-slung, hi-backed driver's seat. To the left, a commuter train roared past on the raised tracks that formed a dead-end to the alleyway. Once it passed, he turned the key to hear the Del Sol's engine purr on, reached under the seat and affixed the CD player's detachable control panel face. The Gipsy Kings. Blasted.

Within minutes, Dan turned onto a quiet street in Evanston. She was waiting, and smiled as he approached. "Downtown okay?" he asked, as she climbed in. She nodded yes.

Speeding south down Lake Shore Drive toward the Loop in a low-to-the-ground red convertible with the music loud on a sunny but not too hot summer day, in the dangerous outside lane, two Altoids melting under your tongue, with rushing air rewarding your face, and the woman in the passenger seat squinting into the wind with a smile she hopes you can't see, and a furl of blond hair streaking behind her like soft flames from a flying torch, this is good.

Politically patched potholes, asphalt buckles, gentle hills, and shoreline curves make "the Drive" a Chicago experience. On the right, Dan saw towering lakeshore high-rises planted behind lush, lagooned Lincoln Park, Chicago's self-deceptive effort to paint this length of design and dignity as its authentic face, regardless of the gritty world just behind it. To the left sprawled Lake Michigan, the only thing Chicagoans call a natural wonder. And wondrous it was in a city where the stockyards and five-foot snowdrifts at every intersection constituted a collective memory for all who lived here even if they had never seen a steer or a blizzard, where once upon a time outdoor cafes, private swimming pools, inflatable balls at the beach, and anything else that suggested five minutes of frivolity was either illegal or unnecessary.

The Lake belonged to everyone. It was "the beach," an enjoyment *allowed* by Chicago's blue-collar culture. Sure, it was crowded like the subway at rush hour, but once prone on its sand, you had no clock to punch, no red light to beat. Here your only duty was to maintain the slim cut of paradise demarcated by your beach towel. A beach *towel,* mind you, not a blanket. Blankets violated beach etiquette as an act of greediness. Everyone in Chicago knew that.

You couldn't help but belong at the beach because like the schools and the neighborhoods, the polling stations and the cemeteries, Lake Michigan's beaches were stratified and segregated: the well-off white kids at Sheridan Beach and above, the Hispanics at Foster Avenue, the poor white trash from Uptown at Wilson Avenue, the greasers at North Avenue, and at Oak Street the cool people—that is, the rich, skinny ones with fragrant tanning oil and fashionable bikinis. Blacks, of course, were stuck far to the south at Rainbow Beach.

In a city of limitations, where you couldn't drive from north to south without going through downtown, where the Cubs couldn't win, and Republicans couldn't run, the Lake was a mirage without limits, an intriguing canvas where sailboats were always painted in by day, and magical lights floated by like stars at night.

So in that moment, in a south-speeding Del Sol, what could be more uplifting than hurtling confidently between the magnificent Lake on the left and the elegant lakefront on the right? It didn't matter that you came from poor, it didn't matter that one day you didn't have five pennies to get into the State Theater, it didn't matter that you didn't have a friend or you couldn't afford the toys they did, it didn't matter that you had a job or didn't, that you were a Pole who still couldn't speak English, a recent Jewish immigrant who spoke with an accent, a Chicano who tried not to speak in public, an Irishman poor but powerful, a black man poor and powerless, or a WASP who tried to never see any of those people. It didn't matter that you drove a Caddy you couldn't afford, a rusted orange Datsun no one wanted, or a station wagon with a worn-out floorboard, nor did it matter if your radio blared Solti, Cash, the Stones, or Aretha. None of it mattered because anyone, meek or powerful, rich or poor, dark or white, could drive down Lake Shore Drive and be thrilled. It was Chicago-style democracy, paved with potholes.

Dan meandered his car to Lower Wacker Drive, the downtown street below the street, beyond the train tracks, near the Chicago River's edge, to a dark upramp on the left.

"Don't," said Park, as a child's expression came over Dan's face.

"Not again. Don't . . ." she warned, this time more sternly.

His car purred in neutral at the base of the narrow, curving, one-way down ramp used exclusively by *Chicago Sun-Times* delivery trucks above at the Wabash Street loading dock. The trucks sped down the ramp several times daily to cut past traffic and quickly access the expressways. Dan's habit was to race up the steep ramp, hoping not to slam head-on into a truck on its way down. Originally, Dan used the ramp as a reporter's shortcut to dash through downtown traffic. Eventually, it became just a stunt to impress friends, or himself if no friends were present. It was his equivalent of chicken. He first did it for Park only yesterday, the day they met. Her mouth had dropped open as he missed by only a moment a caravan of trucks heading down.

Park wanted nothing to do with it a second time. "Let me out, before!"

No way. He floored the Del Sol up past the warning signs, past the concave mirror, into the unlighted blind curve, beyond the point of any safety. Dan was totally relaxed, but Park, her face tensed, expected the worst. Meanwhile, the Gipsy Kings. Blasted.

Just near the top and out of sight, a *Sun-Times* driver waved to his buddy. "I'm late on the edition," he shouted, as he edged forward on the accelerator and his van lurched. The Del Sol climbed the drastic incline faster and faster and at the top virtually launched onto the driveway just inches from the approaching truck. The driver screeched on his brakes, swearing in Lithuanian, as stacks of string-bound newspapers toppled throughout the truck.

Dan broke into a grin of bravado and pulled out onto Wabash where he stopped casually for a light.

Park jumped from the car. "Oh! Oh!" she sputtered. "You are nuts! Twice in two days. Get away from me. What are you doing tomorrow, jumping a bridge over the Chicago River?" She walked off, with Dan in pursuit. To his entreaties and apologies, she just kept muttering, "Thanks, but no thanks."

Finally, while waiting for a green light at a crosswalk, he convinced her to reconsider. As though salvaging good music on an album suffering from noisome scratches, she set the terms. "No more up the down ramp," Park chided. "You can drive *down* the down ramp . . . *up* the up ramp . . . or no ramp at all. Anytime you want to risk your own life, fine. But if I get back in that car, do not challenge any ramp. Agreed?"

"Agreed," Dan quietly declared with a puppy dog face.

Park lost her anger and laughed.

"Come on," he urged. "I can use the company. Let's just talk. We don't have to drive anywhere." Park saw the side of Dan she liked and climbed back into the car.

Minutes later, the two were inches close, eyes in sync, parked on North State Street. They said very little with their lips but entire conversations were softly murmured with their eyes. He came closer, spoke inaudibly in her ear and kissed her in an inviting place just beyond her cheekbone.

They had met only yesterday. Dan was standing on the corner right in front of his favorite high-rise, Lake Point Towers, contemplating how its parabolic face fulfilled the "form follows function" mandates of the Chicago School of architecture. Park walked up and asked for directions to the building, not knowing she was actually standing in front of it. Blond, not quite thin, her arms were muscular but still feminine. Her hands knew work and weather, and her face offered a palette of both innocence and complication. Immediately, Dan could see past her attractiveness and discerned a hidden history of personal struggle, one in which she had not yet emerged the victor. Struggle in a woman attracted Dan. He had struggled all his life. He felt at home with someone else who had.

Instead of guiding her to the building's obscure entrance just a few feet around the corner, which would have been too easy, he asked a few questions. Decades of experience as an investigative reporter had enabled him to surgically extract more information in moments than anyone wanted to surrender in days. He quickly learned that Park McGuire was at Lake Point Tower to rent a friend's apartment while in Chicago.

Park never made it into the building. Dan responded to her openness. An impulsive cup of coffee at the nearby Starbucks segued into a long, enchanted day, as Dan unsuccessfully tried to steer Park to Rogers Park, where the rent would be cheaper for her, and the location nearer to him.

They began exploring the private Chicago Dan had learned to call his own during years as a journalist in the seventies and eighties, a Chicago now almost overrun with nineties changes. They walked along Olive Park, watched the sun find its way through the magnificent skyline, and viewed surrealist masterpieces at the Art Institute, accompanied by Dan's pedantic explanations. "Salvador Dali's repeated use of one woman's image is no reference to the Madonna. It's his insane fascination with his beautiful lover. Except this one over here . . ."

For lunch, they feasted on a Flukey's hotdog overflowing with bright green piccalilli and short, medium-hot peppers, then thumbed through the soundtrack section at the store that used to be Rose Records, and finally took a long narrated walk that began at the top of Michigan Avenue, wound through the romantic courts and plazas straddling the Chicago River, down the broad steps toward Grant Park, and ended at Buckingham Fountain where they shared a small banana Dan unexpectedly produced from his inside jacket pocket as Park giggled and marveled all at once.

They talked–that is, *Dan talked,* about the journalism business, movie music, the Middle East, Chicago architecture, movie music, the vicissitudes of being a foreign correspondent in Jerusalem, movie music, and everything else Dan wanted to talk about. They talked for hours. Eventually, Park even slipped a few words in about herself, a Kansas girl who developed a knack for computers back when computers were the sole province of boys. It was the only way she could compete as the sole daughter in a family with five sons.

By the time the sun began setting, Dan pulled into the parking lot of the lakeside airport, Meigs Field. Moments later, they sneaked into the pilot's lounge. Floor-to-ceiling windows facing north from this vantage point jutting into the lake, framing the gray, green, and bronze steelglass skyline, made this quite possibly the most romantic dusk in the city, a place where Dan now opened a bag he had hastily assembled at the Oak Street Market while Park waited and wondered in the Del Sol. Out came a plastic checkered tablecloth. Then two tall candles he lit and anchored into some melting wax dripped onto the tablecloth. A small round of Brie, a long baguette, some grapes, clear plastic knives and forks, two cheap plastic cups, and then the bottle of Dom.

Park had never tasted Dom Pérignon in a glass, only sampled the legend in movies. Her eyes widened. They were the eyes of a woman who has seen dust storms and floods, boys who couldn't see past the next farmer's pasture and agribusinessmen who wouldn't take their sights off your acres until they owned them. In those eyes that wanted to say *yes* were memories of Sunday and Wednesday doings in the church rec room, a Bible on every surface in the house and more copies on the shelves and in the closet–sixty-two in all during one count–and the spunk to play hooky from school with a friend one day, jump on a bus to Wichita for an unforgettable first big-city adventure only to know fear and shame when she discovered there was no bus back and her father had to drive four hours in the pickup to fetch her. She had seen a lot, and none of it left the blue depths of her eyes. Yet none of it showed on her face, which was somehow strong and soft, a child still in a woman's body.

That was yesterday.

By now, they had become a pair. Just two people comfortable with each other sitting in a red Del Sol, unaware of the world beyond the parking space. Dan leaned over the Del Sol's black knobbed shift and kissed her a second time beyond the cheek. A passing taxi driver turned his head to enjoy the moment. So did a kid whizzing by on a skateboard. But Dan and Park noticed no one.

"Who are you?" she asked whimsically.

He answered, "You mean who *was* I?"

"All right. Who was you?"

"I used to be me."

Park didn't understand, and reposited: "Well then, who are you *now*?"

"The guy who became me after I was me."

"Right," said Park, quickly becoming impatient. "This is the little boy part where I'm supposed to pull it out of you, am I correct? I thought you were a magazine writer. What's the mystery?"

"Yes, that's what I said, but actually I did a little more than just write articles. I became a publisher and had a few magazines. It was a very lucrative mistake, but I did it. And now I'm out of it."

"How many magazines is a few?"

"Seven," he said almost with embarrassment.

"Seven? Like what?"

"It's really not important, and I prefer not talking about it," Dan answered, but then added without prompting, "I mean, there were some great ones like *Chicago Monthly,* that won a bunch of awards for investigative journalism and made a few headlines here and there back when I was younger. And some you never heard of that didn't make headlines. But they made money."

"Like?"

"Like who cares," he replied evasively, but then again provided the details. "Like *Brain Journal* for neurologists. Like an airport magazine called *Wingtip.* Heard of it, you know, in those elite little airports?"

"No."

"Well . . . so who cares?" he came back, again with a hardened air. "I published 'em and did it. How about *Highstyle,* a sorta healthy lifestyle magazine for women 24 to 35, with a quasi-GenX attitude that I couldn't care less about. Maybe you heard of that one?"

That one she knew. "You published *Highstyle?* I used to read that magazine. Health tips. Good recipes . . . Never subscribed." He shrugged. "Bought it on the newsstand, though. So what happened?"

"I sold them all," said Dan, "to a megabillion multinational mean-ass media conglomerate. Australian."

She looked with slight disbelief. "I get it. So you're rich?"

"Possibly it could be construed that way to a certain extent, but it doesn't matter because that isn't the issue," he stammered self-consciously.

"It *'isn't the issue,'*" she came back, "because . . . because you have money so you can afford to not care if you have it. Is that what you mean to say?" She smiled to put him at ease. "Okay. But I'm just a person working to make ends meet. Starting a new job Thursday. And so is Sal."

"Who is Sal?" he asked.

"See, you don't know me," she replied coyly. "Sal is my son. He's a computer genius. I've been programming for years, but this guy–"

"You have a son? You didn't tell me you had a son."

"Hey, yesterday I couldn't tell you much of anything," she joked. "We spent the whole day listening to you talk 'form follows function' and movie music. I now know more than I ever thought I could about John Barry and Hans Zimmer. Anyway, yeah. Sal starts as a junior programmer too at the same place."

"What's it called again, Drake?" asked Dan, slouching in his car seat.

"Derek. Derek Institute," she answered, swiveling to face him. "They're all into Y2K solutions—"

"Uh, yeah, Millennium Bug stuff . . ." Dan's attention had drifted. Now he was barely interested in what she was saying as much as her animation in saying it.

Until this moment Park had seemed shy, almost reticent. Most of her comments were expressed with eyes that spoke simultaneously of a fear-desire to explore yet another human relationship no matter how badly she had chosen in the past, even though a brute locked the door on her one night and demanded everything until she escaped crying into the night while he was prone with his pants down in the bathroom and she waved down a taxi just as he appeared at the door angry and obscene, and even though her pastor shocked her that Sunday and she then had to face him in silence week after week. And even though she was unprepared as a child for all she had encountered when she was almost a woman. Clearly she wanted love as one wants oxygen. Raised in her sheltered, God-fearing world, Park was unready to breathe in the world beyond the farm. When she tried, the gasps were painful. Every woman carries every heartbreak forever. They briefly reappear at the ceiling each time they meet another man, and the shadow dissipates but oh so slowly. Like a singed candle, ready to be relit, Park offered a gentle quality of caution and willingness that triggered something deep in Dan that had been locked away since New Year's when the worst nightmare came, a nightmare that gripped him still.

He returned to the conversation. ". . . All the computers will crash at the turn of the century."

". . . Right," she continued past his trivial interruption, "and since I had that expertise for a while in Seattle, I was able to get the job. Derek," she continued, "is ramping up for the big push to beat the Year 2000 deadline. One day when the recruiter called, she asked if I knew anyone else in Seattle who could join the team. I just jokingly suggested Sal, and he got on the phone, and within fifteen minutes he was talking to the big cheese–this Dr. Kuebitz. So he's been hired as an intern for the summer. With me. Believe that? Just out of high school. Derek is desperate. Originally, it was a principal Bluestar subcontractor on . . . well, on a project I can't tell you about really."

"Can't tell you" were the most stimulating words in Dan's world. "Of course, you can tell me," he told her. "Who am I not to tell? What's the project?"

Park looked like a woman with a secret she didn't want to keep. "I can't tell," she said with ambivalence. "The whole thing is hush-hush until tomorrow's announcement in Baltimore. Can you wait just a day?"

They exchanged that glance that confirmed to both that if Dan pressed, Park would have yielded the information, but she preferred not to, and therefore wished that Dan would not press. Since it was so clear he could have pressed for the information, Dan folded back his pursuit.

"Oh, I can wait. No big deal," he grinned. "But tomorrow."

"Not tomorrow," she answered, "the day after tomorrow. Wait till then. I'll tell you everything. Promise."

He nodded and they drove off into the rush hour.

2

ZOOM

00:00
00:00
00:00
00:00

*S*izzling red bulbs overhead noisily blinked 00:00 as the waiting crowd giggled and cracked jokes outside the National Aquarium in Baltimore. "Great omen," laughed a chubby man as he gulped a soda.

"It's just a clock that can't tell time," a friend next to him in line deadpanned back. "Like this industry."

A lanky man carrying his jacket over his tote bag didn't see the humor. "Make jokes now," he warned. "I predict: no matter what they say in there, it's gonna end up like that," he said, pointing with his thumb at the clock. "Zero is what our world is coming to. Did you ever think, maybe we're screwed, maybe we just can't fix it?"

00:00 continued blinking above.

This event was billed as "rollout," one of those evangelistic pep rallies the computer industry was famous for. Plenty of music, entertainment, and dazzle for the disk *du jour.* But this rollout was different.

Bluestar had in fact assembled more than eleven hundred retail players and point men as the biggest crisis response team in the industry's history. The prized attendees were several dozen buyers and marketing directors from every major computer and software retailer in the world: Silicon Expressway, CompUSA, Computer City, Radio Shack, Babbages, HyperMedia, EuroDisk, Automatique, Electro Warehouse, MicroSeller, Midnight Surfer, Instant Software, Cheaper Software, and even some of the smaller resellers such as Flee Market and BizDisk–they were all there. This time, the invitation included not just the chain stores, but the catalog houses and the Internet. And not just those based in America, but overseas as well.

More than just the senior decisionmakers, Bluestar wanted to marshal the ranks–regional bosses, key store managers, advertising and promotion execs, even lead salesmen in pivotal high-volume stores, and supervising telephone operators from the 800 lines.

The assembled representatives all thought of themselves as computer-savvy power users, technically adept, and versed in the latest acronyms. In truth, most in the crowd, especially from the larger resellers, comprehended only the most superficial aspects of computer technology. They understood as much about software as car salesmen understood about automotive technology–just enough to sell this week's product to this week's customers. So Bluestar would be careful not to overwhelm the audience with techno-babble that would dilute the support it needed to rally. It was not important that this crowd understand the inner workings of the crisis, just the existence of one.

The outside doors finally opened. Noisy, sweaty, the herd of retailers moved up the canopied exterior escalators into the Aquarium entrance. From there, they were guided past the illuminated glass towers of undulating jellyfish, beyond a pool of stingrays, up a long spiral ramp and through the red metal doors of the natatorium, a great hall, half-encased in a glass dome. Below, a mirrorlike pool, spanned by a narrow bridge, created a waterborne stage. Microminiskirted women, all redheads, all wearing black vests emblazoned with a Z, kept repeating, "Fill the front rows first. Fill the front rows first." When all eleven hundred seats were taken, the red doors closed and the last few hurriedly found an aisle step.

Faint angelic soprano voices piped overhead signaled the show's beginning. Massive mechanized shades began pulling across the glass dome. Row by row, the hall became dark until only the stage pool's faint underwater lights remained. Then even those were turned off. Now only red exit lights in the corners broke the darkness.

Suddenly, a low thudding staccato bass guitar pumped from the rear. People's heads turned. A loud, piercing choir of voices brought the audience's focus back to the front. Tense rhythms from the side, back, then the sides again, kept the crowd guessing.

Thin but powerful towers of dense light shot up from the pool. The music crescendoed and then cut completely. "Ladies and gentlemen," the ceiling speaker declared, "the National Aquarium is proud to introduce . . . Johhhhhn Hector!"

Spotlights crisscrossed over a point stage right and the music boomed again as a potbellied man emerged wearing an orange golf shirt embroidered with a Z. The audience cheered, many stood and hooted with enthusiasm. He walked across the bridge spanning the center of the pool, and waited for the excitement to subside.

"Hello everybody, I'm John Hector."

More applause.

"Thank you, thank you," he said over the cheers, "for coming to this luscious stage, the beautiful Baltimore Aquarium. Of course, no one needs an excuse to come to beautiful Baltimore. However, this is an especially momentous occasion, a day we have been working for this past half decade. Now, I would ask that you settle in and sit back, so we can get right to the point.

"You and I both know that the world is facing the potential for disaster in about eighteen months when the clocks tick in the next century. Call it the Millennium Bug, call it Y2K Compliance, call it the Century Glitch. When the year 2000 comes, nearly every mainframe computer in the world—and many smaller ones—will cease functioning. The world as we know it will stop right along with it. And your companies—and your customers—will surely be in the thick of it.

"Already, people with Visas and MasterCards expiring in the year 2000 can't use them; '00' simply doesn't exist in the authorizing mainframes. Our own convention department can't get a hotel in Las Vegas to book COMDEX reservations in the year 2000 because the reservation systems can't find the year. But when the big moment comes at midnight the morning of January 1, year 2000, our woes will be more than cash only for your cappuccino and a lost suite at the Hilton. It will be a global disaster as destructive as any war."

Not a few of the leading buyers in the front row fidgeted. The woman from Electro Warehouse called out, "Is that a little extreme?"

"We've done the studies," Hector replied. "Our banks will crash. Accounts will disappear off the books. Checks will not clear, especially those involving foreign transactions. Most Asian, African, and Latin American banks haven't even started to repair their systems—now it's too late. Office buildings, now totally operated by central computer systems, will shut down completely, trapping everyone either in or out; every service will malfunction—from HVAC to elevators. Hospitals will become killing centers as computer-driven intensive care units and the rest of modern medical technology simply stops or goes out of control. We don't know if the prison doors will remain shut forever or swing wide open. Certainly, electrical grids will blink off and municipal water districts will stop pumping, throwing our cities into darkness and thirst. Air traffic control will freeze—don't believe otherwise. Many airplanes could actually stop flying—I wouldn't want to be midair when the on-board computers go black. It's not just the ordinary looking computers with screens and keyboards, but the small, unseen, embedded computerized components, especially the older ones. For example, not a few new cars dependent upon tiny microchips will be unable to start. Phones will go off because 90 percent of the local switches are still using technology from the early nineties, some the late eighties. Backups will not work—you can forget those. The Internet will crash. And everything computerized in the government from the post office to military management will crash with it."

The crowd grew stonefaced as Hector continued in a grim tone, "I'm afraid no one even knows whether our nuclear missiles can be controlled. In one DOD study, which Bluestar's FedTech division coordinated, we found that when the clocks aboard Trident submarines—I'm talking the biggest submarines in our fleet—tick in the year 2000 and are unable to locate the correct date, every missile on board may just launch. Try as we might, no one can predict whether the missile targets will be here in America or default to someplace else. No one knows. Nor do we know what the missiles in other countries will do. Hello? Russia? China? Iraq? They all have missiles and nothing even approaching the Y2K rescue program we have in America. Heavens, we don't even know if our own radar systems will be able to see enemy missiles . . . or if they will see missiles that don't even exist. Just don't know. Just don't know, my friends.

"Oh, yes," he went on, " I see the expressions on your faces. Some of you are skeptical and more are probably pretty frightened. I have to tell you, a lot of people have been in techno-denial for some time on this," he paused to allow his words to sink in, "just assuming the cavalry will come riding in with a fix. But if we *can't* make it right, if we *can't* . . . God help us. First our world will stop. Then we will probably blow it up. Doomsday, my friends, now dwells in a disk drive."

A sales manager from BizDisk stood up and yelled with disbelief, "What happened to Miami?"

"The Miami Project didn't work," Hector shot back, "and we all know why. The government thought every program running on every network could be made Y2K-compliant with a big hairy bug fix. A bug fix! But all the projections have concluded that the President's Miami Project is a total failure and I was informed–actually just two hours ago–that within a week Miami is expected to permanently disband on orders from the White House. A waste of money–and worse, a waste of time we didn't have.

"But we at Bluestar were not sleeping." Moving into the hype mode needed to sell this group, Hector insisted, "We at Bluestar *have* a solution, the solution you and your customers have been waiting for. Bluestar, still the giant among all computer names, Bluestar has the resources to answer this challenge first and answer it best. We hold more computer-related patents than any other software manufacturer anywhere. We work with more ISVs, more OEMs, and more VARs and integrators than any other computer company on the planet.

"Every IT and IS manager on the job knows his company's mission critical tasks reliably belong to Bluestar today, and we hope that will continue in the future. You of all people understand that we know how to stuff the channels, gain market entry, and quickly achieve 'best of breed' status while the other guys–and we know who they are–are still issuing press releases about unavoidable delays. They slip. We ship. That's why we're going GA in Q3 with the technology the world needs not only to stay productive, but literally to continue existing."

The crowd reacted, and he shouted to be heard. "That's right. Not next year. But *generally available* with a permanent solution by October of *this* year."

"Miami, ladies and gentlemen, didn't work. But Zooooooom will!"

Hector outstretched his arms holding a shiny glistening Zoom CD for all to see. Twin white velour banners unfurled on cue from the ceiling. The unrolling banners displayed a descending column of stacked Bluestar logos until the larger payoff logo at the bottom appeared: "ZOOM" in massive burnt orange Friz Quadrata letters. "Zoom," roared Hector as a blast of music from an offstage network MIDI console jolted the throng.

Hector stretched out his arms again, and now the pool waters parted as a giant submerged gold-colored inflatable Zoom software box rose from a golden center podium in the pool.

"Showmanship if nothing else," one buyer wryly commented to the man seated next to him.

Suddenly, a dozen thousand pound bottlenose dolphins leaped over the Zoom box. Their gray-green dorsal fins and pectoral flippers whizzed through the air loud enough for people in the first few rows to marvel. One by one, rostrum down, tail fluke curved to the ceiling lights, each dolphin twisted its pink belly into view before triumphantly slicing back through the water and disappearing below. "Zoom," preached Hector. "Zoom, salvation for a computerized world ticking off the minutes to its own irreversible delete star dot star."

Two giant screens on either side of Hector lowered. His presentation began.

"Zoom is more than a utility," he declared, wiping his brow. "More than a mere fixpack, more than a patch for our existing software, Zoom is a whole new operating system."

Groans arose from the audience.

"I know. I know," he quieted them down. "Your customers hate that word. When they come into your stores, that twenty-two-year-old sales associate can't really explain it—*an operating system*—and twelve questions and twenty minutes later you have no sale and a lot of wasted time. Then the four people who really did know what they wanted were sick of waiting to talk to a salesman and went home. You lost all the sales.

"But when I say Zoom is an operating system," Hector continued, "I mean a real *operating system* in the purest sense of the word."

Text began appearing on the TVs.

"I know, the OS Wars have left a lot of people bitter," conceded Hector, "But it never had to be that way. Everyone understood DOS," he said, pointing to the displayed text with his wand. "Hey, DOS was the Disk Operating System that ran every computer, the standard inner workings that made all the software work with your machine. What was to understand? You flipped the big red switch and there was DOS. DOS and PCs were synonymous. Weren't they?"

Some buyers laughed.

"Then came Windgazer Prime, the big boo-boo that wasn't really an operating system at all, but gave DOS computers a very pretty screen. A lot of people thought it was an operating system. Instead, it was just a facelift on the same old soul. But at least it did make people think that one day a great operating system would appear.

"Blue2, now there was a real operating system—and a great one. A better DOS than DOS and certainly a better Windgazer than Windgazer, but put together by a brain-dead dinosaur that provoked jokes and laughter from even its most loyal supporters. Say what you will," Hector emphasized, pointing at the logo graphic, "Blue2 really redefined the way we work with PCs, allowing your mouse to drag-and-drop, allowing every part of all various software packages—from word processing to spreadsheets to phone books—to all work interactively with one another, and simultaneously. That's right: *true multitasking.* Blue2 let your computer do ten things at once—even if you could only keep track of two or three at a time. So Blue2 was good," he paused, "but not good enough, not slick enough to succeed."

"That's a distortion," corrected a Windgazer advocate from Silicon Expressway seated in the front row. "Windgazer multitasked. Tell the truth."

Hector rebutted, "Most experts would beg to differ. Windgazer offered *cooperative* multitasking, *coitus interruptus* for software, stopping your spreadsheet dead in its tracks while your word processor stepped in. Blue2 allowed *preemptive multitasking,* allowing all the programs to run simultaneously. The word is *simultaneously.* But it's moot. Blue2 is history. Bluestar spent too much of its time courting its adversaries and alienating its friends. Hopefully we have learned from our mistakes."

He moved the pointer down a line. "Windgazer Prime was . . . well what was it?"

Several in the group chuckled.

"It was prettier, a lot prettier," he declared. "A GUI to die for. Loved it. But a big, big lie, because what that *graphical user interface*–the screen setup–what it told you on the screen was not what was happening inside the CPU. But for the public, 'pretty' worked. While Blue2 floundered, Windgazer Prime flourished. It became a best-seller.

"Oh yes, people deserved Windgazer," said Hector snidely. "Look, whatever it was," he added matter-of-factly, "Windgazer Prime held people's attention long enough for a high-powered operating system to come along, Windgazer IT–a real industrial strength operating system. Certainly, too much for most computers and probably designed to make everyone buy way more memory than they needed and upgrade to 'overkill software' programs they couldn't use."

Snickers from the retailers could not be suppressed.

"Yeah, that part isn't all that bad," acknowledged Hector, playing to the crowd.

"So look," he continued, "many thought the OS Wars were over earlier this year and every computer would use Windgazer IT the way they once used DOS–*ipso facto*. But not so. Now, all legacy operating systems are expected to perish in eighteen months when the clock catches up with our generation. It's July, we don't even have eighteen months. When the century turns, unless we make it right, it won't matter if you're spinning Unix, Blue2, Mac08, OS/2, Microsoft Windows, Win95, Win98, NT, OS/400, MVS, VMS, or Windgazer–every computer will be a boxcar without a locomotive."

He shook his head, pursed his lips and admitted, "Think of the arrogance, negligence, call it what you will, decades ago, when our code punchers simply never accounted for a year after 1999." Hector seemed to drift. "Was it all going so fast? Were we all so nearsighted, that we lived only for the day, or for so few days?"

A blue-jeaned heckler from the stands called out, "Bluestar shares a big part of the blame. None of you would give up the two bytes."

"That's right," Hector shot back, almost apologizing. "It was a shortcut. Two bytes instead of four to designate a year. But now it's a reality. Without those first two bytes in a date, the system can't recognize the next century. Some systems will think 1900, some won't think at all.

"It's easy to say we at Bluestar did it. But in truth, all of us caused this problem," he countered dramatically. "In the past two years, we have made more progress in computerizing our existence than anyone ever dreamed. Progress has its price, and the discounts were illusory. Even seeing the Millennium Bug before us, no one dared pause, no one dared slow down. We just rushed at it with more better faster sooner. No time to breathe, I'm too busy swimming. Lord, the number of personal computers kept doubling, extending into virtually every facet of our lives from national defense, to personal banking, to home security—all essentially operating on one, repeat one, operating system—Windgazer Prime.

"I say it again," Hector hammered, "Bluestar didn't want one system, but the public bought into one system. Or shall I say one family of systems. Many went kicking and screaming. But many went sleepwalking. So we at Bluestar withdrew our competitive software products and cooperated so at least our hardware was compatible. We owed that to our stockholders, customers, and employees."

"Hiiiiiiinnom," the heckler continued.

"Okay," answered Hector. "Hinnom. He toppled Blue2, true, and all other software that stood in his way. Damn near took us over corporately. But we're not here to talk about Hinnom, we're here to talk about Bluestar."

Someone else stood up from the crowd shouting, "What are we afraid of? We can talk about Hinnom."

Hector waved the agitated crowd down. "When Ben Hinnom wants to rent the Baltimore Aquarium and come announce a product, he can talk about himself," he said. "Bluestar has the stage today and Bluestar has the product.

"So let me talk to you about why we're here . . . about Zoom." The crowd paused and Hector resumed. "As the most advanced operating system ever devised, Zoom will feature 100 percent backward compatibility, working with all previous systems, sitting on top of and actually converting everything we can lay our hands on into a Y2K-compliant, completely voice-activated operating system. When I say everything, I mean *everything,* from the cutest Butterfly to the glass room: 286s running DOS, Pentium IIs and IIIs, AS/400s, RISC 6000s, Sun Sparcstations, DECs, PowerMacs and Newtons, Wizards, Palm IIIs and Go-Techs, the complete Hinnom family from Windgazer Prime to Windgazer IM, and beyond. Big Iron running MVS? No problem. Try any piece of legacy or competitive system you care to throw at us. Whatever it takes. Bluestar will make Zoom available on every medium, from 5-and-a-quarter floppies, to standard 3-and-a-halfs, from Zip and Jaz drives, Syquests, and CD-ROMs to mag tapes. And web sites everywhere will feature buttons allowing incremental downloads in the background so a user doesn't spend extra time online. You name it, we'll utilize it. A true 64-bit system, Zoom will run all comers in emulation and eventually grind into native code.

"The secret," he teased, "is the Zoom Conversion Library—I'm going to simplify here because we don't want to give too much away—that reprograms every known operating system and modifies every computer *config.sys* and instruction set to, shall I say, redraw the computer's date sense to the year 2040. Even when the year 2000 arrives, every computer can enjoy yet another forty years of usability—more than anyone would ever expect. There will be plenty of time for all new software and preloaded CPUs to be Zoom-compliant. ZCL will not only reprogram operating systems, it will rewrite vital calls within software itself and modify all contact with the Internet. In slower machines, this will mean a slight delay when loading a program or logging on to the Net, but only initially. We admit that. But in faster machines, Pentiums IIs, Power PCs and faster, with enough RAM to stand up to the task, users will never see the wait state."

The lights went back up. Both screens receded into the ceiling. A cadre of Z-vested convention models fanned out bearing silvery plastic trays stacked with champagne in squat two-ounce white plastic cups. A second group of models passed out black plastic binders; each was sealed by three tabs and bore a large orange Z embossed on the cover. Hector waited for everyone to get theirs.

"There's plenty to go around," he ribbed. "Wait for yours. The ladies will get to you."

Many in the audience reached almost frantically for their dose and their data. "Don't spill any on the notebooks," joked Hector. "They cost us $1.15 each.

"Okay, now you'll have time to review these later," Hector continued, "and please save your champagne for our toast coming up shortly. But if I can direct your attention to page six. Our plans for proliferation—everyone on page six—require each of you to become an evangelist for Zoom. Adoption and conversion of as many as possible as soon as possible is essential. We are even working on a Zoom 'firewall' if you will. Next year, an update will prohibit any connections with any non-Zoom computers, and indeed any installation of any new software not in the Zoom

Conversion Library. We'll treat non-Zooms like a virus.

"Now we are moving as quickly as possible on this," he explained. "Every minute counts. By midnight tonight, our Developer Adviser program will email Zoom briefings to all software engineers we know of in virtually all countries developing software. The DA web site, hyperlinked to each of those emails, will provide instant access to the toolkits needed for Zoom compliance.

"Every major and minor retail chain," he explained in rapid fire, "Silicon Expressway, CompUSA, Radio Shack, Computer City, Babbages, and yes, the new boys on the block like Flee Market–I see you there–all of you here today will be receiving demo diskettes within three weeks that you can stuff into every retail package, be it a new computer or a Crossword Puzzle CD-ROM. A $65-million advertising program will launch ten days prior to our GA date. We'll own spreads in every major piece of print from *Sports Illustrated* to *Forbes,* the choicest network spots from wrestling to the evening news and from *The Simpsons* to reruns of *Seinfeld.* You'll see billboards outside the washrooms in airports, skywriters above Manhattan, discount coupons in every airline seat pocket and concert program. Twelve state prison systems have been contracted to provide inmates; these guys are going to operate phone banks, telemarketing as many as one million users per day. Our corporate customers will cooperate and indeed Bluestar will be adding Zoomers into every piece of commercial software we sell. Every grocery checkout screen will ask 'Are you Zoomed?' Every bank receipt will carry the message: 'Are you Zoomed?'

"Okay. Numbers time," he continued at a speedy clip. "You see, with PC and minicomputer versions added in, we are talking my friends of three hundred million copies of Zoom at $49 a piece with a 61 percent retail markup. Do the math and then my friends I believe you will agree with me when we say . . ." There was a terrifying pause as eleven-hundred left brains calculated their piece of the behemoth sales campaign. One by one their eyes leveled down and transfixed as they awaited Hector's next words. He held back until no one could wait a moment longer.

". . . Agree with me, agree with me and raise your glasses as we toast the next megabillion dollar phenomenon in retail software, the next jetway to profits, and the answer to mankind's potential destruction, I ask you to join my toast."

He raised his own plastic cup high with one hand while the other waved the Zoom CD from left to right as though a banner in the wind, and then yelled, "Go Zoom!"

Everybody shot from their chairs. The seats whipped back in unison like a monstrous pair of boots snapping to.

"Go Zoom," the crowd toasted enthusiastically.

"Say it again," Hector beckoned almost seductively.

"Go Zoom!" they shouted back in unison as all downed their dose.

Hector raised his hands to eye level and declared in a subdued but dramatic voice, "Now. Go back to all your stores, to your mailing lists and databases, to your catalogs and SKUs, to your universal barcodes, your checkout scanners, your employees, your mothers and fathers, sons and daughters, every live one of them, and grandchildren still waiting to come into a world that works, a world that knows productivity and a world that must and will boot up in the year 2000. Go to them and say, 'Go Zoom.' For without Zoom, things are going to get pretty damn ugly out there. We may just destroy ourselves. But with Zoom—with Zoom—we just may make it."

3

BEN HINNOM

*H*ector, with his assistant Ron behind him, sprang out of the pale blue stretch limo and glided through doors held open by Bluestar doormen. Another aide, Lisa, met them in the lobby, and kept pace while falling all over her briefing notebooks and faxes. "You were magnificent, Mr. Hector," she said.

He strolled past a semicircular reception desk manned by two guards, and then directly to his executive elevator. Fifth-floor, the button simply marked *Bluestar*. "It reminded everyone of the old John Hector," Lisa whispered, uncertain if the compliment would be taken the wrong way. Lisa had been on the executive staff for two years, but it was one of her few personal remarks to her generally aloof boss.

Hector noticed her comment only slightly. Lisa moved and began displaying short memos on her portfolio for him to review in the elevator. In rapid-fire style, he passed on each, sometimes after no more than a glance. To the first one, "No."

She held up another. "I need the documentation."

She held up another. "Fine," as he took out a tiny "JH" stamp and touched it to the signature line.

She held up another. "It's a mistake, but do it," again affixing his stamp.

At the fifth-floor, the door opened and he looked askance at one final document. "Bangkok?" he asked with a grimace. "Send it back," he sneered.

Walking briskly, almost jogging, down the corridor past ceiling-mounted monitors replaying his speech at the Baltimore Zoom debut, he turned to Lisa with impatient expectation: "Have it?" She handed him an unmarked, slightly bulging, yellow-brown memo envelope. Without breaking from his walk, he casually pulled out the inhaler, forced it uncomfortably into his mouth, pressed down on the pump, and breathed in with a barely audible gasp. The device was then stowed back into the envelope, which disappeared into Lisa's shoulder bag.

Lisa and Ron could hardly keep up with the energized Hector. At the end of the corridor, he turned right and walked through the remaining gray passageway, marked by gray doors labeled with uninteresting gray plastic placards: *Room 505, Bathroom Supplies, Room 504.* But at the very end, completely out of place, stood elegant, unmarked mahogany double doors. A flickering ceiling light created brief shadows beneath the doorknobs. "Fix that," Hector barked. Lisa scribbled on her hand.

Swinging open, the doors yielded a massive corner office of Bluestar's triangular glass hi-rise just off Michigan Avenue. Towering floor-to-ceiling windows overlooked a majestic, unobstructed northeast perspective of the Chicago River graced by a water cannon fountain arcing jets across its width, by Navy Pier with its giant Ferris wheel, and by Lake Michigan where no white-dotted sailboat was too small to be noticed. Romantic and exhilarating, this view might be better suited for some heart-filled moment of discovery between lovers, not the private office of the chairman of a computer giant. Here the only romance is the passion for commercial conquest, the arousal that stands hairs on end when a competitor misses a ship date, the sweaty eroticism of fourth-quarter results outstripping projections, massaging the stock upward ever so slightly, then dramatically, until its bar graph ignites a burst of overwhelming joy. Bring on the soft music and decor. The men who inhabit offices like these indeed know love and joy, their virility never falters, their appetite only increases. However, their partners are not fine women, but rather the vixens of profit. In the boudoirs of business, all indiscretion can be covered up, denied, or crassly repeated. Profit is the great redeemer.

Lisa tried to force a few more papers before Hector's wandering attention, but he refused. "That's it," he said. She backed off as Hector's personal secretary, Sarah, briskly walked in from a side office to continue the briefings.

"Nothing but today," he warned as she approached. Sarah closed her full week's portfolio dutifully, leaving just a small sheet out with the day's agenda. "The delay at BWI and the drive down the Kennedy put us an hour behind," she reported matter-of-factly. "The sit-down with AT&T was therefore delayed until a week from Thursday. They said either today or not for another week. So I have them for July 16."

Hector seemed uninterested. "What time is it?"

"You have time," Sarah replied, checking her watch. "It's only 4:40. In between, you must, and I mean *must,* address the worldwide managers."

"How long?" he asked, pulling off his orange Zoom golf shirt, revealing a sagging, white-haired trunk marked by a small incision scar near his heart.

"Six minutes. Seven if you like," she answered, handing him a green golf shirt emblazoned "Networking Magic." Hector was struggling into it, when from the inside he saw the logo. "What's this?" he bellowed. "Wrong logo!"

"Sorry, sorry, sorry," she said, running to the closet, where she quickly surveyed three tall stacks of golf shirts, each a different color, each with a different embroidered corporate logo. She pulled out the next to the bottom, the navy blue one marked "Bluestar Worldwide Leadership."

Hector tossed the never-worn green one in the wastepaper basket. As she helped him on with the navy blue "Worldwide Leadership" shirt, their eyes met. "What?" he demanded gruffly.

Sarah spoke in a subdued voice, "You were great at the Zoom rollout, John. I haven't seen you like that for years—no one has. The whole building was mesmerized."

"I admit I felt wonderful, empowered again," Hector came back with a weak smile. "For a while I almost lost them, but by the time it was over, I had the audience, they had me. We were fused in a moment of excitement. I haven't . . . well, it's just that, well not since April have I really gotten excited like that about anything, Sarah."

Sarah put her scheduling notebooks down, and said softly, "It's been difficult."

He drew back. "Don't Vienna me."

"I'm not going to 'Vienna' you," Sarah meekly replied.

"Well then don't," he snapped defensively. "It's been April since I felt like leading anything, and I admit that. Okay. So big deal. People screw

up for decades and nobody ever notices until the division gets sold. I had
a few crummy months. So? Bluestar stayed solid."

He began mindlessly checking email. "Yeah, the stock tanked to sixty-
eight but that only let the big boys buy in lower than they could have ever
dreamed. We're back up now–triple-digit again. Hah! Our smart stockholders made millions on my mistakes."

Sarah motioned to the anteroom and ushered Hector in. He double-
checked his golf shirt. It was the right one.

There was nothing in the room except a tall-backed chair, a mahogany
desk, and a phone. A blue-walled blue Chromakey screen descended
from the ceiling, obscuring the window. A three-man video crew came in
from a side entrance. Focusing in on Hector, the producer punched some
keys on a console sourcing a visual library. On the monitor, Chicago's
skyline appeared behind Hector, the very same view seen naturally
through the anteroom window. But in the digital version, the sky was
bluer. Stationary clouds were digitally added behind the John Hancock
Center as an afterthought. The producer punched a few more keys. The
cameraman checked one final time and nodded readiness.

"Not yet," said Hector, "Hold 'em." Sarah frowned. On a second monitor, a Bluestar manager in London, standing before a clearly artificial
photo of the Houses of Parliament, had already announced, "We are honored today to receive principal remarks by our company's chairman,
John Hector, coming to you live from the company's worldwide headquarters in Chicago. Are you there, John?"

Hector did nothing. The crew was silent.

"Are you there, John?"

No response. Fifteen seconds, thirty seconds.

"Are you there, John?"

"Anticipation, my dear, is everything," Hector chirped with a wink.
Sarah smiled reluctantly.

"Ohhhhkay," Hector nodded to the video operator who counted
down: three . . . and a-two . . . and you're *on*." The camera's tiny dome
light blinked red.

Through the anteroom's closed soundproof glass doors, Hector could
be seen speaking vigorously to the camera, gesturing with both hands. For
all his antics, the gathered staff was impressed with his new vitality.
"Zoom seems to have done it for him," said Sarah. "Things got so bad in

April. Lucy was everything to him."

Lisa agreed, "It was a great loss. But he seems to have bounced back quickly."

Sarah turned to her. "I know John. In his mind, nothing will take Lucy's place. They would run together mornings along the lake. He loved to run his fingers through her hair."

Ron asked, "What's after this?"

"The usual five o'clock," said Sarah, trying to hide her disapproval. Lisa looked away, Sarah pretended not to notice. "It should be coming in shortly."

Just then, the camera operator could be seen gesturing his exaggerated countdown: three fingers, two fingers, then a fist. The camera's red light went off, the Chromakey blue screen receded into the ceiling, and the crew disappeared through a side door.

Hector immediately turned to the clock. It was just before five. Eyes open wide, he stuck his head out of the glass doors, and instructed, "Put the call in here."

He tore off his navy blue Leadership golf shirt, threw it into a waste-basket, and reached into a bottom drawer of the desk to grab a brilliant white golf shirt with green trim at the sleeves. Embroidered underneath its Bluestar logo was the name "Chairman John Hector." Just before five, the private line rang. Hector frantically picked up. "Yes," he sang. It wasn't who he expected. "Uh, I'm getting ready for a global leadership confer-ence," he said dismissively. "Please call my appointment secretary. Call her in the morning, okay? Thanks. Bye."

The call he was really expecting buzzed in moments later at precisely five. "Yes," he sang again. He closed the door, sat in his tall-backed seat and turned toward the window so his form was completely obscured.

"That's the call," muttered Sarah. "Every day at five when he's in the country, I think probably even when he's overseas. Local time, wherever he is. He likes five, I guess," she said, almost giggling.

The waiting staff watched the chair back jiggle a few times, and ex-changed glances. "It started last April after Lucy died," Sarah said curtly.

"Umm," Lisa nodded with embarrassment.

In a few moments, Hector emerged, slightly sweated, staring first at the floor, then out across Lake Michigan, then at Sarah and the assembled staffers. "I told her," he assured Sarah, even as he completely ignored the others. He tugged at his sleeve once or twice in discomfort and uncertainty. "That was the last one." he said quietly. "No more calls. She didn't mind. No, she understood. It has been very helpful since . . . since earlier this year." He looked back at the chair in the anteroom, then down at the floor again. "Hah, so what? No harm. I was down, depressed, actually just lonely," he reasoned.

"But now there's work to be done," Hector declared energetically. "I tell you, I'm in love with the program. I'm betrothed to the launch. I'm giving myself–mind and body–to Zoom. I felt it today. I felt that Zoom was everything I had been waiting for, everything Bluestar needs to regain its primacy, and for God's sake, it's what this world needs if it's not going to blow itself up."

The staff listened respectfully at first, but slowly latched onto his enthusiasm.

"Oh, I certainly believe we can do it," Hector railed. "Grind ourselves down and then blow ourselves up? Sure, we can. We've lost too much time by now. It's an emergency by now. But Zoom can fix it. I *know* it can. And I can't afford," he looked at his tall-backed chair, "I can't afford to be distracted in what we can all expect to be a bloody battle with Hinnom." He walked over to the bar, half laughed, reached into the ice bucket and pulled out a box of Windgazer. Tapping the box, he spoke with resignation, "Think he's going to stand by and see Windgazer falter? He would sooner see me and all of Bluestar burn in hell. That man is evil. No wonder everyone hates him. All the sweaters and public relations men in the world won't help."

He began waving the staff away. "Okay, everyone. Out. So I can concentrate. I promised just a bit more than I can deliver this morning in Baltimore, and I better start pedaling."

Five floors below on East Wacker Drive, an old but shiny yellow school bus pulled up to Bluestar headquarters. It parked directly in front of the entrance, blocking all other traffic. No one could see through the black tinted windows. Neither doorman made an effort to wave it away.

"Could that be . . ." wondered the first doorman.

"Sure," the other doorman answered. "The famous license plate . . . look, *June 66*. That's it, the school bus he rode when he was a kid. You know the story."

". . . It's not true, is it?"

"Oh yeah," the other doorman replied. "It's known. The other boys used to pick on him. And the driver wouldn't stop it, he joined in. Like that. So this guy is six years old and calls the bus company and demands they fire the driver. They laugh at him and he says–"

"–you mean the friggin' story *is* true."

"It's true, man," the other doorman insisted. "The brat threatens, 'One day, I'll own this bus and fire the driver.' When he made his first million, he tries to buy the bus–that one. But the company wouldn't sell. So he buys the whole damn company, sends pink slips to the entire staff from the CEO down. Except for the driver. The story goes he fired the driver personally in his private office just three days before the old geezer's pension was to kick in. The driver begged the asshole for forgiveness."

"You know this from where?"

"TV," the other doorman answered, talking more quietly now. "But magazines, too. It's true. The driver begged for forgiveness, and he had a kidney condition, but he still fired the guy. Jerk. I heard the driver became an alcoholic and lost everything. Then this guy closed the company and sold every bus to a scrap house except for the one you're looking at right there. That one he saved, and put that license plate on it with his birthday. Now for special occasions he trucks it across the country in a big semi. It picks him up at airports. Like the president's limo, flown all over the place."

The school bus doors whooshed open. Both doormen fell silent, staring at the darkened, barely discernible driver's seat where no one was sitting. Street noise seemed to stop. Nearby traffic lights turned red and stuck. A street lamp flashed off. Two women at the corner craned to see who was coming. A cat at the curb looked up. Eventually, a slightly built early-thirties guy with unkempt blondish hair swept to one side and a still boyish expression peeked out, smiled almost sweetly and descended. Ben Hinnom had arrived.

Dressed in simple jeans and a blousy shirt with buccaneer sleeves that fluttered briefly in the light breeze, underimpressing as usual, Hinnom spoke meekly at first, "Please forgive me for parking here." He shrugged with a grin at the vehicle, "It's kinda hard to park." Behind Hinnom came Linzer. "We won't be a moment, actually just a half hour, maybe longer," assured Hinnom in that special manner, combining equal parts of deliberate innocence and undisguisable arrogance. "Will you watch the bus?"

He strolled into the building, casually opening his own doors as though he was not the richest man on earth, whose computer empire controlled 94 percent of the world's computers, as though he was not worth $80 billion, as though he had not single-handedly revolutionized all computer use, as though he had not forced scores of major and minor technology companies out of business or banished them to the murky depths of acquisition, as though he had not purchased several of the most important sculptures of Rodin and even some Michelangelo just because, as though he did not own his own $300 million home in the hills outside Seattle, and as though 60,000 people did not work for him. Both building reception and the guards recognized Hinnom at once and began speaking into their walkie-talkies.

The phone in Hector's office rang and simultaneously an email exploded with a ding on his 20-inch LCD flat screen monitor.

From: Security.

To: JHector.

Message: Ben Hinnom is here for his appointment. He wasn't in the book but we sent him up.

Hector scanned the email incredulously, picked up the phone, listened and blurted, "Are you sure it's Hinnom?" He clicked the SECURITY icon on his screen, clicked CAMERAS and then punched F12 on his keyboard bringing Hinnom into view. "It's him at the elevator."

Startled, he shouted, "Sarah. Am I scheduled to see Ben Hinnom today? What the heck?" She ran over to view the camera shot on the flat screen, shook her head and declared, "No, no."

Moving quickly to her computer, she clicked her SCHEDULE icon, and then SEARCH. She typed in "Ben Hinnom," then "Hinnom Computing."

"Nothing," she called out.

"Get me Fields," he shot back. "And get me a proper shirt." Almost in unison, they reacted "Zoom logo?" For a moment, Sarah was reminded of Vienna four years before, when they worked so intensely at a software convention and then discovered something between them, shared a suite for a week after, and only reluctantly flew home to resume their separate lives. "Here, a Zoom shirt," she said, tearing herself away from the memory.

Fields' videocon image popped onto Hector's screen and flickered miserably. "Oh, pick up the damn telephone," demanded Hector, and then as an aside, "Sarah, tell Team Video to make it work *before* it's on my desktop. I'm not a beta site."

The phone buzzed.

"Fields, are you aware that Ben Hinnom is coming up the executive elevator now to see me!" blared Hector. He punched F12 twice more and the elevator view came onto the screen. Hinnom was indeed on his way up. "Well, how do you explain it?" he hung up.

The doors to Hector's suite opened slowly. They waited almost breathlessly.

A matronly executive followed by fifteen Cub Scouts strolled in. "Mr. Hector . . . hope I'm not disturbing."

He looked completely dismayed.

"Bluestar's Cub Pack?" she reminded.

No response.

With some trepidation, she offered, "It's been set up for a year? July 6, 5:15?"

Waving his hands, Hector blabbered, "Sorry, sorry kids. Must be a mistake. Could we do this next week?" Without waiting for a reply, he and all his aides graciously shoved the den mother and her Cub Scouts back out the double doors. Ron escorted her away.

"Lisa, Sarah. Stay, stay," Hector instructed. He nervously looked around the room for confidential data. "Up there," he pointed at a white board with quarterly projections. Lisa ran to it, and pulled a fresh white board over it. Hector punched F12 several times to bring up various views from security cameras, including the double doors to his suite. "Where is he?"

A knock at the door. Hector looked up and muttered, "The evil one is here."

Hinnom walked in slowly. Behind Hinnom was Linzer. Instantly, Hinnom was his animated, puckish self. "Hi, hi, hi, hi, hi," he said to all in the room adding "hi's" even to people who weren't there, walking in and playfully touching every nearby surface, becoming a new reference point in the executive suite, dominating the moment with his usual underimpressing casual exterior. "John Hector, I presume. My pleasure," he extended his hand for a shake but then it turned into a short wave. "Did I tell you I would be in Chicago?" Without pause, he added, "I barely knew myself. But here I am and so flattered that you took a moment to see me. Busy guy, busy guy–I know you."

Hector was almost confused but snapped out of it. "I just got in and was caught off-calendar," began Hector in a businesslike manner. "But, if it's Windgazer vs. Zoom in the marketplace, Bluestar is happy to open a dialogue with Hinnom Computing."

Hinnom cut him off, "No, John, John, John." A little giggle. "You've talked about Windgazer so much already," he said, floating over to the bar. He lifted the ice bucket lid, pulled out the Windgazer box. "Oooh." He put it back.

Hector stared incredulously. How in the hell did he know? As though reading his mind, Hinnom moved to the floor-to-ceiling windows of the suite, stood against the glass, and waved slightly. "Just saying hi to my Optics Integration office. Did you know they were in the Hancock Building," pointing to the skyscraper down the street, "right over *there*. Most of them go home at 4:30, but some of them are just starting at . . ." he paused and flipped an eyebrow at the tall-backed chair in the glass-doored anteroom, ". . . five. Ooh, did I say something wrong?" Fast forwarding, Hinnom abruptly asked, "Hey, can we talk, just us two guys? Ya know, two big execs, just you and me, computer business stuff?"

Hector stiffened. He knew this was a moment unlike any other boardroom challenge he had battled, unlike any global telephonic wars he had waged, unlike the financial chess he was so adept at, unlike the smiling conflicts at COMDEX where worlds and lives are made and destroyed with none the wiser until after New Year's, by which time it's too late to care. This was different. His opponent Hinnom this time was a genuine personality of his own, without concern for money or career, with no family, no roots, no future scruples. Victory was the only option. "Sure," replied Hector.

Lisa and Sarah left. Only when they stepped completely out the door did Linzer follow.

"Just us," said Hinnom, "but can it truly be just *us*. Do me a real favor, just this weensy one. Shut down your CPU." He tapped the tiny microphone and one-inch camera lens attached to the flat screen. "I know you have Voice Buddy and TeleChat installed, both good products moving from one-point-uh-oh into actual usable software. But I want our meeting to be *private*. It's so important."

Hector hit the right mouse button, then the left to choose Shut Down.

A sequence of sound effects ensued as cascading windows closed: lion roars, kitten meows, Porky Pig stutters, and then the final effect signifying shutdown completion, a wav from a quiet but desperate HAL speaking in *2001: A Space Odyssey:* "I know you and Dave were planning to disconnect me, and that is something I can't allow to happen." A small text message appeared, "It is now quite safe to turn off your computer."

A genuinely amused Hinnom smiled broadly, "Cute."

Hector depressed the white button and the power went off altogether. "Now then," said Hector.

"Oooh. . . '*Now then,*'" mocked Hinnom.

"Okay," Hinnom began, walking around the room. "I saw the Zoom launch rollout promo tape today. It was splendid, John. Dolphins. Nice, very nice touch. Personally, I prefer their cousins, mahi mahi pan fried with a white wine and Dijon sauce—did I tell you I love to cook in my new kitchen? But for you they worked magic. Good, good, good. And I think you can beat us to the punch. Oh yes. Zoom might be ready in days, weeks, whatever. You'll ship before we do. But John, will it be a *better* solution than Windgazer 99? Serve the market better than Windgazer 99? Or will it just distract the market from Windgazer 99, flop bigger than Miami, take up precious time with a buggy bastardy V1, and then ruin everything for everyone and especially for Hinnom Computing because I think really John, that Windgazer 99 is the superior product, will solve all the Millennium Bug problems, and make for a seamless transition into the 21st Century—something you and I both want."

Hinnom stopped moving, and conceded with a shrug, "You're faster. We're better. I admit that."

Quite in control of his responses, Hector answered firmly, "I don't. We're faster *and* we're better. I admit *that.* But I do agree that if Bluestar had your cooperation, Zoom would be more effective and run natively in Windgazer, which controls 90-plus percent of the desktops on Earth. Pull with us, Ben, and we can save the planet from self-destruction. The threat is real. I say, the world won't end with a bang or even a whimper, but with an error message. We're ready to work together if you are."

Hinnom moved to a more serious facial expression. "Yes, that's correct," he replied. "See, we agree. Where we disagree is on approach. You think Bluestar will save the world from trashing itself, and in so doing regain the status it held until a few years ago, *Lord of the Computer.* The words 'computer' and 'Bluestar' were synonymous a few years ago, weren't they? But it's all changed today. Hinnom Computing is now the *Savior.* I want teamwork. But it's not a team effort unless the team is . . ." he paused, ". . . *my* team.

"Bluestar can be part of my team," Hinnom continued with a menacing tone. "Zoom has a future, just like Raisin Computing has a future. Ooh, everyone thought Raisin was finished. Raisin," he scoffed. "The folks who virtually invented home computing, took the graphics world by storm, became the standard bearer for art directors and designers—people I have no use for by the way. Too bad these wonderful Raisin folks tried to monopolize their entire following but eventually were quite simply left to the crows like Hungarian grapes rotting in the fields after harvest. Until Hinnom Computing infused bankrupt Raisin with $90 million in cash— and now it lives and thrives as Raisin still. Rotted grapes became Bull's Blood wine. That's a helluva metaphor, John, because that's how you make Bull's Blood—rotted grapes. I knew that. Anyway, now all the little Raisinettes can drag and drop graphics to their hearts' content. The cult lives. Teamwork."

"Except Raisin is actually Hinnom," Hector sneered.

"Depends how you look at it," Hinnom rebutted. "Puerto Rico is Puerto Rico, but it became part of America. I'm offering you something, John. Take Zoom—that big, loud distracting project with the Zorro logo, and move the whole shebang from your Platform Systems Performance division into your Software Standards Group. Spin SSG into a consortium with us. A few weeks later, we acquire it completely. You will be chairman and CEO of the new consortium. I'll pay you $109 million annual salary and all the five o'clock calls you can stand. Plus, I'll give you 12 million stock options at fifteen dollars. I can promise you the consortium's stock will rise to forty-five dollars within a year." He paused. "We can do that."

There was no response from Hector.

Hinnom raised the stakes: "I'll throw in control through nominees of a new company yet to be formed in Malaysia to act as a broker for all Hinnom Computing CD-ROM production for the next five years. Ironclad contract, John. Take it."

No response.

"Okay," giggled Hinnom, "What a tough bargainer. You! I'll funnel the bulk of your income through the Caymans. Your American salary will be just enough to avoid Alternative Minimum Tax imposed by the IRS. The remainder will go through the Caymans, where it will be taxed not at 39 percent with state and federal, but at an effective rate of seven percent. John, within five years, you'll be one of the richest men in the world." Hinnom became very serious now. "And you will have made a contribution to the betterment of all mankind by working with me, by joining me, by transducing the talents of Zoom into the awesome power of Windgazer. We can do it together, John. Join *me*."

Hector ran his hands over his face to wipe away Hinnom's monologue, and answered, "You are the sick bastard they say you are. Do you really believe you can walk in here and buy me off? With your tawdry millions and your Grand Cayman offshore banks, and your puppet chairmanships of your put-up consortiums to scuttle Zoom and help Windgazer 99 screw the world even more than Windgazer vanilla has already screwed it?"

"John, John. This attitude is not helpful," said Hinnom calmly in a soothing voice. "I'm afraid you just don't understand me. I have a vision. We both know the world is run by computers and microchips, and the part that's not will be soon. Some of it is quite crude, like in that cheap watch you're wearing. Some of it is very sophisticated but limited in scope, like your cell phone. Nice phone, by the way. Some don't need any more brains than it takes to tell a toaster to lighten up the whole wheat or a dishwasher to wait until everyone's asleep to start its cycle. And some computers are so complicated and sophisticated they are magnificent challenges to nature itself: the supercomputers used by the National Weather Service to forecast hurricanes and the NSA to crack secret codes. Oh, I love it when they crack codes. I actually have a little inhouse game at our Seattle headquarters where Team Black tries to create an uncrackable code and Team Gray tries to crack it. Better than those silly chess games Bluestar holds, but to each his own.

"Okay, so where are we?" asked Hinnom, getting back on track. "Ohhh, there are computers everywhere you look and only more of them being stamped out every week. Hinnom Computing wants only one thing: to connect them all." Hinnom's face tightened slightly. "All."

Hector's eyes opened wide. He was about to speak when Hinnom cut him off.

"*All*," growled Hinnom. "I want every classroom, government office, corporate enterprise, and military installation, every pocket calculator,

VCR and toaster, every person in every language everywhere who uses or is affected by any appliance or machine or device or desire to have them all connected by one operating system, the Windgazer family of operating systems. For your plain old office computers Windgazer 99; high-end workstations will hum nicely on Windgazer IT; run your mainframes on Windgazer IM; power your pocket computers and laptops on Windgazer TE; for your household appliances–and I mean everything from the phones to the washing machines to the light switches on the wall–we can use Windgazer ME; medical devices will use Windgazer MD; financial transactions, they go on Windgazer FI–and on and on.

"When Windgazer takes hold," Hinnom promised grandiosely, "you'll be able–from work, mind you–to tap into your home system and ask the fridge to scan for bar codes and report whether you have eggs. You're late leaving the office, and you send a message to the VCR to tape the football game. You're driving in the desert and low on gas, so you ask Windgazer VE to moderate gas consumption. Your enemy refuses to obey a binding resolution of the U.N.? Just shut their society down sector by sector until they comply–with Windgazer, you're always just a command line away from compliance. No more wars, no more criminals, no more uncollectible bills. This is no pipe dream. Half of it's in place today, John. Radio frequency commands and the Internet will make it possible for a world completely networked without wires.

"I can make this happen," Hinnom argued passionately, "I just need to connect the dots–and then replace the dots themselves. Then we control the whole picture. Personal convenience, commercial productivity and prosperity, world peace and inner harmony. *This* is my vision."

Laughing, Hector replied derisively, "Tell me this soliloquy isn't for real. Are you nuts? You want one operating system controlling all software and hardware everywhere in the world, all interrelated and interconnected, and dominated by one company–Hinnom Computing."

"Nuts? If there was one cure for cancer would you complain that there was only one?" Hinnom snapped back. "Disorder is a cancer on the world, in this universe. You prefer chaos? You prefer humans scurrying about in ignorance and conflict using their petty minds to run into walls, bleed, bandage, and bash themselves again? Windgazer can wipe the cancer away."

"You don't want to cure cancer," Hector argued back. "You want to addict everyone to your medicine, and then control who gets doses and when. You will decide who will live or die. You want to be God."

"No," pleaded Hinnom. "It's business. You can understand business. It's like a toll booth, but my information highway has a tollbooth on all of life. Like a gas meter on your house, but this is virtual and exists no matter what you do. The government has one, they call it tax. Tax is everywhere—sales tax, use tax, excise tax, value added tax, hidden pass-through tax, you name it, you drink it, drive it or smoke it, and they tax it. Hinnom Computing wants that. And we'll call it pass through royalties, annual licenses and per use fees. There will be a microprice on all this modern magic. Imagine, every time you deposit money in a bank, pay a bill, brew a cup of coffee, drive your car, flush a toilet . . . ooh, I didn't tell you the part about Windgazer TP—we'll save that for another encounter. But imagine a fraction of a penny for every usage and every activity. The pennies mount up. It all gets deducted automatically from your bank account. Hey, so it costs $150 per month for every man, woman, and child to live in a Hinnom world. That's revenue, John."

"That's world domination, you sick post-pubescent hacker," Hector retorted, nodding his head half in pity, half in disgust. "You want to hook everyone on your software, fill it with bugs and problems, and make the planet buy into constant upgrades which are always promised years sooner than they can be reliably delivered, which ruins the market for the companies with real products up and ready now." Raising his voice and cutting in viciously, "Your software stinks, Hinnom. So why standardize the globe on it?"

Sputtering, showing his teeth and unable to contain his sudden rage, Hinnom shook and stammered, "That is . . . that is . . . that is the *worst* piece of *random* crap I have ever heard! Random. Random. You, John Hector, who I tried to communicate with, you are a truly random asshole."

Hector shot back, "Who are you calling *random?*"

"I'm calling *you* random."

Hector's face came to within just inches of Hinnom's, as he announced, "This meeting is over, and you can just go to hell."

"What's your problem with hell?" quipped Hinnom. Hector drew back and looked askance at Hinnom, whose guise became suddenly calm, menacingly calm.

"John, can I share something with you from the secrets of the $80 billion empire," Hinnom began in a low-keyed voice. "Actually, my little nest egg is a lot bigger than $80 billion, but let's use that number because people relate to it. Do you know what Yap is?"

Hector shrugged with annoyance, "Year Application Protocol? I have no idea. What is Yap?"

"No, John, Yap is a little island in Micronesia where I have incorporated a company called Micronesia Medical Development. With a name like that, it's easy to think Micronesia refers to computers. It actually refers to the geographic thing. Anyway, Micronesia Medical Development has acted through its office in Guam, which is part of the good ole United States, to purchase as much advanced medical technology as it can: bone stimulators, evoked potential, brain mapping, myoelectric prostheses, all that. The companies or the divisions—sometimes just the products severed from the original divisions—are generally small and cost a few million here and a few million there to acquire. Throw the exec a bone with a kick upstairs to nowhere, he retires, the company is ours. Well in that group are the pacemakers. There are only three leading companies in that field. And we bought them. All.

"Let's talk ICDs," Hinnom continued. "Nowadays they are commonplace. Close to 150,000 people in the USA alone have implantable cardioverter-defibrillators. And the population is aging, as they say. Pretty soon ICDs will be as ordinary as contact lenses, well maybe not that ordinary. But you have to admit they are so, so cute, just a few ounces. Improved batteries can last a decade and the new models benefit from constant upgrades in analysis, reporting, and adjustment capabilities. Modern Medicine. Love it."

"You're boring me," monotoned Hector. "I know all this. I have an ICD. I developed a heart condition after Lucy died—"

"Oh your beloved collie, Lucy," chimed Hinnom. "Daily runs with the dog, special kennel for traveling on airplanes, blue ribbons at dog shows, lifelong companion, and all that. I heard it devastated you emotionally. Are you over that?"

Impatient with the trivialization, Hector came back, "We done now? I don't want to be rude."

"Almost done. I just want to show you something." Hinnom slid from his pocket a tiny palmtop the size of a tin of mints.

"Oh, the Windy," said Hector, somewhat impressed. "I heard a production quality prototype was available. May I see it?"

Hinnom held back. "Sorry, no touchee. But lookee is okay." Telescoping the screen to twice the lid size, Hinnom gave a short summary. "You can forget your tired Palm IIIs and Wizards, John. The Windy began shortly after the first PDAs made just everyone yawn. Unlike all the other palmtops, the Windy uses a variant of Windgazer TE that can emulate a client of Windgazer 99. Ten gigs of memory, 128 RAM, loaded with standard apps, it both acts like a standalone palmtop and as a fully-capable LAN or WAN client, and can maintain a strong Internet connection, depending upon mode and, of course, signal strength. Our secret is a combo of advanced radio frequency technology, cellular and satellite connections that allow this cookie to transmit and receive instructions and data to and from any CPU, printer, server. Check out the screen, I love the screen."

"Nice stuff," commented Hector. "Beats the Bluepoint's expandable keyboard."

"Yes, *beats* is the whole point," continued Hinnom. "As you well know from your recent surgery, ICDs are now programmable. That's how your doctor adjusts your heart rate. Hey, you heard about the software error they found in some pacemakers last year. Remember, the patients had to report to their doctors for a software correction. Well, here's how it works.

"The pacemaker software, including all the adjustment parameters, are programmed at the central lab. Once upon a time, that programming was done in a Unix-based language. But when my company acquires a medical technology firm, they standardize all development onto Windgazer MD, the operating system we have developed for the medical technology world. So the lab updates the firmware regularly and copies the updates onto standard floppies. Those floppies are given to the detail men—just another name for salesmen—who go out to the doctors. They copy the floppies into the doctor's on-site programming unit, which actually is about the size of a small VCR. The doctor brings up the new program, and adjusts the parameters any way he likes.

"Look," Hinnom showed the screen to Hector. "There's the proprietary parameter adjustment screen for your particular ICD, the Opal manufactured by PulsePlant, formerly of the Midwest and now relocated to Seattle. Actually, not for another three months. But consider them relocated because I own PulsePlant through my little Micronesian company that no one knows is mine."

Hector was becoming uncomfortable as he studied the screen. Involuntarily, he placed his hand over his chest.

"Now listen carefully, John," Hinnom explained. "The way the parameter adjustment gets from the programming unit into your chest is just a plain old RF transmission. You may remember your doctor–let's see his name . . . oh, here it is, Kaufman. Dr. Kaufman would just pass a little RF wand within about four inches of your chest, the ICD would read the information and update itself on the fly without *skipping a beat*–if you'll excuse the expression." He smiled broadly. "Everyone thinks I'm a reformed hacker. Actually, I'm still hacking, but now I've graduated from school records and banks to the ultimate challenge. I can hack the human body."

Hector's face whitened. "You have my pacemaker program on your Windy?"

"Sure," said Hinnom nonchalantly. "And it is so easily programmed when Windgazer MD has a universal back door for the software engineer to check for defects. Let's see. Your heart is currently beating at 70. But not to worry, we can fix that." Hector recoiled in horror as Hinnom typed in 300 and extended his arm closer to Hector's chest. "That should do it."

"What in God's name are you doing?" shrieked Hector, as he felt an immediate pang in his chest and then a pain in his head.

Hinnom spoke calmly: "In the old days, John, the bad guys used guns and bombs. Now we just press buttons." Hector could hear but he was virtually paralyzed. "It's terrible, John. Every month–every month–more than fifty thousand people in this country are struck by sudden cardiac death. It's not a heart attack, mind you. Let's be precise. SCD is much worse. You see, in SCD the heart speeds up so fast that even though there is plenty of blood in the chambers, the darn thing is beating so fast–jeepers–that it can't pump the stuff out. At all! Not even to the brain which after a minute–often much sooner, says: 'phooey, I can't handle this. Let's just . . . die!' Now it's all just electrical impulses, John, and I could offer to reset, but I think you're probably too disenchanted with the program by now to be a part of the team."

Hector's eyes floated up and his lids dropped down. His fingers stretched out as his memory trembled through halls of cheering users, and from there to the scarring loneliness of being left out one day when he lacked the twenty-five-cent admission to attend the high school basketball game, the door slamming in his face as the crowds cheered inside. Hector swooned across a chair, his head crashing into an armrest.

Hinnom calmly typed in an email message.

Outside the office double doors, a ding went off on Linzer's Windy. Linzer slid open the lid, punched a few keys, dispassionately read the message, touched the "del" key, and slid the lid back into position.

Hinnom powered up Hector's personal computer. Within a few moments, it booted up. "Password memorized?" scowled Hinnom. "Executives, they just think they're too good for the rest of us. Next time, use a password and change it periodically," Hinnom chided a dying Hector. As the computer booted up, security apps came online including the Voice Buddy and TeleChat systems. As they did, Hinnom went into action.

"Help! Help! John, are you okay, what's happening?" he shouted. Linzer and Hector's staff came running in. Hinnom punched a few keys and security came onto the screen. "Help, I think John's had a heart attack. Oh, my dear! A thousand people a day suffer this way, a thousand people a day. Someone help him. Does anyone know CPR? Oh dear. And we were so close to an agreement. Call an ambulance. Quick, some-one call 911!"

4

QUERY

*P*ark wondered if she was waiting at the right corner on North Halsted Street. In fact, she wondered if she was waiting in the right city. Just days ago, she thought Chicago might be a fresh start. But things had drastically changed overnight.

Dan was late. She was always uncomfortable when a man she liked was late. With each minute, she imagined she was at the wrong place, that he might stand her up, or didn't value the meeting, or wasn't serious. The ones she didn't care about, they were always early.

So far, Chicago was everything Park thought it might be. Park actually grew up with fantasies of Chicago, so in her own way she was *rediscovering* the city. WGN Radio's clear channel signal was strong enough to reach Kansas. As a young girl living in a world where most roads were unpaved, where no one ate in restaurants, where the nearest neighbor lived miles away, and party line telephones were a fact of life, WGN was a window over the horizon. After her father and brothers listened to the farm reports and stepped into the morning heat, WGN's talk shows would begin. A guest was always chattering about a favorite Near North restaurant, about downtown theater productions, and baseball. Wrigley Field–"beautiful" Wrigley Field, that is–was home to the Cubs. Comiskey Park was the southside park where the White Sox played. Political independents were strong along the lakefront. The Loop was an imaginary circle in central downtown formed by the elevated train. She knew that rush hour was hell. But back then, she couldn't imagine what a rush hour was.

By her first day in high school, Park decided she would never live in Wichita or Kansas City where she would only find everything she wanted to leave, just grown up and relocated. She longed for a truly urban lifestyle, the restaurants, crowds, and the uncertainty of the big city. There was no uncertainty in Kansas, except the weather and the harvest. Yes, Chicago is where she always wanted to be.

But it didn't work out that way. Post-grad recruitment led to a job in her college town of Lawrence, and then to Boulder for a year, and then to Seattle. Seattle was beautiful, but not that different from Boulder. Tall buildings, tall trees, tall mountains, and tall tales from tall men. The opportunity to come to Chicago might have changed all that. But after last night, she wasn't sure.

To keep her mind occupied while standing around, Park enjoyed noticing how Chicago differed from Seattle: men with more intrusive stares who would eat and walk at the same time, women with smaller purses and higher heels wearing designer clothes just going to work, and the Mayor's name on every city truck.

Dan was now fifteen minutes late. It was a mistake agreeing to meet on a street corner instead of inside the restaurant. Park made it obvious to anyone that she was waiting for a friend. Periodically she glanced up the street and checked her watch. She was about to telephone when the red Del Sol appeared down the block trailing behind a large, smoke-belching delivery truck. Dan waved as he passed, then deftly U-turned, and zipped into the parking space right in front of her. One car in oncoming traffic slammed on its brakes, but Dan pretended not to notice. Park thought to herself that it didn't matter if the boys were on the farm or in the city, they were all the same when they stepped into a car.

After apologizing for being late, complaining about a sell-off on the Asian market, dropping compliments about how good she looked in her jeans, asking if she was enjoying Chicago, not waiting for an answer before promising to show her all the right places, and then popping two Altoids, Dan escorted Park to a quaint little coffeehouse located on the second floor of a nearby warehouse.

She ordered cappuccino without mentioning that Chicago coffee was not as bitter as Seattle's, while Dan ordered a scotch for himself and a large fudge brownie to share. Quickly there was a change. Once he relaxed into the armchair and began sipping Laphroaig, the usually hyper Dan appeared to suddenly mellow. She waited for him to talk. But Dan seemed more than oddly quiet.

"That's a new one, scotch and brownie," she said after a minute, trying to start a conversation.

"For sure," Dan mumbled without thought. Indeed, her words barely penetrated. Dan was traveling. Park debated whether this could be very bad, or very good, and tried to discern whether he was ignoring her or whether her presence combined with a Laphroaig set Dan so much at ease that he just lapsed into an untensed state. One minute he was careening into a parking space, the next he was subdued over a snifter. She wanted a man who was complex, but not this complicated. Couldn't anyone just be normal?

Out of nowhere, Dan asked, "You going to settle in Chicago?"

That question, Park was not ready for. Swallowing her first answer before it left her lips, she took a moment before responding, "I just got here. But who knows now." Dan still seemed far off. Was he even listening to her answer?

"Remember the Y2K project I was on?" she reminded him, "with the big thing in Baltimore?" He shrugged, half aware. "It was Zoom, the big conversion program. Really big."

"Zoom?" Dan repeated. ". . . Okay."

"People barely know what's up," she said, "after John Hector died yesterday." The word "died" brought Dan back to attention.

"Died?" he asked. "Hector? The chief suit at Bluestar died?"

"Well, silly, they don't wear suits anymore. Now it's golf shirts. But it's got everyone spooked. It was right in his office downtown in the middle of a big summit meeting with Hinnom when he suffered a heart attack."

"Bad boy Ben Hinnom, the man with $80 billion and a school bus to drive it in?" asked Dan incredulously. "The two most powerful computer giants in the world are in a room yesterday, and one of them dies. Where is *that?*" he said, picking up the *Chicago Tribune* on the next table. The front page was devoted to news stories on highway construction problems, Bosnia, and Mideast terrorism. "Where's the story?"

"Right here," answered Park, pointing to the front page below the fold: "In Business . . . *Bluestar Chief Suffers Heart Attack.*"

"Page 63?" said Dan. They turned to the three-column item on page two of the *Business* section: "*Hector Passing Leaves Bluestar Doubtful.*"

"He's evil," said Park, her lips pursed in distress.

"Hector?" asked Dan.

"No, Hinnom," she replied.

"Well, he's known for that," said Dan. "Everyone from the Justice Department to the European Union has been trying to stop the Hinnom Computing monopoly. I guess he's bigger than the government. Bigger than a bunch of governments."

"No, I don't mean just evil like a phrase. He's *actually* evil. Inside."

"You mean he has a heart made of black slime?" joked Dan.

"I mean," she revealed, "I worked for both Hector and Hinnom in Seattle."

The words sent an electrical pinch to Dan's forehead. His eyes narrowed, his head turned slightly so he could hear better and his voice became just a bit more reportorial. He listened carefully as Park elaborated.

"I know a few things," she began hesitantly. "I was recruited, you know, by Bluestar. Right out of grad school in 1987. Things were a bore until the spring of '91 when Bluestar opened a small Windgazer programming office in Lawrence to help Blue products connect to Windgazer APIs. That was after Hector declared, 'Bluestar will connect to *everything.*' Right after the stock dropped to the bad sixties. Hinnom had won the desktop wars and Bluestar was going to be history unless its software, hardware too, were Hinnom-compatible.

"I was still in lovely Lawrence," she continued, "so I joined up. In 1991, when I started on the project, there were only eleven people in Connect Blue, as it was code-named. Most transferred from Blue branches in Austin and the Hudson Valley. We tried to keep it out of the trade weeklies."

"I don't understand," Dan interrupted, "Tell me, is this tied into . . ."

"I listened to you all day yesterday," retorted Park. "Let me explain it." Dan demurred.

"Eventually," she resumed, "as Hinnom grabbed more and more of the PC market, our office ramped up. By 1993 or maybe '94, in there, Connect Blue was staffed by more than sixty-five people and the news had hit the Internet. So it was public.

"Hinnom resented Connect Blue," Park related, still uncertain if she was speaking to someone she could trust. "He tried not to cooperate. It's not normal, the way he hates Bluestar. I guess it's the one thing he can't possess, or maybe he still hates the company from before he broke away in the eighties when he was just a DOS punk in a garage doing Bluestar's bidding.

"Anyway," Park went on, now feeling a bit more confident about talking, "Bluestar threatened a big antitrust thing unless Hinnom permitted Bluestar programmers to access the APIs that would allow Bluestar software to connect. Hinnom wasn't as strong then as he is now. Even still, he hung tough because all he needed was another six months of vaporware and Bluestar would have lost both the FAA and Pentagon contracts, and who knows what else in the FedTech division due to lack of compatibility because the government everywhere was standardizing on the Hinnom OS preloaded into the new, faster desktop computers being purchased. That would mean all of Bluestar's software—which had been used for years—would almost overnight become unusable once the preloaded computers came on line."

Dan looked a little confused.

"*Vaporware*," Park explained, "is promoting exciting software that doesn't exist or long before it's ready as a tactic so people won't buy your competitor's product. '*Preloaded*' means factory installed software. So, can I go on?"

Without waiting for a reply, she continued. "The night before Blue lawyers were ready to file lawsuits all over the world, and seek injunctions and stuff, a compromise was worked out. Bluestar was afforded the same cooperation every other software manufacturer received, but Connect Blue had to move into a low-profile office on the Hinnom Seattle campus itself. For security's sake, they said. In other words, move in, pay rent, and even take all phone calls through the general Hinnom switchboard."

Park lowered her voice, "Everyone at Connect Blue suspected the lines were incredibly tapped, so we used cell phones to communicate with Bluestar. Even to order pizzas. That lasted about two weeks until somehow the cell signal got scrambled in our office, and no more cellular. It was very stifling in there."

"Now your son, Sal . . ." broke in Dan.

"Wait, I'm talking about Hinnom. Listen," Park interjected. "This story doesn't come easy. About four months ago, after senior Blues figured that the President's Year 2000 Compliance Commission in Miami would collapse, the Connect office began working on Y2K in a big way. I was a team leader. One day, Hinnom's guy, Linzer–the weird guy, no one knows much about him–comes into the Connect office and says Hinnom is building a better Y2K mousetrap and he's willing to pay dollars."

"Dollars?"

"Linzer said everyone's salary would be *tripled* on the spot, no questions asked, and if we signed up then and there and Hinnom made the GA ship date, we'd get a bonus of one month's pay for every month of uninterrupted service on the job, plus a tax-free gift of $10,000, the legal limit, to us–and a second $10,000 tax-free gift to any relative of our choosing. That's another way of saying $20,000."

"Nice job incentive," commented Dan.

"In high-tech, you have it all," agreed Park. "I've seen company cars, schooling, and the dog-walking corporate concierges. Even the guy who flew his entire company to Disneyland for making GA. Believe me, Silicon Valley recruiters are cruising gay bars and pool halls Saturday nights to find talent. But tripling our salary was more than anyone could believe."

"Again, remind me, what's GA?" asked Dan.

"That's *generally available,* the announced ship date. GA," she explained. "And API is *application program interface,* which is nerdspeak for compatibility between operating system and software. Got it?"

"Got it. So you went to work for Hinnom?"

"Everyone did. No one in the office reacted right away. No one would even talk about it. It was as though people had been instantaneously corrupted and no one was willing to even look anyone in the eye for shame. By lunch, people were whispering into their phones. And within a few days, we were all Hinnom employees. Except for a few people who said they wouldn't work for Hinnom for any amount of money.

"Me? My son was about to graduate from high school," she asserted, as though trying to justify her decision. "I had barely a pittance put away for college. I took the job. I admit it. For the money. Connect Blue closed, and we all just transferred over to Building 6. Which, by the way, is Bad Ben's building."

Park understood family responsibilities, the duty to provide. When the harvest went bad, she had seen her father take night jobs at the gas station near the highway, and then as a janitor at the overgrown grocery that passed for a supermarket in town, and even three weeks in the mortuary in the next county but nightmares made him quit. When you grow up on the farm you often live between thin wheat and thick debt, in communities where the bankers were friends wearing guilty faces like executioners asking forgiveness in advance, under skies that brought curses in between the blessings and sometimes the other way around. Even in the midst of a farm community, where food was abundantly planted, grown, cut, stored and shipped around the world, it was frighteningly easy to go hungry. Park took the job at Hinnom. No apologies.

"You want a little wine?" asked Dan. He motioned to the waitress, pointed to the Chablis listed on the card and then switched the order to the Chardonnay. "So what happened? How did you get to Chicago?"

"This is the part we didn't get to in between all your sermons on Dali," sighed Park. "I didn't realize how creepy Hinnom was. It was a very difficult experience. There was always talk about his tactics. If he wanted, say, some little innocuous PIM—that's a *personal information manager*, you know, like a scheduler and address book—he would make a reasonable offer to the developers. They would send him all their proprietary marketing plans hoping for a big sale. But he never really wanted a genuine acquisition, just the confidential details. Then he would walk into the programming department and order us to duplicate the software with a few minor variations. Bang, he steals a PIM and markets the heck out of it. That happened with Windgazer Daily.

"I remember one guy from New Hampshire," she recalled, "you know, these developers are very inward, socially dysfunctional guys with really defective radar scopes. Well, he butted heads with Bad Ben. This guy had a nice typeface—nothing all that special—but Hinnom liked the letters, especially the H and the way the ascenders rose. The nerd designer wouldn't sell because Hinnom wanted to rename the face 'He-Man.' Don't ask me why. I think the nerdguy was Johnny something . . . maybe John . . . John Colliton. Right, it was ColliFont. Wasn't much, but the font was all Colliton had in the world. Negotiations fell apart, Hinnom sued him in Seattle for breach of good faith or bad faith negotiations—whatever. The poor nerdguy had no lawyer in Seattle, refused to believe the whole thing was happening in a supposed democracy, and before you know it, Colliton is defaulted. Hinnom won a huge judgment against him."

"How much?" interjected Dan.

"Huge," she replied. "A million, two million, something big. Hinnom seized the company, evicted the Colliton guy from his own office–it was in the middle of that big blizzard in New Hampshire a few years ago–took the font, and renamed it 'He-Man.' Then to top it all, Hinnom sent Colliton a personal letter rubbing it in, something like, "Sorry it had to come to this." And the entire letter was typed in the He-Man font, with the weird H's and everything. Even the Hinnom logo on the letterhead was redone in the font–and they never touch that logo, except this one time that I know of. Colliton put Hinnom's 'salt in the wound' letter on the Internet to show the world the extremes the bastard will go to. It's actually become part of the Hinnom legend. All that because Hinnom liked the way the ascenders rose on an *H*."

"He ruined a man for an *H*?" asked Dan in disbelief.

"Correct. How much can an *H* mean to one person?"

"Depends what the *H* stands for to the person in question," answered Dan. "But this thing, the guy with the font. That was in the papers. Even I read it. Point is, you knew all this before you started working for Hinnom Computing. So why did you leave?"

Park's eyes watered.

Dan skillfully said nothing, allowing the long pause to coax the disclosure.

After glancing around to see if anyone was listening, she slowly revealed her story.

"I received an email one day, an email intended for Bad Ben," Park recounted. "Security was intense at Hinnom. No one was permitted to have a real address, like you would be dlevin@hinnom.com. No. Instead we all had registered names inside the firewall. The computer randomly assigned us a different numerical alias each and every day. To send a message, it's a little tedious. You just bring up the Hinnom corporate phone book refreshed daily and select the name; the assigned numerical alias appears and you just type that in. Understand? I could be H351 on Thursday and H649 on Friday. Everyone was really paranoid about sending or receiving email. And to keep people from harassing him with email he didn't want, Hinnom set up an unlisted address for himself only a select few could access. But he was on the same rotation along with everybody else for numerical aliases. One day," she paused, then stopped. ". . . I can't tell you this."

"Sure, you can tell me this." Dan gently pushed. "Just tell me."

"For one full day I got email intended for Hinnom," Park said. "It came to my box. A lot of people had screwed up mail that day because the mail server went down during a power outage and the UPS as usual didn't hold long enough."

"United Parcel Service?"

"*Uninterruptable power supply*–big batteries attached to all the computers," Park corrected. "Most of the mail was obnoxious junk, financial reports and meeting reminders from managers. I deleted it because I didn't want to be the one to forward Ben's mail. But one email was . . ." she fell silent.

"Go ahead."

"One email was from Linzer on his portable Windy, before he knew of the email server screwup." She lugged a daytimer from her purse, peeled back the pages, and found the date. "It read: 'The very Catholic medical examiner Mr. Torres will discover tomorrow morning that his ancient DOS-loving 486 has caught a virus. All the files on the bitch Rosie were corrupted and unrecoverable.' See, I wrote it down in my book," she said as she trembled into the next statement. "I think . . . I think . . . Linzer or Ben might have been involved in Rosie's death."

"Rosie?"

"Rosie was the sweetest woman," explained Park. "No one ever figured how a sweet and simple black grandmotherly type like her became Hinnom's secretary. One day she was just drafted for the job by one of the HR managers when Hinnom's previous gal quit. Rosie never adopted the Hinnom mindset. She always kept a bowl of fresh apples on her desk and treated everyone with genuine friendship. Staff loved her and brought her flowers on Valentine's Day. Once we all chipped in to get her a day of beauty at Salon Miguel. She loved that and came back with a fancy hairdo and professional makeup. She was so nice–and in her own way, she made Hinnom tolerable to those of us who worked in Building 6. One day she got into some sort of dispute with Hinnom. No one knows what it was about."

"Well, what was it?" pressed Dan. "She saw something? Sexual harassment? He insulted her?"

"There's no use asking," Park assured. "We've all been over it. No one ever figured it out. All anybody knew is one day she resigned and five minutes later walked out carrying all her belongings and desk photos in a box, with her bowl of apples at the top of the heap. She passed me in the corridor and kissed me, kissed me crying. Later that day, it was reported that Rosie committed suicide. But it was unclear—couldn't nail this down—whether she did or did not have a reconciliation meeting with Hinnom at her apartment just before that. One neighbor said he saw Bad Ben's school bus. Another guy said it was just the district school bus. Who knew? Who wanted to know? It was a big whispering shock wave for a few days. Then the medical examiner—the Dr. Torres guy—announced that the results of the autopsy were inconsistent with a suicide, but he needed further tests."

"The law mandates an autopsy for every unnatural death," Dan interjected.

"Exactly," she went on. "So it's the email day. And I get Linzer's message intended for Ben. The next day, sure enough, Torres was on the local news channel saying the tests were inconclusive because of technical problems."

She leaned closer to Dan. "I think his computer and maybe his other equipment was deliberately fried. He lost all the data and everything was irretrievable. That's all we heard. End of story. It was all hushed up and no one wanted to talk about it. Hinnom Computing is a huge employer in Seattle. About fifteen thousand people and no one out there wants to make too much of a wave with Hinnom."

Dan waved his index finger, insisting, "No, no. You can't hush up a big corporate suicide. Where was the follow-up?"

"Of course you can," Park countered. "It happened at Bluestar all the time. A career at Bluestar used to mean a job for life. When Bluestar began its first-ever layoffs in the Hudson Valley a few years back, midlevel managers were committing suicide at an incredible rate. I think there were eighteen in one year. After twenty years of service, no pension or prospects, many of them were totally despondent. Those suicides were hushed up. Corporate suicides are always hushed up. Look, even Hector's death doesn't rate more than a few inches back in *Business*."

"And you think Hinnom or Linzer might have been involved in Rosie's death?" Dan asked incredulously.

"That's why I left," said Park, staring off. "I couldn't stand the place any more. I just had to leave and I took the job here with Derek Institute. I never even heard of Derek. But I was desperate to get away. So I took the position. No one—just Sal and you—knows about the email. And I hope you'll keep it that way."

Dan rested his chin atop folded hands. "You think the heart attack at Hector's office was another Rosie."

Park bit her lip, and nodded. "I try not to think about it."

"This is pretty hard to believe," he admitted haltingly, "but I think I smell something too. What could possibly be driving this man to control and manipulate everything in sight, and with such a vengeance?"

Park shrugged, "No one has ever been able to figure it out. Personally, I think the man had a huge problem with his parents. Huge. He's totally screwed up in the head."

"You mean his mother didn't potty train him right," sneered Dan.

"No, it's not his mom, it's his *dad.*"

"His dad?"

"For sure. The day I got Bad Ben's email, I also got his MTMs."

"Which are?"

"*Memos to Myself,*" she continued. "Lots of Hinnom people would send themselves email reminders through the Windgazer alarm feature. It's basically just a graphical messaging system, so anyone could just launch them at the end of the workday timed to arrive the next morning as a reminder. Well, Hinnom was famous for MTMs. And I was getting them because I was getting his email that day. I was working late, it was maybe eleven o'clock, and suddenly his MTM pops up in my email box. I click on it and I see a string of twenty-five seemingly nonsensical letters. I'm sure this is one of his bizarre randomly selected computer-generated passwords, so I want nothing to do with it. Delete. But first, I wrote it down. Get this."

She flipped to a page in her daytimer, and wrote the string on a napkin.

emevigrofrehtafymllliwnehw

"Means what?" Dan asked.

She held the napkin up to the light so the letters shined through and pointed. "It's really simple. Look at these four letters, the four from the end."

"W-I-L-L," discerned Dan.

"That's what clued me in," she chimed back excitedly. "It was baby stuff to add the spaces. Backwards the whole thing reads: 'when will my father forgive me.'"

Dan's mouth opened slightly. He was briefly speechless. "Come again?"

"'When will my father forgive me,' she repeated. And then after I deleted the message, turns out it came again and again—once per minute for about forty minutes, till close to midnight. I deleted every MTM but over and over, Hinnom is asking 'when will my father forgive me.'"

Dan finished his Laphroaig with a gulp, something he never did. "I'll bear it in mind. Let's go, I'm dropping you home. But dinner tonight. Okay?" He took the napkin.

DAN STEPPED OUT of the Del Sol. He parked in one of the semicircles in front of the *Tribune.* "You okay, Chokky?" he asked the rotund traffic cop who has supervised the circles for decades, making sure only the right people parked illegally in front of the Tribune. Chokky always appreciated the deference—that was protocol—and waved Dan into a parking spot.

As always, when Dan walked into Tribune Tower, he looked up and was impressed with the edifice's bizarre, pseudo-Gothic, architecturally overdressed walls studded with famous stone and rock fragments from such far-flung structures as the Kremlin, the Great Wall of China, and the cathedral at Notre Dame. In the days when Chicago was a four-newspaper town, when reporters dressed badly and wrote well, the *Tribune* was known as "the gray ghost," a newspaper so arrogant about its excellence that it invented its own dictionary. "Through" and "though" were spelled *thru* and *tho* to save lines. But eventually the conservative-owned *Tribune* added color ink, bought the Cubs, went public, spruced up WGN Radio—which stands for the World's Greatest Newspaper—and abandoned its own dictionary. After it redecorated the newsrooms, the paper became more corporate than ever. The *Tribune*—what they did and didn't do—was still the defining standard for all news and non-news in Chicago and for every state that bordered Illinois.

He stopped at lobby reception. "Dan Levin to see Ray Magis." A profoundly overweight guard, neck sagging onto his collar, phoned up to Magis. A moment later, the guard reported, "Voice mail. Is he expecting you?"

"Not really," said Dan, very quietly, "but we know each other. Can you try his direct line instead of the department?"

Expressionless, the guard replied. "If you don't have an appointment, all I can do is leave a message on the departmental voice mail. Do you want me to do that?"

"No, thanks," replied Dan. "I'll just call on my own." He walked over to the house phones on the wall, and asked the operator to speak "directly to the private line of Ray Magis." Departmental voice mail is all he heard.

Dan hung up, and tried the next house phone reaching another operator. "I need to speak to Accounts Receivable." A service rep in AR answered. "Ray Magis, please . . . Oh, did they give me the wrong connection again? Check your directory and I'll dial it . . . No, not the departmental line, his direct phone . . . Thanks."

He flashed back the operator, "3231 please." Magis picked up.

"Ray. Dan Levin . . . Good. Good. Look we need to talk about something . . . Next week is not so good. Actually, I'm downstairs. Can I pop up? . . . A few minutes' time, that's all. Good."

Within moments, the guard answered his phone, and looked up to notice Dan. Dan walked over and innocently said, "Hi." The guard nonchalantly handed him a stick-on visitor's badge. Dan pasted it on his pants just above the pocket. He never wore visitor badges anywhere else.

The fifth-floor conference room was glass-walled, with the names of the *Tribune's* numerous Pulitzer winners frosted into one pane. Dan was ushered in by the fifth-floor receptionist and waited quietly. He always waited quietly and spoke quietly at the *Tribune*. To Dan, it was unnatural to be so mannerly in a journalistic setting. He expected to act and talk like the Chicago street journalists he had worked with over the years—especially the investigative reporters, the ones who hung out in bars and threw darts; the ones who defined an investigative reporter as a guy who thought like a criminal but acted like a cop; the ones who resented editors until they became editors themselves and then they learned to live with the loathing; the ones that laughed at graduates from journalism school and anchormen on TV, both of whom knew little about journalism; the ones who barked at new recruits and guarded old sources like prized possessions. Dan had adapted to the civility at the *Tribune,* but begrudgingly.

Magis walked in, pushing his wire-rimmed glasses back onto the reddened groove atop his nose. He knew Dan from the old days, when the four newspapers competed seven times daily and nothing was more important than "the story," from the days when newspapers set up stings to catch official bribery and reporters masqueraded as just about anyone to get a scoop, from the days when 'undercover' did not mean a hidden camera in a TV producer's briefcase, it meant facing a .357 if discovered. But Magis was now a suit sitting in a conference room that looked like it belonged in a bank. His shirt collar was buttoned too tight and one sock had fallen so low the elastic indentation was showing above his ankle.

"How have you been, Dan?" asked Magis in a low voice, cordially shaking hands. "We heard about New Year's. That was a tragedy. Sorry. It must have been terrible."

"I'm fine now," answered Dan. "Thanks for your concern. Look, I have a story I think would be right for the *Trib*."

Now the pitch: two to three succinct selling sentences, known as a *query*, designed to grab Magis' editorial interest. If he didn't buy the idea in those few sentences, a polite dance of denial would follow, rejecting the query. "Maybe you heard about the death of Bluestar's chairman John Hector yesterday," said Dan in a presentation voice. "Hector was actually in a closed-door, very sensitive meeting with Mr. Hinnom at the time. Hector allegedly died of a heart attack, but there is some suggestion, perhaps, of some sort of. . . I guess *foul play* would be the best word to use."

Magis looked stupefied. His days of innate journalistic suspicion had long ago disappeared, in fact not long after he moved to the suburbs so his kids could attend a better school and his wife could drive instead of walk to the grocery store.

"Foul play?" he responded with a grimace.

"Yes," confirmed Dan, adding softly in a monotone. "I learned all this just two hours ago. It seems that Ben Hinnom, already known for his corporate bad-guy tactics, may actually have been involved in a similar death, or at least another suspicious death, earlier this year. I, personally, see a pattern."

"How did Hector's death become 'suspicious?' He had a heart attack," countered Magis, picking up a *Tribune*, and thumbing to the story in the Business section, " '*Third* heart attack,' it says."

"I don't have all the facts," Dan gently insisted in sales mode. "But, as

I say, I developed a source with direct knowledge, and I learned all this
less than two hours ago. I came here first. I think it warrants looking into.
If it's nothing, it's nothing. But my source tells me this could be one of the
biggest stories of the year. Hinnom is dirty. We just don't know how dirty.
If it *is* a story, I'd like to be there with the *Tribune*."

"Sounds a little far out, Dan," said Magis with quiet condescension.
"Even if it was a hard story, it would be a city piece and the paper would
never let an outsider do an investigative article."

"I used to. What's different today?" asked Dan.

"Twenty years," shot back Magis in a smug but subdued voice.

"This is something I want to do, Ray," said Dan, trying to reach out. "I
haven't jumped feet-first into an investigation for the mass media in years.
I need this, guy."

"Why should you, you're a successful publisher?" Magis questioned,
almost snidely. "Sold your magazines for millions—"

"—well, we don't talk about specifics—" interjected Dan.

". . . But you don't need the money," continued Magis. "You have
enough bylines and awards to fill a bathroom wall. You still keep your
Pulitzer on top of the john, I hear. Your Hinnom story sounds far out and
I'd need more than your feelings and unidentified sources and their 'indi-
cations' to even discuss it with the higher-ups here. It's just not going to
happen," Magis assured.

"If you think Hinnom is dirty in some way—other than in Hector's
death—find some documentation and write a think piece for Perspective.
Write an analysis for Business. Do a profile for the *Sunday Magazine*. Talk
about the antitrust stuff, the vanquished competition. But foul play in
Hector's death? It's far out, Dan. It would take an executive nod from
upstairs to even waste our time on a hard piece with the slant of murder
in the executive suite. It wouldn't be very long before the bosses plain
shut us down for being so wacky with our resources. And frankly—"

"You mean: *that indecision is made at a higher level*?" cut in Dan, still softly but incisively.

Magis declined to react to the remark. "Well, I can only tell you how it
is. We use our investigative material from our own reporters responsible
and accountable to this newspaper, not freelancers. You could take it
across the street. They use freelancers."

"You know I don't work across the street," Dan replied. "But I have produced award-winning investigations for this paper and virtually every other paper, magazine and electronic outlet in this town." Defensive, he began clicking them off: "Taxi cabs?"

"Good stuff. No question," Magis responded. "You broke up the taxi monopoly. Stared down a .357, I know the story. I was there."

"Employment agencies?"

"Nice work," Magis easily conceded. "Undercover. Indictments."

"Senator Steve? Most powerful man in the Senate," Dan reminded, "running how many millions through his downstate construction companies? I took him down essentially by my lonesome while everyone in the mainstream media was busy with the invasion of Panama. Ray?"

"A big one," acknowledged Magis, now showing some impatience. "Official Senate censure, indictment, resignation, you don't need to convince me, Dan."

"The insurance scam, for heaven's sake," said Dan, his palms flexing on the table. "Twelve lawyers in prison, *America's Most Wanted*, and an IRE Award. I was all alone on that. These guys threatened to kill me. I was all alone and took them all down. So I ask: is good old-fashioned investigative journalism in this town dead, unless it deals with political sex and contributions?" pressed Dan, still struggling to keep his voice down. "I have a potential story here, Ray. A *real* story."

"Do an analysis piece, Dan, eight hundred words," Magis offered as a compromise. "Forget about an investigation. If you have something concrete on Hector's death, turn it over to the city desk. We'll have a staff reporter look at it, verify it, and credit your independent inquiry within the first three paragraphs. You have my word on that. We'll pay you a courtesy fee out of respect."

"Within the first three graphs?" Dan retorted, barely concealing his irritation. "Ray, I remember you and me walking out of Alderman Marzanto's office with documents stuffed under our shirts, playing tag team with a Xerox machine to get the goods on the taxi cab scam. I remember a guy who punched out a city editor because you didn't like his attitude on a lead."

"I don't walk out of public offices with documents anymore," defended Magis with decorum, "and the punching incident was an indiscretion. I have been forgiven. No one here even remembers it."

"I do."

"And I remember when you didn't have a suit and your ties were too thin," shot back Magis. "You made a name for yourself as a dedicated young freelance investigative reporter back in the days. Okay. Youngest guy ever to get a major byline in either the *Trib* or the *Times*. Eighteen years old, or was it seventeen. Okay. You wrote a big book, the Holocaust thing. Okay. You were on TV every night for a month. Mentioned in all the gossip columns. *Chicago Monthly*. Nice. Crusading journalist. Struggling muckraking magazine. Foreign correspondent. Israel, Lebanon. Pulitzer Prize. Okay. But then, *then* what happened*?*"

"Meaning?" Dan answered.

"You tell me," Magis pushed back, also careful to keep his voice down. "I guess you became a big publisher. *Brain* was it?"

"You got something against brains?" asked Dan defensively.

"Not if they're used right," Magis responded. "But you used yours to become a general publisher. Lifestyle, medical, airport rags. So that's how we see you."

"You got something against success?" Dan asked.

For just an instant, Dan squinted and made a fist. *His newborn son suddenly opened his eyes, for the first time, for the most important time, and Dan's eyes opened as well, as though for the first time, for the most important time. Less than one minute old, the child reached up and touched Dan's beard as his first act on earth. The doctors, nurses and the delivery room itself, even Jenny swimming in her own sweet sweat and tears, dimmed from view. There was only one event in the universe at that moment—his new son, Simon, making contact, Promethean contact, infusing Dan with the electric renewing glory of newborn innocence. Dan looked up and said to Jenny, "My God, I'm the first thing he ever saw." Dan wept. Jenny wept. Simon just blinked.* Dan unsquinted, his fist disappeared.

"Ray," Dan tried to reason, "I'm like the chef who decided to open a restaurant and by the time I took a deep breath I was so busy hiring waiters, buying tablecloths, setting up franchises, paying bills, I wasn't doing much cooking anymore. The *Trib* runs lousy comics, cheesy horoscopes and tacky singles ads. Am I judgmental? It's still one of the finest papers in the country, for my money finer than *The Washington Post* and *The New York Times*. So cut *me* some slack. Now I sold all my restaurants and I'm going back to what I love."

Dan looked around and spoke even more quietly. "Ray, computer tycoons are the robber barons of our day. Double that in the next century. Hinnom is the biggest and most unscrupulous of any. Look back. America's railroad and mineral empires—and not a few unions—were built on thievery and worse. Adversaries were trampled on and sometimes, Ray, they were killed. Yes, killed.

"The robber barons of the information age don't wear top hats and hire Pinkertons," Dan argued. "They wear golf shirts and hire slick public relations firms. But the stakes are still the same. The compulsion to control lives on. The willingness to commit shameless acts for greed is unchanged. You still think the information war is about who sells the most computer systems. Battle of the keyboards. Wrong, Ray. It's a war for who controls what everyone in the world will know and do forever more. That's why the stakes are worth killing for. And this particular death of one John Hector happened just down the street. It's our responsibility to check it out."

Magis, tired of the debate, declared, "Dan, you're a great writer. No one is disputing that. Do a profile on Ben Hinnom for the *Sunday Magazine*. Quote a few prosecutors saying they're looking into strange occurrences involving corporate misconduct and dump that part into a little sidebar, 250 words. Qualify it. Make it a mystery. But don't try to break news and please don't libel the richest man in the world. Do that, or turn over your evidence—if you have any—to the city desk, and they'll credit you in the first three graphs."

The pitch was over. Dan's side of the denial dance was due. "Well, thank you so much for giving this consideration," Dan said summarily and politely, as though he had just been denied by a loan officer. He quietly left Tribune Tower.

DAN PARKED HIS red Del Sol in front of a plug outside the nondescript warehouse on Illinois Street. No one was on the street except a sign painter adding the words "A Percy-Rogers Publication" beneath the Chicago Monthly logo. Dan briskly pushed open the door, scampered up the long stairway, walked right past the newly hired receptionist who only meekly protested, past a long corridor decorated floor-to-ceiling with past CM magazine covers, and into the new editor's office—that is, Dan's old glass-walled office. His favorite photos from the magazine were still on the wall.

A startled, slender, unmuscular, blue-jeaned young man, surely no older than twenty-two, put down a manuscript and good-naturedly announced: "Well, welcome. Dan Levin, I presume. Welcome to *Chicago Monthly*. Recognized you from your picture," pointing to Dan's last "Memo from the Editor" open on his desk. "I knew you'd come in one day. Welcome."

"You're Alger?" said Dan, trying to hide his disappointment upon seeing his slight, seemingly ineffectual replacement.

"I am," the young man proudly replied.

"You're the new *me*?"

"I am. How do you like me?" said Alger, lifting his hands and rotating femininely. "What brings you to *Chicago Monthly*?"

Alger was exactly the kind of person Dan had chewed up and belched out countless times before. An inexperienced, unseasoned nine-to-fiving lightweight, he struck Dan as the type who typically washed out as an intern after the first week; the type who would bristle at the thought of staying an hour late, let alone putting an issue to bed at 6 A.M. just when everyone else was waking up; the type who had never enjoyed breakfast at midnight, or stared silently into a coffee mug at dawn, searching for the reflection of his own fatigue; the type who never felt dizzy, even sexually aroused after writing a gut-wrenching lead; the type who had never walked into a smoldering building as firemen pulled a charred body from the debris; the type who never strolled through a gang-infested shooting gallery to ask a dope-wasted runaway if she wanted to go back home to Wisconsin; the type who never helped a talented young writer reach into his heart and try again, or fire an incompetent smart-ass who had no business touching a typewriter; and most of all—most detestable of all—Alger was almost certainly a graduate of journalism school.

"Just thought I would say hello and see if I could help out," replied Dan. "You came here from . . ."

"From Medill," he bragged. "Actually, I interned on another Percy book, *Senior Week*. A grocery store giveaway. I used to clip the newspapers for the 'Wrap Up' section editor. So this is really my first real job. I love it. A real city magazine."

Dan did not say at least a dozen outrageous things that came to mind, but simply quipped, "Well, everyone's gotta start somewhere. And you have your very own award-winning investigative city magazine. That's Alger, correct, as in Horatio?"

"No, I wish," replied the young man, folding his arms demonstratively. "It's Alger, short for Algeria. My father was in the foreign service and served in North Africa."

"Gee, you're lucky," cracked Dan. "You could have been called Tuna for Tunisia, or Libby, or Morry."

Alger was really amused, and smiled broadly, "That's good," Alger laughed. "Tuna. I heard you were a jokester."

"Well, humor is a good thing," Dan continued, trying to disguise his condescending tone. "But what's important in a magazine is *teamwork*. Teamwork. You're in charge now. I know I invented this magazine–"

"–and everyone at Percy knows that, and knows you have made an indelible legacy," Alger interjected politely.

"Well, Algie, you are the editor now . . ."

"Algie . . . algae, that's a one-celled organism!"

"Yes," said Dan, with exaggerated enthusiasm, "but you have more than one cell. You are a complex higher organism, a meat eater, a lion waiting to prove to the pride around you and the jungle at large that while this is your first magazine, it is only your *first* magazine."

"You had nine," Alger replied in a singsong.

"Seven. But, focus here," Dan continued, "because I really am committed to helping you keep *Chicago Monthly* strong and impressive, give it a new legacy, the Algie legacy. Gutsy. Tough. Groundbreaking."

"Breaking ground is good," agreed Alger.

"It's excellent, for God's sake," Dan confirmed loudly. "Now, you know that *CM* has always been known for its exclusive investigations. The taxicab series, the glass replacement guy breaking windows–remember that one? S&L scams, the arson thing . . ."

". . . the arson thing was great," agreed Alger. "I read every issue of *CM* and that was my favorite investigation because first you talked about all the families that had been ruined and that one girl who asked the fireman why her father wasn't coming home, and only then you brought in the landlords hiring thugs to burn their own buildings for the insurance. I loved that one."

"Got a public service award," said Dan modestly. For a moment he almost thought Alger had some smarts. "Now, I have a story for you, a story I will personally investigate and write for *Chicago Monthly* and you'll have it in time for the September issue."

Alger looked confused.

"September," Dan repeated. "Next year's advertising budgets? You need a strong ass-kicking issue in September to nail down the '99 budgets which are decided in October and November."

"Oh, well, under Percy policies," Alger explained, "I never get involved in advertising or ad budgets. It's just not something I ever think about. Now most Percy publications do have advertiser-sponsored Help Guides, where the advertiser—you know, a bank or car dealer—agrees to be the sole advertiser and then we run all their press releases with bylines that look like stories. We do that. And our advertisers get to write press releases that we run verbatim in our once-per-year Profiles in Success issue. But that is different and otherwise we are very proud of our separation of church and state."

Dan nodded and took a breath, "I know you are, Alger. But this piece won't need a sponsor. It will be the cover story, and, actually, the magazine sorta sponsors that all on its own."

"Well, let me elucidate something," asserted Alger in a perfectly corporate voice. "I think that what you did for *Chicago Monthly* was magnificent, and we will build on that in our new direction."

Dan looked puzzled.

Alger walked out to the art department just outside his office and turned over a three-foot poster facing the wall, displaying it for Dan. It was a prototype cover of the next *Chicago Monthly* sporting a large gauche headline: "Chicago's Best Cheesecake." Alger held up the three-foot poster, asking, "Do you think the head should be bigger?"

Dan's mouth opened but nothing came out.

Alger turned over another from the stack, this one stating: "Chicago's Best Pizza—Your Vote Counts." He beamed a proud smile.

"After we used up your inventory of editorial," Alger made clear, "stuff like the slave quarters above the Indian restaurant—boy, that was a great investigation—we were able to start running some of the stories that we think will position the magazine where it needs to be within this local market, consistent with Percy-Rogers' traditional city market strategies. If it's anything like Southern California, people really want to know about which restaurants matter, especially when they change ownership or hire a new chef. *Chicago Monthly* intends to fulfill its mandate. Proudly fulfill its mandate."

Dan tried to speak. Finally, he coughed up the word. "Mandate?"

"Yes," responded Alger. "We see our mandate as–"

"Stop!" shouted Dan abruptly. "We used to run an investigation almost every month as a cover story. If it wasn't an investigation, it was a compelling article like the land mine piece, or an exclusive, like the Farrakhan interview. Stories that mattered. Are those going to continue running in *Chicago Monthly*?"

Alger was worried by Dan's tone. "As I'm sure you were to expect," he asserted more corporately, "Percy-Rogers appreciates what you did with *Chicago Monthly* and *Brain Journal* and all your magazines. And we realize that *Chicago Monthly* was the flagship of Levincom. But these seven titles are ours now, part of a family of more than sixty-eight magazines in our division, and just one of hundreds of Percy publications worldwide. We have to put the Percy-Rogers signature on each of them. We feel the pulse of Chicago cries out for pizza and cheesecake. We intend to serve it up."

This was not the *Tribune*. Dan could not restrain himself. He took on a kindly but sarcastic facial expression. "Alger, do you have a girlfriend?"

Alger shrugged daintily, reflecting a bit of unjustified excitement. "I'm new in town. Don't know too many people. So I'm available for dinner."

Dan drolly declared, "Uh, I am not." He began thinking of the possibilities. Suddenly he felt a compulsion to urinate on the posters with sufficient force that the splatter reached across the room.

"Could I just do one little thing?" asked Dan, fingering the zipper on his pants.

"Please," invited Alger.

Dan paused just as the Talon handle of the zipper was positioned between his fingertips. He thought better of it. Instead, he casually announced, "I think there's a news hole in this office."

He motioned for Alger to come close to the wall. "You don't see it?"

Alger good-naturedly nodded no.

"It is right *here*." On the word "here," Dan crashed his right fist straight through the white painted drywall, almost to the other side. The noise sent several assistants running and Alger into shock. Dan calmly walked over to the art department, brought back a thick marker and drew a black portrait-style frame around the hole. Under it he scrawled, "News Hole by Dan Levin," as though the damage was hanging in a gallery. "See, it's a work of art, my final contribution to *Chicago Monthly*."

Then Dan walked over to a bookshelf and pulled out a forgotten pint of Laphroaig hidden behind an unabridged dictionary. "I'll take this."

Stepping around the cover posters laying on the ground, Dan, very self-confidently, and exuding one heckuva smile, sauntered down the corridor and down the steps. Alger ran after him in an uproar.

Dan was at the bottom of the stairwell when Alger shouted down from the top: "That's destruction of property. I'll be calling Sydney. Australia will be called!"

BARRY'S "SCARLET LETTER" was playing. Its yearning violins set a somber but romantic mood. The doorbell rang. It was Park, wearing a sexy short brown leather skirt below a delicate beige blouse with flowing sleeves. She carried a chic box purse from the Art Institute decorated with signatures from Picasso, Chagall and Cézanne.

"I see you went back to do some shopping," he said, welcoming her in.

The lights were dim. She noticed.

"This is pretty romantic," she admitted with a smile. "Expecting someone?"

"Just you," Dan answered. He used a long fireplace match to light two tall candles, and then tossed the nearly consumed stick into the fireplace where it gently ignited an oil dish below several dried logs. Soon the fireplace was roaring.

"Hmm. The full treatment," she joked. "We *are* going out?"

Dan brought out two platters of green fusilli pasta and laid them on the dining table.

"We're *not* going out," she amended.

"I like to cook," he answered, ladling a rich red sauce atop the fusilli in a spiral pattern, and then adding a tomato slice in the middle. Atop the tomato slice, he shaved fresh Peccoro Romano, and then dropped a thick wedge of sautéed portobello mushroom, plus a few green peas for contrast. Dan had embarked upon a small sermon about culinary presentation, which methods were used in which great restaurants, why proper plate painting required several steps of sauce preparation, and whether snipping the nose of a plastic squeeze bottle was a cheap trick or a justifiable shortcut, when Park simply said, "It's pretty."

The Virginia Swedenburg '92 had attained a full forty minutes of aeration. "Just because a wine is old, doesn't make it good," he began. "Each wine has its own clock. Reminds me of scotch. For example, the Laphroaig ten-year is ideal for its peak of peatiness. So you might believe the fifteen-year to be even better. Right? Not right. By the time Laphroaig hits fifteen years, it is a half decade past its peak. So the company that makes Laphroaig allows another bottler to peddle the fifteen year at a premium in a lookalike bottle to unknowing fans, confident that genuine connoisseurs would avoid it because it's downhill by that time."

"I don't drink scotch," said Park shyly.

"It's actually quite the same with red wine," Dan continued, "based on the sugar content, acidity, sulphur and lots of other good information, the vintner, and in turn the wine enthusiast, can predict when a given wine will mature. This Swedenburg–I ordered one of the last cases–has just achieved its peak nose, bouquet, and body. But by next year, it will be over the hill and a candidate for cooking wine."

"Tastes fine to me," said Park, sipping a bit.

As the evening advanced, serene John Barry music played on, the level in the wine bottle lowered, a second helping of pasta was declined but which Dan served anyway and then ate from Park's plate, and finally, the two went into the kitchen where he turned off the lights to flame a copper pan of strawberries sautéed in cherry and chocolate liqueurs, seasoned with–of all things–cracked black Madagascar pepper and then drenched over vanilla ice cream, a fiery creation which Park was at first afraid to taste but which she then admitted was the most satisfying dessert she had ever enjoyed.

"Where did you learn to cook this way?" she asked.

"It's nothing," Dan answered, waiting for more questions. But Park didn't offer any. So he kissed her on the cheek. She smiled shyly, uncertain as to the next moment but unafraid to experience whatever came. Turning toward him, she opened her soul and admitted as much with her eyes.

For just an instant, Dan squinted and made a fist. *337 please report to Special Services. What do you mean, Special Services?* He unsquinted and his fist disappeared.

"Dan?"

"You're sweet," he said.

They sat down atop a cushion before the flickering hearth of the fireplace. For Dan, talking pedantically was like exercising a part of his autonomic system. It was as easy as breathing. Easier. But when he wanted to listen, his mind was like a heat seeker. And now it was time to ask questions. "Okay, I give up. Tell me about Sal. And yourself—married, divorced, single mom, what?"

Park laughed. "Never married, never divorced."

Hesitating at first, Park found it hard to resist his penetrating questions, and began her story. "Sal is a very special person, who came to this earth in a very special way. When I was in my first year of college . . . let me start over. I love children and always wanted to have a child. The University of Kansas was not a great place to meet men. Either the guy was a farmer's son trying to get an MBA, a rich obnoxious Saudi prince learning geology so he could work in the oil fields—Lawrence, you know, had one of the best geology schools around—or he was a future intelligence man. More intelligence people per square inch come from Kansas than anywhere else—except maybe Nebraska, I guess. I just wanted better."

She laughed a bit in embarrassment. "Why am I telling you all this?"

"Because I'm a good listener?" replied Dan.

"No," she asserted, "a good questioner."

Park was never comfortable talking about her personal life, especially this part. But this man made it all so easy, so natural.

"Where was I? Well, I guess I had read all about the great minds of this world," Park recounted. "I grew up with Dickens and Conrad. But I certainly couldn't meet a Conrad in school. And I was broke. I lost my scholarship because they reviewed my family's application and the land—the land my dad ultimately lost to agri-gangsters—those few dusty acres, disqualified us from the means test. I needed money.

"One day I answered an ad I saw in the school paper for a surrogate mother." She watched for a reaction and saw none, so she continued. "All school expenses would be paid, plus $20,000 if I carried a child successfully to term. I signed, gee, a gazillion forms. The whole thing was controlled by this Wichita attorney and a Texas doctor. I would receive the egg of the donor wife fertilized by her real husband. They were both fertile but her womb could not host the fetus. After delivery, I was to place the child up for prearranged adoption by the genetic parents, and I would never know their identity. I agreed."

"Sal was not your child, but you carried him?"

"Exactly," replied Park, comforted by the sense that Dan was accepting her history without judgment.

The music had long ago finished, and Dan was now completely focused on Park's story.

"You carry a child," he said, "become its mother. But all the time you must face the reality that you will give this child away to a stranger. You dealt with that?"

"Yes. Being pregnant, this pregnancy, changed me just as I, as—oh I knew it would," Park said dreamily. She recalled the wonders. "I was never alone from the moment I received Sal. My life had new meaning. I wrote beautiful poetry during those months. Saved it all. And every week I wrote a letter to the biological mother and father telling them what I was feeling so they could share in that joy. I mailed them to the attorney. Heaven knows if he ever forwarded any.

"Every minute I would imagine that my son was destined for greatness and I would be part of his greatness," she remembered wistfully. "Who knows? Maybe he would be a great scientist, or a president, or lead a nation. I didn't know where he would end up . . . what state . . . not even what country. The lawyer hid everything from me. But he was prompt with one thing: the monthly payments, the constant medical checks and testing. That doctor. I used to wake up in a panic some nights because I imagined that if the doctor found something lacking in my baby's condition, they might terminate. They had the right . . . to terminate—if they detected an abnormality."

"But you ending up keeping Sal?"

Park folded her arms as if chilled. "Yes. About three weeks before I was due," she recounted, "the lawyer phoned. Meet him at the hotel room at the Holiday Inn—where we always met. He said Sal's parents had died—it was a terrible car crash. I don't even know if that was true. For all I know they just changed their minds. Either way, the biological adoptive parents would not be there. The lawyer even offered me a chance to terminate. Yeah, they said it could be done even at that late point in the last trimester."

She had trouble releasing the words, but they finally tumbled out. "This was *my* child," she declared, eyes watering. "Maybe he would be a nobody and maybe he would save the world. I didn't know. But Sal and I were brought together for a reason and I knew that this was God's way of telling me we would stay together. I remember what I told that, that, that jerk. I could hardly utter the words and I can barely say them now."

Holding back tears, she recalled, "I told him: 'I am carrying this baby. He is in me. I feel him every time I breathe and will every step I take. I will keep him. He will keep me. The Lord will keep us both.' I told him exactly those words. 'The Lord will keep us both.' I have never forgotten. At that moment, my whole outlook changed, from Sal's temporary protector and guardian angel to truly his mother. After the birth, I went through the paperwork to make Sal legally mine. I named him Sal–Sal for . . . well, for Sal."

Dan hugged her. They kissed in a long soaring moment. Park had surrendered her past to Dan and Dan accepted. His kiss slowed from one of excitement to one of passion and Park felt the difference. Initially, her arms were on his chest, still guarding the realm between their bodies. Then she let them fall to her side. She was now open and inviting.

The hard floor could not be felt, the room could not be sensed. Their passionate discovery became the oxygen in their lungs, the blood in their veins and the arousal in their hearts. Now Park became not only receptive to Dan's touch, but responsive, kissing back and finding Dan. Park came atop him as a woman who had made a decision of intimacy, and he submitted to all her bold, unleashed kissing, first on his face, and then down his chest. *Last of the Mohicans,* cut 8, was playing. He tasted her baby-fine hair, sniffed in the calming scent of her skin, and she melded to his embrace.

Then, for just an instant, Dan squinted and made a fist. *337 please report to Special Services. What do you mean, Special Services?* He unsquinted and his fist disappeared.

But he remained taut.

"What's wrong?" she asked. "Where are you?"

"I'm here," he answered, almost with a laugh. He kissed her once deeply and rolled the two of them to an upright position. "I'm fine."

But the mood was broken. They stared quietly at the fireplace flames snapping across the logs. Their foreheads recorded the heat as they reentered reality. Dan reached for his remote. Zimmer's *Backdraft* came on. She peered into his eyes for an explanation. Nothing was revealed.

"I'm fine," he repeated.

They began talking. He offered to locate the attorney and learn the identity of Sal's parents. Park told him not to bother. Six years ago the alcoholic lawyer died of liver failure. She had already tried to get the records, but all his surrogate pregnancy files were shredded after he retired from practice and before he died. She straightened her blouse slightly.

Dan then offered to track down the Texas doctor. Impossible. She never knew a name beyond "Dr. Tam," and he went back to Thailand after the delivery. Park again tried to probe Dan's eyes, but could not get in.

"So when do I meet this Sal?" asked Dan, trying to talk about anything other than his reaction a few moments before. "Sounds like he has already survived more challenges before birth than most people have in a lifetime."

"We don't start at Derek until Thursday," Park answered. "Tomorrow we can all get together. If you like."

"Are you staying tonight?" Dan ventured in a stammer.

Park's face showed vulnerability as she stumbled over an answer. Sal was home alone and it was midnight.

"I better get back," she whispered reluctantly.

Dan did not challenge her. They kissed again. Park remained open to his touch and let him find her. For Dan, that was good to know. He perceived the acceptance immediately and displayed his exhilaration clearly. A smile of contentment came across his face, that smile of peace that settles in after a man has assured himself he has been accepted physically and emotionally by a woman.

"Sure you're okay?" she asked.

"I'm fine, really. Come on, I'll take you home," he said lovingly, with his hand placed gently on hers. She squeezed his, fingers interlocked.

There was nothing in his mouth, but Dan clearly tasted Laphroaig. No music was playing. But in his mind he heard it unmistakably. The Gipsy Kings. Blasted.

5

TESTIMONY

By nine in the morning, Navy Pier was bustling. Thick crowds of visitors flowed across the traffic circle to the Pier's ornate entrance. Walking the long concourse, you were never more than a few feet from the lapping waters of Lake Michigan, from modern art constructed of every conceivable material from driftwood to aluminum piping, from lemonade, beer and pretzel stands, from the grandest, tallest Ferris Wheel most people had ever seen, and from a child giggling with wonderment. And you were always just a few steps from all manner of vessels: sleek cigarettes sporting beer-drinking drivers, elegant dinner liners ready for tuxedoed wedding parties, and any number of cabin cruisers, sail boats, schooners, and skiffs. But all of them moved aside when the bad boy of Navy Pier roared in, the bright yellow commuter speedboat known as the Sea Dog, its skipper barking like Fido into a megaphone as the craft approached.

Music bubbled along the Pier's entire length. Just beyond the entrance, a jazz quartet warmed things up as an Uncle Sam on stilts bent down and patted a baby's head. Only yards away, a yellow-robed Nigerian percussion team syncopated African rhythms. Further down, a bluegrass trio strummed a toe-tapper. At the rounded tip of the Pier, the Grand Ballroom steps yielded to a picturesque plaza confronting the water's edge. Here, seated on the railing, the morning after both the *Tribune* and *Chicago Monthly* said no, was Dan, peering across the dark green waves, sipping espresso from a paper cup. For Park, the Pier was a short stroll from nearby Lake Point Tower, where, despite Dan's urging to the contrary, she ultimately took up residence at her friend's apartment. When he saw her approaching, he waved at a smile that could be seen over the shoulders of the crowd.

"Where's Sal?" asked Dan.

"Punching code," she answered. "I haven't a clue what he's been working on from one minute to the next." Dan offered a sip of his espresso, which Park found odd. In her experience, people did not share food. "It's not Seattle espresso," he quipped, "but it's the best on Navy Pier."

Park sipped a bit anyway. "Ben Hinnom must be hurting," she said.

Dan looked puzzled. "Meaning?"

"It was on the news this morning," she answered. "He was subpoenaed by the Senate committee looking into the antitrust thing."

"Judiciary?" asked Dan.

"Think so," she replied. "Bad Ben said this was a turning point in his company's ability to innovate, and he's determined to make his stand in Washington. The Senate and the Department of Justice. He is supposed to have some big press conference after . . . his first ever."

Dan, who again felt lazy and mellow, bonding with waves far out in the Lake until they dissolved into the beach, suddenly opened his eyes wide. "Would you like to go to Washington?" he asked Park. "I'm on this Ben Hinnom thing. Dammit, I don't have an assignment yet, but I'm on it." Before Park could respond, he pressed on, "Let's go. Let's go. I'll have you back here Sunday night. It will be a fun weekend. Washington can be beautiful."

Park laughed and listed four reasons very quickly why even the idea was silly and impossible. She and Sal started work at Derek tomorrow, she had no money, and by the time they arrived in Washington, the hearings and press conference would all be over. Dan countered at a rapid clip, "That's where you're wrong. I have the travel agent. And don't sweat the tickets and the lodging. You're my assistant on the story. I'll take care of the expense."

"Uh-uh," rejected Park, slowing things down as nicely as possible. "I have a son. We have jobs. The logistics are *uh-uh*."

"No" was not an option for Dan.

"Don't worry about the discreet logistics," he reassured, referring to the room arrangements. "I'll handle it." Waiting for nothing, he pulled out a dark gray palmsized StarTac cell phone, dialed, then cupped his hand over the mouthpiece to block out the Pier's noise. "Gert? I have a right-now situation. Get me three Southwest walk-up tickets next flight from Midway, or the United hourly at O'Hare, whichever . . . Fine. Other passengers are Park McGuire and Sal McGuire . . . Mother and son . . . I want to board in an hour, ninety minutes max . . . Yes, I have a hearing to catch . . . Get me a three-bedroom suite at the Willard, or try the Jefferson. If you strike out with the suite, just get me adjacent rooms or at least the same floor . . . Send a sedan please to pick me up at Lake Point Tower in about fifteen minutes. Make that a half hour. More instructions from the car *en route* . . . Right. Thanks, dear."

He flipped the phone off and smiled. "That wasn't hard. A good travel agent and a platinum MasterCard is all it takes."

He downed the last of his espresso, and boyishly asked, as if the matter had been discussed and agreed to long ago, "Ready to fly to our nation's capital?"

Park's mouth was open. Certainly the spontaneity of it all was igniting, the sense of the unexpected, even the dangerous in Dan, excited her more than anyone else she had ever met. But she questioned whether it was all real. She desperately wanted to go. Washington D.C. Never been there. Why not? She was totally ready and could be packed in minutes.

"How about asking *me?*" she responded with irritation in her voice. "I don't have the clothes. I'm not a successful publisher counting his money. There's just no way. I would have to be back here by tonight. And I could *not* sleep over. I have a job tomorrow and I'm not going to make a lousy impression by missing my first day."

Dan handed her the StarTac. "Call Derek," he said, ushering her down the Pier toward home. "You have five minutes to make this happen." Park froze until Dan forcefully followed with, "Go. I have confidence in you."

She didn't know what was more weird, Dan's incredible presumptive pushiness or the prospect of dinner on impulse in Washington. She took the phone, sheepishly asking, "Do we get to tour the White House?"

"No," he shot back, "that's for tourists," tossing his empty espresso cup into a trash can. "Tell Derek you're just settling in, new city, new home, all that. You need Thursday and Friday, and could you start on Monday all fresh."

"They'll dock me," she answered.

"No they won't," he scoffed. "Tell them you need two personal days. That's paid. My employees did it to me all the time. It was unnerving. Couldn't stand it. But, hey."

When the supervisor at Derek came on the line, Park took a totally different tack, telling him in a subdued voice that Ben Hinnom would be testifying before Congress about monopoly yes, but also about the Millennium Bug. She had arranged transportation and lodging through a friend, and . . . looking at Dan for confirmation . . . the press conference as well–he nodded–and wouldn't it be a big boost to her team and Derek if she brought back her own report on the hearings and the press conference? And Sal of course would have to go with for obvious reasons. All she wanted was permission.

Park was kept on hold as she walked along the Pier, past the stairs to the Ferris Wheel, past the bicycle rental shop, past the balloon vendor, past the last lemonade stand. Her supervisor came back just as Park was crossing the noisy traffic circle. Unable to hear over the road din, she kept repeating, "Say it again, please." She couldn't hear. "Just a minute, let me cross the street."

They jaunted to the other side. "Okay, go ahead . . . Yes. Okay . . . I understand . . . That's interesting . . . Really . . . Really. Really? . . . Thank you." Park handed the phone back.

"So really *what*?" asked Dan.

"Strange," Park related. "My supervisor–he thought the whole thing made no sense. Every minute counts on the program and they want me in tomorrow bright and early. Period. But he said he would check anyway. Finally–long delay–he comes back on. Says he asked his manager but the question was for some reason kicked up to Kuebitz, the head guy, remember, who actually interviewed me and Sal way back in Seattle. I told you about him."

"The guy who hired you," Dan replied.

"Correct. And Dr. Kuebitz says to the supervisor that it would be helpful for me to go to Washington and get a firsthand impression. Derek Institute would reimburse any expenses not covered elsewhere."

"Great. So we're on," said Dan, mentally packing his bags.

"Then he says," Park added, "Kuebitz thinks it is important for Sal to also go, not to leave him home. And if there is any problem getting Sal into the hearing room and press conference to call Kuebitz' secretary."

"Him? Kuebitz?" said Dan defensively. "Who needs him for access? You have me."

"Well, the whole shebang is fine and dandy with me, but why all the sudden cooperation?" asked Park.

"Computer companies are stupid," answered Dan. "It's all touchy-feely stuff. In my day, if you hit your boss in the head, first he'd slug you back, then you'd be out of a job. It would be six months before anyone would take you back. Today, they define that as a job stress-related syndrome, you get paid leave, counseling on the company's tab, and a guaranteed return to your original job path when you come back from the shrink. Park, if you said you wanted to climb a mountain in Nepal to see if rarefied air and chanting Tibetan hymns enhances software programming, they'd authorize it and write you up in the employee newsletter."

Dan's StarTac rang. It was Gert. Three flights were booked, departing in two hours.

"Okay," he told Park, "the sedan will pick you up in the lobby and then drive to me."

"Wait, wait," Park interposed, still trying to slow everything down. "What am I packing? How do people dress for the Senate?"

"Bring nice stuff. We'll go out afterwards to a nice restaurant," Dan said, trailing off toward the garage to get his car.

"Nice stuff?" a flustered Park mumbled. She collected herself and declared in frustration, "Okay, *nice* stuff."

She stood there, still dumbfounded, watching Dan walk off to his car. Just after he disappeared around the corner of the garage entrance, Dan stuck his head back into view, and shouted, "This is fun, isn't it?"

Her jaw dropped slightly as she wondered just what she was getting into. Then she dashed for the elevator.

DAN THREW ON his Armani, and crushed two Bill Blass tuxedo shirts into his suitcase. While throwing in socks and underwear, he issued voice commands to his computer. "Create Directory: Hinnom." Then "DSL Connect Web."

"Load Alta Vista." The search engine loaded. "Search Ben Hinnom." Alta Vista discovered 1,976,328 items.

"Delete under 60 percent relevance." 71,630 remained.

"Delete under 70 percent relevance." 53,412 remained.

Dan laid five ties across his luggage, and then added a sixth one.

"Save Results Page as Hinnom backslash Hinnom Web Unedited."

While dropping miniature bottles of Laphroaig and Dalwhinnie into his bag, he spoke additional commands. "Open Bloodhound." A large bloodhound with adorable brown ears appeared on his screen with a growling sound, and then gruffly declared, "Bloodhound is r-r-r-r-ready. What am I searching for?"

Dan instructed: "Master field equals *Ben Hinnom*. Variables equal: *crime* tab *improper* tab *allegation* tab *suicide* tab *murder* tab *kill* tab *accuse*. End." He thought again: "Additional variable: *Linzer L-I-N-Z-E-R.*"

His zipped his bag.

Bloodhound spoke back: "This is a very long search. It will take. . ." He paused from packing and waited as the computer calculated and then declared ". . . sixty-three minutes. Bloodhound is r-r-r-r-ready. Proceed, cancel, or reschedule?"

"Reschedule," Dan replied. "Commence in five minutes. Minimize and search in background."

Dan opened a black IBM Butterfly notebook. As he did, its collapsible keyboard spread and locked into position. He plugged in a blue Ethernet connection, typed a few commands and then spoke the following instruction: "Copy Hinnom folder plus contents to Butterfly." An icon of the Butterfly came up as files floated across the screen.

The Butterfly confirmed: "Copy complete. 2.6 Gigabytes remaining."

A black sedan beeped outside. He slipped several music CDs into a side pocket of the bag, then punched up Hinnom on the Butterfly. There was the Hinnom folder with its web search file, and there was the Bloodhound command ready to execute within a few minutes. Dan voice instructed Bloodhound: "Pause until web connection reestablished." He snapped the lid shut, watching the keyboard retract. The search would resume once Dan plugged into the Washington hotel's phone line.

Just as Dan was leaving, he spoke to his main computer: "Security Arm. Five Minute Delay. D.Levin. Password: *Hans Zimmer is a swimmer.*" He closed the door, then stuck his hand back in to turn off the lights. The main LCD flat screen still shone in the darkness, displaying the security command with a countdown. Dan came back in, and spoke "Security

Disarm D.Levin. Password: *John Barry is not scary.*" He grabbed two additional StarTac phones from a drawer, checked the power remaining, added a few more batteries, and declared again, "Security Arm. Five Minute Delay. D.Levin. Password: *Hans Zimmer is a swimmer.*"

Again, Dan closed the front door, and again he stuck his hand back in as an afterthought to turn off the lights.

Dan lifted his bag into the sedan's open trunk. Looking through the windows, he could see Park, but not Sal. "Hi, where's your son?"

She sighed, "I couldn't pull him away from his database programming. I packed his stuff. It's in the trunk. But he said he needed twenty more minutes and he preferred to take the subway to O'Hare and meet us at the gate."

Dan breathed in with uncertainty, remarking, "Hmm. Let's hope he gets there on time. The hearing is at 3:30 and the press conference is at six to make the evening broadcasts—not the least of which is the network Hinnom partially owns. We need to make that plane."

The sedan sped off down Touhy Avenue taking sidestreets to the airport, bypassing all the construction on the Kennedy Expressway. Park had never been chauffeured to the airport. Buses, subways, even taxis when she could afford it. But never in a sedan. She didn't even know chauffeured sedans existed. A sedan looked pretty much like any other car. No one would suspect that someone in the back seat was being chauffeured.

Park thought, now was a good time. "You know a lot about me, mister," she began. "But I know, I'd say, nothing about you."

"Me," replied Dan, "just a guy with a compulsion to write."

"Naw, that's too easy," Park countered. "There are a few things I don't understand, and this would be a wonderful time to tell me since we'll be spending a weekend together in Washington and I don't even know you."

Dan tilted his head and waited.

"Hello, you're supposed to be a rich publisher who has all this money because you just sold your magazines. You're retired, but you aren't. So why are you living in a really small townhouse in a crummy neighborhood? Don't get me wrong. I love it. It's cute. But it's not a millionaire's dwelling. And I need to ask—well, I've told you all about me—so are you like. . . like married or divorced or separated . . . where are you with that?"

Then, for just an instant, Dan squinted and made a fist. *Jenny was in the bathtub. She emerged, dripping water off her tanned body, and towelled herself as they communicated visually. Dan knew the look, and stepped into the hall to make sure Simon was asleep. He was a strong young boy, and his blond hair stood out against the blue pillow. Dan half-closed Simon's door, and returned to the bedroom. Jenny was laying in bed with the towel wrapped like a turban around her wet hair. He closed the bedroom door, flipped the lock. As he laid down next to her, she moved toward him, reached for a snifter of cognac at the bed's edge, and whispered, "In a week our world changes forever." He embraced and answered, "Only part of it changes. The best part of it stays the same." She reached for him, saying, "You have done great. I love you."* Dan blinked several times and his fist disappeared.

"Hello?" said Park. "We haven't taken off yet and you look like you're flying already."

Dan shrugged off the remark, answering her previous question. "Me? I'm just a guy with a lot of heavy baggage and some personal storylines that you don't need to know right now because it's just a big bore. I'm not married, have no family."

The driver pretended not to notice the conversation.

Park looked disappointed and unsatisfied with the answer. Why so much mystery?

"I'm a writer," he added to assuage the frustration on her face. "That's a pretty lonely occupation right there. I share everything with the world when I write, but very little with those close to me. But I am here now," he said offhandedly. "So are you. And I'm only making plans from now until Sunday night. So let's have fun. We'll talk. Later, I'll give you some boring details. I promise. Okay?"

Park still could not get past the guardhouse of his mind. Dan misinterpreted her silence as acquiescence. But in truth, his enigmatic and erratic manner troubled her far more than she revealed. Like the painted lines on the highway, her thoughts flashed and blurred: Too much mystery was not such a good thing. What was she doing? Washington D.C. for the weekend with a stranger? Her son *en route* to the airport, too late to say "let's turn around." But who wants to turn around? But what is this strange man afraid of? Why does he electrify his fences?

She smiled.

Dan smiled back. He didn't understand.

The driver made excellent time. Within twenty-six minutes he had pulled up to the United terminal. He popped out of the vehicle to open the doors, assist with luggage and hand Dan an envelope with the tickets and itinerary details. Dan accepted the envelope without looking, as though he had been handed such an envelope hundreds of times in the past.

The two of them raced to the United gate, their luggage flapping behind them, then stood nervously in line, looking for Sal. The line had just reached the counter when the last boarding call was announced.

For just an instant, Dan's eyes narrowed, and his hands tightened. *Is this Special Services? I'm waiting for 337. I'm waiting for 337. I'm waiting for 337.* He jerked his head and blinked rapidly.

The United gate manager's phone rang. "Gate 41," he answered. "It's leaving right now, sir, in about 90 seconds . . . Sir, you are in the wrong terminal, way the heck over on the other side of the airport . . . No sir, it will take you at least ten minutes to get here . . . I can't do that. Take the next flight, it's wide open . . . I *can* do that. What do they look like? . . . I see her, black blazer, red brooch. Okay, but get over here . . . Don't miss the next one."

The gate manager approached Park. "You are Park McGuire?"

She nodded.

"Your son just called. He's at the International Terminal, don't ask me how. We have another flight to DCA leaving in forty minutes. I'll put him on it if you'll just hand me his ticket."

Park looked at Dan, thought for an instant about skipping this flight, but then smiled and said, "Sounds familiar. The ticket," she said, handing it over.

Sal had missed the plane the last two flights. Refusing to pull himself away from a coding session meant he was always a late arrival. So Park was getting used to it. He had forty dollars in his pocket. That would do. She pulled the ticket back from the gate manager for a moment to write on the folder, "Meet us at the Jefferson Hotel. Take a taxi—it's about $10."

Dan interjected, "Make it $15."

She marked $10-15 and then wrote down cell phone numbers for Dan's StarTac and hers.

"Now. Right now," demanded the gate manager. As they hustled themselves aboard, Dan said, "Gee, do I ever get to meet Sal?"

Park giggled and said, "Tonight for dinner, I guess."

United's jetway door shut after them, and moments later the Boeing 777 lifted off the tarmac.

A YELLOW SCHOOL bus pulled up to the guard station on the driveway leading to the Capitol. Large concrete flower pots obstructed the way. A marksman with the Capitol Protection Service dressed in black fatigues, a 9 MM Beretta strapped to his leg, accompanied the regular uniformed officer as they slowly walked around the barricades. "Morning briefing said this might happen," mumbled the uniformed officer. He tapped on the door and entered as the marksman walked cautiously around the back. No one could be seen inside.

Suddenly, Ben Hinnom appeared, all smiles, waving his right hand in a small semicircle. "Hello, hello, it's just me," he sang out. "Don't be bashful. You can come in, except it's just not done, so let me see if I can help you from there. Stay where you are." The officer peered in enough to see only Hinnom and Linzer, then referred to his clipboard, saying, "Mr.–"

"Yes, you have it right," Hinnom interrupted. "Ben Hinnom of Hinnom Computing, reporting to the Senate to testify before the Judiciary Committee as requested–actually subpoenaed–but that's just a formality. Hey, you're nobody these days in Washington unless you've been subpoenaed. Am I right? My day has come."

The uniformed officer nodded, "Yes, sir." The marksman waved approval from the rear of the bus.

"Please drive the vehicle to that location," the uniformed officer pointed, "and leave the keys in the ignition. We'll handle it from there."

"Sure," said Hinnom. "No problem no problem no problem. Except I don't use keys. Is that a problem? I just ask nicely and the bus obeys," he added in half-giggle. "Voice recognition has such potential. Park where? Over there? Can do."

The vehicle lumbered to the designated space. Ben Hinnom and Linzer emerged. As they did a small crowd gathered around. The richest and most powerful man on earth had just descended to walk amongst the ordinary. People craned to see. Linzer preceded Hinnom to speak to security people at the Senate entrance to smooth his boss' passage through the hallway checkpoint.

"Hello, hello, everyone," said Hinnom as he walked the few steps from the doors to the checkpoint. He walked through the metal detector. No buzzer. "Maybe you should change the settings," he said with aplomb, as he demonstratively pulled out his Windy. "Missed this." The guard asked him to place it through the x-ray scanner. "No problem, no problem," he chirped as he laid the palmsized computer on the conveyer belt. To the guard's dismay, it did not even register on the x-ray screen. "Sir, please activate the device, so I see it active on the screen," the guard asked.

"Oh, golly, that's easy." He flipped the Windy open, the screen telescoped. He clicked several strokes and pointed it at the officer. "I don't see anything," she remarked in a security monotone.

"Hmmm," replied Hinnom in an exaggerated voice. He whispered into the Windy. The officer's face, captured close-up by the computer's tiny camera, suddenly flashed full screen, replaying her just spoken words, "I don't see anything." Hinnom clicked several keys and hit Enter, declaring, "Maybe this is better."

The Windy again replayed the officer's recorded voice, but this time inside out, saying, "Don't I see anything?" The guard and her team were amazed. "That is wonderful," she said, as though Hinnom had just dropped off a plate of chocolate cookies.

"That, madam guard, is the power of Windgazer," announced Hinnom dramatically. "See this tiny lens and microphone," Hinnom said, pointing to a corner of the lid. "Well, our speech recognition program converts the spoken word to type. That's not news. A certain blue-colored company introduced the technology years ago. But we have improved upon it. And when *we* improve something, it *is* news. Now I can simply retype your own words, nothing too exotic to start with, and play it back to sound very very different from how you said it." Out of the machine popped a tiny diskette containing the guard's image and modified voice file. Hinnom handed it to her, chirping, "Here. It's you."

"This little thing?" she said in wonderment, holding the tiny diskette up to the light. A small crowd of onlookers applauded as Hinnom charismatically walked away. Linzer was behind him.

On the way to the hearing, Hinnom took a detour into the men's room. Linzer routinely checked the stalls, making sure they were empty, and then busied himself on his Windy. Hinnom looked in a mirror, adjusted his hair, and blew his nose into a paper towel. But when Hinnom opened his eyes, he was shocked to see a janitor smiling directly at him. It was Raymond.

Raymond possessed an extra 21st chromosome. He was one out of a thousand, and only four thousand like him are born every year. But that is exactly what made him special. Some do better than others, and Raymond was in the better half.

Looking all dapper in his gray janitor's aide smock, Raymond was proud that he could empty out the wastebaskets, meet people, and express his joy at being alive. He understood so much about people, far more than anyone gave him credit for. Raymond excitedly tried to share his feelings any chance he could. No one could feel threatened by him.

But when Hinnom saw Raymond, he froze.

For an instant there was no sound. Hustle from the corridors, dripping faucets, even the automatic odorizer spraying mist every forty seconds—none of it could be heard. Hinnom was shaking with fear, speechless. Linzer finally looked up at the quiet, saw a petrified Hinnom and quickly interposed himself, pushing Raymond aside.

Hinnom now managed to utter a breathy syllable: "Down." Getting stronger as Raymond was moved away by Linzer, Hinnom summoned the strength to stammer: "Down. Down. Down. Get that Mongoloid son-of-a-whoring-bitch Down syndrome misfit away. From *me!* Away!"

Linzer tried to push Raymond out the door, but Raymond insisted, "I am cleaning. I was not bad."

Linzer, formal yet forceful, kept shoving, "Out, now. Be a good boy. Out."

"I *am* a good boy," protested Raymond with his immutable smiling expression. Looking at Hinnom and then at Linzer, he could not transmit his feelings to his face, or summon all the words. But Raymond had long understood the difference between himself and nearly everyone else. He loved everyone and often wondered why everyone did not love him back. Love made him feel good. "I am cleaning. Can I clean?" he innocently asked.

Linzer shoved him out completely, saying, "Yes, you can clean this one later. Clean the one upstairs now, and then come back down here later. It's fine." One final shove, "Upstairs. Okay?"

Peeking through the door to make sure Raymond had indeed walked off, Linzer turned to a still trembling Hinnom. Arms spread wide with reassurance, Linzer tried to calm Hinnom, almost as a parent would calm a distraught child. "It's fine. He's gone. It's fine now."

Trying to overcome his anxiety, Hinnom spoke softly at first, "Tycoons and senators. You know. The Chinese party chairman last year. Bankers, I don't mind. *You* know I don't mind. Bring them on. But I have told you," and now his voice escalated in ferocity, "I have told *you*," emphasizing with a raised knuckle, "no Down son-of-a-whoring-bitch bastard syndrome cretins get near me." Only slightly more subdued, he prattled on, "I told you, not a one. Not a one. Keep their putrid, smiling, potato-head faces and the awkward bodies they are pasted to . . . away from me. I don't want to . . ."

Linzer, arms still wide, slowly brought them to rest on Hinnom's shoulders to reassure him: "I know. It's okay. Who knew the little bugger would be in here cleaning? It's the Senate. Who in the world knew? But he is gone." He pointed to the door and shrugged, "Look. He's not here. The little bugger bastard is gone."

Hinnom straightened his tie, cupped a hand under the urinal's replenishing faucet for some water, threw it against his cold skin, did it again, and then drank a bit. While Linzer blocked the door with his knee so no one else could enter, Hinnom dried off with paper towels. "Better?" asked Linzer, "Good. Now we have a hearing."

SENATOR PROVO'S STATELY Judiciary Committee hearing room degraded into a noisy circus as four high-powered computer company executives and their entourages, including Bill Gates, founder of Microsoft, milled around the witness table, chatting off the record with several dozen journalists. Press photographers wearing multiple Nikon bodies and khaki-netted gadget vests staked out spots in the well to crouch and load their film. Senator Provo's gavel abruptly stopped the clatter, sending everyone to their assigned places. C-SPAN cameras and network videocams began rolling. Motor drives whirred like tiny robots dancing. And the pencil press ardently scribbled into spiral steno notebooks as they nervously eyed audio levels on their tape recorders.

For a half hour, the four initial witnesses and the senators bickered over the precise definition of the term *monopoly,* and whether Hinnom Computing had one, or indeed could have one. At one point, Senator Provo asked Richard Waggin, CEO of Browser Media Corp., Hinnom's arch-rival on the web, to explain a contradiction.

"Well, sir," posited Senator Provo, "you say Hinnom has a monopoly, and that they are using their Windgazer operating system to squeeze you out of the market. Yet your browser, which is, for the sake of the record, the software that people use to navigate the world wide web, that is, the graphical portion of the Internet, *your* browser is the monopoly now. You have 80 percent of the market. So who has the real monopoly?"

"BMC Webcruise *had* 80 percent of the market three months ago," Waggin snapped back, "and that's because we created something people *chose* to download and install. As of June 30 of this year, Webcruise has 59 percent of the market and within a year, if not sooner, we will be wiped out completely because of the widespread prevalence of the Windgazer OS, the Hinnom operating system, which as I outlined, is preloaded into every computer you or virtually any other American buys. Even Bill Gates of Microsoft, seated next to me, has been surpassed by Ben Hinnom. That's because Windgazer now includes Webgazer in every new computer. A newer version of Webgazer now being developed automatically pops up and deletes our program from your drive."

"Can it not be restored?" asked Senator Provo.

"Yes," replied Waggin testily, "but only after a complicated restore process that frankly many on my own staff find so annoying they just give up. It will be a lot easier for the average person to just use Webgazer. Anyone who attempts to add our product, Webcruise, in a web download or even from a regular install, or access a web page not optimized for Hinnom's Webgazer software, will discover that the built-in Webgazer program is incompatible with all other browsers, including ours. We will be frozen out of the market. In the process, Ben Hinnom gets to decide what people see and say. He will own the web, the main street and meet-inghouse of the next generation, indeed this generation."

"Why is that?" asked Senator Provo.

Waggin explained, "Because, as I said, only sites compatible with Webgazer will be viewable. Soon, every connection on the web will actually go through Hinnom's central site distributor. All the technology we ourselves advocated so passionately, that is, the software used by schools and libraries and even online services such as AOL to screen out and block pornographic and racist content on the web has been profoundly enhanced by Hinnom Computing. Using his central site distributor, and the automatic dialup in Windgazer, Mr. Hinnom will be able to block any site he disagrees with. He can even filter for specific words. Everything will be blocked from Seattle. Browser Media estimates Hinnom is less than two years from that point.

"If you disagree with AOL," stressed Waggin, "you can go to Compu-Serve, Delphi, or GEnie, use other services, or connect directly through the Internet. But that will all change with Webgazer. And few will even be aware that Hinnom is controlling their access. You may think you are connecting directly to the Senate Home Page, but in fact, Hinnom operates the switchboard. In the flash of a moment, one man at Hinnom headquarters can type a few words into a blocking protocol. Type in 'Senator Provo' and all mention of you, Senator, would disappear. If the site is the First Amendment Home Page and Mr. Hinnom does not like what it says, when the user logs on, he or she will simply receive an error message.

"Remember," Waggin emphasized, "if Hinnom's Webgazer takes hold, we're no longer talking about a diverse jumble of interconnected autonomous pathways constituting for better or for worse what we know as the Internet, a freewheeling system not unlike America's freewheeling system of roads: huge interstate highways, fast local expressways, main boulevards, side streets and even alleys and driveways. If Hinnom succeeds, the current chaotic, competitive system will be replaced with a controllable system which through pervasive, monopolistic, preloaded technology will funnel all communications through one hub. In the first century, they used to say all roads lead to Rome. In the 21st Century, all informational roads will lead to Hinnom."

"Because of innovation or because of monopoly?" asked Senator Provo skeptically, looking askance at his colleagues. "That is the only question this committee can consider. So I ask again, how do you define *monopoly?*"

Waggin turned to the assembled audience and announced, "I define it this way. All of you present, if you use a PC, please raise your hands."

Some hands slowly went up.

"No, everyone," he urged. "Come on. Raise your hands if you use a PC."

Virtually the entire gallery held hands up high. "Now, if you use Hinnom Computing's Windgazer OS, please lower your hands." The assemblage all dropped their hands. Not one palm remained in the air.

"Mr. Chairman," asserted Waggin, "that is a monopoly. Defined."

"Not in my book," declared a bubbly voice from the back. It was Hinnom, making his way through the gallery and the reporters. "Sorry sorry sorry I am late. I was stuck in the little boy's room. Believe that? But I'm here. I'm here." Senator Provo gaveled a brief recess to allow the hearing to compose itself. As Hinnom walked down the aisle, nearby spectators enthusiastically shook his hand. Playing to the crowd, he gave them all a black Windgazer demo disk. "You'll love it," he theatrically told each recipient. When Hinnom passed Bill Gates, Hinnom just pretended not to notice him.

Most, but not all, of the senators—Patton, Kearny, and even Provo—left their seat behind the curved committee desk to greet Hinnom—now the richest man in the world. With awkward aplomb, Hinnom used both hands to shake as many of theirs as possible. Each of them made a cute, self-conscious remark about computers, such as "wish I had a faster computer" or "I don't know my REM from my RAM" or "when I have a problem, my six-year-old helps me out." To each of these remarks, Hinnom would grandly offer a diagnostic diskette and say, "Load this. Hit F10 then F4, it will help."

Senator Provo cheerily complained, "They say I have a memory leak and my drive is constantly running out of swapper. I wish I knew what that meant." Hinnom launched into a dazzling reply, when a self-conscious Senator Provo abruptly said, "Well . . . can we start the hearing now?"

Hinnom astutely switched to his politically savvy voice, "All of us need to understand the significant challenges ahead. I hope this unprecedented hearing will help. Yes, Senator, I'm ready."

Senator Provo gaveled the hearing back to order and swore in Hinnom. Suddenly, just as Senator Provo began his introduction, the proceedings were disrupted. Three protesters stood up in silence. Dramatically, they removed their ties, then their shirts, exposing shaved chests bearing messages in thick black paint. The first chest: DEFEND. The second chest: OUR. The third chest: DATA. The protesters stood silently as the room exploded in an uproar. Sympathizers hooted their approval. Clicking cameras sounded like locusts swarming as reporters pressed around to ask questions.

The three stiff protesters would not reply or even turn their heads.

Gaveling loudly to restore order, Senator Provo directed security to remove the three. They stood fast, staring straight at Hinnom, as security climbed over others in the aisle to pull them away. Eventually, the tumult settled down.

Senator Provo proceeded to ask several simple questions, which Hinnom deftly answered with exquisite, well-phrased, well-rehearsed responses. The testimony was going well. Hinnom could not help but wink at Linzer.

But when Senator Provo was done, the feisty Senator Eltz of North Carolina was recognized. Almost a century old, Senator Eltz was clearly the oldest member of the Senate and proud of it. With a mindset first developed in the Great War, molded forever by the Second World War, tried by the Korean War, scarred by the Vietnam War, hardened by the Cold War, and vindicated by the Gulf War, few thought Senator Eltz up-to-date enough to comprehend this latest conflagration, the OS War. On the contrary, he understood perfectly that this new conflict was a battle not for territory, possessions, or ethnicity, but a fight to the finish to control global information and in the process, seize the human identity itself. The old man would surprise them.

"Mr. Hinnom," Senator Eltz began, "I hope you will permit me to ask you a question. You know I'm not as stupid as I look." The audience respectfully laughed. "Oh yeah, I drove a Model T in Raleigh, and I was elected by salt of the earth farming people who knew the difference between living off the sweat of your own brow and living off the sweat of someone else's.

"However, since my first automobile," he continued, "things have changed a bit. Raleigh and other North Carolina locales have become high-tech centers. A lot of my constituents now make a living in technology. A lot of financial contributors as well, I don't mind telling you." Again the audience laughed.

"I know," Senator Eltz asserted, "the difference between the Model T made by the Ford Motor Company and a T-1 high speed data line that will transmit faster than a few dozen ISDNs wrapped together with a red bow ribbon. I even know that a T-3 outperforms a bucket of T-1s. Wish to heck I had one in my district office. So now that we have that straight, let me ask a few questions and with your permission, I'll just struggle to understand your replies.

"Mr. Hinnom," bellowed Senator Eltz, "how do you answer the charge that you are creating a global media monopoly?"

Hinnom was put off guard. "My company owns no newspapers or radio stations," he defended, "no film studios, and our paperback division only publishes self-help and technical computer books. True, we are a 50 percent owner together with one of the major networks in one cable news entity, HCTV, which is Internet interactive. But we are just one of scores of cable stations. And frankly, HCTV is not doing very well. We are hardly an international media monopoly," Hinnom smiled as some laughter wafted through the audience. He looked back to acknowledge the hubbub with some satisfaction. "If we were," Hinnom added to additional transient audience approval, "I'd get better press."

"Sir, I read *The Washington Post* and *The New York Times* every day," Senator Eltz stated. "And I watch the morning and evening news on TV. But isn't it a fact that you, Hinnom Computing, have been quietly buying up both the cable technology and internet technology needed to turn TV sets into computerized information consoles all operating through the Internet? And the Internet is something you are also poised to control. Eventually, if you have your way, Mr. Hinnom, the TV set that I grew up with in Raleigh will be far more than *The Honeymooners* and *Mickey Mouse* in black and white. It will be an all-purpose combination communications device."

Hinnom did not reply.

"Let's see," Senator Eltz continued, checking through some papers almost absentmindedly, and then reaching into his pocket for a napkin with writing on it. "That TV set in your family den will be a high-definition, multimodal, entertainment and information center with an interactive phone, and a wireless computer and a keyboard attached to it, along with a color printer. The whole setup will access and transmit information—just about everything creative mankind can write or draw, from daily newspapers and monthly magazines, to all forms of voice and image data. This so-called TV will be hooked up to every appliance in your home, every room in the house, and every office in the building. The personal network will even travel with you. I hear you have personal identity chips planned for the heels in people's shoes that will make a connection when people shake hands. That is not in the far distant future, sir. I saw a demo at MIT. For heaven's sake, your computer will know everyone anyone has met and everything about them.

"In fact," Senator Eltz continued, "everyone will be connected everywhere. They will all be connected. Through you!"

Senator Eltz raised his voice slightly, "Sir. Do you not believe that the Internet is the only media that counts in the 21st Century?"

Hinnom could not help but answer, "I do."

"You know, Mr. Hinnom, no one person or company ever controlled the printing presses, the airwaves, or even the cable lines in the United States. Radio tried to replace paper and failed—it could only compete for the public's ear. Did a damn good job. My generation knows that. TV tried to replace radio and it failed—again because it had to compete in an open environment and people were free to choose what they saw. The last generation knows that. But if you control the Internet, Mr. Hinnom, the age of competition in information and communications will be over. Your generation, I believe, knows that. So I ask you again, good sir: Are you not well on your way to becoming a global media monopoly? Is it not true we will all be connected through *you*? And you will have the ability, at the stroke of a key, to disconnect us at will?"

A clearly rattled Hinnom tried to maintain his cool. "Do you want to replace Hinnom Computing?" he retorted with agitation. "Are you trying to stifle our innovation or punish us for innovating? The universe abhors random action. It cherishes organized thought."

Hinnom was becoming snide when he caught himself. He licked his upper lip, took a deep breath, and turned to Senator Provo, whom he viewed as an ally on the Committee.

Reverting to polished mode, Hinnom asserted, "Senator. Our nation is built on the strength of our ideas. The American way rewards creative and inventive thought—and the enterprising spirit. American law protects that spirit and creates an environment for it to flourish." Senator Provo's eye met Hinnom's. They connected. "The hour is late in this century to prepare for the next. Men such as yourself have the vision." Hinnom stared hypnotically at Senator Provo. "Men such as yourself have the vision. I have a vision, gentlemen. My vision is to stand at the threshold of another vision. Someone else can solve today's problems. You and I must seek tomorrow's solutions."

Turning now to Senator Eltz, Hinnom softly chimed, "We at Hinnom join those facing the challenges of helping mankind walk to the next plateau. . ." Senator Eltz seemed disinterested. His mind wandered when confronted by speechmaking. Hinnom glanced back at Linzer who nodded slightly, and then ceremoniously pointed his finger down to hit the Enter key on his Windy. Hinnom ever so subtly looked at his Windy screen. He continued without a pause. ". . . And if I was a boy and I was crying in the barn, a red barn with one broken door, and my father had beat me with a strap for missing school. . ." Senator Eltz perked up like a nail had been driven into his psyche. ". . . well, then I would understand that today we confront opportunities to explore beyond the horizon, opportunities no different from those facing Christopher Columbus, Lewis and Clark, and John Glenn."

Senator Eltz seemed confused. He doubted the words he had heard.

Hinnom continued, ". . . In our exploration we must reach out unselfishly so that, yes, our technical accomplishments temporarily enrich those who pioneer them, but so they also empower the user to acquire long term personal riches, whether that person is a business tycoon or just a boy locked in a closet stuffed with garden tools crying for forgiveness, hurting from a bruised knee . . ."

Senator Eltz was stunned. He stood up slowly, his left arm shook almost uncontrollably.

". . . Because the great and the gritty among us will all be equalized when technology completes the final process of a democratic society. Only technology is truly blind to religion, race, and national origin. Technology will free this world. This is my gift to mankind. I offer you the fruit of my technology garden. I invite you to freely bite."

Most in the room were taken with Hinnom's remarks and barely noticed his oratorical departures. Senator Eltz' face turned white. His aides ran up and he seemed to swoon. He pushed them off, but then almost fell limp. He pushed them off a second time. Steadying himself, the senator, eyes fixed on Hinnom, requested in a tremble, "Mr. Chairman, I am feeling a bit shaky. I ask for a recess. May we please resume Monday."

Senator Provo agreed, but even as he did, Senator Eltz raised his hand, actually just a few fingers, pointed at Hinnom and warned in a stern if quivering voice, "Sir, you have not heard the last of me, and not the last of the American people." A barrage of clicking cameras sounded like the locusts had returned. Scores of people all speaking at once created a muf-

6

WINDGAZER 99

Some regard the historic Willard as Washington's official hotel. Lincoln slept here awaiting inauguration. The term "lobbyist" was invented when special interest groups began pressuring President Grant while he smoked cigars and snifted brandy in the Willard lobby. Foreign dignitaries have conducted sensitive international affairs of state while ensconced in its elegant guestrooms. Peace treaties have been hammered out in its cloistered bars. Celebrities make this their address in Washington just to add their name to the Willard's legendary guest list.

Architecturally, the stately Willard looks like it was plucked from Paris' Left Bank as a visual gift to the nation's capital. Redesigned at the beginning of the twentieth century by the same architect who created New York's Plaza and Waldorf-Astoria hotels, the Willard, with its mansard roofs, ornate crestings, and elaborate chimney stacks represents the capital's quintessential Second French Empire Beaux-Arts structure. But the hotel is distinctly American within. Its exquisite lobby is graced by the great seals of all fifty states painted into its ceiling. Quiet bars, decorated like plush private clubs and hidden in niches, cater to the contemporary powerful just as they once did to railroad barons and shipping magnates. And a turn-of-the-century mahogany front desk, which might be seen in any frontier bank, speaks eloquently of the Willard's own sense of small-town Americana.

Constantly cluttered with taxis, stretch limos, stout men in tuxes and lean women in diamonds, the tempo of the Willard front door understandably paused as a yellow school bus pulled up. Car jockeys dressed in blue windbreakers, accustomed to accepting the keys for sleek Masseratis, Ducatis, Cords, and even an occasional Silver Phantom, thought the laughable vehicle belonged on a country road, rather than obstructing the Willard's front driveway.

But the veteran doormen knew better. They immediately understood who the special visitor was. As he stepped down, Hinnom ceremoniously bestowed upon them autographed Windgazer CDs as tips. Linzer eyed them carefully. And a crowd of hotel guests hustling in and out came to a standstill and gawked.

The Willard's hotel manager came out to escort Hinnom and Linzer inside. Standing to the side was an entourage of press handlers and corporate managers who had followed in their own van. Up they all went to the second floor where a small ballroom had been converted into a temporary press setting. There the group was greeted by an advance team of more press relations specialists uniformly dressed in dark slacks and beige golf shirts sporting a "thumbs-up" logo.

The ballroom would host the actual press conference. Bluejeaned techies hurried to finish stringing, clamping, and taping down the cable needed to run the event. A small adjacent meeting room door would be used as a makeshift headquarters. A piece of Hinnom Computing letterhead, with a handscrawled "Hinnom Press Conference HQ," was affixed to its door. Inside, more techies continued setting up the usual equipment deployed for major media gatherings: two fax machines—one inbound, one outbound, as well as four laptops linked by a radio frequency network to a lunchbox server, connected in turn to a series of color and black and white laser printers, all neatly lined against the wall. A squadron of walkie-talkies near the door stood erect, juiced, and blinking in their chargers.

Complementing the *de rigeur* communications gear were the trinkets and trash every such media event requires. Stacked in a corner were two freshly opened boxes of black Windgazer T-shirts and baseball caps embroidered with a logo exclaiming, "Our Clock Will Not Stop Ticking," superimposed over an image of a "January 1, 2000" calendar page. Boxes of logo-stamped Windgazer mousepads, demo disks, and fully functional Windgazer samples were everywhere, ready to be distributed.

PR specialists established the customary perimeter just forward of the press conference suite by positioning a reception table across the hallway. Under the table sat a just-FedExed cardboard box brimming with glossy folders, emblazoned with the Windgazer logo and the "Our Clock Will Not Stop Ticking" motto. Each folder contained a photograph of Ben Hinnom, a Windgazer fact sheet, a demo disk, and a carefully edited transcript of Hinnom's remarks before the Judiciary Committee, finalized, copied, and stuffed just moments before. In the right-hand folder pocket was a small, sealed white envelope marked "NDA." Paperclipped to each kit was a stick-on ID tag bearing a reporter's name imprinted by the portable badging system in the hall.

On cue, a miniskirted media management intern named Jan began arranging media kits alphabetically in rows across the reception table, according to her list of invited journalists. Each reporter would claim his folder when checking in. A few unreserved folders were available for unexpected press who might drop in. Those names would be written on badges by hand. It would be Jan's job to make sure only properly credentialed media entered the room. Assisted by a low-level security guard obtained from a local agency, she would carefully check everyone for a "Working Press" pass issued either by the Senate Gallery or by a local police department if the reporter came from out of town. No press pass, no entry. That was the rule.

When the elevator doors opened, Dan and Park, along with many others, were welcomed by two media managers directing them to the reception table to the left.

"We don't have credentials," Dan whispered to Park as they walked toward the table, preparing her for the unexpected.

"I thought you were a journalist," she nervously whispered back. "You must have a press pass."

"After I sold the magazines," Dan explained with some embarrassment, "I had to give my credentials back to the Chicago Police Department. They issue press passes. Without that card, I can't get in anywhere." He added haltingly, "I suppose I can reactivate it."

"Well?" she asked.

"Yeah," he stumbled, "well, it would take weeks. It goes before a committee and all."

The press line moved closer to the reception table.

"So how are we getting in?" she came back in a quiet singsong.

"No problem," he mumbled, adding, "just stay in line and be cool." Dan pulled a handheld Sony tape recorder out of his bag. "Here. Hold this." He raised her hand, "Hold it up higher—in plain view—so they can see it." With that he floated through the crowd over to the reception table besieged with reporters trying to get in. Overwhelmed, Jan struggled to verify credentials, answer queries, and graciously hand out media kits to the crush of reporters. Amidst all this confusion, out of nowhere, Dan stuck his hand on Jan's shoulder and abruptly commanded: "Jan." She looked up for an off-balance instant. "Jan!" he instructed. "See that gal over there with the tape recorder, the dark blazer with the tape recorder? She's with me. Give her an extra media kit and send her in."

Jan, flustered by twelve people talking to her simultaneously, visually fixed for a moment on Park, smiled corporately at Dan, and said, "Sure."

Dan grabbed a media kit for himself and walked in unchallenged, stopping long enough to tap the security guard on the shoulder and mention, "That broad over there is with me." A few moments later, Park came to the reception desk and said, "I'm handling the tape recorder for that guy." Jan sent her in.

Standing close to Dan in the crowded room, oblivious to the media din, Park looked up with lifted eyebrow at Dan and asked, "You break the rules often?"

Dan brushed off the question naughtily with a curt, "No." Park didn't even try to believe him.

As she saw the others unfolding their computer notebooks and laptops, she asked Dan, "You seem to have a working knowledge of computers. But do you really know the nitty gritty?"

"I do have a working knowledge," Dan replied with a facade of shallow braggadocio, "A damn good working knowledge. My whole house is networked and automated. I've installed voice technology, search engines, multimedia, sophisticated schedulers. Certainly, I'm a power user." He paused, and then reluctantly conceded, "But this stuff is . . . uh, it's deep. I *use* computers, I don't program them. All this talk about an OS and APIs and all the rest. . . yeah, it confuses me. . . just a tiny, little," he admitted.

"In the business, you're known as an *end-user*," Park explained as though tutoring. "A person who uses the computer and even uses it well, but doesn't necessarily understand the first thing about the way it works."

"Fine. I'm an end-user," acknowledged Dan almost defensively. "My old IT manager–from the magazine–did all my setup. When anything goes bad, I still call him. So is that bad? I drive my car, but when there's a problem, I take it to the mechanic. Don't worry, I know the basics about Windgazer," he reassured. "It's an *operating system*. That's like the computer's transmission. Right? It connects the computer to all the software applications. You can make the best motor in the world and the best word processor, but if the computer's transmission won't connect, it's worthless. See, I understand."

Park nodded in agreement. "That's as good an explanation as any," she assured, adding, "now imagine a transmission with all sorts of secret circuits and fuses that change constantly and without warning. Without compatibility to those secret circuits, your motor will short out. The car just won't work. And if you manufacture the motors, you won't be able to sell any. It's the same with Hinnom Computing. If you don't connect to him, you don't connect–period. And Windgazer is preloaded from the manufacturer on all the computers right out of the box."

"How did *that* come about?" Dan asked.

"This may be news to you," she cautioned, "and a few hundred million like you, but not the people who travel in my circles. It's well known to the computer world."

"Got it," said Dan, fluttering his fingers in encouragement, waiting to hear more.

"Hinnom cut deals with all the computer manufacturers, way back when," she outlined. "He offered Windgazer at an incredibly cheap rate, so long as the companies paid a royalty on each and every computer they manufactured. These deals are so ironclad, no one could get out of them if they tried. Hinnom Computing has more lawyers than programmers just about. In a word, the manufacturers have to pay a royalty on every machine they sell, even if they don't preload Windgazer. So they passed on other operating systems and just preloaded Windgazer for everything. Voilà, all the computers have Windgazer. That's the chicken. Then comes the egg."

"The egg?"

"It doesn't stop there," Park continued. "Then Hinnom goes to all the highly cutthroat competitive software manufacturers and tells them all the new computers are now running on Windgazer; everyone will need to license his technology to be compatible or be locked out of the market. So all the major software makers convert their systems to Windgazer because, at the time, the Windgazer *interface*–that's the way the computer screen appears, you know, all the icons and the way you drag and drop stuff–it all looked very, very pretty and easy to use. That pretty Windgazer interface made computing graphical and user friendly for the average person. It helped bring millions upon millions of new users to the PC. That created a brand-new chicken. Which led to a brand-new egg.

"Today," she continued, "so many millions of people are using Windgazer-compatible software, no computer manufacturer dares make a computer that can't run the most popular software. Otherwise they would be selling a computer no one can use. The eggs and chickens keep going until the whole world is running on Windgazer and all software and hardware is forced to be Windgazer compatible. Worse, Hinnom develops his own software . . ."

"Like Windphraser . . ." Dan cut in, to show he understood.

". . . Like Windphraser, the leading word processor in America, and several dozen more just like it in graphics, databasing, and personal productivity. And these Hinnom programs all have the inside track on the secret compatibility stuff inside Windgazer. It only takes a tiny, minor change to make all other software run slower. Drivers for example."

"Drivers?" asked Dan.

"Yes, not chauffeurs, *drivers*. These are the very overlooked but absolutely critical software add-ons that connect the software to the operating system and the computer, the printer, really all the peripherals. Monitors, scanners, disk drives. Drivers are taken for granted but they actually take a very long time to make, and you need slightly different ones for every software to hardware connection. It's like trying to spell without vowels. Drivers complete the commands. So between the software compatibility issue and the drivers that Hinnom controls, Hinnom software enjoys an edge over other developers." Park grabbed a quick breath. "That's it in sixty seconds. And all this power-grab occurred within about the last ten years. Bang. Here we are."

"Yeah, it's a monopoly," confirmed Dan, resolutely repeating the sentiment in the Senate hearing.

"It's like we were so busy eating the fruit on the tree," she responded, "we never noticed quicksand underfoot. Hinnom is now so entrenched, no one can get in. And no one can oust him."

Glancing around to detect whether she was being overhead, Park continued, "Many have tried. Even Bluestar was knocked out of the running. They had Blue2, which most people in the know acknowledged was a vastly superior operating system. But no one can get a competing operating system preloaded, especially when the compatible software does not exist, not even the once-mighty Bluestar. If any computer maker tries to go with another OS, they risk excluding themselves from virtually the entire market for a year or two. It's suicide."

"So who knows all this?" asked Dan.

"Just about everybody in the technology community, a few million people on the Internet, every member of the computer press . . . and now *you,*" answered Park dryly. "But the tech community can't do any more than moan and groan. Which they do every day. It is generally assumed that the overwhelming majority of the computer rags–the guys who understand all this best–are just too dependent on Hinnom to buck him." She leaned close and whispered, "Look at the name badges on these guys."

Dan looked around him. *Windgazer Monthly, Windgazer Sources, Windgazer Update.*

"They seem like independent magazines but they are named for, created to serve, and editorially devoted to one product line, *Windgazer.* They need Hinnom advertising. They need the advance technology briefings, like this one we're at right now. They need the free evaluation equipment and software–like the free software everyone is going to walk out of here with. The Internet is filled with complaints about the computer press. So all this is old hat to someone like me. But not many in the general media–including you, mister–pay any attention. All that most of the computer press wants to do is promote the stuff they write about and sell a lot of expensive advertising in the process."

"They're all in bed together," said Dan.

"Not all," she answered. "But quite a few, I guess. And the courageous ones have been known to suffer. In the corner over there," she nonchalantly pointed with her elbow, "are the guys from *Megabyte* and their big competitor *Gigabyte.* They're sorta independent, but they don't have much sway."

"Wait, I see lot of other mainstream publications in the room," Dan observed. "Newspapers, networks, business press. Hey, there's *CNN, Wall Street Journal, ABC News* . . . see over there, the guy from *The Washington Post*. Come on. They're gonna ask the tough questions about monopolistic practices."

"Sure," answered Park, "but I wonder how many of them really understand the technology the way these computer press guys do. Even if they did–and I guess some of them do–how many of the regular press would write about the technology? It's too complex for the average person. The general media would rather cover a sex scandal in the White House or a bombing in the heartland. But unless the public understands the technology, they can't understand the crime being committed under their very noses. So it's a toss-up between a computer press that knows the technology but is too consumed with it to report on the consequences, and the regular press that probably cares about the consequences but just doesn't know the technology or finds it too complicated to bore their editors and readers with."

"You're right," said Dan with an admiring nod. "That's why I need you. We're a team."

"That's why you got me," she replied with a smile that caused a connection in Dan that he felt, looked away from, and then returned to. "You look excited," she added, feeling good for the moment. "I think you like all this excitement. Am I right?" Dan flashed a sheepish grin and pointed her to the front.

The press conference was called to order by a Hinnom media manager. Hinnom suddenly swaggered in from a service door at the rear. The manager introduced him without flourish. He stood at his own lectern, smiling widely, feeling the power of deciding how much he would tell the assembled journalists.

One by one, the media manager recognized questions from the computer press people she knew best. They asked about beta releases, fixpacks, GA dates, cross-platform integration, something called phase three implementation, and software versions years away from release. Their readers craved the answers to such questions because they were single-tracked technology managers whose day-to-day success or failure depended upon understanding not only today's systems, but the world's long-term technology path. They were obsessed with avoiding sudden obsolescence.

Nothing else mattered.

Hinnom glibly answered the questions using arcane abbreviations and spec babble comprehensible only to the trade press–OLE, DLL, OO, GUI, MPLS, 64-bit, PCI buses, 512 cache. And as he did, mainstream reporters began looking at their watches, calculating how much time they had before their deadlines, and wondering if they needed anything beyond the sound bytes from the Judiciary hearing and comments from senatorial aides.

Dan was fidgeting as well. "We need some action," he said, showing the frustration. "No one is getting to the meat." He mischievously nudged Park, "What do you want Hinnom to say?"

Park looked askance. "Me?" she asked. "What do you mean?"

"I can make him say whatever you want to hear."

Laughing in disbelief, she answered, "Sure. Make him say . . . make him say, 'Goofy.' No, make him say, 'My software ain't goofy. Goofy is a dog.' Just like that."

When the next question was finished, Dan raised one finger high, and declared loudly before the next reporter could speak, "Levincom. Question." The media manager at the podium pointed back in recognition.

"Mr. Hinnom. I saw a cartoon on the Internet. It was Goofy the cat and the caption was, 'Hinnom should give us software that *ain't* goofy, software that works.' Why is there this perception that whatever software Hinnom Computing releases, it will have bugs requiring expensive upgrades?"

Hinnom responded immediately. "The Internet is so valuable. Very, very," Hinnom declared diplomatically. "I learn from it every day. But it is also so amusing because it is free speech at its best. I love it. Our software satisfies millions here and abroad who use it. But we can't satisfy everyone. If we have a choice between delaying software for years, and continuing on-going development with upgrades, we will do the latter. I assure you, my software *ain't* goofy."

Dan made a slight turn toward Park.

"And by the way," added Hinnom with a hint of arrogance, "Goofy is a dog."

Dan turned again and smiled immodestly. Park's mouth dropped open in amazement. "Follow-up, sir. Your point on software is well taken. But what will the effect of the death of Bluestar's John Hector have on your future software development plans? Uh, it's a two-part follow-up, and the second part is, can you add any insight into his unexpected death while the two of you were meeting in his office in Chicago? What really happened?"

Linzer looked up. Without moving his head or showing any reaction, he slowly reached for the press list, positioning it front and center, and glanced down. He strained his eyes to look for a name badge on Dan's chest, and didn't see one. He looked at his watch, pulled out his Windy and sent himself an MTM: "Check tape: 7:03 P.M."

Without pausing, Hinnom replied, "Hinnom Computing has always tried to both compete and cooperate with others in the computer industry, whether they are small enterprises working out of basements—as I once was—or giants like Bluestar. We call it *coopetition*. I love inventing new words. *Coopetition*. It's healthy for our free-market system. John was a good man. Good man, good man," he continued, "and we were working toward common ground. His untimely death is a tragedy for all of us, for the entire world of technology. But it will not deter Hinnom and Windgazer from doing what we can to serve our customers. Our customers are first."

"And the details of his death?" shot back Dan.

Hinnom seemed at a loss for words. "Oh golly, I'm no doctor. I just called 911."

Linzer icily pointed the camera in his Windy at Dan.

The media manager called on the next reporter. The mainstream press began asking obligatory questions about the monopoly hearing and whether the Congress and Justice Department were interfering with his company's willingness to innovate. At some point, the media manager declared, "Last two questions." Two more were asked.

"Now we are moving to the NDA portion," announced the media manager. The mainstream reporters all left. Only the tech press remained. Dan tapped an overweight reporter next to him, "Uh, NDA?" The reporter, wearing a nametag, "Luke Allison, *Windgazer Retailer*," took a bite out of his Snickers, held up his palmsized computer, and still chewing answered: "PDA? It means Personal Digital Assistant."

Dan came back, "Uh, no, *NDA*. NDA."

Luke pulled the white envelope marked NDA out of the media kit and tapped it. Dan checked his folder and found one too. He almost never looked at the contents of media kits. Inside the envelope was a short contract entitled "Non-Disclosure Agreement" offering to provide details of "the proprietary software known as Windgazer 99" in exchange for agreeing to neither publish nor discuss any details prior to Hinnom Computing's explicit written permission, and requiring the publication to take its own legal action against any employee or related party that might attempt to prematurely disclose it.

Dan's eyes widened. "You nuts?" he asked Luke. "Who would sign this?"

"We all sign it," said Luke nonchalantly. "It means zippo, and if it helps me get access to the information months before it's released, I have to do that for my readers."

"And if I don't sign it?" asked Dan.

"No problem," answered Luke, offering a bite of his unfinished Snickers. Dan declined. "They just ask you to leave," Luke explained. "Plenty of people won't sign. A lot of times the weeklies won't sign. Sometimes they do. Of course, they can afford not to because up until Wednesday at 4 P.M., they can still make their weekend editions. A monthly like us, on the other hand, like most of the people in this room, we have three-month lead times. What are we gonna do, learn about it in January and report it in April, three months after it's been discussed to death and changed? You're obviously not from the technology press."

Dan confirmed that with a nod.

Luke finished his Snickers and said, "My suggestion is: pay no attention and sign it. We all know what the NDA covers anyway. It's Windgazer 99 and Y2K compliance. If you want the details, sign."

"This is standard?" asked Dan in disbelief. "A contract governing coverage?"

"Don't exaggerate," rebutted Luke. "It doesn't govern coverage. You can say anything you want, good or lousy. Just you can't say it until Hinnom is ready."

Park heard the exchange and added in a whisper, "It's not just the press. It's everyone employed at Hinnom, and everyone employed at all the other software companies with access to Windgazer details."

"So if I am an independent software manufacturer," asked a still incredulous Dan, "making a word processor or a personal scheduler, and I want to make my stuff compatible to Windgazer, I have to sign this document and so do all my employees? Under penalty of profound legal action including," he pointed to a clause, "*Confession of Judgment,* allowing Hinnom attorneys to walk into any court in any jurisdiction and appear in your name–in lieu of you–and plead guilty?"

"Commonplace," said Park. "Everyone in the industry. I signed one myself just to work there."

Just then, a smiling Jan came by to pick up Dan's signed copy.

"Oh sure," said Dan. He scribbled "Sorry, Can't Agree" with the flourish of a bureaucratic signature. To distract her, he pointed to Hinnom, "Gee, look at Ben's profile." Jan turned. "Ah, you missed it," he lamented. She took his NDA, and without looking at it, tucked it away in a folder with the others.

Park noticed and again asked Dan, "You always do this kind of thing?"

Again Dan looked innocent, and curtly said, "No." Park didn't even try to believe him.

The lights dimmed to commence the NDA briefing. Two monitors mounted on six-foot towers flashed on, immediately faded to black screens which first fizzled into Windgazer 99 logos, and then morphed into the thumbs-up logo. Then it all transitioned into a January 01, 2000 calendar sheet with "Our Clock Will Not Stop Ticking" zipping over it from the side to complete the image.

Soft lighting illuminated the podium area. A media manager stepped up to announce: "Mr. Hinnom is now speaking pursuant to your NDA." He stepped back to the lectern, waited for everyone to settle down, and then began.

"Zoom is dead," Hinnom declared audaciously. He paused to let the words sink in. "The misguided effort by Bluestar, admittedly our chief rival in the OS War–it's just not going to happen. From everything I have been able to detect, Zoom was dependent upon code from a number of independent software vendors–and that code will not be available. Those vendors have had to make a choice: work with a proven winner–guess who–or take a chance on starting from scratch with Zoom. Although a number of these key ISVs did initially agree to join the Zoom team, including Nelumbo Software, which is actually a mega-acquisition of the declining Bluestar empire, and although Bluestar had indeed hoped that the others would just fall into line . . . oopsy, it just didn't happen."

Hinnom saw one reporter scribbling as fast as he could, and paused to let him catch up. "Got it? Good," said Hinnom to the rushing scribbler. "Next time try Windvoicer. Look ma, no hands," he held up his hands with a pencil wedged horizontally between his fingers.

Turning back to the topic. "So where were we? We were . . ." he paused dramatically, "looking the 21st century smack dab in the mandibles. That's right. We cannot run from the Millennium Bug. That bug will bite us right on the tooshiola. But we now have something to bite it back. Forget about all the rumors. Today you will learn the reality of our new product, Windgazer 99, due out in January. Codenamed *Ravine Dance*. Umm, *Ravine Dance*. I like it. Don't you get bored with silly codenames, like *Sunspot, Tractor Beam,* and *Twinkle Twinkle?* But *Ravine Dance*–now that's down to Earth. Really down."

Hinnom began clicking off his new product's attributes. "You want voice. We heard you. Windgazer 99 will implement the most advanced voice technology any company has ever devised, more than 165,000 words in its dictionary, and most amazingly, it functions in fourteen different languages. Windvoicer technology can not only transcribe discreet sentences, dialect- sensitive–that's fourteen major ones in England alone–it can translate them into speech or text. All from a laptop."

He took out his Windy to demonstrate. The audience ooed as he showed off the enviable compact device. "Lookee no touchee," he chirped. "Let's see Windvoicer in action." Hinnom threw the program a difficult sentence. "'Send these two letters to Bishop Tutu, too.' Replay in French." The Windy broadcast back through the room speakers: *"Envoyez aussi ces deux lettres à Monseigneur Tutu."*

The audience marveled.

He continued the demo. "You wanted easy-to-use. We took notice. Windgazer 99 employs our new Windwatcher technology, a unique ability to watch your facial emotions and compare that to a gallery of your voiceprints and a library of your own human factor averages to better comprehend your nonverbal instructions or even recognize if you are stressed. Human factors have been studied for years. Well, we finally have the breakthrough that will make computers become the very user-friendly humancentric machines we all want. Did I say user-*friendly?* Windwatcher makes computers downright sociable."

To demonstrate, Hinnom turned to a monitor with a tiny mounted camera. "Okay, let's say I'm driving. I'm lost and, frankly, I'm too flustered to ask for directions, the three kids are screaming in the background and the radio is playing. That's a toughie. You all know computers still have a hard time discriminating voice commands in a noisy environment. No problem with Windgazer 99. If you're using one of our GPS-based navigation units, which soon will be standard equipment in top-model Cadillacs, Audis and Saabs, you simply plug in your laptop–or your Windy, if you can get one," he ostentatiously held up his prized Windy "plug it into the nav unit. Well then, Windwatcher can observe distress on your face.

"We have a demo set up," he continued, "to act as though I'm driving from Santa Monica to Tarzana–which ain't easy if you know the tricky transition from the 405 to the 101. Golly, that's a doozy." A driver's ed simulator came up on Hinnom's demo monitor with an inset picture of the navigation unit screen. This same image was duped to the two tower monitors for all to see. Hinnom drove with a joy stick. Suddenly, as he neared the correct exit on the 405, he shook with histrionic frustration.

The system responded with a large screen message. "Don't worry, Ben. There are three exit lanes. Be sure to stay in the middle lane. Then bear left at the fork in the ramp. Relax, Ben."

The audience applauded. Hinnom quieted them down with a gentle wave of his hand. "Okay, now there's more." Turning to the tech crew, "Can you load Windgraphics with Windbrush? Good. Now is Windwatcher watching?" A crew member pointed yes.

An advertising mock-up for Hinnom Computing appeared on the screens. "Okey-dokey. Gee, I'm not sure I like the way this advertisement looks," he said with exaggeration. "Can you please move the Windgazer logo . . ." He motioned with his head to move it up, and then a little to the left. Windwatcher observed. As he did, the Hinnom Computing logo moved up and to the left.

"Okay, now it's a white logo and we want to make it . . . make it . . . make it *red*," he instructed with a flourish. The system changed the white logotype to a pink. He nodded disapproval with his head and wiggled his fingers to gesture *more*. The logo turned to burnt red. He nodded and gestured disapproval again, and the logo turned fire engine red. It was as though Windgazer 99 could read his mind.

The crowd clapped and hooted. "In the next century, you may never need to worry about getting things right," predicted Hinnom, "because Windgazer 99 will be watching you just about everywhere." Park turned to Dan. Her eyes reflecting sudden fear met his. Dan returned the expression. She wrapped her goosebumped arms together. He bit his lip for a moment.

"I could tell you much more about the power and productivity of Windgazer 99," said Hinnom, saving the best for last. "But perhaps the most important component is the built-in Y2K crisis killer that will inoculate all computers against the Millennium Bug and ensure our world does not blow itself up. Oooh, who needs *that* on a Saturday morning? We call it Centurygazer. I love our names. Yes, Centurygazer, and our motto is . . ." he paused for the monitors to sync with him, " 'Our Clock will Not Stop Ticking.' Sorry, no dolphins. Hah! Just the assurance of a thumbs-up that comes Saturday morning, January the first, 2000, when every computer running Windgazer 99 will continue running without skipping so much as a nanosecond. Indeed, we see this as the final solution to the software problem."

Final solution. Now Dan also got goosebumps.

For just an instant, Dan pressed his forehead. *The man with hypnotic eyes and the Swastika armband brushed his black hair to one side of his forehead and stepped to the window. There he heard the crowd assembled in the plaza below chanting in unison: Seig Heil! Seig Heil! Suddenly a woman's voice cried from a corner. It was Dan's mother, moaning "I was shot. I was buried. I was dead. But we survived. Why us?" Dan was a child, and replied helplessly, "I don't know." Dan's father chimed in, "You know. You just don't know that you know." Terrified, Dan, still a child, ran down the back steps of an apartment building, and raced down the alley, but now as a grown man. Seig Heil! Seig Heil! Dan placed his hands protectively over his ears and screamed, "I don't know." His father appeared in the bricks of the building and insisted, "You know. You just don't know that you know." Dan took a pencil and painfully drove it like a spike into his left palm. He held up his hand and the blood dripped not from the wound, but from his eyes. Again he heard the admonition, "You know. You just don't know that you know." Dan* shook it off and glanced obliquely at Park to see if she had noticed. He was relieved to see she was still looking straight ahead, and he mentally rejoined the briefing.

"Windgazer 99," insisted Hinnom, "with our nifty Centurygazer technology, will be the only cross-platform, inter-inoculating, completely seamless, truly Y2K-compliant operating system. Therefore, all new computers to be sold–starting early next year–will run Windgazer 99. We have seen to that with our many partners in the manufacturing community, all of whom share our enthusiasm for this latest phase in computer evolution. At the same time, all new software revs will feature Centurygazer modules–which we are now licensing–thus allowing them to run on these new computers. If you have an old computer, as millions around the world do, and it is running any version of Windgazer, you can purchase an access code for $29 to download the 99 version. If you do not have a personal computer that runs Windgazer . . . well, oopsy, I guess you'll need to purchase one. All is fair in love and technology." Hinnom savored the comment. "Ummm, I love an upgrade.

"As far as all the big legacy machines," Hinnom continued, "–that's everything from your minis to mainframes to supers–Hinnom Computing will be offering Centurygazer technology in a special legacy inoculation campaign that we hope to have completed by the middle of next year. We'll be hitting every major financial institution, medical organization, corporation, and government in the world. We already have our teams in place to work with the United Nations, the Islamic League, the Nonaligned Counties, NATO. . . gee, the Organization of African States, the European Union. I could go on, but it is all organized on a global basis. Even the Bluestar legacy people have consented because, heck, they don't want their mainframes to grind to a halt any more than we do. Really, we think that between the Internet, the slipstreams of all software vendors, and special teams of Windgazer 99 inoculation commandos, we can reach virtually every computer in the world–well, every one that matters. We have already arranged for all email that transmits through Windgazer 99 computers to carry an extended attribute reminding the recipient to upgrade. More than just email. . ."

Suddenly, Dan was tapped on the shoulder. "Mr. *Agree,* is it?"

Dan turned around. It was Linzer. "I help oversee security at Hinnom," Linzer said quietly but firmly, "and this briefing is strictly for those members of the media who have executed the standard Non-Disclosure Agreement. Is your first name *'Sorry?'* "

"Hah!" replied Dan with a smile. "You guys are great. Just checking your efficiency. NDAs are such a bore, I sometimes wonder if anyone ever checks 'em."

"We did," responded Linzer in a monotone, sizing up Dan.

"Hey, if it's a problem," said Dan, "I'll–"

"Could I kindly see your press pass and know what publication you are from?" asked Linzer.

"No problem. Levincom," replied Dan smoothly, extending his business card. "We formerly published the award-winning *Chicago Monthly*. That unit was just spun off along with a number of other titles, allowing us to concentrate on the technology side of the market we feel is more suited to our 21st Century emphasis. We'll be launching a series of web-based E-zines, weekly high-tech broadcast fax newsletters, and perhaps one or two niched print monthlies for the IT community. I'm very impressed with what I have seen here. Hinnom is doing quite a job. Very futuristic."

Park was silent and pretended not to know Dan, acting as though she was focusing on the Hinnom presentation.

"No press credential, Mr. Levin?" asked Linzer.

"We'll be relocating soon," Dan replied glibly in corporate voice, "so we're in transition, and until we do, we won't apply for new credentials. Hey, these days it's either to the Silicon Valley or perhaps the Seattle area, where the action really is. Coffee's a lot better in Seattle, I hear."

Linzer showed impatience.

"Really, it's a toss-up," continued Dan with barely a breath. "Tax breaks, property values, enterprise zones. That kinda thing. As soon as HR and our company's site team make their final recommendation, we'll be there in a virtual minute. And I'm sure we'll be working very closely with you. So thanks for all your help." Dan turned away to concentrate on the briefing.

"Asking questions about the unfortunate tragedy involving Mr. Hector," commented Linzer, still in monotone, "now that is unusual for a technology-based reporter."

"Ahh," Dan dismissed himself, "it's just my old hard news background poking through the clouds." He laughed it off. Seizing the opportunity to extricate himself, "So look, Mister . . . Mister–"

"Yes?" interjected Linzer.

"–Mister Hinnom Computing official," Dan went on, "I'm here to get the details on Windgazer 99, not talk about our new zip code." He pulled out a pen and signed his NDA properly. "Keep the card and let me pay attention to the briefing," he added with feigned arrogance. "Or don't complain if I get it wrong in print."

With that, Dan ceremoniously turned toward Hinnom and began scribbling notes.

Linzer fed the card into his Windy, which scanned its contents, and gave it back to Dan. Aiming his Windy at Park, who was pretending to be oblivious to the encounter, Linzer almost asked her a question. She kept her back to him, dedicating her attention to Hinnom at the podium and the tape recorder in her hands.

Linzer moved a few inches until his Windy could photograph her face at a better angle. Then he couldn't help himself. "Do we know each other? You are?"

Park turned around looking a little stupid, like she had just shipped in as recycled trailer trash. "Bug off, buddy. I'm just running the tape recorder here for this guy," she snapped. "If you have a question, ask him. *Geez,* you computer guys think you can just hit on any woman in sight. You want my name, call the temp agency. And back off before I call security." Loudly under her breath, she babbled, "Think I don't know about all your Internet pornography. I have a TV set, ya know. I watch *60 Minutes.* I'm not a moron."

Linzer moved away. His Windy had captured a side shot of her face. He clicked a few keys on his device, and walked back to the podium, leaving Dan and Park to take notes and fastidiously check their tape recorder. In the corner of his eye, Dan could see Linzer still punching the keypad.

Across the country, in a darkened office in the nerve center of Hinnom Computing headquarters, just around the corner from the executive suite in Building 6, a black computer tower whirred away beneath a small monitor filled with icons.

Suddenly, the system remotely highlighted Datagazer's icon, a Jolly Roger motif with a skull and two magnifying glasses for crossbones. The program loaded. Datagazer's opening screen appeared with icons for a dozen options. *Personal Identity* was one of them. It remotely highlighted. Three menu possibilities appeared: BioData, Account Number, or Photo. Photo remotely highlighted. A red background popped up. Then the photo of Park taken at the press conference by Linzer's Windy appeared in a green outline box labeled "Source Image."

Slightly off-kilter, and providing only a partial profile, the image would not be easy to match. Under the Park photo, a menu listed several dozen database search options. A checkmark remotely appeared in front of "Motor Vehicle Departments." New screen. Each state and territorial DMV, including Puerto Rico, Guam and the Northern Marianna islands, appeared in three alphabetical columns. The unmarked entry after *Wyoming* was "ALL." A check remotely appeared in front of ALL. The parameter "Female" was checked as the final instruction.

Datagazer's massive search launched.

Abruptly, the screen dissolved into two images. Steady on the left was the source picture of Park. Flashing on the right, one by one, were the candidate comparison photographs of every licensed female driver on America soil. The endless stutter of faces created a frenzied whirring among the disk drives and a hypnotic flicker on the screen.

Above this stroboscopic sight pulsed the words, DATA MINING 183,131,860 IMAGES.

7

MIDNIGHT
AT TEL AVIV CAFE

*F*rom the massive brown lacquered dining room table in the Jefferson Hotel's presidential suite, Dan could just barely see through the master bedroom door left slightly open. At the far end of the bedroom, the bathroom door was ajar. Through that he could see Park's slender, muscular body slip into the jacuzzi. He took another sip of coffee. By now it had turned tepid and bitter.

"This is the place!" Park called out from the steaming tub. "I've decided it's okay for retired publishers to ask me to come to Washington. Spur of the moment is fine." She sighed with content as the soothing water reached her neck. "Ask me back in a week," she sang out dreamily.

Dan felt a sense of satisfaction because Park was enjoying herself. He walked into his bedroom, one of three in the elegant suite, and busied himself rearranging his clothes in the closet and making sure all hangers faced one direction. Skimming through a selection of CDs, he picked one, then another, but finally settled on Goldsmith's *Congo*. It was a lousy film but proof in Dan's mind that great soundtrack composers write their best music for bad movies. He unflipped his StarTac, and while walking through the suite, checked his voice messages, discarding and saving them by depressing buttons, displaying the same look of disdain he always had about his messages. He used the StarTac to call out because he had long ago calculated that even after roaming charges, it was cheaper to make long distance calls from a hotel room with a cellular than by using the hotel's phone. Hotel phone charges bothered Dan. And he was now bored.

"Are you cold?" he called out to Park through the doors.

"I'm fine."

"You hungry?" he asked.

"I'm just fine," she answered, trying to just soak for a moment without engaging in conversation.

"Well, I can't stand that chilled room effect these hotels insist on," he shouted across the suite. "The thermostat won't work. I'm freezing . . . I called the desk." He looked with irritation at a clock. "That was a half hour ago."

"Okay," she said, not hearing all of what Dan said.

The suite's doorbell rang. A tall, slender young man in a T-shirt, looking barely old enough to drive, stood there holding a small bag, his arms dangling from shoulders that almost furled like the beginnings of a cocoon. "Good," said Dan. "Get this damn thing to work."

For the next few moments, Dan explained in detail what he had done to make the digital thermostat work, pointing to the buttons, and how nothing had helped, and for heaven's sake it's an expensive suite to be cold in. "If you guys would just put an old-fashioned thermostat in here with a dull, round dial that goes up and down with a twist," he complained with not a little sarcasm, "I could regulate the heat. But you need modern ones. And that's okay. Because I believe in modern things even though you have the suite decked out like an eighteenth-century chateau. But when a guy like me, who knows modern computers and works with them every day, can't push enough buttons on this modern thermostat to make it work, maybe it's time to step back in time to recent antiquity, say ten years, for the sake of warmth."

The young man unfurled one shoulder to lift the cosmetic panel on the thermostat. He pressed RESET, then three buttons, then ON. Silence.

Dan listened for the heat. In a moment it switched on. He dropped his fingers down to the floor vent and felt the warmth blowing. "Nice going. Thank you so much," said Dan with thin politeness. He gave the young man a dollar, and escorted him to the door. "I appreciate it."

During the next five minutes, Dan peeked through the bedroom door once more, set up his Butterfly, ran a phone cord from the notebook to the phone, checked his stocks, and decided to go to the lobby. "I'm running down to talk to the manager to say hello. I know him from way back," Dan shouted over to Park. He heard no answer.

When he opened the suite door, there stood the man who repaired the thermostat, arms defensively strung across his length, palms curved out, a look of uncertainty on his face. Surprised at his presence, Dan said, "Excuse me. How long have you been standing there?" The young man was too flustered by Dan to say anything. "Excuse me?" No response.

"Habla Espanol?" No response.

"Uh, I was just going to talk to the GM, so should I mention maybe your name or are you going to tell me why you're standing there?" said Dan, gesturing with his hands in a circular fashion.

Impatient, Dan finally said, "Okay, may I please have your name." He dreaded having to revisit old times with the hotel manager by starting with a complaint, so he hoped the young man would simply go away. "I'm ready now. What is your name?" asked Dan in a command voice.

The young man's head dropped to one side as he mustered a reply: "Sal."

Dan shut his eyes in pain, as though he had just walked out of his house without pants. "Oh dear, Sal. My silly, silly error." He graciously ushered Sal back into the suite, taking his bag. After calling out to Park that Sal had arrived–"Good. I'll be right out"–and offering him any number of juices, sodas, and candies, all of which were declined, Dan tried to engage Sal in conversation. How was the flight? Miss planes a lot, I hear. Any trouble getting to the hotel? Your programming reputation precedes you. You really showed me on that thermostat. To each of these statements, Sal seemed to wince in worried silence.

Every time he came close to replying–and that could take thirty to sixty seconds–an impatient Dan would give up and ask yet another question, which would only restart Sal's slow process. Sal abhorred verbal answers because of their great potential for error. *How are you?* Answering *fine,* could be somewhat inaccurate. *Want a pizza?* He did at the moment, but if he changed his mind, the order would have already been set in motion, and maybe he really wanted something else not yet offered. Calculations did not lie. They were immune to the frailties of life and impervious to misinterpretation. 300 minus 1 was 299 whether recited by a Bantu in Africa or a broker in Manhattan. Sal found shelter in the strength and power of numbers and by extension the art of programming, and the ecstasy of physics. But sentences were designed to deceive. Ask any four people. That's why, for Sal, even simple questions launched complex calculations weighing the possibilities and facts. He wanted to lie as little as possible. Lying was unholy. If God had wanted men to lie, he would not have created numbers.

More often than not, Sal felt that the social requirement to speak was little more than an intrusion upon his intelligence and integrity, trying to force the imprecision of language upon him when the exactitude of a formula or the immutable reality of nature's own power spoke volumes. Words only caused trouble. Math never did. For this reason, Sal volunteered almost nothing, and answered little. Many misperceived Sal's exaggerated sense of precision for dullness and in some cases retardation. If you can't judge a computer by its gray case, then everything about Sal's presence was misleading. In truth, Sal's mind constantly whirred with a cacophony of explosive perceptions, alluring comparisons and enticing projections. But like many standalones, he found output taxing to his system.

Sal's way was more than tolerated by his mother, Park, who in her own non-computer moments also found glibness an unwelcome attribute. But for Dan, who used words like weapons, whether spoken or written, it would take some time to comprehend a person who expressed himself in a vocabulary of silence.

"Talk much?" asked Dan, determined to wait for a reply. After a long, anxious pause, Sal finally managed to answer, "Yes."

Dan's eyes lit up as he turned his head to narrow his focus on Sal. They made eye contact, and Dan felt he was beginning to communicate. He positioned his Butterfly in front of Sal as an offering, and opened it to show off its expandible keyboard. "I hear you know your computers."

Sal didn't smile; it was more like a swallow that could have been a smile if it wasn't actually a swallow. But Dan took the sight of Sal's bobbing Adam's Apple as a sort of internalized gesture of goodwill, a form of dialogue. Sal glanced for a moment at the exquisite Butterfly notebook, but then wordlessly reached into his bag. Out came a tiny palmsized computer. Sal opened it, and as the screen telescoped, an embarrassed partial smile actually did reach Sal's face. Dan's mouth dropped. "You have a Windy? Hinnom hasn't released it yet."

"Rosie made me a beta tester," interjected Park, appearing at the door wearing a plush Jefferson Hotel bathrobe. Sal's nearly smiling demeanor receded. "But I don't think anyone knew that and heck, I forgot to give it back when I left the company," she explained with a wry smirk.

Sal's head and shoulders clenched as a full smile erupted.

"It's one of three fully functional production candidate models created," explained Park. "It's very powerful. Preloaded with all the Hinnom access phone numbers, the test labs and databanks, the works. It probably still remotely calls in for updates. It's a doozy."

Dan's attention became riveted. Sal noticed and quietly cringed. "This device," Dan pointed as he spoke emphatically, "is connected to Hinnom's headquarters?"

Park nodded and Sal nonverbally displayed his agreement as well. "It's connected to lots more things than Hinnom headquarters," added Park. "We haven't even checked out all the sites nailed into the system."

"Can I see it?" Dan asked. Sal's lips pressed tightly.

"Uh, I think Sal's got all sorts of hot keys programmed in," Park answered for her son. "He doesn't let anyone touch it. Those keys are so small, you could accidentally touch one and whew, there goes some of Sal's routines."

"Like maybe F9 starts the cappuccino steaming and we could get all fogged up here in a matter of minutes?" Dan joked.

"Exactly," Park came back.

Dan rubbed his forehead, dragged his hand over his eyes, and then wiped it past the side of his head in exasperation. "Well maybe not now," he declared, "but eventually, I think we should use the Windy for everything it's worth. Maybe we could click into some of Hinnom's files. That would be a good thing. Huh?"

Park did not respond. Sal seemed to fold his shoulders even closer together. The room became very unreceptive. "I think it's Sal's decision," said Park. "He feels pretty personal about his Windy."

Dan grimaced and wrinkled his forehead. "Right," said Dan switching the subject. "I'm hungry, anyone for dinner?"

Park smiled again and the three of them went down to grab a cab.

PULSING GUITARS AND a Latin rhythm electrified the Bethesda night air around the Tel Aviv Cafe as Gipsy Kings music pumped through the restaurant's speaker system and out onto the street. Traffic barely crawled past the address, only increasing the interest nearby. If you weren't pulling up for valet parking, you were driving elsewhere but stopping in front to yell greetings to Udi, the affable restaurant owner who knew every guest by name and many guests who preferred no name at all. The restaurant only minimally catered to the Jewish and Israeli crowds. It quickly became a hangout for the openly and the quietly empowered of all walks and runs of life. Spies, ex-spies, and future spies felt comfortable rubbing elbows with lobbyists, artists, financiers, diplomats, and journalists. Sleek, beautiful women, ever present, regularly tested the nerves of men who tried not to turn their heads midsentence. Festive platters of Israeli, Moroccan, and Mediterranean dishes constantly floated back and forth atop the spread fingers of waiters who carried the perfumed presentations like exotic scarves blowing in the wind. And when other nearby restaurants closed at eleven, it was here that their owners came for a late-night drink.

Some patrons of Tel Aviv Cafe always preferred to sit outside and become part of the street scene, weather permitting. But there were always those who preferred sitting inside, even at the back. Not Dan. His favorite spot was Table One, right in front where the seating met the sidewalk.

As chance would have it, Table One opened just as Dan's taxi pulled up. Dan, Park, and Sal had barely emerged from the vehicle when Udi, from deep within the restaurant, recognized his old friend approaching. Udi motioned to the petite, doll-like hostess; she looked to the front, also recognized Dan, and understood. In a moment, busboys descended on Table One. The Italian commercial attaché and his wife were waiting, but the hostess bypassed them, seating Dan and his party instead. Dan pretended not to notice the chagrin of the attaché's wife, who was offered a drink on the house for her extra wait.

Udi was a debonair pony-tailed Moroccan Israeli who spoke impeccable French, Hebrew, Arabic, and English. He had seen much and done more during his service in an elite Israeli commando unit and later, said some, in the Mossad. Dan first met Udi during his foreign correspondent days while touring Maronite enclaves in South Lebanon. Dan's vehicle had separated from the military-escorted group. Udi was dispatched by Israeli intelligence to search for Dan and lead him back across the border before Amal gunmen seeking fresh hostages discovered him wandering about.

Dan stood with an expression of genuine joy, and they greeted each other with a kiss on either cheek and a hug. *"Shaaalom, chaver,"* said Udi.

"Hello friend," replied Dan. He whispered a joke in Udi's ear. Udi whispered back. They laughed.

"And this is?" he asked. Dan introduced Park and Sal. Park shook hands enthusiastically. Sal blinked a few times as a greeting and tilted his head away.

Dan and Udi exchanged quick resumes of the recent past, and then Udi said, "You're recovering from New Year's?"

"Recovered," said Dan curtly. "I am starvin'. Bring on the food."

Udi ordered a sumptuous feast of Moroccan, Israeli, and Continental dishes. It began with cigarim, falafel, hummus, and tehina appetizers arranged in concentric circles on exquisite Bedouin earthenware, plus a plate of pita, trimmed with a small clay vessel of zesty green *zattar*, a spicy bowl of *hariff*, and olive oil. The barman uncorked a fine Merlot. He checked the display for scotches and couldn't find Laphroaig. Udi thought, and then reached for a shelf in the back. A small smile spread across Dan's face when the familiar black-and-white labeled bottle appeared.

"Still only half gone?" asked Dan.

"You're the only one who drinks it," Udi jabbed back.

The loud thumping music and the constant flow of people created its own excitement. The cuisine Dan took for granted, having eaten it for years before and after his time in Israel, was a completely new experience for Park. She loved it, and even sampled from the *hariff* bowl, declaring with a gasp after a smidgen of the thick, sinus-clearing pepper paste, "Yow! That's kinda good."

Sal refused to venture into the condiments, but did slide his pita once or twice into the hummus. He accepted the shishlik, which to him tasted more like a hamburger. At one point, the waiter brushed up against the vinegar and oil, and some vinegar spilled on one of the spice bowls. It happened just as Sal dipped his finger in for a sample. He winced, smeared it off his finger and wiped it away with a napkin.

Sal grimaced, "What is it?"

"Oh *that*." said Dan. "I know it. I'm just not sure of the Arabic name.

In English, it's called *hyssop*. You ate this with vinegar?"

Sal nodded.

"Yeah," Dan continued. "Weird on salads or minced eggplant. You gotta develop a taste for it. Ever had it before?" Sal shrugged no.

"Maybe in another life," Dan joked.

As the evening edged toward midnight, the music became louder. The adjacent bar thickened with patrons. When an elderly gentleman in a dapper, if slightly out of date, gray suit and a tie knot pulled crooked walked in, Dan couldn't believe it. "I have to leave you for a minute," Dan told Park and Sal. "It's business—and it could be terribly important to me. Might just be a minute, but it might be a lot longer. I'll explain after." He motioned to Udi to pay some extra attention to the table in his absence. Dan then approached and waited for the right moment.

"Ted?" Dan asked. "It's you?"

Theodore Steeple pulled his glasses from his inside pocket, hooked them into position, looked at Dan for a moment, focused, remembered, and then blurted out, "You're what's his name . . . Levine . . . Lewin . . ."

"Dan Levin," corrected Dan cordially.

"I can't tell one Jewish name from another," he barked back. "You can. But I can't. Levin. All right, Levin. I knew that. I just needed a minute. Dan, how in heck are you?"

Ted Steeple was one of the New York literary establishment's elder statesmen, and just about the only person Dan allowed to bark at him. That was Steeple's way. If Steeple didn't speak with derision, he really didn't care about you. In his not quite absentminded seventies, not unacquainted with the lesser forms of scotch, and proud of his tennis game, his home in the Hamptons, and his WASP heritage, politeness was Steeple's form of condescension. But with fifty years in the business, editor to the great authors, a man who stood up to prissy book executives to push important projects and enjoyed vindication every time, Steeple wrote his own rules and chose his own game. It was Steeple who three decades before had discovered a young, overenthusiastic, unpolished Dan Levin and battered him emotionally and editorially until five years later Levin produced his bestselling masterpiece, *Reich Dollars*, an investigation of Nazi finances that made international headlines and first put Levin on the map. You can grow, but never in the mind of your mentor. To Steeple, Levin was still a precocious kid with a sharp pencil in his ear and a dull fire in his chest. In truth, Levin had changed. He was no longer a kid.

"I'm fine, Ted," said Dan. "It's wonderful seeing you after, after I don't know, twenty years, fifteen years. What brings you to Tel Aviv Cafe?"

"Why? Is there a sign up there that says Jews only?" snapped Steeple with his good-natured brusqueness. "Look around. Do you think I'm the only WASP here?" No matter what was said, Dan never won with Steeple, whose conversations with Dan were often laced with blunt Jewish references that might seem anti-Semitic to just about anyone else. But Ted had championed and published more than two dozen of the most important Holocaust books in print. His credentials for Jewish causes on the field of literary battle were well established. And inside that scaly WASP exterior, there bled a man whose outrage over the Holocaust never faded. Dan and he shared that in common. "You here alone?" asked Steeple.

Dan motioned to Park and Sal at the table.

"My friend and her son. We're just here for the weekend."

"Duh weekend?" mocked Steeple. "When in Crisname are you going to speak correctly and not like a punk from a Chicago street gang?" He flailed a bit and over-mimiced Chicagoese: "Deez and dooz and dare four dis tree." He swigged the lesser scotch and jabbed, "Can you e-nunciate and say *these,* and *those,* and *therefore this three.*"

There was no arguing with him. "There is nothing that I cannot pronounce in the fashion you are accustomed to hearing them, so there," replied Dan in a monotone, accentuating his *th* sounds.

"That's better," Steeple relented, proving once again that he could begin any conversation with a conquest. "Now, how the heck are you did you say?"

"Actually, I'm not fine. I'm a little ticked," said Dan, as he waved another Laphroaig from the bar man.

Steeple interrupted, "Before you tell me your boring story, how are you inside? I heard about New Year's Day with Jenny and your boy Simon. You want to talk about that? You can talk to me. Deep down I care about you."

For just an instant, Dan pressed his thumbs into fists. *337 please report to Special Services. What do you mean, Special Services? Excuse me, what do you mean, Special Services? Sir, please follow me. She took him by the arm to a door off a special ramp which shortcut to a dimly lit windowless room with twelve rows of chairs. What's in there? She squeezed his arm. Please step in.*

What the hell is in there? He looked in and saw people weeping. He tried to pull away. Please step in. Dan's fists unfolded.

"Yeah, I'm just fine," he said, pausing for a breath. "But I'm a little ticked right now. You know, I sold all my magazines."

"Ten magazines," said Steeple.

". . . Seven," Dan corrected. "Now they're being run by a bunch of derivative idiots."

"Well, I have no use for derivative idiots," agreed Steeple.

"But the derivatives are taking over the world," complained Dan.

"Okay, okay. How about you? Now you're ready to goddamn retire, a rich bastard," said Steeple. "I think that's a mistake, young man. Look at me. They tried to retire me and I kicked 'em on their ass."

"I'm not trying to retire," Dan explained. "I sold my rags and I'm back to serious writing."

Dan glanced back to the table, and saw Park watching from afar. He winked and subtly touched a finger to his lip and threw a kiss no one could detect. Across the restaurant, Park smiled and subtly ran her hand across her cheek to indicate the kiss had landed.

"Okay, let's talk about it," said Steeple. "What type of writing do you want to do? You know, I told you a thousand times that book on the Czar, another investigative history is where you need to be. It's your strong suit."

"Nah," Dan responded, "I'm not there anymore. I did historical investigation. It was nice. What I really want to do is go back to Holocaust. Maybe this time write my parents' story."

"Judaica?" said Steeple. "I know Judaica. It's awfully important. I published many a Holocaust book. But that's narrow interest. No money. You're a whiz at investigative reporting. What happened? You diverted yourself with those silly magazines you published. What was it? *Brain?* That kind of stuff is not going to help your career, kiddo."

"You have a problem with the brain?" rebutted Dan defensively. "Dyslexia, memory, Alzheimer's, motor function, attention deficit disorder, Parkinson's, inherited traits of violence. These are big topics. It's three pounds of tissue smack between our ears that most people don't know how to use correctly. Fifty million Americans suffer from brain-related disorders. In case you don't have the number handy, that translates to $305 billion in annual treatment, rehabilitation, and associated costs per year. So how did I go wrong? By adding some hard-edge report-ing to a field plagued by boring literature that would put any lobe to sleep? Give me a minor break."

"Okay, write a book about the brain," said Steeple dismissively.

Dan shook his head in frustration. "I don't want to write a book about the brain. I'm sick of the brain."

"Then start another magazine," grumbled Steeple.

"Ten years," Dan shot back. "I'm tired of the 3 A.M. calls from pressmen with a color question. Tired of working on three issues at once for seven titles. I'm tired."

"It should be easy for a guy like you," came back Steeple. "What hap-pened to that photographic memory?"

"I'm out of film," Dan retorted. "Even if I wasn't, I put all that behind me when I sold my titles. And I can't do a mag without Jenny. Now I have a few dollars and I want to write the one book my father challenged me to write that I never did: their true story. I've really wanted to all my life. I just couldn't get started. Too busy with everything else."

Dan stopped his digression. "Ironically, my head is still elsewhere. I'm actually trying to develop an investigative piece and I've been making the rounds working on a story. My plan, Ted, is to get a few high-profile mag-azine articles, splash a few headlines again, and then make the leap back to books."

"I have known a few great Judaica writers," Steeple bragged with con-descension. "I edited Holocaust books, including yours, and published bios on all the great Israeli leaders. They were all great books. But I don't want your next effort to be just another survivor account ending up on the Judaica shelf at Barnes and Noble, two copies per store. Do you under-stand the first flying thing about what I am saying? You can do better."

Dan lifted his snifter for a taste. "Ted, I see images," Dan explained. "I see images constantly and they tear at me. Some of them are beautiful, some of them are painful, many horrifying. I write them down on little scraps of paper or just sear them into my memory. After a while, I paste them together and make a scene, and when I read it back, it's alive. It burns to read, and burns to write. I'm still struggling just to understand the process." He sipped again and opened his soul to the one person he still trusted. "My mind divides the world up into images it won't let in . . . and images it won't let out."

"How do you deal with that?" asked Steeple.

"I turn up the stereo, get in front of the keyboard," Dan responded. "The result comes out on paper. Fundamentally, I guess nothing has changed for me. The world is a very black place with a black past. People fumble around in fear pretending they're not lost, pretending they can't see what just happened. I want to light their way in the dark. That's the giving part of me."

"And the ego part of you?" Steeple asked flippantly.

"Maybe a few people will notice the source of the light," Dan acknowledged self-consciously with a slight grin.

"Okay, now listen to the following," Steeple barked. Whenever he began a sentence with those words, Dan knew something important was going to be said. "The horse's asses that tried to retire me," growled Steeple, "in the midst of their ill-advised mergers have learned the errors of their ways. Have you been following the book market?" Without waiting for answer, he continued, "Because I know you haven't. But the old families that ran the houses are gone. Judgment is gone. The little bookstore guy on the corner with his wine and cheeseboard, that is essentially gone, although I still buy all my books from my bookseller down the street. Now it's all big corporations—publishers and retailers both. The Germans and Brits own everything, and the Chinese control a vast market everyone wants to tap into so execs quake when the Chinese speak. It's not the important books anymore. It's the gimmick books or the proven names that dominate. Books by the numbers. Like Hollywood. But eventually, the public demands better, and eventually, one of these international media moguls decides for all the wrong reasons to do the right thing. He asserts himself like an arrogant sonofabitch and says 'We're gonna do things the right way' just *because*.

"You know about Castlebank Books and you know about Manhattan-Billings Street Press?" continued Steeple. "Those two—which have merged up and down the street, are themselves going to merge next week and the whole shebang will now be a monster division of Wolf Multi."

"The Italians?" interjected Dan.

"My boy," corrected Steeple, "when you're as big as Angelo Wolf, you're no longer Italian, German, British, or American. You're just Wolf Multi. Now don't distract me and listen. Castlebank Manhattan Publishing will be the new name. Billings is finished. Do you have that?

Castlebank Manhattan. But the old fart from Castlebank who was kept at some ridiculous salary he doesn't deserve as publisher asked me to come on as editor-in-chief at an equally ridiculous salary which I *do* deserve. My job is to develop a list of great books." Dan was silent. When Steeple was talking like this, the best thing was to be silent.

"Leave it to me, my boy," said Steeple.

That comment was always a good thing. Dan usually just complied when he heard Steeple say those words.

"Now maybe you can do justice to your parents' story and maybe you can't. Or maybe you should leave it to mister moviemaker, Steven what's-his-name," Steeple continued. "I hired that overstuffed Markowitz from Soho Meridian Press to handle my Judaica list. That's his call. But I'll phone him Monday and tell him to listen to anything you have to say. Give us three chapters that don't put half of New York to sleep and maybe you two can revive Holocaust titles."

"I understand," said Dan cautiously.

"Hang on! First, you deliver a hard-edged investigation to help out my Fall 99 list. Go into your black bag, find something juicy that you have a head start on, give me enough solid reporting and meat for 80,000-plus words—I think that's probably 270-300 pages—deliver it in eight weeks on a disk and then you can dance with Markowitz and pretend you're writing the great American novel. But first I get an investigation."

Dan swallowed hard and looked at the floor, "The Czar Nicholas thing?"

Steeple finished his scotch and tapped the glass rim to signal another shot. "The Czar thing is fine," he said. "I'll tell you, though, if you could use that noggin of yours, Dan my boy, to combine what you know about technology—computers and that sort of thing—I think the market is ready for that kind of book. Got anything about computer fraud or slave labor in manufacturing out there in Malaysia? Now listen, I'm not asking for a future society vision book," he waved his hands in crystal ball mockery, "or a how-to. But I do want people to know how prone they are depending upon all these goddamn computers. They're vulnerable. The world's independence is dribbling away like saliva. I'd like the public to know just how terribly wrong it can all go. I need a shocker to scare their pants off."

Dan looked up. "I might maybe have a book idea," he said quietly.

From Park's vantage point back at the table, she could barely see Dan and the man he was talking to across the restaurant and over the shoulders of customers. Dan was now animated, gesturing with his hands. The other man was just listening and writing an occasional note. Periodically their glasses would come north for a moment and then return to the bar slightly lighter. Park couldn't wait to learn what was being discussed.

But Sal was bored. He checked his Windy for email and found a message from a fellow traveler at the Capital Database Collective inviting him to stop by for some Jolt cola and corn chips as a prelude to some exotic table normalization and row updating in multitable views.

After making sure her son had cash for a Metro card, and extracting a promise that he would be back at the hotel before dawn, Park blew him a kiss on the end of her finger and waved good-bye. That left her sitting alone, and on the verge of becoming annoyed. But Dan and Steeple seemed to be reaching a critical moment, so she tolerated the wait.

"Is this on the level about Hinnom?" asked Steeple.

"At first I wasn't sure," replied Dan. "But now I believe the guy is some kind of dark genius bent on controlling the world with tools no other conqueror in history has had at his disposal. I speak not of wielding spears and legions to control whole populations and territory but the passive act of withholding passwords and updates that will subjugate humanity just as effectively. When you hear bombs bursting, you feel a blast and see fires burning. But when Hinnom attacks, his battles are waged with the whir of a hard drive, the barely audible click of a keystroke. Ultimately, it is silence that signals final defeat."

"Well, you stupid sonofabitch," blurted Steeple. "Can you write it like that?"

"Yes," said Dan, excitement welling up in his eyes.

"Okay," Steeple said. "$40,000 now and $40,000 on complete and final. Delivery in sixty days. Working title . . . how about . . . *Hinnom–The Untold Story.*"

"The title is boring enough. The money is putrid," Dan retorted. "But I'll live with both."

Steeple shook Dan's hand. Dan hugged him. Steeple tried to extricate himself. "Come on, come on. It's a public place for cryin' out loud."

Dan sauntered back to Park, being careful not to run. He uncontrollably stuffed a large kubeh in his mouth—a whole one—and washed it down with Merlot.

"Out," he whispered in her ear. "We're going back to the hotel."

"What in God's name . . ." Park protested.

"Full story coming up. When we're out of here. Hey. What happened to Sal?"

"He connected with a local users group," she replied, "and they're going to stay up all night dismantling and reassembling databases. Who was that man over there?"

"Did you give Sal money to take care of himself?"

"Yes, yes," Park answered, "but tell me tell me who is that guy?"

"He's Ted Steeple," explained Dan, talking loud enough to be heard over the music, "the old man of great book publishing. And we need to leave before he changes his mind. I got the assignment. A book. A *book*," said Dan, raising his eyebrows to indicate Steeple back at the bar who had just lit up a Monte Cristo #2 Udi smuggled in from Havana. "When it's this good, you leave. Let's go."

"A book on what?" asked Park in a loud whisper barely audible over the music.

"Our buddy, Bad Ben," he answered. "We got him! It's a book on Hinnom and his whole corrupt, vomitus empire. And this guy Steeple will make it happen–and big." Dan clenched his hands in front of him so only she could see. "It's what I wanted. I'm back."

Park smiled as though the victory was not Dan's alone but hers as well, as though she was as much a part of the start and finish of this odyssey as Dan's own struggle to undertake it. She grabbed his hand and squeezed it tight.

He dropped a new hundred dollar bill on the table, swigged the remnants of his glass of wine, and escorted her to the door. Udi saw the exit, motioned for the waiter to take the money, and yelled after Dan, "Next time let me know when you're coming."

Dan turned and blew Udi a fist of friendship. "See you soon, Udi," Dan called out as he bolted for a taxi.

～

AS THE TAXI drove away, Dan directed the driver, "Take the Parkway."

"Wisconsin is faster. The Parkway is roundabout," the driver pointed out with some irritation.

"The Parkway," Dan repeated.

Twenty minutes later, the cab had turned onto the George Washington Parkway, that surreal stone-trimmed, tree-lined highway without lights that courses idyllically above the Potomac, built to provide the CIA with a ten-minute access to National Airport and, in the process, offering all a reminder that the political chaos of the nation's capital ironically resides within a setting of peaceful natural serenity. When the night is clear, when the stars are sprinkled just right, when the moon hovers to both illuminate the way and sparkle its image atop the river below, then the gleaming Washington Monument, the Kennedy Center, the Jefferson Memorial, the twinkling from the Virginia side, and the excitement of jet planes twisting and banking toward the nearby runways–it all makes this ten-minute drive an exhilarating one that promises something special is in store.

From the distance, the cab could be seen passing the far-off glint of the Washington Monument, that beckoning white Egyptian obelisk said to derive its sleek towering shape from ancient fertility worship. Its tall and erect commanding presence came into sight for only an instant when the Parkway edged through a clearing in the trees. But once glimpsed, the landmark's imposing visage remained with Dan and Park, even when out of view.

For the longest time, Dan was silent. Finally, he emotionally admitted, "Things are happening. So much is happening."

Park almost replied, but decided to listen.

"I was buried," said Dan. "But now this book on Hinnom . . . this is a great development for me. Goodness. It's my chance to go after a bad guy. Again. Like the old days."

Dan turned to her and saw a partner. "Don't think I'm unaware that you're the source of it all. It was you, Park. The Hinnom stuff. Fantastic. It was as though you pulled me from a grave and nourished me back with information and support and companionship, that I had no idea–no damn idea–I would need so desperately."

The taxi's headlights cut through wisps of fog drifting across the unlighted roadway as deer along the shoulder stood passive except for the fire in their reflective eyes.

"You understand I can't do this alone," continued Dan, with uncharacteristic trepidation. "It's an *us* thing. You have to be with me. You know this stuff–computers. My idea of hard drive is a guy being chased by his past."

"It's just data storage," she retorted with a chuckle.

"Same difference," he laughed, still suppressing the emotion of the moment. "Park, I'm gonna need help here. Real help. Every step of the way." Help was a word Dan uttered with difficulty.

"I'm willing," answered Park, seeing into his heart, "if you'll open up and let me. Sometimes I think you have a hard time doing that."

Dan folded his hands calmly and confessed with a faint gasp, "I need . . . I need to need. I admit that. But it's been so impossible for me for so long."

"We're opening possibilities up for each other," she replied, nudging his hand almost imperceptibly. "Sal and I have been living in a corner forever. I'm not used to unconditional acceptance."

"Acceptance?"

"We've had no one," she recounted. "My family, my friends, they all vanished when Sal appeared. From their point of view, either I sold my body for money, or had an illegitimate child and was lying to cover it up. Nobody wanted to understand. My dad, my brothers, the pastor . . . even Mom. No one wanted me to come close. And that's no problem because I don't need any of them. We had our own life and I raised a precious son. Just two of us for Thanksgiving and Christmas. Two is good enough. No problem."

"No problem?"

"None." She paused. "But three wouldn't be bad."

"Hard drive is a guy being chased by his past," he repeated.

"Yeah, well sometimes too much data storage crashes the system," she replied.

He leaned over and kissed her on the neck just to connect. She quivered slightly at the touch. He felt her response.

The Washington Monument was long out of sight. But they could see it shining nonetheless, just up ahead.

8

HAKOL LAVAN

*S*he was frightened. Dan was new, terribly new. But soon she would be floating. Everything was too perfect: the way he softly stroked her neck in the taxi, this magnificent three-bedroom suite at the Jefferson, Dan's triumphant moment with Ted Steeple at Tel Aviv Cafe, the lingering visuals of monuments along the Parkway, and the pure romance of Washington, a city where dreams suddenly become realities, and realities suddenly become dreams. She couldn't tell which was which in her relationship with Dan. But she knew that soon, too soon, she would be floating.

Park looked across the suite and noticed Dan flipping through CDs he had brought from home. He selected *Swept from the Sea*, a little-known John Barry soundtrack to a forgotten romance about two lovers who struggle to find themselves amidst a sea of confusion and animosity. Violins traced a beautiful and romantic theme. The lights were dim. Washington's intoxication flowed through the open window. Dan approached and his face broadcast his expectations.

Ready but still unready, she inhaled Dan's boyish yet worldly air even as it clashed with bad memories of insensitive brutes and hurtful men who said anything, and one night gave her no choice and she showered until dawn, and another who laughed on the phone the next day, and so many she turned from in the past. How could she now turn to love this man when the pulsing apparitions of all these other men stood before her? How could she reach past the pain and let this moment attain itself in spite of every other moment both of them would never forget?

She shivered once and simply decided she would be the woman summoned by the moment. Dan spoke no words because words would only interfere with the dialogue between their eyes. And now his lips were finding the angles of her face and she allowed it. As his arms pulled her close enough to be his breath, Park closed her eyes and submitted to a river running swiftly past flowers on the hillside and children waving from the bank. Her childhood home in Kansas flashed in and then receded. But finally she joined Dan. Strong and compelling, he held and guided her.

From the window to the nearby couch, they moved like an animated vine. The music swelled. He unbuttoned her, and unlike any time before, she unbuttoned in return. She knew this was new—and he sensed the same. Covering him with desperate kisses, she willingly escalated from the minute's passion to a desperate longing for love and union. This time and never again; this time and always again. All reluctance now fell away.

Dan removed her clothing not in arrogance but with the slow, silent, and subtle permission of consensual lovers. And now he found her body. They were locked and receptive.

Dan tensed for a moment. Park saw the change. "Where are you going?" she asked.

He shook it off. "Right here," said Dan smoothly with a small smile, resuming their embrace and aggressively kissing her, almost artificially, to bring back the moment. Fingers intertwined, he straddled from above and then moved into the current of their intimacy. The confluence lay enticingly ahead. She released herself to accept him, join him, become him, float with him.

Just then, Dan's head pulled back. His body became taut, his leg muscles visibly tensed, his face furrowed with hesitation, no, with shame. "I can't," he panted. "Oh, God," he gasped, running his hands across his forehead and back over his throbbing skull. He rolled off Park, her sweat and scent still with him, and sat up, leaving her exposed. She pulled her blouse back on, but lovingly stayed with Dan, as though they had walked through a thousand such late night crises and now she would steer him through yet another. As though cradling a child, she wrapped her arms around his naked shoulders.

"Why are you burning?" she whispered. "Talk to me."

Dan shook, unable to catch a full breath. All personal pretense and composure dripped away revealing his molten anguish. He squinted hard, very hard, made a fist and started babbling, in and out of cogency. At first Park couldn't understand the fragments. But slowly Dan's story began to emerge.

In a long narrow boardroom lit only at the far end beneath its display screen, somewhere in the King's Gate section of Sydney, Dan faced down coldboned Mark O'Cook, Percy-Rogers' vice president of acquisition. Three lean assistants lurked silently in the background, saying nothing, taking notes, not infrequently looking up to assess facial expressions.

"You said $11.34 million," protested Dan. "I have it in writing in the Letter of Intent. It's in writing."

"We said eleven dot three four," replied O'Cook with no difficulty, "because we thought it was worth eleven dot three four at the time. Maybe it still is. But our new chairman has instituted an acquisition policy that values magazines not for what they are worth to us to buy, but what the properties are worth to you to sell. That pegs the sale not to our ability to turn a profit but your ability to get out of debt."

Dan could hardly muster words as he listened.

"We did additional research," O'Cook went on. "You, sir, owe printers and banks four dot four million and you're fighting them off with funny stories. You're desperate. We know you exude that tantalizing air of utter confidence and bravado, the dashing editor and publisher. And that's fine. That helps value the publications for the advertisers and the readership. But this is the real world of mergers and acquisition where we pay our bills with bank cheques not braggadocio. So we now revise our offer to six dot eight seven million. Take it or leave it."

Allowing Dan no time to respond, O'Cook jackhammered the harsh realities: "Leave it, and we move board consideration to the next scheduled buyout. Leave it, and you go back to Chicago with no deal. We know what that means. We checked. You're ruined. Which shovel of coal is heaved next into our financial furnace matters little to us, Mr. Levin. We've done twelve buys this year and we're rushing to do several more before Jan One to finish 1997 with a flourish. Remember, there are other owners of other enterprises waiting their turn to be rewarded for their years of sacrifice. You're not the only one who has labored long and suffered a sleepless life waiting for this moment.

"On the other hand, you can take the six dot eight seven," continued O'Cook,

staring Dan directly in the eye. "We get the titles free and clear, you keep Levincom as an empty shell as originally planned. Pay off your banks, printers, and other creditors. Make and enjoy as much interest as you can on the two dot four after-debt-pre-tax. Give the tax man his due, would you please, which would be dot six two and change. You keep one dot eight million plus your net of investments at the end of the day. No worries, if you know what I mean."

"We've been talking now for six months," said Dan slowly. "You told me not to secure 1999 because you had your own strategy. You bet, I've lost too much time. You stand still in the magazine business you sink quickly. You're right, I would be ruined."

"Listen to us," chided O'Cook. "We know what we're doing. While you were getting your interesting but uncompelling sweat-driven company ready for acquisition by Percy-Rogers, you never got the 1999 pharm and food budgets you needed for Wingtip. Under Levincom Wingtip is finished. We know that. But we—Percy Rogers—can fill those pages with multiple magazine buys from our other magazine reps. While you've been spending our money in your mind, our reps have been lining up European accounts you've never even heard of. German drug companies, French vitamin producers, Italian designers, Austrian ski lodges. We even have Swedish crackers. They're all ready to break into the American market through Wingtip. We can make it grow into a powerful publication reaching more than a million people in airports across America. And would you believe American pharmaceutical companies are willing to purchase an extra 100,000 copies per issue of Brain Journal to send to the Chinese, Korean, and Indian medical establishments. We're taking an international approach to all your properties, sir. You haven't a clue what global magazine publishing is about. We do."

"I can't sell seven magazines for six-eight," Dan remonstrated again. "I'd be left after tax and debt with . . . with $1.8 million. I took almost no salary and zero distribution all this time building my magazines. It's been ten years of hell that aged me thirty. It stole my wife's youth, robbed my son of a daddy. And this was to be the payoff, a proper sale to a proper organization, negotiated with all the best lawyers and accountant firms. Months of reps and warranties."

O'Cook was unmoved.

"I fly Qantas all day and all night," appealed Dan. "My jetlag is ready to crack my head, I didn't sleep the two days before I got to the airport responding to your late night faxes. I can barely stand. And now, with you fresh from a good night's sleep and a rousing morning at the health club, you ask me to take just

about half the promised money or nothing? You ask it here . . . at the signing ceremony? You ask it now . . . after months of working it all out. What kind of monsters are you?"

"Publicly traded monsters," O'Cook snapped. "Don't complain to us. Grandmothers and benevolent organizations own our stock. They ask for auto-graphed copies of our annual report. They love us—but only when the stock clicks north. It's the system. Everyone is happy!"

"But me," spoke a dejected Dan.

"But you . . . Every cigar leaves its ash," sneered O'Cook. "No offense, once we flick you away, no one will even remember. Take the offer, Mr. Levin. You won't be a wealthy man when you arrive in Chicago. That's right. But you won't be poor either. We both know being a millionaire isn't all it's cracked up to be. But you'll be fine. Invest your one dot eight net after-tax-after-debt money wisely; you'll take home, I figure, $108,000 per annum without drawing down your principal—more if you're willing to risk short term losses in equities."

The dim lights seemed to shine brighter, and now angled in his eyes. He turned away slightly.

"Question of the day. Can you live on that, Mr. Levin?" asked O'Cook force-fully. "It's retirement, college tuition for your boy, a good life for you and the mis-sis. Do you walk away, Mr. Levin, with $108,000 per year guaranteed for life and almost two million in the bank to pay for your nursing home twenty years hence or to bestow to your wife and son who will outlive you? Or do you go back to your messy office in Chicago after six months of due diligence and tough nego-tiations that you always thought you were excelling at—but now with nothing to show for it?"

"My wife and boy are flying to London," Dan said, almost to himself. The lights seemed to increase to a glare. "Probably, by now, they are somewhere in New York waiting for a plane." He pulled a ticket out of his vest pocket, and confirmed their schedule. Demoralized, he went on, trying to find the humanity in his impatient opponent. "See, this was to be the climax to a life of work. We never wanted to be publishers. Jenny and I were writers, journalists, and we got thrown into publishing with Chicago Monthly, and then one thing led to anoth-er and, my God, then there were seven magazines and sixty-one employees, and forty-thousand-dollar convention booths. Forget all the hype and the glitz and the TV columns. We still live in the same tiny two-bedroom townhouse we have all these years, making it from paycheck to paycheck—still on an $800 per month mortgage from the old days. We could have sold out long ago to the advertisers.

But we were true to our readers. Editorial first, integrity first. Always trying to help the little guy, standing up for the causes, asking the tough questions and hurting often ourselves because the truth hurts the truthsayer first—and then everybody else second and third. So after ten years and just about nothing in the bank, mortgaged up to our wrists and hanging on for dear life . . . you're stealing our company. You've engineered the theft of the family business. If I were in Iowa it would have been the family farm."

Dan paused and looked around the room as if someone was standing next to him. But there was no one. "She's meeting me," he said. "We're meeting in London. She's flying east from Chicago through New York, with Simon, and I'm flying west from here. Get it, meeting in the middle. I have a suite waiting at the Dorchester. Afternoon tea, little cucumber sandwiches with clotted cream. Everything first class."

"Yes, you spent our money well. But too soon," said O'Cook, nodding in agreement with himself.

"These papers were just to be a formality," Dan defended, getting some energy back. "I paid $35,000 in legal fees and you probably three times that much just to get all the papers in order. It was months. The contract is fourteen hundred pages long with exhibits. The dollars were agreed on long ago. That's the one part we agreed on early. Now you're trying to rob me."

"It's not robbery, it's an acquisition," replied O'Cook defensively. "And we are acting within the law. Our Letter of Intent specifically states that nothing we offer shall be binding until adopted by both our USA board and our Australian board," repeated O'Cook. "You read it. Your lawyers read it. Our USA board said yes, but our Australian board is balking."

"This smacks of bad faith," said Dan. "I've spent a lifetime exposing financial scams, putting lawyers and politicians in jail. Am I really the one you want to do this to? I have recourse for bad-faith bargaining."

"Call your lawyers," dared O'Cook. "Spend a few hundred thousand and the next decade on legal fees fighting us on two continents. You'll be broke long before trial, certainly before the appeal. Look, last week we purchased a small chain of American movie theaters for $619 million. Next week, we buy a string of Latin American dailies and their radio stations for $204 million. I think there's a convention hall somewhere in Mexico as part of the deal. For us, Levincom is just a mildly curious bit of routine acquisition—not a big event. I'm afraid our board doesn't even know you exist. Six dot this and whatever dot that . . . you're not even on their radar screen, Mr. Levin. I'm just going to slip them the signa-

ture sheet of that fourteen hundred page contract and recommend the board rat-
ify and affix three authorizing signatures. And if I don't march into that board-
room on the fourth floor in nine minutes, you'll be off the agenda and neither of
us can get you back on.

"Nothing personal, Mr. Levin," O'Cook said in an almost soothing voice. But
then he tightened up again. "Make your decision please. Go home penniless and
spend the next ten years a victimized plaintiff, or meet your family for cham-
pagne and caviar in a nice suite at the Dorchester, a hotel, by the way, that no
one here would dream of patronizing. I could recommend the Intercontinental or
the Hyde Park Hilton or a dozen others. My secretary could even help you with
a reservation . . . But first we need a decision."

"Nine dot," said Dan, trying to find a compromise.

"Six dot eight seven," answered O'Cook, polishing his glasses and not even
looking up. And that offer is withdrawn in sixty seconds because the board will
be convening."

"Nine dot," repeated Dan, unwilling to bid against himself. But O'Cook was
silent, expressionless, unwavering.

Dan's mouth became dust-dry. He stiffened. Those youthful assistants dressed
nattily in black, standing back to the side, were taking notes to create whatever
evidentiary record they wanted to exist. Dan knew that. He looked at them and
then away. He had been a winner all his life. A hard guy. Given enough time
and energy, he could do anything. He was proud, a fighter, a crusader like his
father, a partisan in the forest. Now Dan felt like he was walking into the pit,
naked and chilled, his hands cupped over his genitals.

"Where do I sign?"

One of the assistants from the back suddenly came to life. She sprang forward
with several bound contract volumes, noisily stacked them in front of Dan, and
began opening to signature page after signature page, pointing to flagged lines
and securing Dan's initials and signatures, initials and signatures, initials and
signatures. Here. And here. No here. Here also. One here and one also here. Here.
Here. These two and here. Here. Here. Here.

O'Cook watched carefully during the several minutes it took to sign and ini-
tial all the key pages. "Nothing personal, Mr. Levin," he assured with a proud
smile. "Trust me there, nothing personal. Just business. Like I said. Everybody is
happy! And this acquisition," he stacked the contracts neatly at the side of the
table, "we are all delighted to say, will be ratified in a few moments. Then our
bank in Boston—you will be delighted to know—will be authorized to wire yours

in Chicago. I'll issue the papers right after the board meeting or in any event before the end of business today, Sydney time. Good-bye, Mr. Levin."

Dan drank some water. His eyes opened, then drifted. Park took his cold, sweaty palms and rubbed them for warmth. She knew there was much more and didn't know if she should ask, or wait for Dan to speak. He began a gentle rocking motion as his face tightened and loosened in waves. Then he calmed, and said, "Could I have some more water?" She went to the minibar, poured a small Evian, and carefully placed the glass in his hand. Dan looked with confusion at Park, accepted the glass, but then did not drink.

"Maybe you want some scotch?" Park asked. He nodded no in a brief, rapid motion. "If there is more you want to talk about, whatever it is . . . I can't figure what's going on in your life. Long way from it. But I can't help if you won't let me in."

He squinted hard, harder than ever before and his fisted hands turned white from pressure even as sweat beads popped from the curl of his thumb and fingers. Once more, it began as a babbling account, but again his story slowly came together.

NEW YEAR'S DAY. Heathrow International. A million eight at the end of the day was not so bad. It was not the $4.5 million after tax and debt they had hoped for. It was not enough to let them take a badly needed few years off, traveling and writing. It would not create a principal investment that would itself generate about a half million annually, and allow them to purchase the home of their dreams on Jerusalem's Jaffa Road across from the Old City gates, and allow them to fly back and forth between Chicago and Israel, and live the life that they had always dreamed of. But they were out from under their horrific commercial obligations, no longer answerable to their own demanding organization, and they could concentrate, in financial security, on Simon and themselves. They were at the physical and fiscal breaking point when Percy-Rogers approached, and Dan knew he did the right thing by accepting the revised offer. What was important was Jenny and Simon. They were healthy, they were happy, and they could all live like a family. Tonight he would sleep sounder than any night of his life. Tonight he again belonged only to himself, to Jenny and to Simon.

As he waited for Flight 337 from New York to arrive, Dan walked among the chic shops of Heathrow's International Concourse. He saw a child running, gig-

gling. Looked like Simon. Dan looked again. But it wasn't. The child darted out again. Dan looked. The boy ran down the concourse and disappeared in the crowd.

For a moment, Dan stood still, folded his arms for warmth, felt a copy of the final signature in his suit pocket, and again debated his decision. Take the money? Fight the money? Jenny's face appeared. For a long instant, he shuddered, and in that instant it felt as if the very terminal had shuddered with him, as though the earth itself had been pummeled by a giant weight. Next to him was a jewelry stand. The name tags were swaying. He looked again. The name tags stopped swaying.

Dan diverted himself along the concourse. He sniffed handrolled Havanas in the smoke shop, priced the Monte Cristos and Cohibas, and laughed at the discreet sign saying they were for sale but illegal to bring into America. Next door, he sampled the wondrous scotches at the whiskey shop, where wee tastes for travelers are a tradition, and traded stories with other scotch snobs about highland peats, estate bottled Macallen, and overaged Laphroaig. He was sipping a glass of San Peligrino and cutting into a thick slice of Scottish salmon topped with chopped onions and capers at the caviar bar when he heard the announcement.

"Will those friends and family members waiting for Flight 337 please report to Special Services. We repeat: Will those friends and family members waiting for Flight 337 please report to Special Services."

Dan sauntered over to the nearby gate and asked an attendant, "What do you mean, Special Services?" The gate attendant glanced briefly at her partner and answered, "You are expecting someone on Flight 337? The name, please." Dan answered: "Jenny and Simon Levin."

"Sir, please follow me to Special Services."

"Excuse me, what do you mean, 'Special Services?'"

"Sir, please follow me." She took him by the arm to a door off a special ramp which shortcut to a dimly lit windowless room with twelve rows of chairs. "What's in there?"

She patted his arm. "Please step in."

He looked again. It was an interdenominational chapel. On its wall was a crucifix, a crescent, and a Star of David. "What the hell is in there?" he said with a fright. In the dim light, he saw people weeping. He tried to pull away. "Please step in."

"Tell me now," he demanded. "Jenny and Simon Levin. Passengers on 337 . . ." he stopped in midsentence. "Don't you dare . . . don't you dare . . ." Dan

grabbed his face with both hands.

"Sir," an airline official told him, "there has been a terrible, terrible accident, moments ago. Flight 337 from New York in its final landing approach almost struck another outbound plane. No one knows much. The pilot tried to avoid the collision and made what we believe was a desperate attempt to pull up. It worked briefly, but then the plane . . . We don't know much of anything at this early stage. Except 337 crashed in the fields just beyond the runway. Rescue crews are just getting there now. And we're hoping for as many survivors as our dear Lord in heaven will permit. That includes your loved ones. Now, what is important—"

Dan turned and ran from the chapel to the nearest gate across the corridor. Through the window, over the shoulders of the crowd, he could see the tail of a jumbo jet in the distance just beyond the runway surrounded by black billows of smoke. At the tarmac edge nearest to the crash, a half dozen green emergency trucks sprayed chemicals and foam, paramedics were racing in, and everywhere red, blue, and yellow emergency lights angrily flashed.

Suddenly, Dan bolted. Through the nearby door to the jetway and down the ramp. No plane was parked at the gate, so the jetway's docking canopy opened onto the air. Faint burning flesh, fire, smoke, airport exhaust and de-icing fluid, all chilled together by the winter morning, stung his eyes and nostrils. Two or three airport security people and a gate attendant ran after him, calling. The stairway door was unlocked. He went through it, clanging down the metal steps leading to the runway itself.

"Stop. I order you to stop!" an officer demanded, chasing after him, and blowing his whistle. Dan ran as fast as he could directly toward the crash site. Now several other runway security men joined in the pursuit. Dan sprinted around a fuel vehicle, jumped over its connecting hose, and landed in a skid on the slimed surface. A catering truck stopped short, nearly hitting him while prone on the ground.

Dan pulled himself up, ran a few steps almost dazed, and stumbled into a long tractor-pulled baggage train. It was too long to go around. He scrambled over it, tumbling off the car with suitcases and boxes falling in his wake. Insensate to the January wind slapping at his cheek, he was equally oblivious to the great airplanes taxiing back and forth all around him. Over the roar of deafening engines, he could feel but not hear his own screams: "Jenny! Simon!" Even so, the frigid air made his cries bizarrely visible as bursts of frosted breath exploded from his mouth and lungs.

With a screech, a white runway security car pulled up, directly blocking his path. Uniformed Officer Doyle, dispatched by the gate attendants, jumped out, opened his arms wide as though a barricade, shouting, "Mr. Levin. Come here."

Panting and crying amidst his own cloud of breath, Dan stopped and fell into a vaporous heap on the runway. The elderly officer came over and put his arms around him, saying, "Sir, this is not the way. We are doing everything possible. Now then, please come with me."

Dan gripped his arm and squeezed hard. Doyle propped Dan up compassionately.

"Now then, come along," Doyle repeated.

Wet with tears, Dan looked up at the sky, then over at the grassy embankment just beyond the runway. The other security men were catching up, closing in from all directions. He saw emergency medical vehicles.

"They're alive!" Flailing his arms, he broke free from Doyle, who lost his footing, and slipped on an ice slick. Dan rushed into the security car, motor running, and gunned it. Doyle chased after it a few steps, yelling, then gave up, and reported into the radio slung over his shoulder.

Swerving the white security car past airport support vehicles, Dan steered left then right. Suddenly, he came within yards of the landing gear of a Japan Air 747 rolling away from the gate. He hit the brakes, then resumed racing toward the crash site just ahead, beyond an unused part of the runway. Right off the tarmac. Down with a big bump. Onto the moist and icing earth. Up the ridge as close as he could get before the car's spinning wheels finally dug into the mud. Personnel ran toward him from both the crash site and from the runway. He jumped out and scrambled to the top of the ridge.

He saw below him a valley of death. Shattered bodies and parts of bodies were everywhere, strewn around the fractured fuselage. Close by, one hand, detached from any arm, gripped a small book. Beyond that, a body, clothes and skin completely burned off, mouth wide open, teeth bared, scorched arms curved as though wrapped around some now vanished object. Papers and clothing littered the destruction everywhere as though sprinkled capriciously by some great hand from above. Emergency response staff moved gingerly from person to person. Beside each dead body, they planted a small yellow marker flag. Beside each unattached body part was a small blue flag. Paramedics administered first aid to survivors. Yes, survivors—some wailing, some incapable of sound and barely of breath. Chilled, visual moans steaming through the debris brought rescuers scurrying to their side.

Jenny and Simon would be among them. They had to be.

Dan commanded himself back to reality. He had covered the great American Airlines crash in Chicago years before. This one was amazingly similar. Think. His eyes narrowed and he scanned the terrain. Tail section, an abysmal smoldering horror, over there to the right. Wing parts here, there, and straight in front, some small flames still visible, just being extinguished by firemen. First class . . . first class. First class! Over there to the left. Large brown leather chairs, the shattered nose cone partially furrowed into the earth just beyond. That's it! Dan raced down the embankment.

"Jenny! Jenny! Simon!" His arms and legs dug into the slope as he half tumbled down, encountering bits of strewn effects and debris along the way.

Workers began moving toward him, watching their footfalls to avoid stepping on evidence. Some shouted. "Hey there!" Whistles blew.

Dan came upon a bulky first-class seat on its side with blood flowing from its bottom. "Jenny!" he shouted. He raced around and saw a form. It was an elderly man—alive—bleeding profusely from his head, a deep gash in one arm, the other twisted completely backward as though someone had attached it incorrectly to a doll—except that bone was protruding through the skin. Still strapped in, the helpless man moaned indecipherable sounds.

"Here's a live one," yelled Dan. "This man needs help! He's alive." Dan smeared blood off the fellow's forehead with part of the survivor's torn shirt. "They're coming," Dan told him, stroking his face.

He continued searching.

A few steps away, through a billow of smoke, Dan saw it. One first-class seat flat atop another. He ran to it. A body was clearly trapped in between.

"Jenny? Simon?"

The victim's skin was burned black on the only side he could see. Rescue workers and security officers finally caught up and tackled him. "Stay down now, sir," they said, lashing his hands with nylon wrist restraints.

"That's her," Dan begged, "that's her and Simon. Help them, they might be alive." He knew that emergency response to disasters was rarely frantic, always methodical. He knew that more would survive if only they were not written off as dead, but instead rushed at a reduced body temperature to a surgical suite for life saving. He had covered that story years ago, and fought with the Chicago Police about their procedures. He knew that damn story. And now here, on a bloodstained field at Heathrow, it was the same.

"I think that's her. She's alive!" he cried.

Doyle by now had caught up. "Mr. Levin," he said, taking custody of Dan's bound hands, "we don't know if that is your wife and son. As I speak, the medics are checking whoever that is, and will do all in their power. Now I'm going to bring you around for a look. But please . . ."

Doyle and Dan slowly circled around to the other side, as workers pulled away a blanket. "Life signs!" one of them yelled. Two of three other medics moved in. Dan craned to see from a few feet. Whoever it was, they had been protected by being sandwiched in between the two massive overcushioned first class seats. Then he saw it in the seat pocket. A copy of Chicago Monthly. "That's her!" he screamed. "That's Jenny! Sy? Sy? Are you there kid!"

Doyle cut Dan's nylon cuffs as the men pried the two seats apart.

"Stand back, sir," a medic shouted. "We need space,"

Now he could see her clearly. She was conscious, his beautiful Jenny, her shredded arms wrapped protectively around a lifeless Simon who was embedded by the impact into her crushed chest, now slowly oozing away the final moments of her life. She opened one eye just long enough to focus on Dan. Their eyes met. She moved her head just slightly, just an inch, acknowledging him, and as if to say, "I love you, Dan. I have always loved you, Dan. And I have loved this miracle of a son we conceived, our Simon. I tried to protect him again, to guard him, and tried to give my life to save him . . . Simon is in a good place. But he needs me there too . . . I will miss you. But one day you and I, my love, and our miracle son, shall be together again."

As Dan saw her head move that inch, and her eye suddenly become motionless, he heard each unspoken word again in his mind, as though it had been whispered by an angelic form softly stroking his face with one hand, and holding a child in the other.

The paramedic checked her, and blurted, "She's gone, I'm sorry. The boy also. Sorry." They quickly moved on to the other first class passenger still alive a few yards away. Someone planted two yellow flags next to their expired bodies.

Dan stepped forward, as the men stood back to give him room. He crouched down and ran his finger across Simon's fluid-encrusted hair. "Oh, you beautiful young man, you hero, you miracle child." He bent over and kissed the boy. And then bent over and kissed the white lips of Jenny. "Not long, honey," he promised in tears. "I'll be there, honey." His mouth opened wide in a silent scream as he whispered in her ear, "Save my place, honey. There is no life for me without you."

Doyle gripped Dan's shoulder and tried to console him. Dan turned his eyes to the sky, looked straight up, and screamed to the heavens, this time so loud that not even the roaring aircraft could drown out his anguish. He shook his fist at God and demanded, "Take me! What is wrong with you? He had so much life in front of him. She was so pure. Why couldn't you take me?" Doyle hugged him with straight jacket arms. In numbing disconsolation, Dan repeated his request. "I'll make the switch right now," he offered. "Give them back and take me. I'm ready. Take me!"

Dan stared straight ahead, and occasional shivers still swept over his body. Park wiped both their tears with her blouse.

"I need help," mumbled Dan. "I thought I could take it. But I just can't get over it. I will never get over it." He shook his head violently. "No, I see them still. I see them still!"

Park came around directly in front of Dan, grabbed his head and cried, "Look at me. I am here. It is me. They wanted you to live. They loved you. Then live."

"I can't live," he answered back as he raced for the window and opened it wider. He peered at the sidewalk below. "Not without them. I can't live."

"Sit down, please," Park spoke softly. "Come away from there and sit down."

Dan placed one foot outside the window. "They were much higher when God took them," he argued maniacally. "This height is nothing, it's an insult to their death. It's a cheap imitation," he scoffed. "But it's the best I can do tonight," he added with a short, insane laugh.

Park's face became serene as she stretched out her arm, and murmured, "Dan, come back and take my hand."

"But . . . but . . ."

"Take my hand."

"No."

"Yes, take my hand."

The dementia slowly drifted off his face. His eyes darted from side to side, and down to the sidewalk again, and then to Park. Inch by inch, he edged away from the window. Weak, he collapsed into a sitting position on the floor. Several minutes of wordless tension ensued, broken only by the unexpected crunches of the refrigerator ice machine replenishing. The noise startled him back to stability.

"Okay," he shrugged. "I'm fine. Forget it." He scratched his head. "Yeah, hard drive is a guy being chased by his past."

"Too much data can crash the system," she replied.

He half laughed. Suddenly it was indeed as though nothing had happened. He wiped the tears off his nose and chin, dried his eyes with the back of his hand and closed the window.

"Gee, it's late, where's Sal?" Dan asked nonchalantly. "He should check in. Want me to call him on the cell?"

Park pursed her lips and swallowed. She drank some water and looked at Dan, not believing he could flash back to normal so quickly. She took a deep breath, sat in a chair, looked at him again, and answered, "Uh, cell? No. Not necessary."

AT 3:30 A.M., SAL swiped his plastic key card into the suite door and nudged it open just enough to slip in. He closed it as quietly as possible. Night lights were on throughout the room. Sal checked the illuminated dial of the thermostat. He almost smiled, but didn't. Shoulders still furled like a serape, he checked the minibar for a snack. M&Ms. He brought out a large bag, tore off the top and poured the colored contents into a wine glass. Then he drank the M&Ms as though root beer.

A note from Park left in the middle of the dining table reminded Sal to take the corner bedroom. He dragged himself there, spotted his suitcase contents on the bed, neatly laid out by his mother. Instead of putting them away, he laid down next to them in a slender line on the edge of the mattress. A moment later, he got up, tore his clothes off down to his jockeys, and resumed his narrow position in bed. Exhausted, he began fading into sleep. Within minutes, he was completely motionless.

The suite was quiet, save the ticking of the antique Regulator grandfather clock in the main parlor. Park and Dan were each in their own rooms. The window was closed and no street noise could be heard. All was still.

Sal, still asleep, began running his left index finger over his left eyelid. After a few seconds, his eyes slowly opened. It was always a problem for Sal to sleep in a new bed, but exhaustion usually compensated. Time? No clock. Still dark, though. Sal sat up. He reached into his bag and pulled out his Windy. As it opened, the articulated screen snapped into its larger format. He clicked his email icon. Only one inbound appeared. He clicked.

> **FROM: Kuebitz, Derek Institute**
> **SUBJECT: Change in Plans**
> **TO: Relevant Staff:**
> Due to the untimely death of John Hector, we expect that Bluestar will soon cancel plans to finalize Zoom, and instead join forces with Hinnom Computing. Hector's successor has already hinted as much in a briefing yesterday. The millennium problem remains. Windgazer 99 is not the answer. We have decided therefore to close our Chicago lab and consolidate all our efforts full throttle at our headquarters in Israel. You and a small elite cadre of specialists are being transferred to Jerusalem forthwith. Not expected to last more than several months. Call the corporate travel desk to arrange airfare. Your name preauthorized. Our account will be charged and we will be notified. $500 transit expenses will be advanced same day upon arrival in Israel. Travel bonus and per diem to be worked out. Housing will be arranged by Derek in Jerusalem. For further questions, call the Chicago office. Relocation counselors are standing by. Kuebitz.

Israel? Who knew Derek was an Israeli company? Sal thought about the possibilities and didn't believe that he or Park wanted to move to Israel. He was about to reply in the negative when a second email icon appeared. He clicked it.

> **FROM: Kuebitz, Derek Institute**
> **SUBJECT: Sal McGuire–Personal**
> You and your mother are crucial to our project. Your participation is indispensable. But you have understandable doubts. So check the attached site. Kuebitz.

Appended to the bottom of Kuebitz' email was the usual blue text hyperlink to a web site. By clicking it, Sal's computer would automatically enter the location. But Sal did not recognize the URL form. There was no www, not even an http:// at the beginning of the address. In fact, Sal had to strain to make out the letters and numbers. They seemed to pixilate on the screen. He clicked anyway. The unknown site began to load.

Sal felt strange. First he was chilled, then he grew warm. He could hear his own heart pounding. He placed his hand on his chest and felt it softly thumping. The Windy was now playing tricks on him. It seemed to vibrate. He almost laughed, but then held the Windy and felt the vibration himself. He wondered if the drive might be spinning out of whack. No, that made no sense. He raised his head and listened to the quiet. The suite was noiseless. Not even the Regulator clock was ticking.

"Strange sequence of anomalies," Sal said aloud.

The mystery site was still loading, according to the rotating browser icon on his Windy screen. Abruptly, the icon stopped. But Sal couldn't see anything. At first.

Whiteness all at once appeared in the middle of the screen. Initially, the image was no larger than a thick dot. Quickly it grew larger. Very large. Eventually, the large white dot reached the limits of the screen edge. But it would not stop there. Now, the powerful luminescence extended its glow and engulfed Sal in its strange, spreading radiance. Soon, much of the room was filled with a blinding, throbbing whiteness. At first Sal shielded his eyes, but then dropped his hands and looked directly into the screen. He could not move.

The whiteness transfixed Sal, who found its unfathomable layers of exquisite brilliance fundamentally perfect. The essence of perfection itself confounded Sal, and his face showed the conflict.

From deep within the formless white, Sal then heard a sound. Yes, he heard it distinctly–yet understood that he and only he could. Suddenly, he was overcome. He opened his mouth wide and wept like a child.

Without warning, everything shut down. All whiteness receded into a disappearing dot. A standard disconnect message appeared on the screen: "Server site down. Try again later." Dark and quiet returned to the suite. The Regulator could be heard ticking once more. Sal noticed his cheeks were wet from tears. "Very strange sequence of anomalies," he panted.

Sal walked to his mother's bedroom, "Get up. Get up." Then to Dan's door, "Get up. Get up."

Both, wearing their night clothes, straggled into the main parlor.

"What?" yawned Dan, half asleep.

Sal showed a printout of the email from Kuebitz relocating elite staff.

"Israel," said Park. "Derek is an Israeli company? How did Derek become Israeli?"

Sleepy Dan now became alert. "Israel? What's Israel?" He also read the email. "Derek is Israeli?" he asked, "Just like that you're transferred to Israel. Can they do that?"

"I knew friends who were transferred so often they call their company *I Been Moved*," answered Park, rubbing her eyes. "At least this is temporary. Says a few months." She stopped. "But overseas . . . that's unusual." She thought about it some more, rearranged her sleeping shirt, thought again and said, "Nah, not that unusual. It's a global world. But . . ."

She turned to Sal and as a foregone conclusion declared, "We can't do it. No way. It's crazy."

"Yes, we can," Sal replied staunchly and without his customary pause.

"Just like that?" countered Park. "Just *yes*. No discussion? Do you or I know one thing about Jerusalem?"

"I know a thing about it," Dan chimed in.

"I logged onto a hyperlinked site from Kuebitz," Sal responded with his head initially angled but then straight. "It was in the second email. I can't describe it. It was . . . it was all white. Awesome, like I had just touched . . . touched a holy place . . . or logged onto one."

Sal began to say more, but the additional words never formed.

"Holy?" asked a confused Park. "Holy how?"

"Maybe–" started Dan.

"Let *him* tell me," interrupted Park. "Did you say *holy?*"

Sal pursed his lips and after a long pause tried to explain: "It was all so monumentally complicated, I just can't verbalize it. Maybe I was still dreaming."

Dan and Park exchanged a glance in the simultaneous recognition that suddenly Sal was speaking in full sentences.

"Sal, how much Jolt cola did you have last night?" asked Dan. Sal's face cringed and he became self-conscious. "Kidding," appended Dan.

"The email says just 'a few months,'" reminded Park, "and a bonus." She scratched her head, "What time is it? Uh, do we need to decide right now? Let's go back to sleep and work it out in the morning."

Sal looked up and surprised them by insisting forcefully, "No. Let's decide right now." He tapered off, "We don't want to be excluded from the team. Call the office like they said."

Taken aback, Park eyed Sal and walked over to the phone. "Now, at this hour?"

Seeing Sal's unexpected agitation, Park dialed Derek's line in Chicago. "Voice mail," she said. *Relocation counselors* was a voice menu option. She pressed a button. "I think it's forwarding," she reported. A counselor picked up the phone. Park covered the mouthpiece, whispering "Foreign accent. Israeli, I'm guessing." Park asked one or two questions but was then silent for two or three minutes as she listened to all the details.

"We'll let you know in a few days," Park told the counselor.

Sal came up close and fervently nodded in disagreement. "Now. Decide *now*," he urged. Park shushed him so she could hear the counselor who was saying the same thing.

"Why now?" Park asked the counselor, protesting, "It's Saturday morning, not even dawn." Park paused as she listened. She turned toward the clock. "Strategic decisions . . . when? After Sabbath in Israel?"

"That would be in a few hours, Israeli time," said Dan.

Park tried to explain, "I'm a new recruit and I wasn't at the staff meeting in Chicago on Thursday, which was to be my first day of work, actually . . . Uh, I was given permission to be in Washington by Kuebitz' office. I *did* get explicit permission."

Sal folded his hands demonstratively and repeated, "Now. Decide now."

Park waved him away so she could concentrate. "How much bonus? . . . that's for me, and my son, Sal McGuire, is extra. That's a double bonus, right? . . . Less than six weeks? . . . All expenses, you're sure?" She looked at Dan, who sat expressionless watching the exchange unfold.

Sal again dramatically begged with his folded hands.

Park motioned at Dan for his opinion. He grabbed a folded linen napkin and wrote on it: "Can I come with?"

She wrote back, "Hinnom book?"

Dan scrawled back, "Butterfly," and pointed to his notebook. She smiled.

". . . No, I don't need to call back," Park abruptly decided. "Nothing will change in three hours. We'll go." Dan's eyes became watery. Sal almost smiled but just nodded instead.

"Got it," she confirmed to the Derek counselor. "TWA . . . That soon . . . Yes, fax it all to me care of the Jefferson Hotel in Washington."

Park hung up the phone and looked at Dan who was grinning broadly. "I'm not here. I don't know where I am," she said with exasperation. "A few days ago I was in Seattle, then I'm in Chicago, now I'm in Washington and before you know it we're flying to Jerusalem. And I am completely sleep-deprived."

"We're going to have a great time in Israel," said Dan. "I love it there and you will too. The whole place is one hypnotic struggle." He glanced outside and noticed the sun was coming up. He shook his head slightly. "I'm not ready for this," he chortled. "I can't believe I'm going back."

"I can't believe we're going in the first place," Park deadpanned.

He scratched his head, "It's dawn. Let's get some sleep." Park and Dan walked back to their bedroom doors.

Dan turned to Sal, "You ready for Israel?"

Sal paused as expected, but now his face became strangely peaceful. Park couldn't help but notice the change. Dan repeated: "You ready?"

Sal closed his eyes for an instant, opened them wide and serenely replied, "Yes."

"You know what Derek means?" Dan asked Sal pedantically.

"I thought it's like a big steel crane," offered Park.

"No, that's *derrick* with two Rs," corrected Dan, "which is named for the sixteenth-century English hangman. Derek, I'm guessing, is related to the same Hebrew word *direct* comes from."

"I know what it means," said Sal.

"Which is?" Dan asked.

"It means *the way*," Sal answered.

"Yes, it does," returned Dan. "'The way,' in Hebrew. How did you know that?"

Sal tilted his head slightly, hesitated, but then answered, "I don't know. I just did."

PART TWO

DISCOVERY

9

JERUSALEM

Step out onto your balcony. Look in all directions. Smell the chill.

When the dawning sun finally pushes up beyond the gray-green Judean Hills, Jerusalem's dense morning sunlight will wend tortuously through the ancient new city, illuminating its roads, alleys, parks and rocky lots, one by one, as though unlocking a series of visual doors in magical sequence. Behold, in this place, all light and dark is delivered by the finger of God. Only He understands.

On cue, the bus motors collectively ignite to begin their growling routes. Like mechanized muezzins, they cry to the faithful and faithless all, signaling the start of another frenzied day. Soon the majestic gold shimmer of the Dome of the Rock, the gleaming white mass of the Knesset, and the glow the Old City ramparts come alive.

Jaffa Road belches and groans with activity. Market stalls clang open. Boxes of fruits, vegetables and dry goods slam from surface to surface. The thuds of commerce eventually give way to the rasp of currency, and the chinkle of coinage. Arabs go to the *shuk*. Israelis go to Mahane Yehuda.

Jerusalem is electric. Feel it. The very ground is charged with the anguish and aspirations of centuries. Quiver within its awesome energy.

Jewish or Arab, religious or secular, empowered or impoverished, hopeful or hopeless, the tenacious residents of this eternal City of Peace, gripped by anger and fear, and fortified by resolute defiance, will stand against all forces just to be, that is, to be *here*. In Jerusalem, *to be* is to triumph.

No wonder spiritual compromise is impermissible for the many contending groups that lay claim to this city's mystic soul. Tears, blood, and sweat are everywhere joined as the lacquer coating all things living and dead. Every inch of existence boasts its own saga of dispute. Every footfall creates a political statement. Are you visiting Al Aksa Mosque or Yad Vashem? Are you buying bread from an Arab baker, or an Israeli one, or from an Israeli vendor selling Arab bread? Are you having lunch in West Jerusalem or East? Priests in rival churches clash for the right to sweep floors and wash mantels. Housekeeping implies ownership.

Close your eyes.

Now open them. Listen.

Wooden flutes, violin lamentations, bagpipes, drums, electric guitar, an accordion, fleeting strains of symphony, bells–tinkled by fingers or reverberating from church towers, they all crescendo together at the whoosh of a cappuccino machine.

Lay your flattened palms against the Wailing Wall, inhale its centuries. Move, as the Arab boy pushes his cart of dates and dried apricots fullspeed right at you through the narrow stone steps of The Old City. Take it in the ribs, as a chubby Russian woman elbows past you to stuff four tomatoes and an eggplant in a green netted bag. Step aside, as an Israeli general, beret stuffed within his epaulet, swaggers from a Defense Ministry office to his Peugeot command car, its curtains pulled. Look away, as a weathered and stubbly beggar stares deeply with his one diseased eye. Smile and wonder, as six Jewish children in uniform race down the sidewalk, bookbags flagging at their backs, their faces filled with joy and promise. Envy, as the terraced maze of exquisite Yemin Moshe townhouses built into the hill bubble with the energy of artisans and thinkers.

Listen, the muezzins are calling Koranic prayers, black-hatted rabbis are twirling their beards, a Greek Orthodox priest bends to light a tall, thin candle.

Fold your hands and look to the sky, wrap your fingers in phylacteries, lay your head upon them and prostrate, grip the rosary, pass your fingers across some ancient stone engraving, punch the keypad of an adding machine, pull the safety on a gun, roll a bullet beneath your thumb, rub your eyes in amazement and happiness, discover the nipple of a woman you love or a new mother giving milk, hold just one finger up and wonder, does it stand for unity or a dividing line?

Step in Jerusalem and step toward eternity. For here it began and here it shall end. Humble yourself.

~

POSITIONED AT THE busiest intersection in Jerusalem, at the edge of town, where the main road becomes the highway to Tel Aviv, his hand-drawn sign could not be missed. Its large letters begged:

Please do not drive on Shabbat!!!
If every Jew will observe the Shabbat for
two weeks, the Messiah shall return

Behind the placard, standing on a five-foot-wide concrete island beside a stoplight was a weeping orthodox Jew. Gaunt face, bulbous red nose, eyebrows reaching into his forehead, the Shabbos Rebbe completed his image, despite the oppressive heat, with black linen Hassidic attire topped by a broad furry hat or *straymel*. As each car drove past, he tearfully waved his arms, not in haughty reproach as so many *haredim* do, but in supplication.

"Please don't drive," he moaned. "Please, please," he begged. None complied.

The whooshing was incessant. Many scorned with offensive gestures his efforts to stop them from driving on Saturday. The war between the observant and the secular was a hot one. The religious often threw stones and shouted condemnation at cars profaning Shabbat. Drivers honked back. But the Shabbos Rebbe was different. He did not insult or threaten in the name of God. He was almost unique for humbly beseeching those he saw as the defilers of God's Holy Day. Thousands of cars passed his post, and he tried to make eye contact with each and every driver. He took each anonymous rejection as a profoundly singular, deeply personal failure. His disconsolation exceeded the limits of facial sadness.

Dan was driving into Jerusalem from the hills in a large white van. After six emails, three telephone calls and two confirming faxes, he has been convinced that the rental agency's promise of a red Honda Del Sol would be kept. But when he arrived at the rental car desk at Ben Gurion Airport, he was told that such cars simply do not exist in Israel, "no matter what you were told by someone who had no right to do so." To compensate for the mix-up, the agency gave him a spacious van. Very spacious–large enough to seat fifteen people. Dan looked with shock at the huge vehicle. It looked like an airport shuttle and would be impossible to navigate through most of Jerusalem's narrow streets. At first, laughing in disbelief, he refused to accept it. But after the agency declared they now had no other vehicle available, and would have to charge him anyway because his reservation was noncancellable during the high season, Dan reluctantly took the keys with the understanding that he could trade in the behemoth for a smaller car as soon as one became free.

As the Shabbos Rebbe came into view, Dan chuckled in amazement, "This guy is still here." He explained to Park that the Shabbos Rebbe had been a fixture of Saturday traffic years ago during his days as a foreign correspondent.

Dan pulled over.

"Leave him alone," said Park, uncomfortable with the idea of stopping to deal with a fanatic. Sal winced. Dan ignored their reluctance.

"It's fine," he assured. "I've seen him forever. I've just never stopped. He'll enjoy the attention."

Dan maneuvered the van into the nearby concert hall parking lot, paid the attendant a few sheklim to watch the vehicle, and then dodged traffic running to the island. Initially, he urged Park to accompany him, but then asked her to stay, recognizing that the Hassid would be offended by close proximity to a woman. Dan found it difficult to explain to Park perverse Hassidic idiosyncrasies about contact with women, and she cautiously did not press the question. Sal was happy just to remain in the van and read pamphlets about the history of the Holy Land.

The Shabbos Rebbe eyed Dan from the moment he parked, and watched him cross the highway. When Dan jumped onto the island, the Rebbe's mournful expression turned to one of complete joy.

"English?" asked Dan.

"Yes, Inglish," replied the Shabbos Rebbe. "Come, we'll have tea."

"I just wanted to ask you a few questions," said Dan, flashing his old Foreign Press pass, an ID everyone in Israel deferred to. He renewed it the last time he was in Israel, and no one cared about expiration dates.

"Put it away," the Shabbos Rebbe said, waving at the pass. "I live not far. Come with me," he said, tugging with glee at Dan's shirt.

"Whoa, whoa. *Ich kannicht,*" Dan declined, partially in Yiddish.

"*Doff nicht Yiddish,*" replied the Shabbos Rebbe joyfully, "speak Inglish. Come my house."

Dan tried to explain he had people waiting for him in the van, that he could only park for a few moments, and he just wanted to set a time after the Sabbath when the two could talk. How about tomorrow?

"No, no, leave the car," argued the Shabbos Rebbe demonstratively. "Don't touch the car. Let it sit. Shabbos. Shabbos."

"I know," said Dan respectfully, "but I can't leave the car there. Can I meet you tomorrow?"

The Rebbe's face became a mournful frown. Tears appeared. "Please don't drive. *Moschiach.* Come, we'll have fun. We'll talk, we'll drink. Please don't drive."

Dan again politely disagreed, but the old man kept moaning, "Please."

Dan pulled his cell phone out of his pocket as the Rebbe looked off in pain. He phoned across the street to Park and Sal. "Give the guy there a few sheklim like five," instructed Dan. "Tell him we have a problem with the ignition. It goes on, it goes off—unpredictable. Use your hands when you talk . . . That's right." He waved at her across the traffic. "Then grab a taxi to the hotel, have them take in the luggage. Check in. They know me." He added, "If it's an Arab taxi, act like you've been here many times . . . exactly, so you don't get driven by way of East Kishinev."

Park thought for an instant. "Wait, this is Israel," she protested. "You're leaving me on the outskirts of Jerusalem to bother a religious guy? What am I supposed to do? I thought we were here together."

"It's Jerusalem, not Uganda," answered Dan, turning away so the old man wouldn't hear. "Just walk in like you would at the Chicago Hilton and say, 'Hello, may I check in?' They speak English. If you want to make a nice impression say, '*Shalom,* may I check in?'"

"What if there's a question?" asked Park.

"What question? Just check in, I'll be there shortly . . . OK, I have an idea. Go into my travel bag, in the inside pocket, and you'll see a bunch of business cards. One of them is Shlaemi, the taxi driver I use in Jerusalem. Call him and he'll come get you. Tell him to charge the hotel, we'll settle later. If he can't come, he'll send a pal."

"Fine," Park said with a slight chill. "See you at the hotel. Call us please, if you get delayed."

"Hey, can you understand," Dan tried to explain, muffling his words from the Shabbos Rebbe. "I just finally met this individual who I have seen for years but never approached. You can't ever find him except on Saturdays. I have him. I just want to talk to the guy."

Park was still a bit distant.

"I don't put things off anymore," he said.

"Alright." She stepped out of the van to see Dan better. Still on cellular, she asked, "You'll be back soon?"

He held up his thumb and index finger horizontally and close together, the Israeli hand signal for a short time frame. "I'll make it back for dinner with you guys and Motke. Gotta go." He threw her a kiss. She caught it and threw one back. "Gotta go. Bye." He turned toward the old man with a smile.

The Shabbos Rebbe exploded in happiness. He hung his sign from a bolt on the island's stoplight, stood back, then tilted his head a few times to adjust the poster one last time. "Come, come," he beckoned.

Dan and the Rebbe walked past the shuttered shops of Jaffa Road, past the natural ice cream vendor from Dimona, past the dogs sniffing at garbage strewn along the curb, beyond concert billboards, to Mea Shearim, the ultra-orthodox Hassidic enclave that functioned almost as a city within a city. It was very unusual for a black hat and a nonreligious to walk together, especially on Shabbat. Not a few Hassidim turned their heads in clear disgust, and even some secular Israelis thought it was odd.

At the entrance to the quarter, Dan recognized the weathered sign broadcasting its unmistakable warning: "Women—cover yourself and conduct yourself modestly." Many secular Israelis would not dare enter Mea Shearim, and not a few tourists have been stoned for trying to take pictures, dressing in short sleeves, or interacting inappropriately with the residents. But without hesitation, Dan followed the old man up the main walkway, around two side paths, across another street, down some steps, along an alley, and through a narrow gangway. At the end of the gangway was a courtyard walled in by back doors and old stone balconies, not unlike the old European Jewish ghettos.

The Shabbos Rebbe waved his arms grandly, "My home."

"Your home is where?" asked Dan.

"Just there," the Shabbos Rebbe replied, pointing to a small rusted metal plate hinged to the stone. It was held shut by a thick chain strung between gaping holes punched through the plate and a frame, and then secured tight by a large padlock. The hinged plate was no bigger than a casement on a coal bin. The Shabbos Rebbe playfully uncurled from his white stocking a long cord with a thin metal holder attached. He flipped open the holder and pulled out a key on a retractable wire which he inserted into the padlock. It unlocked with the sound of a prison cell.

The old man noisily pulled the heavy chain through the holes, and slowly creaked open the rusted plate door. The small, dank chamber within was completely dark. As the door opened, the invading light revealed first a crude floor mattress stuffed with crumpled newspapers, then two old towels from the Jerusalem Hilton rolled together and bound with a rubber band to create a makeshift pillow. Streams of slime on the rough-hewn stone walls reflected rays of daylight as the plate door was fully opened. It seemed to Dan not to be someone's willing abode, but rather a dungeon. To the Shabbos Rebbe, however, this austere hovel provided all he needed on this earth.

"*Bevakasha,*" chirped the Shabbos Rebbe, extending the traditional Israeli phrase of welcome.

Bending, Dan stepped through the opening. A horrific urinacious stench gripped him as he entered. The low ceiling forced him to crouch. Stacked alongside the floor mattress were sacred books with gold lettering on their covers, many with bits of paper protruding to mark important passages of mystic text.

"Sit," invited the Shabbos Rebbe, as he plunked himself down on his mattress.

Dan crossed his legs and angled his feet so his body descended vertically into a powwow sitting position on the floor. He shooed away a few cockroaches with a nearby slipper. There weren't two slippers, only one, and it seemed to be used exclusively as a fly and roach swatter.

The Rebbe mumbled prayers as he closed the door and in an automatic motion with his foot shoved a brick forward to keep it shut. The chamber returned to complete darkness. Quickly, the old man rotated a small piece of metal bolted to the wall. Once swiveled, it exposed spaces between the stonework allowing in a modicum of light and ventilation. He did it as effortlessly as one would pull the chain dangling from a lamp.

Light and shadow blended across the Rebbe's face.

For an hour they talked. Dan was fascinated. He lived for such encounters. The Shabbos Rebbe was a character he would one day write into his novel. He made mental notes of every detail.

But the Shabbos Rebbe seemed to have no name, no family, and no history—at least none he would reveal. To each question, he shrugged and declared, "Don't know" or in Yiddish, "*vays nicht.*" Dan knew only that for years the old man had been a Saturday morning landmark at the outskirts of Jerusalem, warning and pleading with the masses to stop driving and observe the Sabbath.

The Rebbe smiled almost impishly and eased out a book from near the bottom of one stack. Turning to a page he clearly knew well, he pointed at a line of Hebrew text and read it aloud expressively. Passing into English, "Man always has choice. He always choose way of no faith, way of evil." He stopped himself, "Good Inglish?"

Dan answered yes.

"Why does man always choose like this? Even to choose for *Moschiach,*" the Rebbe continued, "for Messiah—Inglish. The Holy One commands man observe the Sabbath. One day. There are six more for work. Just one day to rest." He pointed his finger to the heavens.

"The Heavenly Father shows how evil man is," he lamented. "He even offers to bring perfect order, to bring *Moschiach* to Jerusalem, if only Jews will observe two *Shabbatot* straight. Just two." Again the Rebbe checked, "Inglish okay?"

"Very good."

"But no," the Rebbe wailed. "He needs to drive. To where? To a pizza, to a friend, to a football game, to shameless women. What are a pizza and shameless women compared to *Moschiach?* You see—this is the way of man.

"Oy, oy, oy," the Rebbe moaned, rocking his head, eyes closed, and mumbling a prayer. "But there is always chance. Always. And I remind, so the Holy One can see and all persons can see. Man is gived chance for *Moschiach,* but makes pizza. Oy."

"Why, Rebbe? Why do you think?" asked Dan.

"Man is gived chance for *Moschiach,*" the Rebbe repeated, "but always choose evil. It is said, *hakol tsafuy vehareshut netuna.*"

"Yes, the old saying: *everything is predetermined, but permission is granted.* But what does it mean?"

The Rebbe replied with a sudden stare, "You need to figure out."

"So when is *Moschiach* coming?" asked Dan, seeking an impossible answer.

The Rebbe broke out in joy. "Oh soon. Very soon," he declared, gesturing to the heavens with both hands.

"Will you see him?" asked Dan.

"Yes, very soon. But not here. *They* will see him here. They will play at his side."

"*They?*" asked Dan.

The old man motioned with his misshapen thumb to the courtyard outside, "The *kinder,* the children. Ask them. Can't you hear them singing?"

Dan turned his head. He listened. There was no sound. "Who?"

Kicking away the brick against the plate door, the Rebbe stepped back into the courtyard. Dan followed. It was empty.

"How joyous they sing!" the Rebbe beamed.

"*Ha rav,* there is no one here," Dan delicately pointed out, gesturing first toward the courtyard's empty corners and shadows and then up at the peopleless balconies. "Nothing."

"Louder, children, he can't hear you," the Rebbe called out.

Dan looked down and suddenly, everywhere, there were children gleefully dancing and singing, maybe two dozen of them, touching the old man's breeches, twirling their curls, racing round and round. Dan's eyes watered as he beheld the uncanny frolic.

"*Moschiach, Moschiach, Moschiach, Moschiach, Moschiach,*" they chanted. Their pace quickened, their dance became more dizzying.

Dan subtly reached into his gadget jacket, found the red record button on his microcasette recorder, and pressed down. The Rebbe noticed the move and furiously objected. He grabbed Dan by the head and pulled his face flush against his coat. "No, no, no," the old man cried.

Dan pulled away. Suddenly, the children were gone. The courtyard became silent. "Where are the kids?" The Rebbe said nothing, and frowned. "The *kinder,*" said Dan, "they were here one second ago!"

The balconies–empty. All the doors–still shuttered. Some discarded newspaper blew in the wind. Dan ran through the gangway. On the other side he looked both ways. No children.

A small, old woman in a babushka hurried into a doorway.

"*Gzen kinder?*" Dan asked her in Yiddish. "Little children, did you see some boys?"

She ignored him and proceeded into her house.

Dan frantically searched through adjacent alleys and walkways, but still no children. Soon he was lost in the maze-like byways of Mea Shearim. He tried to retrace his steps to find the Shabbos Rebbe's hovel, but he could not. After wrong turn upon wrong turn, Dan gave up. Eventually, he recognized a walkway to the Mea Shearim entrance, and exited the quarter.

THEY SAID IT couldn't be done. Virtually down street from Jaffa Gate, facing the ramparts of the Old City, stood the exquisite Dan Pearl Hotel–a modern wonder in ancient Jerusalem. It took years to take it from master plan to masterpiece. Audacious for its location, this structure was power politics manifesting as design poetry.

Architectonically, the Dan Pearl was perfect. At the door, steps led down to a somewhat sunken lobby and up to a dining room. Tapering perspectives swept across the guest floors. The shimmering swimming pool was underground, as in Herodian times. Every angle and its intersection with each surface pleased the eye no matter where you stood, or what direction you turned. It was as though an artisan had redrawn the interior a thousand times from every conceivable vantage point to make sure every sightline was harmonious.

Each room was an elegant suite, appointed with more amenities and sophisticated gadgets than any other luxury accommodation in the country. Every guest was presented with a unique view of the Old City that constantly intrigued. During the day, the sun beat down on the rough, white stones, creating a special radiance interrupted only by the constant flicker of buses, cars, trucks, and taxis that kept the ancient walled center vibrant. At night, the romantic lights of David's Citadel, the soft floodlit walls, and the periodic flashing lights of the Mishtarah patroling in blue police cars and the Mishmar Hagvul patroling in green Border Patrol jeeps commanded by elite Druze soldiers reminded that the Old City rarely slept, and when it did, never soundly.

Sal was busy in the main parlor clicking through satellite TV, channel-surfing from New Delhi music videos to the CNN *Travel Report* to a BBC documentary on the Shroud of Turin. Park and Dan were each in their own glass-doored bedrooms, curtains pulled, unpacking suitcases and changing into fresh clothing.

The phone rang. It was Motke.

"Ah, you want Park. *Rak rega, bevakasha,*" said Dan, asking him in Hebrew to wait just a moment.

Park spoke briefly on her bedroom extension, knocked on Dan's door, and peeked in. "It's Motke. He wants to meet on something called the *midrekhov,*" said Park, "at some place called Atara. Tonight after sundown."

Dan smiled broadly, "The Atara. Cool!"

After she hung up, Dan explained all about what was loosely called the *midrekhov,* the serpentine pedestrian mall of outdoor cafes, hummus joints, stylish boutiques, ethnic restaurants, antiquity shops, street vendors, ice cream stands, artists, musicians, and general wall-to-wall people that made Jerusalem at night an unforgettable communal experience–especially Saturday night when the Sabbath concluded. It wasn't enough to extol the *midrekhov's* excitement. Dan pedantically traced the zone's step-by-step expansion from 1970, when he first found the area as a depot street for intercity taxis, and then a bricked over street dotted with coffeehouses. Each war and ensuing pause in belligerence had its own impact on the mall's expansion until it finally became a sprawling complex of social exuberance, each night attracting thousands of people to its narrow confines. After describing the owners and establishments along the main and side streets, past and present, who sold out to whom, what Zionist pioneers used to sip turkish at Atara Cafe, the irreparable damage when McDonald's and Burger King appeared, which falafel joints served the best hot sauce, which no longer served the best hot sauce, which T-shirt places should be avoided, which art galleries have been there forever and which were converted from pharmacies, which cafes baked their own pastries, which served delivered goods that looked great and tasted lousy, after doing all this for about ten minutes, Park finally said, "Okay."

Sal looked up for a moment, and then back at the TV.

Noting the reaction, Dan explained, "I just want you to have a good time and understand a few things." Park said she understood and went back to her room to finish dressing.

A few hours later, Dan and Park took the long scenic route, walking down the hill past the Moslem cemetery and Independence Park, past the Beit Agron foreign press center, past a path that led to a place where Mama Mia restaurant used to be, past where vendors had laid out blankets filled with handcrafted jewelry, hats, scarves, imitation bedouin robes, past the caricaturists and starving artists working in ceramic, wood and stone, past the pack of tourists surrounding the Moroccan folk trio, to the beginning of the *midrekhov* proper. As they wandered through the carefree crowds, where everyone connected as extended family, where all present seemed to share the common belief that the pinnacle of Jewish self-determination was the right to sip thick, black coffee and talk politics in the Jerusalem night air without being molested, as Dan and Park plunged closer and closer to the epicenter of the mall, it became almost impossible to move.

After a while, they boldly burrowed their way to Atara Cafe. When a table opened, Dan grabbed it, apologizing, "I grab this table not in the name of the Atara that stands here, but the Atara that once was and is no more."

Park thought the scene idyllic and didn't understand Dan's protest.

The coffee and dainty cakes were just being served when a heavyset man with mangy hair approached. He wore an XX Large T-shirt with the message, "Time is Running Out." Waving and pushing, he finally bullied sideways through the chattering masses until he arrived at their table.

"Park from Chicago?" he asked as introduction, and extending a handshake. "I'm Motke, from Derek."

"I am," answered Park with surprise. "How did you know?"

Motke unfolded from his back pocket a fax of Park's Derek employment photo. "I had this. And you also look like this is your first night here. Welcome to Israel. I am supposed to, pardon the expression, 'take care of you.' That means—in my book—make sure you eat well and show up on time."

"I can do both of those with a little practice," replied Park.

"But where is the young man, Sal?" Park explained that he was surfing the net back in the hotel room. "A good sign," said Motke agreeably.

Dan introduced himself, and liked Motke immediately, but sat back, restraining his urge to join the conversation as Motke and Park chatted about her new assignment.

Motke described Derek Institute as an Israeli government-sponsored think tank set up shortly after Independence to investigate military technology. Originally, they were located in a warehouse at kibbutz Neve Eitan, famous for contributing several major generals to the IDF. Eventually, Derek drifted into commercial projects, then relocated to the Technion campus. Not long after, it opened branches in the United States, England and Germany, working closely with the embassies.

"Several years ago, Kuebitz entered the scene," continued Motke. "No one knows much about him. He's a strange one."

"I spoke to him originally," said Park. "He hired me, and my son."

"Yes, and he has very special plans for you, I hear," Motke said.

"Meaning?"

"Meaning," Motke replied, "that while me and about two dozen other programmers are punching code twenty-three hours a day, he has you and Sal assigned to the Development Oversight Group."

"Dare I ask what that is?" said Park.

"It's not quite as bad as it sounds," Motke clarified. "I'm the Program Development team leader. I have two dozen programmers under me, ten of whom know what they are doing. The rest are just frightened little debuggers. The Development Oversight Group, the DOG—or, as I call it, DOGMA—is just three or four people under the direct supervision of Mr. Mystery."

"Kuebitz?" she asked.

"But of course. It's Kuebitz and a few of his friends who are equally mysterious. A few years ago, when they embarked upon this ambitious Millennium Bug project, the whole operation moved from Technion to a basement complex about three blocks from here." He pointed, "Just beyond there, a block or two over is Hillel Street. It's there. I'll take you in the morning. We can meet here for coffee."

Park nodded agreement.

"There's no sign in front," he continued, "and you'll never find it through all the doors and stairways. But Park, if you're smart, you'll do all your work from a laptop and avoid the place."

"You said Kuebitz has plans for me and Sal?"

"Yes. You are the only one here who has ever worked for Hinnom Computing *and* Bluestar on their Y2K programs. So Kuebitz wants you looking at the pieces we are assembling and compare them to what you know from America. It's an easy job. Enjoy it until he decides to make you work for your salary."

"And Sal?" she asked.

"This part might be really smart," said Motke. "Everyone on my team has been in the trenches for years. I'm sure you too. Kuebitz believes our team needs fresh perspective, uncorrupted outlook, from someone who wasn't brought up on the byte-schlepper mentality, the eight-dot-three filenames or the whole glass-house *meshugaas*–craziness, I mean–that got us messed up in the first place. We need a *pisher*. That, Mrs. McGuire, is your son, Sal."

"A *pisher*?" she asked, glancing for a clue at Dan, who just winked. "A thinker?"

"Close enough," said Motke. "Maybe he'll have an earth-shattering thought? But no more with the job. This is Israel. Let's eat and have a good time."

Dan jumped in. Using a little broken Hebrew, interspersed with fragments of Yiddish and long English segues, he could no longer delay establishing rapport with Motke. The two talked and talked, sharing their common hope for a Mideast peace that seemed to never come, complaining about the right-wing government holding on by a thread, laughing about applications for telephone service that used to take so long they were passed from father to son as legacies, giggling about cell phones now hanging from every pants belt in the country, marveling about changes in Israeli society, technologic, political and spiritual, ridiculing Israeli drivers, remembering great Arab restaurants they used to frequent in East Jerusalem, and paying homage to an Israeli society that still cherished its openness and freedom in the midst of a siege mindset that made every person nervous about every paper bag on every street . . . was it a bomb or just someone's half-eaten lunch?

Israelis were divided into those who were extremely rude and arrogant, and those who were so genuinely gracious and open that they forged instant relationships. Motke was of the latter group–you met him once and it was as though you had known him forever.

Happy to find a soulmate in Dan, Motke was nonetheless careful not to exclude Park. Dan made the same effort and constantly involved her in every exchange.

"I'm reminded of the time I was driving down from Hebron," Dan recalled. "Someone threw a hand grenade at my car."

Motke nonchalantly replied, "Nu?"

"It missed," answered Dan, with that special dropping inflection that made it a joke.

They both laughed.

Park didn't understand the humor in a hand grenade, and just tried to chuckle along.

Quickly, Park received a crash course in Israeli attitude, history, social divisions, religious strife, and the telephone system. Nothing was what she expected. For her, Israel was not a country of kibbutzim and commandos, but the land of the Bible. She revered the same sand and dust that touched the feet of Jesus and Moses. To her, the Children of Israel were not kids in baggy jeans on skateboards carrying portable CD players in their backpacks, they were the Chosen People. She was confused and amazed by everything she saw and heard. Park tried to forget her Bible Belt heritage, the stereotypical drawings of shepherds with lambs in Sunday school workbooks, and the images of Christ, his blond hair flowing gently, printed into oval picture frames and hung above the fireplace. But she remained confused and amazed.

For Park, everything in Israel seemed like it should be a holy endeavor. She looked around. Everyone was partying. She knew nothing about the Hebrew language, but thought surely it should be reserved for the tablets of the Ten Commandments, or those age-old handcrafted Torah scrolls and sacred liturgical expressions written down in religious books. But Hebrew here was a modern language like any other. Bazooka comics, fashion magazines, coffee cans, and even pornography—they were all written in Hebrew. The radios shouted Hebrew promos for cheap movies, Nescafé, Levis, and Burger King. It all sounded like the hyped-up used car TV ads back home.

Dan sensed some of her emotions. "Hey, I freaked the first time I came to Israel," he laughed. "I spent years as a kid praying in Hebrew School. Who knew you could use those words to tell dirty jokes!"

Motke extended his palm, Dan casually slapped five.

"Hebrew is the language of truth," asserted Motke with an intense expression. "That is, unless spoken by Netanyahu," he cracked.

Dan poked his index finger at Motke's extended palm, offering a one-digit version of five.

A braless waitress came by and asked if another round was needed.

Dan answered in a deep voice, "*Lama lo.*" In Israel, Dan always preferred to answer *lama lo*, Hebrew for "why not?" instead of *yes*. He thought a simple "yes" was just too curt.

This time the coffee was *turki im hel*, that is, sweet turkish coffee seasoned with freshly ground cardamom.

Dan sipped and savored its exotic aroma. He shivered with fulfillment, leaned back, and loudly exclaimed, *"Oy!"*

"*Oy*, I'm not sure about *oy*," inquired Park. "I never know what you mean when you say *oy*. Sometimes it's good and sometimes bad. So what does it mean?"

"*Oy* is a cumulative expression," Dan replied authoritatively. "Each *oy* uttered by a Jew incorporates all previous utterances of *oy* by any Jew throughout time all over the world. Depending upon its inflection and its context, and the strength, age, and mentality of the utterer, *oy* can be an expression of exasperation, amazement, ennui, fear, or several dozen other emotions Jews have known or can know, with the understanding that each *oy* linguistically benefits from and builds on the previous *oys*, and in turn makes its contribution to the *oys* of the future."

"*Oy,*" said Motke signifying how impressed he was with the definition, adding, "You know your *oys*."

Dan extended his flat palm. Motke slid his five fingers across.

"Could you repeat that?" asked Park.

"No," answered Dan. "That was an inspired spontaneous definition that could transmogrify with the next generation of *oys*. It would be a betrayal of its place in the continuum of Jewish thought to suffer it the ravages of reiteration." He sipped a bit more *turki*.

"You're awfully comfortable, aren't you?" observed Park.

"Yes, I am," Dan confirmed. "It's seventy-two degrees, no humidity, and I'm sipping coffee in Jerusalem."

"What amazes me," she observed, "is you two have just met, and you act as though you were raised together on the same block."

"The same mental block," explained Dan. "Happens all the time. Two Jews, they never knew each other, come together like they grew up in one house. It's our common agony."

"It's agonizing," confirmed Motke.

"We're like blood brothers—it starts at circumcision," revealed Dan.

They all laughed and Park was just beginning to feel at home. By now, the crowds were thinning slightly, which meant the throng had reduced itself to bands of merrymakers, some Israeli, some foreign. The green command jeeps of the Mishmar Hagvul, their tall radio antennas lashed downward to the front, could now be seen at the top of Ben Yehuda Street. In the midst of all the frivolity, stoney-faced anti-terror soldiers, rifles slung low just below their hips, stood by vigilantly scrutinizing all that occurred.

A portly man in Hassidic garb, his face barely visible beneath his hat brim, could be seen walking slowly and bent over. His long gray beard came down over his breast in stringy strands. He seemed disoriented. First, he walked toward a coffee bar, then away from it, and then over to a music shop where teenagers were sampling the latest hit songs. He came within a few inches of a girl, stared at her for a moment, then moved next to a concrete planter. Fidgeting about in a circle, he seemed unsure where his next step would land. Eventually, he stumbled into a tourist from America wheeling his infant daughter in a small blue stroller.

The portly Hassid appeared bewildered. So, many people on the mall ignored him, just as they ignored other bizarre characters wandering any night along the *midrekhov*. But now he seemed to be staring at the infant. His head came up for a moment and beneath the hat, a young, high-cheeked face could be seen.

With his knee, Dan nudged Motke. "Check out the Jew."

"The Hassidic dude?" asked Motke barely looking.

"He's no Hassid," Dan replied in a deadly serious monotone.

Now the portly man wandered toward their table.

"Honey, do as I say," Dan whispered to Park. "Get up and walk into the ladies room in the Atara." He pressed her arm. "Do as I say. Right now. Right now."

Motke steeled his sight onto the man and agreed, "No Jew."

Dan caught the eye of a soldier and communicated with his eyes that the portly Hassid was trouble. Park stood up and left the table as instructed. The soldier stared intensely at the suspect and spoke into his headset microphone.

Within a moment, a dozen heads—some soldiers, some undercover Israeli security men—turned to look at the suspect. Initially, the American with the baby stroller gabbed unaware on his cell phone. But when the Hassid began slowly circling the stroller, the American couldn't help but notice. At first, the American smiled, but as his eyes met the portly Hassid's, the smile shrunk away. Park could not get past a pastry cart blocking the door to the Atara. Dan saw she was stuck. Soldiers and security men began to move from all corners of the mall.

The portly Hassid gestured to the infant in the stroller and spoke goo-goo with an Arab accent: "Babee. Babee." Then he began to tremble terribly.

Terribly, until he tore off the false beard and hat, and opened his heavy coat revealing the body of a slender, young Arab man wearing a white vest sewn with numerous long narrow pockets, each fitted with a slender plastique charge all wired together.

"Aaaallaaah Akbar!" he cried, "Death to the sons of pigs and monkeys!"

He stretched his right arm out, revealing a rudimentary plunger connected to a wire run through his coatsleeve and clearly leading to the charges around his belly.

A soldier advanced.

"Stop!" the terrorist yelled, waving a finger in a semicircle barely an inch over the plunger button. The soldier froze.

"No move, no step," he yelled. "No step. I bomb myself."

The crowd broke for cover on the ground, hid behind flimsy cafe tables, in shallow doorways, and nowhere at all. Whimpering was everywhere. Anyone on the periphery slipped away to safety.

With his other hand the bomber brought out a cellular phone, very slowly, demonstratively. "No move. I bomb myself," he repeated. He raised the phone high above his head for all to see. A piece of cardboard with writing on it was attached to the side of the phone. Slowly, he brought the phone down to his cheek to show he was going to use it for a call. He touched a button, calling Israel Radio.

The American with the baby stroller begged, "Let me take my daughter away, just my daughter."

"Babee," agreed the bomber. "Not you. Babee," he motioned to a teenage girl. Trembling, she pulled herself up from the ground, took charge of the stroller, and rolled it away around the corner as the father looked on helplessly.

Shouting into the phone, the bomber began reading for Israel Radio and all to hear a prepared English statement written for him on the cardboard. "I am commando 12 of Deir Yassin Revenge Unit," he announced, referring to the Deir Yassin massacre of Arabs during the War of Independence. "Tape this message," he instructed. "You cannot stop me. I bomb myself. More friends will come with bombs tomorrow, another day, another week, another year. You kill many Arab children. Not just my brother. Many brothers. So I cannot sleep. Now I bomb myself. Not just me but many friends will bomb themself. So you cannot sleep."

Dan stood up and spoke softly to the bomber just a few feet away. "*Salaam Aleikum*, my friend."

A soldier shouted in English, "Sit down."

Motke mumbled, "Stop, Dan."

Park cowered against the pastry cart and shook in complete fear.

Dan persisted, "No, I want this man to know he is not going to heaven, but to *Gehennem* if he bombs himself."

The terrorist was taken aback to hear Dan's traditional Islamic greeting, as well as the Arabic word for Hell, *Gehennem,* coming from an American Jew.

"Oh yes, I know the Koran, I studied the Koran," said Dan, while he had the bomber's attention. "And I know that you have been fed a pack of lies by your buddies who told you that you would have a thousand virgins in heaven and sit at Allah's right hand. But that is a lie. You are going straight to *Gehennem,*" he insisted, crackling the word *Gehennem* with acidic emphasis.

> Position one, atop a command jeep just yards away, radioed quietly to command. "Yosef, I see enough plastique to kill two hundred people including our unit. Everyone here. Subject wants to make a statement, or we would all be dead now. Subject is not fully committed, he might negotiate. He is now talking to a crazy American." The terrorist was completely within his Galil sniperscope. "Estimate just a few ounces pressure to set off the device. Even after a head shot, subject will detonate."

"I bomb myself," shouted the young terrorist, probably no older than sixteen. He waved his finger back and forth across the plunger. "Shoot, I bomb myself," he yelled, with a tremolo, suggesting that, in truth, he wanted to live, that deep within, he feared the dark moment of explosion.

"You deserve better," continued Dan. "You understand English . . . Your mother is a good woman and she deserves to be with you. You have a sister and you want to protect her, see her again. Do you want your mother in heaven where she belongs–and you in Hell–*Gehennem*–which is where you're going to go if you push that button. You will never see her again. You don't have to push the button. No button." Dan's racing mind thought back to *Brain Monthly*. He knew that even a bullet to the head would probably not stop a nervous impulse through the neural pathways to the fingertips, setting off the bomb.

The young terrorist read the English statement again into the phone. "Israh-el Radio. Do you hear me? I am commando 12 of Deir Yassin Revenge Unit. Tape this message." He began tossing his head and shaking, but continued in a rage, "You cannot stop me. I bomb myself."

Some in the crowd tried to slip away. "No move! No step! No step!" he screamed, waving his hand and the plunger.

Even still, the hostages continued to thin as those out of sight escaped.

The bomber resumed his message: "More friends will come with bombs tomorrow, another day, another week, another year. You kill many Arab children. Not just my brother. Many brothers. So I cannot sleep. Now I bomb myself. Not just me but many friends will bomb themself. So you cannot sleep."

> Position One to Command: "Yosef, I have a clear shot, but the bomb trigger will be depressed. Repeat: Detonation likely even after a clean shot to the head. Recommend Thief Maneuver if triangulation ready."

> Position Two to Command: "I agree, but I'm not ready." He wedged himself against a wall with the terrorist in his scope, and reported. "Ready for Thief Maneuver."

> Yosef radioed back: "Position Three?"

> Position Three to Command: "Not ready," the young Druze soldier replied, sprawled along the ground, his rifle tripoded against his elbows. He spread his legs to further anchor himself, and shook the sweat off his forehead to clear his vision. But he was not ready.

"*Gehennem,*" repeated Dan.

The terrorist looked directly into Dan's eyes.

They connected.

He continued speaking into the cell phone and answering Dan at the same time. "No *Gehennem*. Allah. Allah"

"You are wrong," shouted Dan, "It's *Gehennem,* straight to the fires of Hell."

"Okay, *Gehennem,"* bellowed the terrorist, "but you go too." With that he tossed the cell phone to the side, closed his eyes, and began praying in Arabic.

Park pushed further into the unmoving pastry cart as she prayed silently, her lips moving rapidly and emphatically. Motke tightened his jaw, fixed on the terrorist's hand, and read Torah in his mind, his head bobbing ever so slightly.

Back in Seattle, the computer matching millions of driver's license photos suddenly stopped on one name. It flashed twice and then a red box highlighted it. Linzer walked over to the screen and read the name aloud: "Park McGuire . . . Park McGuire?" He punched a few buttons and her employee records at Hinnom Computing flashed on another monitor. "Park McGuire," he nodded. The Nazi laughed and Chaim screamed out in quiet agony as the Luger pressed into his temple. Chaim waited for the bullet and tried to find God. Dan ran down the debris-strewn embankment yelling, "Jenny! Simon!" He smelled burning flesh, turned and saw Park ready to die in a doorway. His father spoke: "You know, you just don't know that you know." Back at the Dan Pearl, Sal abruptly looked up from his Windy at though someone had tapped him on the shoulder. Startled, he ran to the balcony and looked outside. The young terrorist's prayers were getting louder. Sal strained to hear something but he did not know what. Louder. The prayers became louder.

Yosef asked again: "Position Three? Are you ready?"

Position One to Command: "I am ready for Thief Maneuver."

Position Two to Command: "I am ready for Thief Maneuver."

Yosef again: "I ask Position Three?"

Position Three to Command: "Not ready." He moved one final time a few inches to the left.

Yosef again: "Position Three?"

Position Three to Command: "Yes, ready for Thief Maneuver."

The terrorist stopped his prayers, fisted his face, opened his eyes, focused on the plunger beneath his index finger, looked up, found the stars sparkling above, saw his mother hugging his photo and now kissing it once softly, and prepared to explode his plastique.

Yosef to all positions: "Punish the Thief."

Simultaneously, as though one mind, each of the three soldiers flipped the targeting switch on their Galil .233 rifles, lined the terrorist within the crosshairs of their night scopes, and then painted his wrist with FA-4 red laser sighting dots no larger than .23 square inch. Each thought the same words as they squeezed their triggers: "You stole our peace of mind." All at once, three triangulated shots that sounded like one blasted through the narrows of Ben Yehuda street, streaking toward the terrorist's wrist. All three found their target. The hand was completely severed from the flexor tendons in the forearm. No muscle pressure was possible against the plunger. As the hand flew away, the plunger dangled harmlessly from the coatsleeve. The terrorist looked in shock at his arm without a hand. Two more shots were fired, burning into his left shoulder as three plainclothes security men jumped forward to grip the plunger and restrain the wounded man.

"Get away! Get away!" one of the security men yelled in Hebrew and English.

The crowd ran in all directions.

Soldiers had taken over various shops around the corners out of view to gather fleeing people and see to any injuries. One security man ran up, pulled a silk bag from his back pocket and pulled it roughly over the terrorist's head. Another wrapped a table cloth around the man's blood-spurting wrist. A paramedic under the direction of police scooped up the severed hand with a handkerchief, dropping it in a plastic evidence bag. The bomber was hustled away to a waiting police van with another paramedic attending to his wounds.

Motke, Park, and Dan did not run like the rest. Park stood up slowly, watching until the terrorist disappeared behind the slamming doors of the van, screeching away, its blue light flashing. The mall became a cacophony of crackling two-way radios and ringing cell phones. Israel TV, Magen David Adom–the Israeli equivalent of the Red Cross–and more police descended upon the chaos. The bomb squad checked for booby traps in garbage cans. A police officer walked up to Dan: "We need to talk to you. Do you know this maniac?"

Dan muttered back in a monotone, *"Itonayee"* and showed his foreign press card.

The policeman said, "Okay, journalist. Still, we need to talk to you."

Park gripped his arm, and, still shaking, almost broke into tears. But instead, she just bit her lip and steeled herself.

A Mishmar Hagvul commander approached Dan. He asked, "Is this the crazy American?" The soldier from Position One walked up and nodded.

"I am Yosef," said the commander to Dan. "So. You are a hero. You bought us the time we needed by talking to this killer." Dan's face was a rock as he comprehended all that had occurred. Yosef shook Dan's hand, "I don't know what went in your head. Tonight you are a hero, but please don't do it again. Let *us* be the heroes. Not you."

Dan kissed Park. Motke gripped Dan's other palm in a heartfelt handshake of comradeship.

"I'll bear that in mind," said Dan.

"Yes," said Yosef, "bear it."

10

DEREK

"**Y**ou're right, I don't see anything," Park admitted to Motke, as she and Sal stood with him in front of a series of shops on Hillel Street.

"Yes, it's invisible," chuckled Motke. He waited a moment, drank a little more of the freshly squeezed carrot juice he had picked up on the *midrekhov*, and smugly asked, "Give up?"

Park gave up.

"It's right before you," Motke said, pointing to a cramped, dirty vestibule hosting old-fashioned mailboxes stuffed with flyers and newspapers. Just big enough for one person to turn around in, the vestibule gave way to a dark staircase leading up. Motke switched on the hallway lights. Several black office placards lettered in Hebrew and English were illuminated, revealing a travel agent, two barristers, and an accountant.

"It's up there?" asked Park.

"No," he replied, but then added with false surprise, "Wait. What's here, behind the stairs?"

Park and Sal looked just behind the stairwell. A small sign reading "D.I.L. Parking" pointed to a doorway. She looked askance. "This way?"

"Very good," said Motke. "So let's go down." The three walked through the doorway to a noisy metal staircase that descended through a three-level parking garage. Motke led them down only one flight. "Down there is for parking," he said. "Here is for staff." He opened a door, which led to an adjacent stairway, walked up two steps, around through another entrance, and straight across a short catwalk overlooking the parked cars. At the end of the catwalk was a heavy-duty steel door with a mounted speaker observed by a small TV camera. A chipped black placard on the door read "Derek Institute Ltd."

Sal manifested the beginnings of a smile. He liked the maze, and took an extra bite out of an Elite candy bar he had been enjoying since the hotel lobby.

"Ohhhhkay," smiled Park. "It's a secret?"

"Nothing so exciting," answered Motke. "Just an old building. Before the State, there were many such buildings built with very complicated passages in and out. If you go to the Jewish Agency just a few blocks from here, you can see a nice white building with a pretty entrance. Yes. But until just a few years ago, it had the original facade designed to confuse the British. The Mandate officers would walk in the front entrance with the big sign 'Jewish Agency' and all the flags waving. It went to nothing but a few worthless offices. The real way in and out to the nerve center of the Jewish Agency was through the parking lot in the rear. Little unmarked doors going in, then up and down a few steps, and around corners. No secret passageways. Just *real* confusing if you don't know."

"Why?" asked Park, who knew little of Israeli history.

"They were hiding things about immigration, about guns–things they didn't want the British to know," explained Motke. He rang the Derek buzzer, the camera audibly zoomed once, paused, and the door clicked open. They stepped into a standing-room only chamber. The first door closed behind them. Then the second door clicked open to the Derek offices.

"Quite a security system," commented Park quietly.

"It's nothing, just an old two-door chamber system from the old days," pooh-poohed Motke. "The World Zionist Organization uses the same system in their building on Park Avenue in New York. So does every bank in France. I'd like to see some nice stuff: retinal scans, face and body imaging, thermal and voice signature matching."

Sal perked up.

"But," said Motke, "who has the money and the time?"

As the three emerged from the entry chamber, they encountered a long, dilapidated table manned by an aging veteran acting as auxiliary security looking for bombs. Men like him stood guard at buildings, malls, cinemas, and public places all over Israel. This gentleman wore a black beret, ordinary street clothes, and by his side was the WWII vintage Czech bolt-action rifle he used in 1948. A crude Jewish Star under the name, "Lodz," was carved into the battered wooden butt. He stuck his finger into Motke's tote bag and peered, then did the same to Park's purse.

"*Shaaalom,*" chimed Motke with deep friendship. The man nodded slightly in appreciation.

"Known him long?" asked Park.

"First day here," answered Motke.

The three walked down a long corridor lined with old pre-State veneer doors, many warped with exfoliated patches. At the end of the corridor, double doors led to a large room with narrow windows running along the top for natural light. A large blackboard stretched along one side. Several dozen rickety wooden chairs, like those used in grade schools, too small for most adults, were organized around a collection of card and picnic tables, creating one large horizontal surface. Several developers chatted quietly in a corner. Others drifted in until the room was filled and noisy. Transplanted from Derek offices around the world, they were anxious to know where the Y2K project would go next. Motke was asked questions in a variety of languages, mostly Hebrew, sometimes in French, and occasionally in German. He answered each with a short English response, "Please wait for the briefing. We'll answer everything," reminding, "and English, please."

Conversation turned to who was where when the terrorist incident occurred last night, whether it was still safe to sip coffee on the *midrekhov,* and stories about what the crazy American did and did not do. Motke and Park listened silently and tried to avoid the subject.

Eventually, Ronit, the administrative secretary, signaled Motke.

"Okay, *hevre, sheket, bevakasha,*" Motke announced, adding, "please sit, and let's come to order. English only, please. It's late, almost eight," he said, bringing them to order.

An old woman wearing a formless faded blue dress and slippers shuffled in with a tray of glasses filled with boiling water, each with a Wissotzky teabag hanging over the rim. Motke graciously thanked her as she methodically laid the glasses atop the table. Needing several more, she motioned to her little granddaughter, who dutifully brought in a second tray with additional glasses.

"Todah," said Motke, thanking her one final time.

"We start now," said Motke. "Can Dr. Kuebitz come in please?" he asked Ronit.

Speaking in Hebrew, she surprised Motke with the news that Kuebitz and his associates on the Development Oversight Group were stuck in Tel Aviv at Hakirya, Israel's Pentagon. He would be joining the meeting via speakerphone at 8:15.

"Okay, why not?" said Motke, looking at the clock, seeing the call would come in a few moments. Quickly, they went to Kuebitz' office and began stringing his speakerphone via six-foot phone wire extensions until it reached into the meeting room. It didn't quite stretch to the tables, so they rested it on a chair. At 8:15 sharp, Ronit motioned that the call was ready.

"Are you there, Dr. Kuebitz?" asked Motke.

"Yes, proceed," replied the voice of Kuebitz. "I am sorry, I am not there, but I am here." Sal liked the statement, and thought about it for a moment.

Motke began the briefing. "Zoom at Bluestar will not happen for sure. After Hector died from the heart attack, Bluestar, we think, really fell apart. It seems Hinnom may now succeed in pushing Windgazer 99 on the world. We think this is not good. Windgazer has never been stable, not even Windgazer Prime. Yet this new version Windgazer 99 is being rushed to the marketplace, again sacrificing stability. No one will know until it is too late because Hinnom Computing is the master of the beautiful but false user interface. Your screen says the system is finished copying, but it's not. Your screen says it has finished installing, but it has not. Your screen says the task is done, but it's just beginning inside the CPU. Later on, you get the error messages, lost documents, corrupted files, and incompatible routines. Then come the costly bug fixes. Updates. Why sell the software just one time when it is finally finished—when you can sell it piece by piece over and over again?

"Zoom, we think, would have worked," Motke continued. "Why? First of all, I was working on it."

The group laughed.

"Second, our partner Bluestar was committed to inclusion of all operating systems, all software, all users, including competitors. Hinnom wants to succeed, but only for Windgazer systems. He says: 'You can breathe but only if you breathe from my oxygen tank.'"

Motke lifted his still boiling tea glass with two fingers, a napkin cling-
ing underneath, sipped a bit and exhaled with satisfaction. He turned to
the speakerphone, "You can hear still?"

"Continue. I'm fine," replied the voice of Kuebitz.

"Zoom might be dead for Bluestar, but not for us," said Motke. "Much
of the key development was done by Derek. We only licensed the technology to Bluestar. A few little bits and pieces were contributed by some
independents, but Derek purchased those. Our agreement with Bluestar
called not only for us to retain our rights to the core code, but to the
enhancements added during the Zoom project should they never be used.
So, even though Bluestar is out of the picture, Derek has the ability to finish the job. We have no right to the "Zoom" name, however, because
Bluestar trademarked that.

"So today–" Motke turned to the speakerphone to seek authority to
reveal the project. "I can continue?"

"Continue, it is time," replied the voice of Kuebitz.

"So today," he resumed, "we announce Operation Ohr. *Ohr* is the
Hebrew word for light. Most of you recall the story of Hanukkah, when
the Israelites had oil only for one night. They held out for a miracle and
the oil lasted for eight nights. *Hevre,* the world is running out of time and
it only has enough oil for one night. Our job is to keep the lights burning.

"It will take a miracle. Here is where you come in," Motke explained.
"Y2K is far more serious than anyone knows except for those of us in this
nerve-wracking business. Some people in the computer world believe that
faster development takes place if executed globally. Okay, in theory the
project never sleeps. When Cambridge, Massachusetts, programmers are
done for the day, Seattle takes over. When Seattle is finished, New Delhi
picks up until it starts back at Cambridge. Yes, a lot of work gets done that
way, but when do people get to put their heads together to compare notes
and look each other in the eye? The human element has been lost. We
believe computers and modems have been used in this way not to bring
talented people together but to keep them separate.

"Derek is taking a different approach," continued Motke. "We're
putting everyone together in one place–in this building, or at your homes
within walking distance of here, on the laptops provided. We will finish
the job. In the end, there is less sleep and more code for everyone."

The group laughed.

"But, also in the end," emphasized Motke, "Derek will have a real product that really works. We will call it Ohr 2000–the millennial light for all computers."

An Israeli programmer asked, "Do I understand that we now continue with the identical development program as Zoom, but under Derek?"

"More or less," replied Motke, adding "but be ready for the unexpected. Remember, each man or woman in our elite group is indispensable. Every one of you has the ability to make us fail or succeed."

"Is the team structure the same?" asked a Nigerian.

"Yes," Motke responded good-naturedly, "until we change it."

He nodded to Park and Sal. "And now I will introduce two more Americans who come to us. First, Park McGuire, who worked on both projects: Zoom for Bluestar and Windgazer 99 for Hinnom Computing." The crowd was impressed. "She and her son, Sal, the young man over there eating candy bars"–smiles all around–"have been added to Development Oversight. They will work with Dr. Kuebitz' group. So they will say a few words. Park, please say hello."

She pushed back her chair to stand, shook the blond hair out of her eyes, and appeared overwhelmed. Unready and unwilling to take a leadership role, she began slowly, "I don't really know what to say because I wasn't prepared for any of this." She cleared her throat. "And jetlag is just setting in. But I'll do my best to give my view." As she spoke, she became animated. Quickly she captured the entire room's attention.

"Fundamentally, Hinnom and Bluestar follow completely different management approaches," she outlined. "Bluestar prefers to field a number of diversified teams with a lot of overlap and no one cares about a few extra million lines of code.

"Hinnom, on the other hand, stresses personal ingenuity," she continued. "His company thrives on code stars, leading–no actually *dominating* the teams. So it would be one man on integration, one man on interface, one man on reliability, one man on throughput, everyone serving that team master but with the game plan really emanating from the very top– Ben Hinnom himself. His will on any question is ordained and then implemented by his closest followers, the chief programmers. At Hinnom you get to goal quickly. They tolerate no bloated code. People are shamed for excess lines. That sounds great to the lean mean programmer in us, but in point of fact, at Hinnom, reliability always took a back seat to getting to market before the other guy and giving the chief programmer justification for his bonus—whether or not the software was ready. We used to joke, we'll get it right in Rev N-Plus One."

"Rev N-Plus One is my favorite," laughed Motke. For those who don't know, it means 'next time.'"

"Exactly," smiled Park. "Derek should, in my view, import the best of both those worlds, and export the worst of them. Spare no code to make Ohr 2000 solid, reliable, and effective. But the heck with look, feel, and marketability. This is an emergency. Fat code engenders its own instability and becomes a resource hog that inevitably collapses under its own weight."

"You have specifics?" asked Motke.

"Probably the same as everyone else. I think we should have three goals: modularity, reliability, and throughput—roughly in that order. As you would expect, system security will be enhanced through N-turnkey routines with one-way encrypted signatures on all components. One-way encryption, of course, allows people to decrypt inbound to verify legitimate system-level compliance, but not to encrypt outbound allowing just anyone to fake it. Hence, it will be that much harder for a virus or noncompliant data to creep in.

"Every public interface," she continued, "must pass a rigorous automated test of all boundary conditions as well as randomly selected verification data sets. Testing, testing, testing—and then more testing. Because we are dealing with so many different types of software, hardware, applications, and even time zones and languages spread across the international network enterprise, every programming possibility will have to be calculated and recalculated to the nth degree for every circumstance. Zoom—excuse me, Ohr 2000—will probably be most vulnerable where general software is always most vulnerable: the minimums, the maximums, and critical transitions, such as those from negative to positive numbers, unexpected conditions. Identifying those in and of itself will be different for every system. It could be one-byte or two. Old mainframes, for example, use 128 number possibilities: that is, 0-127—or in fact, any combination of 128 negative to positive numbers. But in one-byte systems, the number is stored hexadecimally, and the range would be zero-zero to nine-nine. So our teams will need to check for two-byte strings, one-byte packed decimals, signed and unsigned char types, you name it. I guess we'll have to unbabble Babel."

"What was that?" the voice of Kuebitz asked.

"The Bible said it in Genesis 11:9," explained Park, looking first at the speakerphone and then back at the group. "Once," she recounted with some self-conscious, "all the world knew only one language, but man was arrogant and tried to build a tower so tall it would challenge the heavens. Quoting Scripture now: *The Lord came down to see the tower, which mortals had built. And the Lord said: Look, they are one people, and they all have one language; and this is only the beginning of what they will do; nothing that they propose to do will now be impossible for them.* Then the Lord confounded their language, condemning them to speak many tongues. So when one man asked for a brick, the man next to him misunderstood and gave him a hammer. Eventually, the men building the tower fought with each other and scattered across the face of the Earth. The tower was never finished. God called that place 'Babel,' because that was where he confounded the language of the Earth. I guess we still have the problem," she smiled.

But no one smiled with her as the comparison sunk in.

"You know the story well," remarked the voice of Kuebitz.

"Basic Sunday school," responded Park, a little uncomfortable with the somber reaction she had evoked.

Motke broke the short silence. "That was good. That was good," he commented, adding, "And for those who know the Arabic, Babel means *Gate to God.* So the moral of the story is reach high—but not too high, eh?"

He looked across the table at Sal. "So, maybe now we could hear from the younger generation. Sal, if you can finish the milk chocolate . . ."

Sal looked up from a lanky body folded like a cape around himself. He said nothing for some time.

The group waited, patiently, and Motke brightly repeated his invitation. "Sal, just introduce yourself."

But the most Sal did was tense his jaw in preparation for the possible utterance of a word. Park looked across the table proudly, displaying no pressure, understanding the thoughts stacking through her son's logic set.

"Sal, please pick up," requested the voice of Kuebitz.

Motke handed the individual phone to Sal. He eyed it suspiciously and pursed his lips. He unveiled one arm to accept the handset, and put it to his ear. The voice of Kuebitz spoke to him. A moment later, Sal, his eyes moist and fearful, gave the phone back. Motke switched Kuebitz back to speakerphone.

Sal walked over to the side of the room. There on the ground he saw a pointer. He picked it up with one hand, gripping it tensely. With the other hand he took a piece of white chalk. Still in silence he took his hand to the blackboard and drew a large dot. Eying the speakerphone and the group alternately, he aimed the pointer at the dot.

"I think the solution will come," Sal said quietly, ". . . but it isn't here yet."

The others leaned forward, straining to understand.

"We don't know the answer yet, or even the form it will take. Yes, it will require a miracle. The definition of a miracle is a process not yet understood by people. Flying was a miracle, until we understood the principles of lift and drag." Sal looked at Park for guidance and she motioned encouragement. "Rain was a miracle until we understood the moisture content of clouds and condensation. Birth was a miracle until we understood the interaction of sperm and ovum, and the process of gestation. We need a miracle of understanding. We need to be open to receive it. Copernicus wasn't determined to find a certain number of heavenly bodies. Copernicus opened his eyes and searched the heavens. Then he discovered.

"Our problem," he again pointed at the dot, "might be as simple as the contents of this dot. No one really knows what is within this point in time and space. No one cares because it looks so simple. But consider the possibilities. Maybe our answer is as simple as a white dot. We must wait until it reveals itself to us." He scrunched his eyes with those last words and looked back nervously at the speakerphone.

"Sal, please pick up," the voice of Kuebitz requested.

Motke again handed Sal the handset. Sal's hand shook nervously as he again brought the phone to his ear. He listened a bit and then mustered a meek, "Thank you." Sal gave the phone back to Motke, reporting, "Dr. Kuebitz said it was a good meeting, he had to go."

Motke spoke into the phone, trying to find Kuebitz. But nothing. Dial tone.

"Okay, team," said Motke. "A good meeting. Let's all go to work. Sal and Park, Ronit will show you to your little offices. And please, everyone," he quipped with a laugh, "be on the lookout for a *revealing thing.*"

Motke balanced his head in a cupped hand atop folded arms. He thought for a moment as people filed out of the room, and called to Sal, "Hey, let me know if something gets revealed to you." Sal nervously twitched his face and nodded that he would.

~

JERUSALEM'S MORNING SUN was intense when Dan stepped out of the Dan Pearl. As usual, Jaffa Road air admixed the unique aroma of heated Jerusalem limestone with the diesel fumes of heavy-duty construction trucks, bus propane and gasoline exhaust, along with Mideast spices blended with bodily perspiration. Wafting all together, it became the fragrance of Jerusalem.

Dan walked up the steep street, sidestepping construction planks and mud puddles until he could cross over to the Old City walls and toward Jaffa Gate. Along the way, the usual assortment of Arab peddlers jumped at him, offering tours, necklaces, religious objects, postcards, sweets, and cool drinks.

One noisome peddler pushing tours would not give up: "I give you good price, show you all Holy places, Juish too, not to worry."

Just then, a large ornate Mercedes taxi pulled up. Out came a slightly heavyset Arab gentleman, impeccably dressed, a copy of the *Financial Times* and *Al Kuds* under his arm. They immediately recognized each other.

"Abu Sayeed," said Dan with joy. *"Salaam."* Sayeed grasped Dan's extended hand, kissed his left, then right cheek in the traditional Arab greeting. As he did so, Sayeed locked eyes with the peddler, who shrank away.

"You are back, my brother," said Sayeed, with his characteristic trilling of r's. "Why not you call me? Or fax. Come my shop. We drink tea."

Dan walked with him right past a collection of soldiers who took notice, as they always did when Jews and Arabs showed amity. Sayeed strolled very slowly down narrow David Street with Dan at his side. It was less a stroll than a procession. As Sayeed passed through the cluttered gauntlet of Arab shopkeepers accustomed to abrasively hawking wares to all who passed within their midst, each demurred with a deferential *salaam aleikum.* In the tight, hectic confines of David Street, Sayeed's zone of respect extended to Dan, who received the same nod of deference from all they passed. At one point an Arab boy came crashing down the street with a cart of bread, screaming, "Allo! Allo!" expecting startled tourists to jump out of the way. As the boy approached on a collision course with Dan, he observed Sayeed, abruptly braked, perilously backed his cart into a stall selling scarves, and allowed the two men to slowly pass.

Halfway up the sloping stone walkway of David Street, on the right-hand side, barely visible amongst the hanging carpets, racks of cheap crucifixes and Jewish stars, camel carvings, and fake artifacts, stood a tiny stall barely big enough for three people to stand in. Sayeed graciously welcomed Dan within.

Dan had been in the Occidental Jewelry Shop many times. He first made Sayeed's acquaintance in the mid-1970s, after the Yom Kippur War, when Dan was on assignment and looking for voices of moderation within the Arab community. Sayeed was a former Jordanian minister, loyal to King Hussein, and a pillar of Jerusalem's Arab community. A caring family man and successful merchant, first he suffered through and survived the heel of the Israeli occupation and then endured the scorn of Palestinian militants who rejected his moderation. Each time Dan returned to Jerusalem, he met with Sayeed.

Now, as always, Dan verbally admired the many racks of Roman glass pendants, silver and gem earrings, delicate embroidered Bedouin-style vests, and ornamental beaten brass bracelets. Sayeed graciously accepted the compliments. The Arab man behind the counter was taken aback by Dan's brotherly appearance at Sayeed's side, but respectfully did not question it.

"You will have tea with *naana*?" offered Sayeed, as they sat on small stools.

It was rude to not accept what was offered, but Dan thought this one time he would ask for something different. "Could I have hot *zachleb?*" *Zachleb* was a heartwarming goat milk and coconut drink, reserved for cold winter mornings.

"Oh, it is too hot now," answered Sayeed. "No one makes it anymore. But okay. We shall have it." He whispered to the man behind the counter who obediently pulled out a cell phone, ringing up anyone in the Casbah who could quickly cook some *zachleb*. Sayeed pointed to two old-fashioned rotary phones plugged into the wall. "These two do not work," he said. "But mobile does. I have my own," he said, placing his phone on the glass countertop. Telephones were one of the things Old City Arabs could point to with pride. Theirs were as up to date as any the Israelis carried. Achieving equality even in cellular was an act of defiance. The other man's phone rang, he mumbled, and Sayeed assured, "*Zachleb* will yes be here. Very soon."

The two became engrossed in political discussion. Both men cherished their ability to overcome the great gulfs between them and speak honestly.

Dan, as usual, tried to discern the political leanings of the Arab community. "Everything is very bad now," said Sayeed. "There is no money for the shops. For anyone. They take many Juish taxes, so we close our stores to protest. Now there is very little." Sayeed conceded, "I have given up. We will exist. That is all. Just exist. It is very hopeless. Last night there was another incident on the *midrekhov*. A bomb I have heard."

"I was there," said Dan. "Actually, I'm the one who spoke to the guy face-to-face."

Sayeed was astonished. "You! You were the crazy American I heard about."

Dan confirmed it and the two delved back into intense discussion, first about the incident, and then more about the state of peace negotiations with Palestinians. They agreed there was nothing encouraging. "Too many people are hypnotized by the past," said Dan.

"Now the past is all we have to look forward to tomorrow," Sayeed agreed sadly.

There was good news, however. Sayeed's three sons, who had emigrated to Dearborn, Michigan, where they had established several thriving grocery stores, were now back to help the family through their latest economic crisis. Sayeed went to a display case, fingered past most of the items hanging, and found one exquisite piece of bruised green Roman glass set in hammered silver. "This one is real," said Sayeed. "For Jenny." Picking up a carved wooden dreidel, "And for your boy I have this."

For just an instant, Dan flinched and looked away. Sayeed noticed and reached for Dan. "My brother, what happened?"

"Jenny and Simon are gone," said Dan, tightening his face. He related a few details. Sayeed gripped Dan's arm in condolence. "They are with God," said Sayeed, pointing up with one hand. He spoke softly in Arabic to the other man. Both mouthed a quiet prayer.

"You will come to my home for dinner." Dan explained he had a friend with him, and her son. "They are *welcome*," he said with that accent and energy Jerusalem Arabs typically place on the word *welcome*. Dan became a little misty-eyed.

A little boy in torn clothes wearing plastic sandals rushed in with *zachleb* swinging from a bronze tray. Dan sipped the hot drink through the next moments of awkward silence.

"I'm going now to the *Kotel*," said Dan, finishing his drink and adding a traditional Arabic blessing "*Ma'a salaamah*."

"Dan, do you wish the Roman glass for your friend?" offered Sayeed.

"No," he answered, shaking Sayeed's hand. He took Sayeed's new business card with the cell phone number on it. "*Ma'a salaamah*."

Dan stepped out and strolled through the cramped Old City's side streets toward the *Kotel,* the Wailing Wall. He deliberately took the short cut, the one through alleyways and around corners where Jews *en route* had been knifed several times in recent weeks. People always spoke of the most recent knifings. Almost no Jews went this way any more. In case any Arabs had any doubts that he might just be a Christian pilgrim, Dan pulled a *yarmulke* from his back pocket. Now that Sayeed was not at his side, he stood out. He could feel the broiling contempt from Arab eyes as he passed their stalls jammed top to bottom with pots, pans, clocks, baskets, and skinned goats, hung from hooks dripping blood.

Unlike many Jews who preferred to look away from the hostile gaze, Dan looked each Arab in the face. No fear, no anger, just eye contact. Aware that he was vulnerable, he also imperceptibly scrutinized their hands, looking for sudden movements. On occasion, he stopped to examine a hanging scarf or carpet. Actually, he was checking over his shoulder. Dan felt that walking tall in the Old City, looking Arabs in the eye as human beings, was a duty for Jews.

At the checkpoint overlooking the Western Wall plaza, an Israeli soldier made a brief visual check, and then waved him in.

He walked down the steps and suddenly the magnificent white structure came into view: *HaKotel.* He approached and the closer he drew, the more he was enveloped in its awesome presence. The gleaming Second Temple stones towered over him, not just physically, but spiritually. He felt small. Wondrous cracks and crevices, each and every one a neural path to the Almighty, were, as always, crammed with small handwritten notes, personal prayers directly to the eyes of God, one squeezed atop another, like so many people pushing against a locked door to escape as the gas drifted down. Any Jew could peer into his soul at this place because every Jewish soul was stored here. Deep within these massive blocks dwelt the Jewish experience.

Dan looked to his left and right. Hassidic Jews within an inch of the Wall prayed in ecstatic cadence, rocking and twisting from side to side. Soldiers on leave, knitted *yarmulkes* atop their heads, their Galils and Uzis slung across their backs, peering over small prayer books, standing, as fighters before them had stood centuries ago, prayed for strength and forgiveness. A nondescript old man sauntered straight to the Wall, apprehensively touched his palm to it, uttered a short prayer, and walked away satisfied. Gaggles of Jewish tourists from Boston, New York, and Cleveland, donned cardboard *yarmulkes* provided at the gate; as they looked and tried to comprehend, not a few became sullen coming to grips with the enormity of what they did not understand. From this place, Jews had been expelled, and then decimated. Jews had to fight, splashing frenetically through their own pools of blood and destruction, just to once again stand humbly in the Wall's presence beneath the direct sight of the Holy One.

The Jewish Continuum is not linear. Its circle begins and concludes at this spot. A Jew cannot go forward without first returning.

A young, smooth-skinned Hassid approached Dan. "Do you want I should pray for you?"

"Money?" asked Dan.

"Not much, twenty shekel," answered the Hassid.

"Get away from me," Dan snarled with revulsion.

Condescendingly, the Hassid retorted, "Now I'll pray for you anyway . . . for free."

"Get a job," snapped Dan. As the Hassid walked away, he added, "Better yet, join the army." Instantly, regretting the outburst, Dan reached into his pocket for some prayer money, ready to apologize. But the Hassid had blended into the crowd. Now Dan was alone with his regret, actually hoping another pious man would approach. None did.

Dan stepped closer to the Wall. He could feel the magnetism. When he was just a few paces from it, Dan felt his chest moving irresistibly forward. His eyelids became weighted. Slowly his form touched the stones, first his body, then his outstretched arms, palms down, then his forehead. As though merging with its power, he gently rubbed his head to the right, over the stony texture until the ancient rock was flush with the side of his face. Then he asked the same question, the one question, he has asked all his life, each and every time he came to *HaKotel*.

"Why?"

Dan listened within.

It sounded like a piston cycling. Train wheels.

He listened again. Ground his head closer to the stone. Now he felt the continuous, deadly, swaying. One flattened hand curled into a fist. He pounded the wooden sides and squeezed his eyes shut.

EVERYTHING WITHIN WAS dark, illuminated this moonlit night only by the desperate eyes and drawn faces of dozens of petrified Jews who had been loaded into the boxcar. Most stood, some squatted if they could. A few could not help but lie on the floor, some in their own defecation.

The train sounded like a piston cycling. It swayed rhythmically as it sped toward Treblinka.

"I'm sorry," an old Polish Jew said softly as he became the latest in the car to soil his clothes. He had held himself for three hours, and now his frail body gave way. The added stench caused another woman to vomit, and the sounds of her aching heaves penetrated even the numbed souls among them.

A thin, twelve-year-old girl sat quietly on the floor, listening to the thudding rail ties, trying to understand the stream of terrible events befalling her family. First they lost their house in Bialystok. It was a nice home, a small garden, a fence around it. Nothing big, but a nice home for her and her brothers. Such a pretty white wooden fence, with flowers along the edge. Then the Germans came with papers moving them to the ghetto, to an apartment with six other families. Everyone was confused. So many terrifying rumors. Then several days ago, her father was taken away in the middle of the night. No one knew where. She and her mother could not avoid the aktion this afternoon. Everyone on her block, and the next block, and the next block after them, and many more from elsewhere in the ghetto, were all herded into wagons and driven to the train station. No one would explain. Maybe she could sleep now and get away from this nightmare. She wanted it to end.

Her mother nudged and whispered, "Don't fall asleep, Rivke. We know where this train is going. The Pollockis showed us," She ran her finger across her throat as she had seen several Polish farmers and children do just as the Jews were being loaded into the boxcars. Rivke did not understand.

"You're a skinny one, always a skinny one," her mother said patting her hair down as she anxiously eyed the tiny vent at the top of the boxcar. "Quickly, up there," she said suddenly. "Rivke, go through." Rivke looked at the dark vent outlined by moonlight. Her mother repeated urgently, "Quickly, I said."

Two men nearby helped. They pulled and pulled until the first wooden slats broke. Piece by piece, they yanked it in until the entire grille was off allowing a portal of escape.

"I can't get through that little opening," pleaded Rivke.

"You'll get through" said one of the men. "We'll push you."

"Use my towel," her mother said.

"Up now. Up!" they commanded, as they hoisted Rivke upon their shoulders. "One of us is getting out. So be the one." As the train rocked, the men lifted Rivke's legs through first, then forced her protruding hips, and pushed some more until she rested on her stomach, half in half out of the speeding boxcar. Her legs kicked in the wind as she looked down at her mother's determined face.

"We'll let you down slowly. Hold onto the towel," her mother said.

"I can't do this. I can't leave you," begged Rivke.

"Where I'll see you again, the Nazis can't touch us," her mother said bravely.

Rivke inched out of the vent and down the horizontal wooden slats of the boxcar's exterior until her elbows and then finally her wrists cleared. Now with one foot resting on an exterior bolt, and hanging onto the towel against the wind, Rivke cried out in terror, "Take me back up. I can't do it."

The men nodded to Rivke's mother.

"Get ready," her mother instructed. "When you hit the ground, run, Rivke, run. And tell someone. Tell someone what is happening."

"I can't do it! Pull me up!" Rivke screamed.

"Now or not!" the men shouted at her mother, "And we didn't help you if they ask." She released the towel.

Rivke went flying off the speeding train. Flesh tore from her knees as she slammed into the gravel along the siding, and then tumbled several feet. Dazed, she stood sensing but not feeling blood run down the side of her head.

Bullets flew around her as she ducked, then ran straight across the field to uncertainty beneath the August night. She looked back once and saw the moonlit train fading in the distance. Rivke strained to see the boxcar her mother was in. Nothing.

Everything behind her was gone. Everything in front of her was to be.

The field shed was to be. It was Rivke's world for months. She hid between the hay bales during the day, and didn't make a peep when the farmer came in. At night, she gathered what she could for food, once in a while garbage at the house when she could sneak up, but more often grass. She drank from the cows what she could. Sometimes milk, sometimes urine. Once the winter came, she drank snow. That was better. But she had to watch her steps outside when she buried her own waste. She spoke stories aloud to herself, initially so she could fall asleep, but eventually so she would remember she was human.

One day, a band of men came to the shed. "Jews in there, come out!"

She held still, afraid even to breathe. "We know you are there," they called from outside. "We're Jews going back to the ghetto to meet up with others."

The ghetto. Others. Oh yes, perhaps her father, her mother, one of her brothers, someone was back there. She fearfully crept from her hiding place in the corner of the shed with a direct view through the window. The four armed Armia Krajowa militiamen leading the group were not Jews, but they greeted her warmly. More than two dozen Polish Jews who been rounded up stood off to the side.

When she joined them, one woman gave her a crust of bread. "I'm giving you this," snapped the woman. "But you'll have to pay me back when we get to the ghetto. This is from me, remember." Rivke fearfully agreed, flaked off and tasted a piece, and then devoured it all. She washed it down with a fistful of snow.

As they marched through the snowy field, past the farmhouse, Rivke saw the family within. The woman came to the window and glared until her husband pulled her away. Rivke tried not to look.

For an hour the group walked, first on the road, and then along a trail deep into the woods. "We have to be careful," one of the militiamen assured the group. "Wait here until we check ahead. Sit, in a circle over there."

The Jews huddled on the ground for warmth and whispered amongst themselves. "Which A.K. group is this?" asked a man. "The one that hates the Germans, or the one that hates the Russians?"

"It's the one that hates the Jews," another chimed in.

"Thank God they came for us," a man said in defense of the soldiers. "I couldn't hold out this way much longer. Who cares who they hate?"

"There's still a price on our heads," one added. "Is it fifty pounds of sugar for one dead Jew? People said it. That's double three months ago."

Suddenly, bolt action was heard all around. The A.K. militiamen were back, aiming their rifles at the group. "Poland for the Polish!" one of the A.K. men muttered before spitting at the Jews. Without another word, the A.K. fired into the group from three directions. Over and over again. First Jews seated on the outside dropped, then the ones inside. Some squirmed to escape. But after the last volley, a militiaman lobbed a German potato masher grenade. It tore through the bleeding bodies of those not yet dead, finishing the job. Blood splattered all around the wintry ground.

It snowed again that night.

The next morning, two Jewish teenage forest fighters, Moishe and Yoshke, were walking through the woods, guns in their belts, duffel bags tied to their backs with yarn. They happened upon the dead Jews. For a moment they studied the murdered arms and legs protruding from the snow.

"Fools," said Moishe.

"A.K.?" asked Yoshke.

"No," said Moishe as he pulled up bits of bodies to estimate the number of dead. "Wait, maybe. Ah, look, a grenade was used," he said, fingering a piece of shrapnel in one victim's skull. "Like last week on the other side of the village. Yes, it's that same bunch. They say they are A.K."

"Who knows anymore, A.K., not A.K.?" replied Yoshke. "These are dead Jews."

"They didn't take the bodies to claim the reward, so maybe it's A.K.," answered Moishe. "Who buries them, me or you?"

"You do it," said Yoshke. "I'll look ahead."

Moishe scooped handfuls of snow atop the bodily rubble covering as much as possible. "Might need this," he said, removing a hat from one dead man and stowing it under his coat. He patted the snow in some places to form a mound.

"I'm not dead yet."

Moishe drew his gun and froze.

"Don't bury me, I'm not dead yet."

He scrambled over the corpses until he saw a slender but motionless thigh in the snow, its flesh ripped back to the buttocks by shrapnel as though torn by a monster's claw. Not far from that a finger moved within the carnage. Frantically, Moishe cleared the snow, pried away the dead man on top, and saw her eyes blinking.

"You spoke Yiddish," she moaned helplessly.

"Yes, yes. I'm Moishe," he said, pulling her away from the death.

"I'm numb. I can't feel anything."

"Okay, okay. Don't talk. I'm taking care of you now."

Gangrene was spreading across her thigh.

"There's no time. What's your name?" he asked to distract her as he brought a bottle of brandy and a straight razor out of his bag, and then unbuckled his belt. She told him, Rivke. *"Drink a touch,"* he instructed. *"Now bite on my belt."* He splashed brandy on the wound, blew off debris and cleared some away with his finger before deftly cutting the gangrene, then flinging the diseased flesh hatefully to the side. Rivke weakly murmured in pain and squeezed his arm, but did not move until he was finished. Then he gently packed the bleeding site with a clump of pig's fat retrieved from his bag, and then ice until the gushing stopped.

"Rivke, from now on, you're with me," assured Moishe, stroking her long brown hair. *"I'm taking care of you. Nazis, Pollockis, A.K.—leave them to me."*

Still shivering from the cold, she nodded, wondering what was happening.

"You need to trust someone," he went on as he propped her into a more comfortable position. *"That's me. No one else. Not even Yoshke up there. He'll be back in a second. If the Nazis catch him, they'll torture him and I promise you he'll bring them right to us. Understand?"*

She nodded.

He then pedantically explained the ways of survival in the forest. *"First, we don't move in a full moon. That's suicide. I've seen people die that way. If you do walk, step on trees, roots, stones. Hide your tracks. Second, we don't sleep any more than three nights in one place, then we move. Third, no groups. See,"* he pointed to the corpses, *"this is a group. They're dead. No groups. More than four is a group. Next, when you relieve yourself, walk far away in a zigzag and bury it. Never close by to where you sleep. I can walk two miles to pee. I don't care."*

She nodded.

He methodically replaced the razor and the brandy, after a sip. *"Don't eat everything when you get a piece of food. Not so fast. Tomorrow's another day. Don't trust farmers. They'll make a deal: you can clean up for food. Sure, until they decide they want the reward—then it's a bullet. Understand?"*

She nodded.

Yoshke could be seen returning in the distance. *"Now in a minute,"* Moishe continued, *"Yoshke will come back to tell us the road is clear, God willing. He'll be worried when he sees you. You say nothing. Not a word. I'll do all the talking. Understand?"*

Rivke hugged Moishe tightly. *"Not a word,"* she murmured, adding, *"You saved me. I'm never leaving you."*

"Good," answered Moishe, with a smile. "I'm not leaving you either. Any questions?"

"Maybe you can tell me why?" she asked, shaking her head.

"Why what?" asked Moishe. "Why I found you in a grave? Why am I even alive to find you? Why the Pollockis and the Nazis are trying to kill us? Why what?"

Rivke could not answer.

"Maybe we know," said Moishe, "we just don't know that we know."

Dan's fist disappeared, his hand flattened, and he leaned away from the Wall. Despite Jerusalem's sweltering sunshine, Dan's head felt iced. The faint odor of alcohol was somewhere nearby, but he couldn't sense where. He reached into his pants pocket, and extracted a Levincom business card. After tearing away the top, bottom, and sides of the card, all that was left was a tiny fragment printed with his name: DAN LEVIN. He flipped the fragment over, uncapped a pen, and wrote one word on it. Then he rolled it into a ball, kissed it, and pressed it into a crack.

11

THE GLOBAL INSTALL

"**W**e can't make it work," Motke conceded, as an Atara waitress brought *cafe hafuch.* "Everyone thought it would be over by Rosh Hashanah. I did."

Park stirred some sugar into her tea, and nodded in agreement. She methodically reviewed all the progress made on Ohr 2000. The millennium cure was made compatible with as many software platforms as anyone could identify. But every time Derek came close to compatibility with Windgazer itself, Hinnom released another update with slightly different API calls, many undocumented, causing Ohr 2000 to crash. As soon as Ohr 2000 was fixed to work with the new Windgazer rev, Windgazer changed once again.

"Yesterday, I heard that unless we can make Ohr foolproof," said Park, "Derek may disband the team. I don't know if it's a rumor or not. But it isn't the team's fault. It's Hinnom Computing. Business as usual. The API calls keep shifting. It's like changing the roads after we print the map. We just need to stay one step ahead of Bad Ben."

"I'm tired," yawned Motke. "I haven't been sleeping. I'd rather live under the cruel thumb of Ben Hinnom than lose any more sleep."

Dan appeared on the *midrekhov* carrying a falafel sandwich stuffed with more trimmings than anyone had witnessed in recent memory: chopped tomatoes and cucumbers, shredded lettuce, slices of bitter pickle, slivers of sumac-stained onions, brine peppers, two types of minced eggplant salad, all topped with drizzles of spicy red *hariff,* tangy green *skhug,* coarse beige *hummus* and silky white *tehina.* He joined the group at the Atara, jiggling the table as he sat down, causing the coffee and tea to spill.

"Is the sandwich big enough?" asked Park.

Motke stared in admiration. "I trust a man who can eat."

"I have been putting this off for months," responded Dan. "I'm pigging. I earned it." He successfully stretched his mouth over the packed pita as Park and Motke shielded their faces, expecting torrents of squished food splatter. Eyes closed, Dan chomped down, sinking his teeth into virtually every flavor variant in the sandwich. They watched in awe as a jagged circular section was subtracted from the original structure. He chewed a bit, swallowed with a loud tracheal sound, and then demonstratively washed it down with the remnants of her tea, the tea Park had worked so diligently to flavor with two types of mint and just the right amount of cube sugar, a skill that had taken her three months in Israel to master and that was now finally perfected in this one particular cup of tea before her. This was not how people broke bread in Kansas.

"Good work," congratulated Motke.

"It's not the view of God that separates Christians and Jews," jabbed Park. "It's the view of food." Neither Motke nor Dan understood. Park ordered another tea to start again.

"I'm entitled," said Dan. "While you guys have been busy saving the world, I'm making significant headway on the Ben book. The web search I launched in Chicago was a gem. Things got dicey as I followed up. But the book is now all completely outlined and I can start writing chapters. In total, I found nineteen candidates of really severe criminal conduct creating an identifiable pattern. Nineteen cases."

"You told me sixteen," interjected Park.

"I had sixteen, but three more, Asian stuff, panned out in the end."

"This is the secret book you won't talk about?" asked Motke.

"It's not a big secret, but it's an investigation in progress. So this is not to go beyond the *midrekhov.*"

Motke looked at the crowds. "The several thousand people around us are all sworn to secrecy."

"Right," continued Dan, eager to summarize his progress. "So I have these nineteen horror stories of continuing criminal conduct by Ben Hinnom in the accretion of his fortune and construction of his empire.

Not just commercial takeovers, theft of software, infringement deals—
chalk those shenanigans up to cutthroat business. I mean the *real* evil stuff,
in the category of Rosie's death and Hector's death."

"John Hector?" Motke perked up. "I'm listening."

"You're listening and not repeating, right?" Dan underscored.

"Yes, yes. I'm all ears and no tongue," assured Motke.

Park leaned forward to hear the details as well.

"I kept running into web sites where some outraged or beat-down victim or relative of a victim would post an incredible accusation against
Hinnom. Ten years ago, this stuff would have been buried in a file drawer. Today, the Internet can turn a little dissatisfaction into global news in
minutes. There were hundreds of anti-Hinnom sites, but I isolated these
nineteen hot cases.

"Get this," said Dan, leaning closer. "In several cases, I find good stuff
on Hinnom at a web site. A few days later I go back to check for an
update—the page is black, shut down, site moved. I had one site in Japan,
some outfit called PacRim Human Justice Group. One of their activists
was investigating this island Ben Hinnom bought lock, stock, and
seashore in the Pacific. He gathered children—or should I say purchased
them—from Thailand, Africa, Indonesia. Now he's breeding them into
some sort of slave race or human guinea pig collective. One of the nurses
on the project went crazy altogether. During a supply trip to Tokyo, she
ran off and contacted PacRim. One day her story is on the web, huge nar-
rative exposing all. A few days later, the site says PacRim has merged with
Micronesian Public Medical Alliance and its site is being reconstructed. I
can't find squat on Micronesian Public, whoever they are. Fortunately, I
downloaded the nurse's story the second I spotted it. But PacRim itself is
gone. Vanished."

"This is one of the Asian things?" asked Park.

"Asia is just the beginning. The list is long and odious," answered Dan.
Holding up fingers to tabulate each crime, he started with two. "Let's start
with the death of Rosie, now add the death of Hector." He raised a third
finger. "Add a building inspector who halted work on Ben's house because
construction exceeded the permit. This man is blinded with glass fragments in the eye when his computer monitor explodes in his face. His
office records and the permit originals disappear. Then an amended permit is suddenly issued. Construction resumes. I know monitors can

explode, people get blinded. But if you're an enemy of Hinnom, the odds go up.

"There's more. Two lawyers sued Hinnom Computing on separate but similar infringement cases. It was early nineties. Very pivotal litigation. Megamillion-dollar stuff. One day, this Boston attorney finds that $3 million in client funds awaiting settlement on another case has been transferred to a mysterious bank account in Liechtenstein which gets wired back in six-digit increments to this Boston lawyer's personal bank account. It's discovered. How? In a sudden audit by the IRS. The Boston attorney swears he knows nothing about the money, that he is being framed, grants interviews to the *Boston Globe*, goes super public. But he is dismissed as a nut job. The law firm is broken up, the attorney is now in federal prison at Allentown on embezzlement, money laundering, and criminal tax evasion.

"And surprise," continued Dan ominously. "A very similar thing happened to the second attorney in Austin, Texas. He too embezzles money–this time from the law firm itself. He too denies it. He too is now doing federal time. The two infringement cases were dropped when Hinnom lawyers swooped in with dismissal motions during the chaos. These guys never connected their misfortune to Hinnom. But I do."

Dan held up two more fingers, showing all five.

"I'm not gonna list it all now," he continued, "because that's the book. Isn't it amazing, though, how this man's enemies–real or perceived–end up ruined, framed and sent to prison, or dead? And yes, I have more dead bodies. Not just Rosie and Hector. Dig the timing: Hinnom's accountant for years offers to cooperate with tax auditors; he dies of E. coli from a bad hamburger three days before the auditors arrive. A wrinkled, old geezer swears that as long as he lives he won't sell the very land Building 6 now sits on. No problem. He dies of electrocution trying to fix his TV. Hello Building 6."

"So who's going to stop this person?" asked Park, shaking her head in disgust.

"Not Congress," snapped Dan. "Everybody seated? Senator Eltz . . ."

". . . Who is Senator Eltz?" Motke asked quietly.

"Senator Eltz," answered Dan, tossing his magnificent half-eaten falafel sandwich in a nearby trash can, "is the man on Judiciary who stood up to Ben Hinnom. He was America's last chance to stop the Hinnom monopoly by forcing Webgazer's Internet hegemony out of Windgazer 99."

"So?" said Park.

Dan wiped his hands on a napkin, and pulled from his back pocket a folded page of the morning _Jerusalem Post_. Pointing to a small wire story at the bottom, Dan summed it up: "Eltz committed suicide late yesterday at his boyhood home in North Carolina. Hung himself in the barn. The article says, 'A rambling suicide note talked about haunting childhood memories.' Notice: it says the suicide note was not handwritten, but computer typed and of course unsigned. Suicides always sign their notes. I almost signed one myself once. Trust me, the Judiciary Committee will be in disarray over Eltz's death and adjourn for the elections in November. Windgazer 99, here we go."

"I don't believe what I have heard here," said Motke.

"I will crush his balls!" Dan barked, slamming the table. People turned to look around. Dan quieted himself. "You think I'm afraid of this faggot-ass killer nerd? He will fall. The evidence is scant. Admittedly. Each and every case has been covered up. Admittedly. And I can't investigate all these cases, solve them all, and make my book deadline. I could do it if I had the time. No problem. I mean, it would take a year. But I don't have that. So it's the art of the possible. The book is now called _The Hinnom Curse: Deadly Luck or Deadly Deeds_. The object is to raise all these issues, line them up in a neat row before the world—this string of heinous coincidences—and let the public react. I already sent a fax to my editor, Steeples."

"I'm not believing this," insisted Motke, but preempting Dan, he quickly reassured, "and of course I'm not repeating what I'm not believing." He reflected a moment, "Okay, why not? Maybe I _do_ believe it."

"Hey, it's a great book," said Park cautiously, a frightened look descending upon her face. "But do you think for one minute that the Hinnom you have uncovered will let you get away with this? He could turn on you, Dan."

"You think I can't handle this guy?" countered Dan. "I've been threatened by experts: the CIA, the mob, a combination of both, powerful senators, taxi hoodlums, the Klan. Worry for Hinnom, not for me. You guys at Derek can futz all you want with Ohr this and Ohr that. Windgazer 99 is probably gonna ship. He has you beat. But I tell you, that software ships and the world becomes enslaved to Hinnom. We will all be on life support and his hands will be on the plug. He will have the power. We already know he believes Windgazer transcends governments, transcends languages, transcends borders, and functions as a law and authority unto itself. Ben says that openly. You know, 'Software is the Great Equalizer.' But hear me, when he is ready he'll be able to destroy whole societies. Motke, look at your shirt. Time *is* running out.'"

Dan's eyes stung as though he were running through a field of fire and smoke. "Everything has been taken from me," he blistered. "My wife–I loved her so much. I'm empty without her. My wonderful son–bless his innocent heart–he's waiting on me to justify myself so I can get where he is. My fortune, my magazines, my career. All crashed and burned. So I have what left? Nothing . . . nothing but money I don't need and opportunities I refuse to pass. Maybe I've stumbled across an opportunity now that no one has ever faced. I have gone against bad guys and bastards, but never one like this. I honestly believe I have a chance to save the world from this monster."

Park tried to calm him down. "I didn't mean you lacked–"

Dan kept boiling over. "You think God let my mother squeeze out of a boxcar on the way to Treblinka and my father pull her frozen body . . ."

". . . Settle down . . ." whispered Park, looking around at those turning their heads.

". . . pulled her from the snow, dead–but she wasn't. You think any of that happened without a reason?"

A somewhat distressed waitress stepped in. "Anything wrong? I can get you something?"

"Nothing, I'm fine," snapped Dan, turning back to Motke and Park. "They didn't survive the shooting pit, the train, the woods, Pollock militiamen, and Hitler to raise a son who wasn't going to stand up to a maniac trying to do with data and digits what a hundred dictators before him were unable to accomplish with bullets and bombs."

"Sir," the Atara's disquieted manager said. "If you are done, please pay the bill and give up the table to others who are waiting."

"Get your paw off my arm," snarled Dan. He turned back to Motke and Park. "Is that why they survived, so I could lack courage when the world is on the brink? Is that *why?*" He squinted, saw the *Kotel,* and made a tight fist.

MOISHE APPEARED NOT far from the dugout where they were hiding. He was carrying a thirty-pound pig around his shoulders. "Rivkele, this runt of the litter will last us a week if we keep it cold," he said, heaving it to the ground.

"A pig again," observed Rivke, nodding regret. "We need to ask forgiveness. My father told us—"

"Ask forgiveness after we eat," Moishe cut her off. "This is what I could find. So yes, pig again. It's only the third time."

Moishe and Rivke had hidden in many places during the past two years. This cave had been home for almost a week, longer than Moishe felt safe. But they were both so tired of moving. He looked around for a flat place a distance away from their hideout to prepare the feast. "That way," he pointed. "There, by the stream. See?" He hoisted the pig back over his shoulders and trekked in a circular path to the spot. Rivke followed him with the one bowl, one spoon, one fork, and two rags that constituted their marital property.

At the spot near the stream, Moishe began slicing the carcass. Rivke grimaced as he casually peeled away the animal's hide and carved large sheaves of pink muscle which he hung on nearby branches. As he did, he explained with a bit of defensiveness, "I can't ask for chickens when I'm offered a pig. They'll know I'm a Jew. I have blond hair, so I can come to the farmers like any A.K. Pollocki. What do they know? This Jew-hater from the farm thinks I got lost running from the Russians. I worked three mornings stacking his bags. He offered the sickly pig before it dies and I took it. Period."

Rivke burrowed with her fingers, burying the offal from sight, and demured, "I'm not complaining." She washed her hands with water from the stream, shook them dry, and busied herself with the cut meat.

"I heard something today," said Moishe as he gathered nearby sticks for the fire. "I've heard this before, but this time I think maybe it's true. So listen. The Pollocki at the farm heard from some Russians that the Russian Army is inside Berlin. Berlin itself. Also the American Army. The Pollocki heard the same thing from BBC shortwave. He has a radio. They said the War is . . ."

Rivke looked up expectantly.

". . . maybe the War might be over."

"Oy, Moishe." She broke into tears, looking around to see if anyone was about. "My father, my mother. My brothers. Can we find them?"

"We're finding no one for now," said Moishe. "Not from your family, not from mine. Here's the plan. Number one, we do nothing. Eat the pig, survive another night, and then nothing. I'll wait a few more days, go back to the farm,

and then maybe into the village. If it's okay, we'll take a little chance and try to blend in. Go somewhere. Who knows where? I'm sure my little town of Chowsk is no more a town. They took everyone in trucks to be shot. So we can't go back there."

"Bialystok?" asked Rivke.

"Get it straight," he answered. "Bialystok Ghetto is finished. All the ghettos are finished. Who didn't die in the ghetto, died in the camps. Who didn't die in the camps, died in the woods from the A.K. or other Jew-killers. After two years, I'm sure Yoshke is dead. I'm sure. I told him not to go with a group. But he went."

"So there are no more Jews?" asked Rivke.

"Jews are finished," he insisted. "The world wanted them dead—and they are dead. Millions. Everywhere. Those that did not die, decided not to be Jews anymore. Because why should they? Jews are finished."

"So what are we?" asked Rivke.

"We?" replied Moishe. He looked at the ground, at the trees and then into Rivke's eyes. "We stay Jews. Just us two. We're it, Rivkele. In a few days, God should grant, we will walk out of these woods to the main road and meet up with people. Pollockis, Russians, I don't know. They will be Christian, Catholic, whatever. But we will not be like them. We will stay Jews. I don't believe in all your nonsense with blessing this and blessing that. You know that already so it's not news. But if there is a God, the same God who turned from us during this terrible time, then this is also the same God that allowed us for some reason to survive.

"Ask yourself why?" said Moishe painfully, trying to look away as his eyes became moist. "Why did the Nazis, and the Polish, and the Russians—all these bastards everywhere in Hungary, Rumania, I can't name them all—why did they try so hard to kill our people? Why did God save us two pisherkees when he let so many millions die? Your family, my family—all the towns and ghettos. So, if they tried that hard to kill us, and God tried that hard to save us, we, Rivkele, must be special. We—who knows—might be the last Jews on Earth. If we are, so then we are. We will walk out of the forest as Jews, and stay alive—as Jews— waiting for whatever is in front of us."

Rivke hugged Moishe tightly, wiping her streaming tears on his shoulder, and murmured, "Why, why, why? Why did these black black things happen to us?"

Moishe looked off and shrugged. "We know—we just don't know that we know."

Dan unsquinted and his fist disappeared. A policeman came over. "It's a problem? You are making a noise," he stated.

"No, it's not a problem. I'm just talking to my *hevre,* explaining a few things about a maniac I have to bring down," he replied. The policeman waited for Dan to return to normal, and then moved away.

"Dan," said Park softly. He did not respond.

"Dan?"

"Don't give me *Dan* like I'm a nut," he reacted. "I'm no nut. *Why* you ask? I'll tell you why! I see it. I really do. Everything with a purpose. The *why* will reveal itself–and soon." Park and Motke paused for a moment and both thought back to a comment Sal made months before.

"Okay. Okay," said Motke. He motioned to the waitress to bring a round of *turki.* "Dan, you do your thing with the book, and I'll do mine with the software. I wasn't supposed to release this yet. Park, you are half right. Derek's international programming group is disbanding, going back to their homes. But I'm sure Derek will keep me on the project until Windgazer 99 actually ships. And the Israeli guys are not going any place in any event. So for me, Ohr 2000 stays alive."

"I'm not going any place either," added Park.

"I thought you said only six weeks," asked Motke. "It's already been double that."

"Dan and I have talked it out," said Park, speaking for both of them. "We will stay if . . . if Derek wants me and can pay my per diem."

"The Dan Pearl is racking up quite a tab," added Dan, "but we're looking for an apartment. Sal can either take some time off or enroll at one of the universities, maybe Tel Aviv. Frankly, he's been on his secret Y2K program. Not a word on it. And I think he'll be happy with that till Kingdom Come."

"Might be sooner than any of us think," Motke offered.

"Can't argue," replied Dan. "Point is, I see no reason to leave Israel. To finish my Hinnom book I can fly back to America once or twice like other foreign writers. That's why they have airplanes. Park wants to stay. Where do I need to go?"

"I'm here," she confirmed. Motke patted her hand in approval. "Okay, we stay a team," she promised. "Sal can stay holed up with the Windy. My thought is we need to wait for Windgazer to finally ship. Grab the code the best we can, get compatible with the latest API, wait for it to fail, and zoom in–no pun intended–with Ohr 2000."

"But who knows when this guy will ship," warned Motke. "For Hinnom, the later the better, the less choice people have. Correct?" He pointed to the message on his T-shirt.

"That's his style," agreed Dan.

"All his ship dates have slipped," said Motke. "Fall was the big time that he originally advertised. You see it, Rosh Hashanah is in a few days and nothing will happen. He's blaming your Justice Department. So I expect him any minute to announce that Hinnom Computing will ship at the end of 1998–not before."

"Okay. More time for us to prepare," said Park matter-of-factly. "But I frankly wonder if he will be even later than that. Sal said he tapped into a Hinnom internal development site with his Windy and one schedule said next summer. He tried a second time and the schedule was gone. Now he's not sure."

"Summer '99? That late?" asked Dan.

"He's done this so many times," replied Park. "Vaporware is his specialty. Competition can't develop because they are waiting for him to ship on a given Monday. But a hundred Mondays pass and he never does. Can you move your book up a few months to coincide with his ship date?"

"Never," said Dan. "Publishing is slow. Distribution takes months."

"So," said Motke, "we wait. We work and we wait."

"We wait," Park and Dan toasted, clicking coffee demitasses.

ON THE EIGHTH day of the sixth month of the year 1999, on a day when wind could not be felt and birds could not be heard; when doldrums silently deadened the seas; when 144 whales beached themselves on a California coast; when a band of vicious monkeys attacked tourists at a Japanese resort village; when vultures swooped down and killed a herd of sheep in the Scottish highlands; when ants everywhere invaded homes and offices and swarmed into the shoes of those who walked; when spontaneous rainforest fires in Mexico and Malaysia billowed thick smoke across the world, blotting out the sun; when deranged high school students in six American rural towns without warning shot their teachers and classmates; and when rats in many places crawled out of their filthy holes to stand fearlessly on their hind legs; on this black day, at noon Pacific Savings Time, Windgazer 99 shipped.

Operation Dark Wind began. Shiny gold master CDs in special static-free pouches were couriered to computer manufacturers around the world so Windgazer 99 could be blown into new PCs on the assembly line. Boxes of already-built units were gingerly opened and utility devices attached to CPU serial ports, allowing the new Windgazer to overwrite the old version. Installation completed only when the words *Screen Saver Enabled* appeared.

Special 72-hour transmission sites were set up across the Internet, allowing leading computer retailers to download copy-protected versions into store inventory. One by one, units were brought to the repair desk and plugged into T-1 lines for the vital transmission. Sales associates eagerly watched and welcomed each appearance of *Screen Saver Enabled*. CD pressing plants throughout the world began stamping product. Hundreds of thousands of Windgazer 99 copies rolled out hour after hour. Jewel cases fitted with disks were stacked at boxing stations, stuffed, and sent along for stickering. At the end of the conveyer belts, minimum wage piece workers grabbed six of the black and yellow boxes at a time, methodically filling transit pallets. Completed pallets were forklifted to loading dock aprons, then transferred into semitrailers boasting large yellow and black Windgazer 99 promo stickers.

Bypassing distribution warehouses, the trucks were dispatched directly to retail centers. As the semis rolled into parking lots, consumers who had camped out overnight cheered the arrival. Managers cordially met drivers at the entrance offering handshakes, sometimes a cold beer, not infrequently a bottle of champagne. Local TV crews in many cities recorded the event. Newscameras ceremoniously followed the cargo through the front door as frenzied users pushed and shoved to get theirs. Holding the precious box in their hands, all gleefully read the instructions: "Type install. Installation is completed when you see the words *Screen Saver Enabled*."

Users in countries everywhere logged onto consumer web sites to begin several hours of downloads so their computers could ingest the new operating system. LAN and WAN administrators downloaded the network version into their servers, preparing to systematically update connected clients throughout the enterprise. Mainframe managers typed in the codes allowing their systems to integrate the OS, sector by sector, on the fly. As the long, tedious download proceeded some busied themselves with other work. But most watched, some with excitement, some with suspicion. The sectors hypnotically counted down, one by one, as the system read once, then verified. Installation completion occurred when the words *Screen Saver Enabled* appeared.

Computers were only the beginning.

Small yellow and black boxes, nicknamed "the Gazer Phaser," were velcroed to the backs, fronts, sides, and underbellies of electronic gear of all sorts: VCRs, medical equipment, cockpit instrumentation, telephone switches, missile launch consoles, automobiles, bank vaults–any electronic device operating off microchips or microcontrollers with date and year references. Such devices did not work with monitors or keyboards, but they were computers nonetheless, and vulnerable to Y2K. The yellow and black boxes emitted RF signals with Year 2000 time-date emulation. Even people and companies with devices that did not require them velcroed "Gazer Phasers" to every device in sight–what the heck–purchasing them by the fistful as though they were batteries to be hoarded before the storm. Some hung them from doorways like cloves of garlic to announce their office was Windgazer-compliant.

Room by room, device by device, network by network, the world was systemically converted to Windgazer 99. Numbers continuously flowed into the Hinnom Computing War Room in Seattle. Each country was listed on a giant score board with ever-increasing percentages reporting the level of national installation.

Brazil 18% . . .
China 31% . . .
France 39% . . .
United States 51% . . .

As the hours passed, the percentages became larger and larger.

Brazil 26% . . .
China 61% . . .
France 69% . . .
United States 82% . . .

Hinnom employees watched in jubilation, cheering every tenth million in total installation. Special toasts of champagne were raised when a national score rolled to 100 percent of target.

Argentina 100% . . .
Germany 100% . . .
Morocco 100% . . .

After the third day and night, it was done. The Global Installation was over. The world belonged to Windgazer 99.

It rained. Hinnom screensavers appeared before the eyes of the Earth. An email to all at Derek read: "We have lost. The world is in a Dark Wind. But I beseech you. Return to your computers. Operation Ohr continues." The Shabbos Rebbe felt something strange; he pulled a thin, never-opened leather-bound volume from his stacks; his eyes opened in tearful amazement as he read the words and began fervently chanting, quietly at first–then loudly. Raymond opened a travel brochure and admired the pictures. His mother gently said, "It's the chance of a lifetime." Park took Dan's hand, smiled through tears, squeezed and finally admitted, "We're not even close to stopping Windgazer." Dan turned from his Butterfly, stroked her hair. Sal began punching furiously on his Windy: error, try again, error, try again, error. In Building 6, both doors burst open as Ben Hinnom swaggered onto the balcony outside his executive office. Spreading his arms, he gripped the air with such ferocity that blood vessels in his arms bulged. The tension visibly traveled through his shoulders and neck and then flowed into his fiery eyes. Suddenly his right hand shot straight up at the blackened clouds. The Shabbos Rebbe stopped praying, Sal connected, the Kotel seemed to shake.

With his finger pointed at the Father, Hinnom slowly bellowed: "I don't need you anymore!"

12

THE POINT NINE
UPDATE

*D*iane sat in shock in front of her computer at the Social Security Administration in Baltimore. She refused to touch a key. Tears welled in her eyes. Transfixed, she reached out to press her finger against the screen. Unable to hold back another moment, she asked aloud, "Mother, why did you leave me?"

Chuck, a twelve-year-old, slammed his backpack to the floor after another trying day at Marshall Middle School in Houston. He powered up the newly updated computer in his bedroom, eager to surf the net. Twice he shook his head in disbelief, but the image was still there—his own face superimposed over a view of the cosmos. "Du-ude!" he exclaimed. He hit a key to bring up email, but the screen saver vanished. "Hey, how do I get it back?"

Maureen worked as a claims adjuster in Ft. Lauderdale and lived alone in a three-room apartment overlooking gardens. In her solitary existence, she quietly cultivated roses as personal friends. She grew them in the garden and in window boxes outside her bedroom. Although she loved pale pink Kalinkas, true white Escimos and shocking orange Lambadas, bold reds were her favorite. To Maureen's vivid imagination, reds suggested dashing visitors and grandiose palace events. But she kept her fascination with flowers to herself. That's why she was amazed when she clicked on her office monitor to find her screen magically filled with an abundance of roses, wonderful red roses: dark Cara Mias and bright Kardinals.

Who knew? Who did it?

Mark smirked, looked over his shoulder nervously, blocked the screen from room view, and then tittered with prurient satisfaction. He hit his intercom button and called a coworker, "Hey, pal. Come on, check this out. My Windgazer 99 screen saver is a picture of an awesome bitch with humongous knockers. I can't believe it . . . You do? . . . Ice cream? How come you have ice cream and I have the bitch babe?"

A car dealer in Cleveland Heights enjoyed his favorite scenes from *Star Wars*. A military inventory specialist in Philadelphia beheld a stunning view of Fisher's Monument from his home town near Moab, Utah. A teacher in Los Angeles who loved dogs saw toy terriers playing. A medical assistant in Boise looked in awe as a photograph of her recently deceased brother appeared.

Windgazer 99's screen saver had something special for everybody. Two weeks after the system was installed, the visuals suddenly began switching on. Automatically generated by the operating system and individualized for each user, the screen saver graphics appealed not just to simple preferences, but to deep-seated desires, regrets, and joys. Windgazer 99's Advanced Monitor Protocol used existing computer marketing technology, but stapled together and refined in a way never before dared.

First, the AMP sniffed the user's hard drive for words, phrases, icons, and even graphics. Then it searched the Internet browser's history of accessed web pages. Gathered hard drive and web access information was added to a long list of individual preferences and personal data, including social security number, solicited in the Windgazer 99 registration process. Those who completed the questionnaire were assured that their name would be entered in a million-dollar Hinnom lottery; registrants were told that the winning entry would be disqualified if data could not be verified, thus promoting honest responses. The General User Profile that emerged from registration and drive-sniffing was just the beginning. That information was then subjected to datamining in Hinnom's vast databanks, which yielded a complex, highly detailed User Personality Profile. User Personality Profiles were first submitted to standard personality tests and then linked to existing data warehouses on referenced people, places, topics, and events. Utilizing the same principles perfected in robot web searches and the cookie-based personalized Internet responses, Windgazer 99 manufactured a highly emotional screen graphic calculated to captivate—one individual at a time.

The system was hardly infallible. A Pittsburgh chemist who enjoyed Kentucky bluegrass was amused to suddenly see a tub of Kentucky Fried Chicken on his screen saver. Scores of Lutheran scholars across America giggled when they saw photos of Martin Luther King, Jr., appear. And more than one lover of Dimitri Shostokovich's music was treated to picturesque views of Mt. Shasta. Initially, the screen savers did not have the syntax depth to operate in languages other than English, although multilingual protocols were in the works.

For most English-speaking users, Windgazer 99 traveled far beyond just an operating system. It became an engaging extension of self, a software amalgam people could closely identify with, making their computer more than just an inanimate device to be fought, but rather a friend to be confided in. Friendship itself became a feature. User-friendly. Very friendly.

Screen savers were just the beginning. Windgazer 99 soon began generating likeable, impish cartoon characters with names pegged to the screen saver theme. Diane's "Mom" closely resembled the woman she remembered. Larry's cosmos graphic created "Venus." Mark's soft porn babe yielded a scantily clad voluptuous "Hot Babe." Maureen's flower-adorned screen offered a petal-shaped figure named "Blossom." All these characters did the same thing, they solicited secrets—just in fun, of course, as a stress releaser, of course, but secrets nonetheless. Some of the confessions were spoken into microphone-equipped PC systems, but most were typed in as journal entries. Ostensibly, any entry could be erased at the click of a button, and so all these playful entries were widely considered safe and private. But as many computer advisers had always warned, computers never truly erase, they merely corrupt the first letter of the entry, making it unrecognizable, or move the file to a trash directory. Either way, information in deleted files could be easily undeleted with a few keystrokes.

Sure, the chemist who liked Kentucky bluegrass couldn't help but laugh when an animated piece of fried chicken dubbed "Deep Wing" would waltz onto the screen and chirp, "Hey! What's for dinner tonight?" or "Hey! What didn't you have for dinner last night that you really, really wanted?"

But for most users, the characters became quite serious. Many people developed bizarre cathartic relationships with their screen buddies. "Come on," Hot Babe would seductively urge. "What naughty thing did you do today to someone you know, to your wife, or maybe to yourself? You can tell me." Mark would confess the most intimate details. When he did, he felt good, and looked forward to the next encounter. Soon, he imagined that his acts of dishonesty and infidelity were, in a sense, "cleansed" by the screen. He could commit outrageous deeds now with moral impunity, confess, and repeat them again with even greater boldness.

For Maureen, Blossom's floral-looking character would sometimes be the most encouraging presence of the day. "People just don't understand," Blossom would sympathetically declare. "What happened today?" Maureen would happily confide the latest. Not infrequently, she would not touch the keyboard for eleven minutes six seconds, the time needed for an undisturbed Windgazer 99 to revert to screen saver. If there wasn't time to access Blossom, Maureen would feel forlorn, cheated, even desperate. Once during a power outage, she railed at the office manager. "Get the power up, I need Blossom."

Quickly, more than a few objected to Windgazer 99's screen saver. Corporate managers complained that productivity had dropped because users were constantly allowing their computers to go stagnant for eleven minutes six seconds, thus allowing the screen saver to appear. Parents objected because their children were becoming hypnotized. Spouses protested about their mates' saver, but fought jealously to retain their own.

For three dollars per unit, Hinnom Computing offered to mail, within thirty days, a disabling diskette that would terminate the screen saver. But that meant cost, inconvenience, and delay. Many, especially companies with thousands of stations, chose to tolerate the silliness. Protesters who threatened litigation were warned that their periodic modem refreshes would be blocked, unleashing built-in software timebombs that were restrained only by the updates. Without those updates, their systems would be useless and their data would be lost. Supposedly.

Windgazer 99 machines seemed secure and isolated, but in fact they were all very much connected. Periodically, generally during the middle of the night, phone-connected machines would dial out to Hinnom Central in Seattle, which routed the calls by satellite to the nameless

Pacific island Hinnom had purchased. Once connected, user machines would regularly download the latest fixpacks, device drivers, diagnostics, and virus inoculations needed to optimize their systems. But they would also back up the entire drive, storing the data in broad petatowers arrayed in a massively configured "storchard" on an island hilltop. Each petatower, the size of twenty filing cabinets, hosted more than ten thousand advanced 100 gigabyte drives. As such, Hinnom's storchard was capable of storing all the information in all the computers possessed by all of mankind. A second storchard of petatowers was on the drawing board should the island's storage infrastructure need expansion. In essence, a mirror image of nearly every computer on earth was in Hinnom's control.

Tall red walls lined the corridor in a special research wing of Building 6. Hinnom, dressed in a blowsy black shirt and pants, walked briskly across the bright crimson like a shadow flitting between approaching headlights. He stopped at a black doorway marked "I.T." He placed his left fingers and palm onto the recognition system. It scanned his hand. The LED display flashed: "Welcome B. Hinnom. Please complete steps 2 and 3 to enter I.T. area."

Hinnom slid his security card into the swiper, then punched a code into the pad. He waited for the heavy black door to click open. It did not. "Processing Approval. Please Wait." appeared on the LED display. Bobbing his head rhythmically to kill time, Hinnom at first playfully focused on the flashing "Processing Approval. Please Wait." But his patience soon disappeared. Hinnom finally yelled out and slugged the door, "Hey, let me in, dammit!" No answer. He kicked it several times and then beat on it. "This is Ben Hinnom. Open the damn door! Open the damn door, dammit!"

A moment later the black door to the lab crept open. A shaved head peered out, and, as he recognized Hinnom, quickly deferred, "Oh . . . oh . . . come on in, Mr. Hinnom."

"I've been *trying* to come in," Hinnom sighed sarcastically. "Did *you* program this silly security thingee?"

"No, no, no. That would be security," the shaved head blabbered.

"Yes. Security," droned Hinnom. He pulled out his Windy, popped it open, typed a short email to Linzer and with a ceremonious downward press of his finger sent it hurtling on its electronic way.

Switching schizophrenically to effervescence, Hinnom exclaimed, "So, how is the I.T. Department? On schedule?" He began touching everything in sight: the computers, synthesizers, scanners, strobes, and oscilloscopes stacked chaotically atop one another, all the cables connecting everything, and even floppy drives hanging like so much ornamentation from half-dismantled CPUs. All of it was controlled by a series of digital consoles and Hinnom was sure to touch each of those as well.

"Almost, almost," the shaky shaved head replied, then nodded. "Sure, almost right there on schedule."

Hinnom's face became serious, and one eyebrow raised. "Just tell me we'll have the *right temp,*" Hinnom demanded darkly.

"Eventually. Yes. Soon," the shaved head nervously corrected.

"Question, question, question!" asked Hinnom in an overly dramatic voice. "Can you give me the *right temp* by the target date?"

"Everything will begin uploading end of year," the shaved head haltingly confirmed, "and should complete by January 5 or 6 in the year 2000, after the long weekend. Sure . . . Uh, it's not going to be 100 percent, Mr. Hinnom. It's just too new . . . too diverse a target population. But," he choke-laughed, "it will be impressive."

"Impressive?" parodied Hinnom, adding, "How about *effective.* Because if I have to chose between *impressive* and *effective* . . . I'll take *effective* any day. You see, if it's *effective,"* he paused, "it automatically becomes *impressive.* Okay?" He smiled broadly. "You have my email address. Ping if you need me."

He turned with a flourish, walked out of the lab, vaguely noticed the still flashing "Processing Approval. Please Wait." on the LED display as he passed, and then hustled back down the red corridor from whence he came, his fast-moving black form marked by sleeves flapping behind him.

The shaved head peeped out of the I.T lab, blinked several times, made sure his boss was really gone, and returned to his work chamber.

THE WORLD WAS divided. Many saw Windgazer 99 as a great advance for humanity. Hinnom Computing's software seemed to fix the Y2K crisis, provided periodic overnight updates with the latest improvements and antiviral protection, and, of course, the screen savers were a wonderful toy. But many saw the accretion of all this technologic power into the hands of a single man and the corporation he dominated to be a threat in and of itself. They were appalled at the involuntary overnight refreshes. The Justice Department, the Senate, a consortium of state attorneys general, the European Union, Japanese regulators, and indeed all of them working in concert were unable to rein in Hinnom. Now, through Windgazer 99's command and control of the computers of the world, Hinnom had more authority and dominion than any one person in history. Hinnom reveled in it.

He swaggered in and out of his office, flipped light switches with bravado, drank tall glasses of pineapple juice with a ceremonious tilt of the head, drove his sports car even more recklessly, spit with accuracy into potted plants around the building. Sometimes Hinnom would just stop and shiver from all the power he now wielded.

Linzer, never far from his side, would occasionally try to moderate his master's delight by frankly reminding him, "One day we will encounter the stone."

Hinnom would cackle and sing song, "The stone, the stone, the stone. Get me the *right temp*. I'll handle the stone."

Linzer would reply, "I.T. is on it."

Soon, mesmerizing screen savers began appearing in the Windgazer 99 installations beyond the United States. They were still limited by syntax. So initially, they surfaced only at the computers of English-speaking users in such countries as India, Hong Kong, Nigeria, Finland—wherever English was widely spoken as a second language.

But the breakthrough into other languages did not take long. A French version suddenly appeared, first in France and then in lands where French was also spoken, such as Haiti, Lebanon, Tunisia and Switzerland. When the Spanish version was added, all Latin American countries and Spain were suddenly added to the base. German and Italian versions came next. Soon, users around the world were able to click on their monitors to see captivating visions of their home towns, sweethearts, sexual fantasies, or their own image pasted over a longtime dream. Every day another population would be delighted to discover their computers had been enlivened with Windgazer 99's screen saver, and soon thereafter, a screen buddy.

Many throughout the world could not wait for their screen saver to appear, just as they could not wait for McDonald's, Levi's, or Viagra.

They wanted the ultimate in personal computing. Of course they had Windgazer 99 installed, but felt incomplete without the screen saver and buddy. Nonetheless, Cyrillic, pictographic, Semitic, and other non-Roman alphabets were still beyond the program's power because of inherent linguistic difficulties. To assuage demand, Hinnom Computing publicly promised that development would eventually extend to those language groups as well. The company asked for patience. In the interim, those who could not wait were encouraged to fill out special registration forms, at a nominal fee, that provided Windgazer 99 screen savers in English.

Nearly 300 million computers worldwide installed Windgazer 99 beginning June 8, 1999. Decamillions of those users worshipped the Windgazer 99 screen saver as a gift from the heavens. The naysayers—and they did exist—were in the minority. Hinnom felt confident about confronting his critics, and quieting the rumblings of politicians, regulators, and attorneys.

Rather than answer opponents one by one in the nations of the world, Hinnom offered to rebut them all in a single televised global press conference beamed to forty-five nations. All the leading networks and newspapers of the world were invited to participate in the historic event.

Only reporters teleconferencing with Hinnom's proprietary Windwatcher technology were allowed to participate. Hinnom Computing was able to install Windwatcher in their CPUs via an overnight update. One morning the software . . . just appeared on reporters' machines, completely operational. Recipients only needed to purchase a small miked monitor cam if they didn't already own one. Hinnom Computing remotely executed all configuration.

Any news organizations that did not possess on-site teleconferencing capabilities or have access to any nearby—many in Africa, Asia, and Latin America simply lacked the facilities—were sent by overnight express a small miked cam to mount on a PC, thus creating a temporary telecon center. The miked cams would have to be returned after the press conference, unless the news organizations wanted to pay the $300 to keep them. Hinnom believed many would buy the nifty devices outright as well as the enabling code to extend Windwatcher.

Logistically, the global press conference would be organized into pools similar to those used in war coverage. The most important pools were created for the newspapers, magazines, TV and radio networks, wire services and Internet e-zines within each of the major G7 industrial countries. Secondary mixed media pools were created throughout Asia and Latin America, with tertiary tiers in Africa, the Middle East, and Oceania/Australia. Each pool representative–chosen by colleagues–was invited to pose a question. Hinnom's press relations people would call on one pool reporter at a time, guaranteeing that each national or continental pool would be hit at least once, with G7 pools hit at least twice.

History's biggest press conference was scheduled to begin at noon Seattle-time, June 26. But by 11:45 A.M., the broadcast director started to worry. Hinnom Computing satellite transmitters were readied, aimed, and waiting for the star of the event to appear in the corporate studios. Hinnom, however, could not be found. He was not in the studio green room, nor in his executive suite, not in the Building 6 cafeteria where he sometimes liked to dash in for rice pudding, not in the company cigar lounge, not in its coffee bar, and, of course, not in the fitness center he never visited anyway.

Actually, Hinnom was preparing quite privately for the worldwide appearance. His office balcony enjoyed an unobstructed pastoral view of the rolling hills and berms surrounding the Hinnom Campus. Beyond that, the rugged Cascade mountains rose toward the heavens to inspire. From this vantage point, Hinnom could see no man or woman, and none could see him. A tightly wound, steel, circular staircase spiraled down from his balcony to a narrow, neatly trimmed pebble path which extended several meters from the base of the circular stairs toward a small man-made pond.

Just before noon, as the broadcast crew was still frantically searching for him, Hinnom strode quietly along the path and sat at the pond's edge on soft, tufted grass. A frog jumped out from below a shrub, secured a prime view, and just stared. Hinnom thoughtfully crossed his legs, took a deep breath, and assumed a peaceful visage amid these tranquil surroundings. A small monitor was positioned a few feet away.

In the meantime, Linzer, the only Hinnom staffer who knew of the unannounced switch, was calmly setting up on the balcony. He latched his Windy onto a small pocket tripod anchored to the balcony rail. After verifying a direct sight line with Hinnom, Linzer waved "Okay." The Windy would relay Hinnom's image to nearby office security cameras, which would feed into the corporate studio's broadcast channel. From there, it would be beamed to the world in a split screen format. Hinnom would occupy the left screen half. The other half would be fed by questioning journalists calling from their offices or the telecon centers set up around the world. A Hinnom's public relations specialist would moderate, calling upon questioners and cuing overseas sites in and out of the broadcast.

No one in the studio knew Hinnom would be transmitting his image live from the pond until a few moments before noon when Linzer called a frayed broadcast staff with the news.

"Mr. Hinnom is ready," Linzer sedately reported to the control booth by intercom. "We'll be feeding from his security cameras. I've routed them into your master console . . . See them on the monitor." The control booth acknowledged with relief.

At noon, the broadcast director cued down, three fingers, two fingers, and a final cue to open with a tight shot of Ben Hinnom that slowly widened to show the pond.

"Hello world, I'm Ben Hinnom of Hinnom Computing, speaking to millions of you in forty-five countries through the miracle of a small hand-held computer, called the Windy, an innovation that Hinnom Computing will be mass producing in the near future." He held up a model. "This handheld device includes a tiny miked video camera. It can transmit data, instructions, and images via a combination of radio frequency—we call it RF—bundled with the same technology that makes satellite cellular phones work. My image as you see it is originating not on expensive studio cameras, but from this handheld Windy which is sending the signal on to our corporate broadcast center for global viewing. We're very proud of the Windy.

"I'm here to answer questions about our exciting Windgazer 99 product line, which has saved the world from the millennium crisis and created a regular Internet updating procedure that means you'll never again have to worry about getting the latest software. As we at Hinnom Computing iron out kinks, fix bugs, and refine features, those improvements will automatically load into your computers over telephone lines in an almost daily seamless transition. One day in the near future, there will be no wires or lines connecting any of us. Hinnom towers will simply broadcast the changes and your computers will receive the updates via RF the way you receive AM and FM broadcasts now, or the way your cell phones receive and call out. The TV, the phone, the computer, the cable net-work—it is all one interrelated info network that Hinnom Computing is finally bringing together for the benefit of our customers and consumers everywhere.

"Oh, yes, I'm sure you have all noticed that we also made Windgazer 99 fun and lively. We put a little ooh-la-la back into our boring, mundane computer days with our creative screen saver package and our on-screen animated screen buddies. Even I have a screen buddy—I call him Linzy.

"Because we folded together several existing technologies in new, exciting and cohesive ways, we know there are questions. And I'm ready to answer any of those. So fiiiire away."

A media manager's voice came over the screen.

"Hello, I'm Bruce, and I'll be moderating today on behalf of Hinnom Computing. The first question goes to Clive Simon-Burrows, BBC, London."

Many of us find Windgazer 99 quite exciting, and at the same time quite frightening. Isn't it unusual for comput-ers to call out every night or to be updated with addi-tional programs? For example, many in the media woke up to find we have Windwatcher in our computers. What if a person doesn't want the update or extra software, or what if the update itself has a bug? That commonly hap-pens with fixpacks. You fix one problem only to cause another.

"I'm so happy you asked that question. Oooh, started with a good one. Clive, computers have been polling for years. Polling is calling out auto-matically all by itself. Both commercial computers and personal comput-ers. Chain stores frequently have cash registers transmit their information nightly to central bookkeeping. There is an unnamed company—you can guess who—that makes just about everybody's personal accounting and checking software—no, it's not us—and this software has built-in dialers that check for regular updates. Network managers are accustomed to exe-cuting updates, fixes, and even total deletes and installs all across their enterprise. The companies that sell and service midrange computers use overnight dialogues to monitor usage and performance to ensure opti-mization—and sell you more disk storage when you run low. Clever guys. Two-way remote computing is well-established. Are we doing something that isn't old hat? I think not. Thanks Clive."

"Next question, Joshua Morgenthal of The Washington Post in Washington D.C."

You said that the Y2K problem has been fixed. Wouldn't it have been possible to just provide people the Year 2000 correcting module without radically altering the way the average person relates to and controls their computer? Why was it necessary several weeks ago to bundle Centurygazer in with Windgazer 99?

"Nice, Joshua. A very nice question. First, Centurygazer is the module that corrects the Millennium Bug. Our viewers might need to know that. But in point of fact, we didn't bundle it with Windgazer 99. I know, I know, you thought we did starting June 8 during the Global Install. But we weren't ready. That's the beauty of Windgazer 99, it is actually just a structure for advanced multifaceted computing. Many of its components have not yet been fully completed or even implemented. Centurygazer–the Y2K fix–was one of them. But not to worry. We just completed it. In fact, we didn't begin really loading it into people's computers until just recently.

When was that?

"I think we began yesterday, and the process will take about another week worldwide. As for 'radically altering' . . . Joshua, we didn't 'radically alter' anything. We are innovating. Networking and group sharing was a huge step forward. Cell phones were a huge step forward. Jeepers, how about fax machines? Talk about a step. Fax was a step! Windgazer 99 is just the next step. And not even a big one. Just coordinated."

"We'll take a question from Kyle Kamen at ABC News in Los Angeles."

Many people have been fascinated by the Wind-gazer 99 screen saver and those cute little and sometimes not so cute little screen buddies. But managers report that productivity is actually down because people are waiting the eleven-plus minutes without touching the keyboard needed for the screen saver to resume. How was Hinnom Computing able to create these deeply personal images– which strongly demonstrates the depth of your knowl-

**edge of people's most intimate lives? Can these screen
savers be disabled? And why is it necessary to solicit so
much personal information–the secret story sessions–
from users with these screen characters?**

"Glad you asked that Carl."

Kyle.

"Right, Kyle. Our industry heard these same complaints in the early
nineties when the first operating systems came out with built-in games,
Tetras, Solitaire, Minefield. Hey, that was fun! But then a few squawked
and so eventually, computer companies responded to the marketplace.
Those games became optional. Now it's possible, quite possibly possible,
that people will say, 'Gee, these screen savers are so delicious, it's just a
giant time drain.' Geesch . . . like games used to be. Okay, then I guess
we would tell our programmers to find a way to make it optional. We
could then disable it–at a nominal fee, a very small monthly charge. But,
Kyle, live a little! Remember, these screen buddies help both the computer and user interface better. Humancentric computing is hardly new.

"Now, you had two other questions. Oh. The information. Well, it's
hardly sinister. We use the same databanks that mass marketers use in
direct mail. Two billion credit card mailings each year don't come out of
nowhere. Carl, just about every computer now has a so-called data cookie with all sorts of personal information retained; this information is provided every time you access a web page, whether it's *Time* magazine or
Hinnom Central. I admit we have elevated the art of consumer profiling
to a new height, but that is part of the innovation people have come to
expect from Hinnom Computing, innovation we are dedicated to continuing for the betterment of all.

"Uh, before I forget, Kyle. You asked about our screen buddies. Hey,
world, aren't they adorable? Do you love 'em or do you love 'em! I personally can't figure out why a few people in a minority are bothered by
our effort to humanize the face of computing. We're not the first computer company to program animated characters onto our screens. That's old.
But look at the bigger picture. Millions of Japanese have made personal
friends out of their yamaguchies–those are just very simple computers. In
Poland, they worship the Black Madonna–it's just a painting. We've seen
it here with pet rocks and Beanie Babies. Lighten up, Kyle. People wor-

ship pictures of Elvis, Marilyn Monroe, and now the latest pre-teen coochie-coo, Leo. How about the savings and loan in Florida with dirty windows that people think is the Virgin Mary? Hah! Her of all people. I just think folks want to believe in something even if it's a silly thing–and our screen buddies might be an improvement over an unwashed window."

"Our next question will come from Marcel Loussier of Le Monde in Paris."

This is not Mr. Loussier, but I'll be happy to ask my question.

"Oh goodie. Ask away."

I've been cruising the web lately and I came across a discussion site where someone reposted a message from people in the know about Hinnom development.

"Hah! I wish I had a dollar for everyone who claims to know about our development plans. But I'm all ears."

This message talked about your I.T. Department. That your I.T. Department was engaged in controversial research soon to be completed that would change the history of computing and perhaps the history of mankind itself. What exactly is your I.T. Department?

Hinnom became stonefaced and silent.

Without waiting, Linzer looked at the broadcast monitor and saw only a blank screen next to Hinnom. He ran into the office and punched the phone.

"Control. Sid."

"Sid. That caller," demanded Linzer, "where is that call coming from? The caller!"

"The one now?" said Sid lazily. "Don't know. We hooked in Paris and this other guy came up and we can't get picture–only voice signal."

"Find him!" barked Linzer. "I'm on my way." Linzer raced out of the office, ran to the elevators, slammed the down button with his fist, instantly gave up and stormed down the stairwell, bumping into two or three people on the way. "Excuse me . . . Pardon me . . . Out the way . . . out the way."

Sir? What is your I.T. Department?

Hinnom regained his composure and with some queasiness replied slowly, "Well, gee, everyone in the world knows what I.T means. Every member of the computer press, every corporate manager–millions of people use that term everyday. It's Information Technology," he laughed nervously. "Do you expect Hinnom Computing to be the only computer company in the world that does not have an I.T. Department?"

From the glass walls of the control booth, Linzer was seen dashing through the studio. He exploded through the soundproof control booth doors.

"The caller?" he bellowed. "Where is the guy!" he stammered, clicking buttons on the control panel to isolate the source as helpless technicians looked on.

> **I know what an I.T. Department is. I had one of my own. But Mr. Hinnom, I understand that you have an I.T. Department run by a gentleman named Max? Max from Canada.**

Linzer blanched. He grabbed the phone and called the I.T. Lab.

The shaved head picked up. "Max?" said Linzer gruffly. "Don't take lunch. Mr. Hinnom and I will want to talk to you." Slamming the phone, he turned to the broadcast director and snapped, "Switch to another caller!"

Quickly, the director depressed a button and tried to fade in Rome. There was no change on the screen. "Switch!" demanded Linzer.

"I'm switching!" the director helplessly yelped back. "Nothing."

Linzer pushed the console button himself. And again. The blank half screen beside Hinnom's picture remained.

"We need to switch now to another reporter," coughed Hinnom uncomfortably, his eyes dancing left and right. "Hello, next questioner? I'm listening."

> **Still me, Mr. Hinnom. Why is Max convinced that the world will change forever when the I.T. Depart-ment has mastered "the right temp?" What exactly is the "right temp?"**

Linzer grabbed the broadcast director by the collar, "You switch this bloody thing, you sonofabitch, to Rome, try Melbourne. Cut this guy off and do it now or you'll wish–" Linzer jerked with sudden awareness.

"Patch me in . . . Now!" The broadcast director punched three buttons, pointed to a mike and with his finger cued Linzer.

"Are we speaking to Mr. Levin again?" demanded Linzer, with the whole world listening.

In Jerusalem, Sal unwrapped his arms, and with a smile of complete satisfaction, high-fived Park. He checked a status line on the Windy's screen, and steadied it on the table in their Dan Pearl suite.

Park scrawled on a large notepad: Anything more on right temp?

Sal nodded no.

Motke wrote down, ASK MORE ON *I.T.*

Dan bent his head slightly to speak into the Windy's microphone, making sure the small square of masking tape remained tight over the tiny camera portal blocking the picture.

"Is that you, Mr. Levin?" reiterated Linzer coldly. "Did you think I wouldn't recognize the voice?"

> **Yes indeed it is. And I'm still waiting for an answer. Windgazer 99 is now sitting in the hard drives of hundreds of millions of computers across the globe. People have a right to be suspicious when one unregulated company with your track record now possesses the sole power to configure and disable virtually every computer on the planet with an overnight modem update—or, I might add, the lack of it. Again, I ask: Exactly what is your I.T. Department, and what is their hush-hush research involving the "right temp"? How will it affect Windgazer 99 in our systems?**

"If the right of a free press includes somehow gaining access to our proprietary development trade secrets," Hinnom sneered, "our confidential trade secrets, then there is no need to continue this press conference. Or perhaps we will resume it at a time when we don't suffer illegal hacking into our broadcast operations. I'm thankful we could address some very important questions tonight. I'm asking . . . now asking my studio to please terminate this broadcast. Thank you." Hinnom ran his finger across his throat to signal cutting the broadcast, not knowing the gesture was caught on camera.

With Linzer over his shoulder, the director cued termination to a Hinnom Computing logo and then cut transmission. Hinnom grabbed his

Windy, ran from his spot at the pond, and scrambled up the spiral stair-case to his office.

Linzer phoned an assistant in security, howling, "I want everyone–worldwide–to check every pool broadcast center, anyone we sent a mon-itor cam, anyone at teleconference center we set up. The works . . . Someone found a way to hack into the press conference . . . Daniel Levin is his name . . . Yes we know him, we know him, and he is with a dis-gruntled ex-employee–mark this, named Park McGuire . . . Everywhere . . . Do it now. Berlin. Tokyo. Boston . . . Uh, Chicago, try Chicago first . . . I don't really know his street address, we're trying to run a business here. You do it!"

Hinnom flew into the control booth burning with anger. "What hap-pened!" The broadcast director was trying to mouth a response when Hinnom screamed, "Get out! All of you get out! Everyone"

Linzer herded them all out of the control booth.

"Out! Out! Out!" said Hinnom, jumping up and down in rage. Linzer could not even begin to calm him, extending his arms wide for a moment but then dropping them in resignation.

"Find that man, Levin," growled Hinnom, spitting the words. "But first, get me . . . Max!"

∼

NEITHER LINZER NOR Hinnom made a sound. They just sat on folding chairs in the I.T. Lab as the shaved head seated just a few feet away faced them and pursed his lips nervously . . . completely unaware.

Another minute. Still nothing.

The shaved head swallowed, began to utter a syllable, but then demurred.

Finally Hinnom docilely asked, "Max, do you know why we are here?"

He shook his head ever so slightly left then right, squirmed, and man-aged a "No."

Linzer quietly inquired, "Did you see the worldwide telecon on Windgazer 99?"

Max slowly nodded no. "Have my work to keep me busy. Deadlines, you know."

"We have been very good to you, Max," Hinnom began in a soft tone.

"My goodness. Took care of that little boo-boo in Canada, brought you into this country. Set you up. All the equipment you asked for. Unlimited budget. A spot in history. Even a designated parking place in the lot. And all we asked was that you devotedly continue your I.T. development unmolested by everyday pressures, and give us what we justifiably need—which is, the ability to control the right temp. *Control* is the wrong word. *Enhance* . . . enhance and work with the right temp is better, isn't it? Sort of a cooperative give-and-take arrangement."

"I'm fine with that, Mr. Hinnom . . . Ben," Max replied.

"Don't call me Ben," Hinnom cut in.

"Yes, okay," Max gulped.

"So what's this about leaking the details of the work on the Internet or in emails to friends or something along those lines?" asked Hinnom with a broad smile. Linzer listened without expression.

Max, blinking rapidly, appeared wholly confused. "What are you . . ."

"I mean . . ." Hinnom bellowed volcanically, "that yooooooooou have been—you Max—have been talking outside this organization about your work in clear violation of your NDA, in flagrant contravention of every trade secret law enacted in this state and by the federal government, and most of all in utter *defiance* of the agreement you and I personally established. Is something unclear about that?"

Linzer punched up his Windy. In an emotionless monotone, Linzer announced, "You, Max, have a net worth of $63,512, if we accept as fact an appraisal of your house that is six months old. If we were to move against you for these improper disclosures and obtain a judgment, say, a few million dollars, you would spend the rest of your life regretting it. We would, of course, consider the acts fraudulent and excludable from discharge under bankruptcy, so you couldn't even go bankrupt on such a judgment. I don't know. Maybe you've been making personal long distance calls on the company phone and that is . . . well, I guess that is embezzlement. Maybe the budget in this I.T. operation needs more scrutiny. Maybe crimes have been committed. Maybe you will go to jail for the rest of your life. Maybe you will be raped in jail, three or four times, before you are killed at a moment you least suspect it with a shiv in the neck right *here,*" Linzer pointed to the carotid artery. "Maybe, Max, this is not turning out to be such a good day for you after all."

Max couldn't collect himself. He tried to speak, tried to breathe.

He could only gasp.

"Calm down," said Hinnom gently. "Take one breath . . . good, now another . . . Good. Now tell us."

"I have never said a word to anyone," averred Max. "I don't know what this is about. The only communications I have had with anyone has been you personally, Mr. Hinnom."

"Well that's a scream," countered Hinnom with false laughter, "because we just had the joy of engaging in a worldwide–*LIVE*–press conference in which a certain freelance journalist seemed to say that by surfing the net he was able to come across a few discussion groups which had reposted some emails of yours referring to our I.T. Department and our efforts on the *right temp.*"

"No. No," blurted Max fearfully. "It's not true. I have emailed only one person, I have memoed only one person. You, Mr. Hinnom, and never through the main server for security purposes. Always, as you instructed, directly on the closed Windy channel. The only one who could have access to any of our discussions or the directories in which they are residing is a person with a Windy and there are only two prototype Windies, and they are both in this room in your hands."

Linzer and Hinnom turned to each other.

"Rosie, our suicidal secretary," said Hinnom. "We never found the third Windy."

"Rosie to Park McGuire," said Linzer coldly. "Park McGuire to Dan Levin and who knows where else?"

Both men furiously punched their keypads looking for telltale traces of unauthorized entry. "Can't tell," said Linzer, adding, "Check the I.T. files."

"The Windy is unstoppable," reminded Hinnom. "It unlocks everything, slices through every firewall."

"There is very little there even if someone were able to hack in," Max assured them enthusiastically. "I always spoke in code and never ever very directly about the project and what it was doing. There are some references to the 'right temp' but never exactly what we are doing."

"Okay," Hinnom relented. "No breach of security, no lawsuit, no jail, no anal rape, no problem. What can anyone do anyway? We're too far along. The Update will be announced in a matter of days–July 4. And you're on schedule for the end of the century. Right?"

"May I bring up some fascinating items on the monitor?" asked Max.

"No," Hinnom responded. "I don't need the graphics. But think about this more important question. The I.T. cat is out of the plastic bag. If someone were to ask, did we at Hinnom Computing invent the I.T. program . . . well, it wasn't us, was it?" he demanded furiously. "How would you answer?"

"Us? Oh not us," said a shaking Max. "The term is relatively new, but the concept is hardly new. Hardly new."

"Ah!" Hinnom said, seizing on the words, and suddenly displaying a docile, almost comforting demeanor. " 'The concept is hardly new,' you say. That's good, Max. So, specifically, if called upon, you could trace the history. Because the media is going to ask. You bet they will. And you can certainly verify that the history of I.T. predates this company. You could give all the historical overviews and insights. Correct?"

"Oh yes," assured Max. He launched into the subject, relieved he was allowed an opportunity to explain. "Stop me if I become too academic."

"Get on with it," interjected Hinnom, struggling to maintain his encouraging guise.

"Yes," explained Max. "It is true that *Influence Technology* is the term behavior scientists have been collectively using for the past five years or so to group all the mind control, riot control, and nonlethal weapon developments including electromagnetic, radio frequency, visual, acoustic–the whole group. But in reality, this research actually began in Auschwitz and Dachau–the experiments of Dr. Heinhem, the so-called Dark Angel. The Japanese also were spending I think several million Yen per year during the Second World War to perfect a death ray that could kill a man miles away by projecting radio waves.

"America entered the field after the War," Max's discourse continued, "because the Navy thought the experiments could be perfected for our own military needs. The Navy absorbed the Nazi doctors via Operation Chatterbox in Potsdam. These guys were then transferred to U.S. military labs through Operation Paperclip. Heh, that's how we got to the moon. Nazi rocket scientists. Fortunately for our endeavor, not all of them were aiming for the stars, some were aiming a little closer to home," said Max, tapping his head.

"The right temporal lobe," acknowledged Hinnom.

"Well, the right temp was not recognized early on," corrected Max.

"Early investigators did know that waves less than a few meters could zap brain cells. Research evolved from killing the man to manipulating the mind, but only in the sixties and seventies. Influence technology programs were conducted mainly under black military and CIA auspices, usually through outside research grants. Plenty of it done up at Canadian universities. Again," Max added with a bit of embarrassment, "this was where I got involved.

"When some of these I.T. projects lost funding," Max went on with a tightened jaw, "the scientists–especially the Canadians–applied their knowledge to the medical sphere or to commercial undertakings. I, as you know, did not succeed in relocating into medicine or the corporate setting. And after my incident–I'm still sorry that happened, Mr. Hinnom, always sorry about that . . . I ended up here and am thankful for that. Oh, so thankful."

"So RF research, mind manipulation, whatever–it's all widely known," concluded Hinnom confidently. "That's what I wanted to know. Widely known. Very, very widely known. No one will start ranting or raving. It's national security. Hey, national security."

"Actually, it has only been in the nineties," Max continued, "that much of this has leaked out. But yeah, it's out there for anyone who wants to pay attention. For heaven's sake, CNN, *Time, U.S. News*–they have all done major stories on military and CIA mind control using radio frequency. People went a little hyper. President Clinton, of course, signed Executive Order 12975–on October 3, 1995, which is by the way my birthday–creating the National Bioethics Advisory Commission for the Protection of Human Research Subjects. The focus shifted for a while. Lots of good things, good things, have happened in epilepsy treatment by right temporal lobe surgery, and correlating defective lobes to glucose levels."

Hinnom clapped his hands for emphasis, declaring, "There you have it. We can save lives, better humanity, do a good thing."

"But in recent years," Max went on, "it has swung back the other way as well. The non-lethality movement in the Pentagon has seen big funding. Big resurgence. So there are now plenty of projects. They finally realized the Russians were way ahead of the West. The Soviets used their Lido machine in those insane asylums–where very few were insane, at least when they went in. This little box, the Lido, would transmit words and sounds into the right temporal lobe–sort of reprogramming the old-fashioned way. "I say old-fashioned," explained Max, "because the Soviet Lido box relied on old-fashioned wires, you know, electrodes hooked up," he pointed near his ear, "to the right temporal lobe, which is the center of speech, sight, and sound analysis.

"Nowadays we can accomplish the same thing with radio frequency. Distance is still a problem. But we can either convey the message through a cell phone or the monitor of a computer if the person stays within about eighteen inches. I think that distance can lengthen perhaps as time goes on. Eventually, when Windgazer screen buddies start to whisper and as people come closer to the monitor to hear, our results will become more reliable."

"You stated there were several different approaches," asked Hinnom. "Have you come to any conclusions?"

"Different strokes for different folks," answered Max, a little more comfortable with his audience. "It depends what the goal is. We have captured the brain waves of people in stress and in extreme relaxation, fear, sexual arousal, shame—you name it. So we can pipe those in *prerecorded,* if you will," he said with a little nervous giggle. "So police can either pacify or disorient in a hostage situation—stop me if this is too much detail—and the military can subdue both combatants and noncombatants in your low-intensity highly-localized conflicts: your Haitis, Bosnias, southern Iraqs—whatever. I know advance Seal units were trying to get psycho-warfare weapons ready for use in Somalia and the Gulf War. The ones in Somalia were laser-activitated devices and actually deployed, but I guess the commander chose not to use them. A second approach, however, is to simply stimulate portions of the right temp responsible for analysis of light, sound, and movement—and achieve the desired effect.

"Here we get into the spiritual part of things, " ventured Max. "Gets a little spooky. The most telling cases come from children, tribespeople, regular Joes and Janes—just anyone who encounters the near-death experience. All these people see the same thing. The white light, the tunnel, the faces of loved ones, all that cliché stuff from the movies. Well, that near-death experience is basically an electromagnetic overstimulation of the right temporal lobe that occurs during the dying moment, cessation of lung and brain activity, a bunch of good stuff. You see, it's such a predictable psycho-physiological response, we already know what the sensation is going to be. So it's neat. Some of the near-death survivors continue to emanate RF, so much that a few have reported their computers did not work right when they sat down."

"Ah ha! That's how Hinnom Computing got involved. Very innocent. Very innocent," said Hinnom. "Just trying to fix a computing problem. Voilà, we established our own I.T. Department."

"Bonus," added Linzer. "We backward-engineered the solution."

"I think," Max said, "don't get freaked, but I think God talks to man through his temporal lobe. We can track it, brain map it, analyze it in evoked potential. *Déjà vu,* voices, personality changes, perception of faces, unrestrained talking. These kids who go berserk and shoot their parents, the mothers who kill their babies . . . they all say 'the devil made me do it.' They say, 'I hear voices in my head.' Well they hear them in the right temp.

"When we are done here, Windgazer 99 will theoretically–I suppose–be able to control the right temp," Max asserted. "I suppose if you were a bad guy, you could control the world." Max laughed nervously, "You could even become a God."

"Thank you for the explanation, Max," said Hinnom. "You're a good boy. And you say we'll be ready by end of year, with the Update, right?"

"Yes, yes," assured Max. "I'm sorry about this stuff today–"

"Enough," Hinnom stopped him. "I.T. needs you. Back to work."

Linzer and Hinnom left the lab quietly, almost breathlessly. At the elevator, Hinnom looked both ways, and seeing they were alone, tears appeared in his eyes. Sobbing, he hugged Linzer, "Oh, yes. Oh yes."

"I presume we are ready?" asked Linzer.

"Yes. Issue a press release, a release to the world, to everyone. Tell them we have unexpectedly found a terrible bug in Windgazer 99. Our millennium program is flawed. As it stands, every computer in the world will crash–*absolutely,* not maybe–on January 1, 2000. Those whose computers were already Y2K-compliant through independent means, we have inadvertently and to our deep deep regret undone their compliance with our glitch. But we can fix it. Oh yes, we can fix it. A special Update, the Point Nine Update, will be issued–free of charge, I might add. The final solution to the Y2K problem will be transmitted and downloaded to all of mankind on December 31, 1999 amid the biggest celebration in human history. No more problems for anyone–once they install Windgazer 99.9."

13

THE COPPER SCROLL

M*otke*, Sal, and Park hustled into the Hillel Street vestibule, through the stairwell door to an adjacent stairway, up two steps, around to another entrance, and straight across the short catwalk to the Derek offices. *"Nu?"* Motke asked the security camera. The heavy steel door clicked open. They passed through the two-door chamber. A congenial black-bereted veteran inspected their bags.

"Shaaalom," chimed Motke.

"Shalumm," added Park.

Sal nodded his head in polite agreement.

The smiling old fighter lifted his polished and oiled M-1 to wave back.

"New guy?" she whispered to Motke.

"First time I've seen him."

The trio briskly paced over to the conference room where the few remaining Ohr 2000 programmers were slouched in chairs, barely noticing the old woman in slippers shuffling in with her tray laden with glasses of tea.

"Kuebitz?" asked Motke as Ronit passed in the corridor.

"Stuck at Hakirya again," Ronit reported, devoid of interest. "Speaker call in ten minutes," she added as she melted into an anteroom.

"What else is new?" Motke muttered. He strung the speakerphone wire from Kuebitz' bare office to the conference room. The call came in but, this time, with Windgazer 99 installed worldwide, the glum programmers assembled hardly lifted their attention.

"Good morning. Are you there, Dr. Kuebitz?" asked Motke.

"Yes, proceed," replied the voice of Kuebitz.

"Okay," said Motke, unfolding a fax. "We start. There isn't much I can say. Yesterday, when everyone in the States was busy with the American July fourth, Hinnom Computing issued their press release. You all know it by now. It made a big shock worldwide and they will not comment more than what they said. Windgazer 99 is a *fake*–this is my word. By them, they said Windgazer 99 has a *glitch* no one could detect. Windgazer 99 will not fix the Millennium Bug; in fact, it guarantees it. Hinnom 'apologizes for the inconvenience.' This is a quote from the press release. Sure, they say they will have it all fixed hunky dory in Windgazer 99.9, the big new Update–but not until December 31, 1999, which is, coincidentally, the final Shabbat of the twentieth century.

"What a situation," bemoaned Motke. "Now is July 6 and no one company or even consortium of companies can mount another development program to replace Windgazer. Derek of course has the Ohr project, but we also have no chance. We still have the same problem today we have had for months. The Windgazer APIs that govern compatibility change every few days in Hinnom's overnight updates. We can't program to convert them because they are not uniform. It seems Windgazer employs three or four such APIs and they rotate among individual PCs in a hit-or-miss way. On any given day, one man's computer could be refreshed with one version of the API and the computer next to it in the same room could have a second version. In a week, it changes the other way around. And it varies between countries. We find one set of rotating APIs in America, another set in Canada, and a third set in Denmark. No one can predict where they will pop up. It's not complex. Really, it's simple–like a random number generator."

"That's it," Park interjected excitedly. "That's actually it. Hinnom has a system not that different from the email code generator he used back at headquarters. It generates a different identification every day for each user. Bad Ben must have created a few million of these random codes–"

"This is not hard," declared one of the other programmers without looking up. "I could do it." Others lazily nodded in agreement.

". . . And," Park continued, "Hinnom's system must randomly assign every computer in the world a different alias each day. One day your alias is such and such, then a new one is embedded in the overnight refresh. You're right—it's not complicated. Just devious."

"It's basic cryptography," another programmer volunteered. "It's less. It's like the keys to your car—all just a chance distribution of thirty or forty types. In any parking lot filled with Toyotas, one key will open several cars."

"For sure," concurred Motke. "We just need the key. Take all the numbers . . ."

"Or even better," Park broke in, "discover the common structure of all the numbers. Then Ohr's antidote tells the PC that from now on, if it receives such a number in a Hinnom refresh, it should convert it to an Ohr number. So let us say the overnight refresh is any combination of fifty digits. We just program a fix to convert any such combination to our own universal enabling code. Of course, our code never changes. We solve the problem permanently."

"Unless he changes the API update from so many digits—fifty, maybe seventy-five—to something we can't predict," challenged Motke. "I think that is exactly what will happen. I wish I knew what is the next move because now it is no longer a fight for commercial control and profits. Now the world fights for survival because we can't rely on Windgazer 99.9 or anything that comes after it from Hinnom Computing."

Park glanced at Sal, sitting like a straight line resisting a curve.

"Sal has made some progress in his research," offered Park.

The group grew silent. What research?

Park explained, "Sal has been cruising some sites normally offbounds."

"Hacking?" asked a programmer with a wee smile.

"Ask not and ye shall not know," quipped Motke. "*Nu?* Tell us, Sal."

Sal turned a bit in toward himself. "I have access to . . ."

The room leaned forward.

". . . to the Hinnom Computing Intranet—their entire enterprise, including a number of special restricted sites. I am able to get in and they can't really stop me. Generally, they can't even see me. Some things I have been able to learn, some other things I am guessing because the company is moving data around. The problem is," he became a bit more confident as he observed the attentiveness of the group, "that Hinnom is in fact using random numbers to refresh computer APIs, but only temporarily. Soon he will switch to radio frequency."

"Switching to RF?" asked Motke. "Timetable?"

"The final enabling technology transmits with the Point Nine Update December 31," replied Sal, twisting his head. "It might have something to do with climate control. His secret new *I.T.* Department is working on a project that requires control of the *right temp.* It's what Dan was asking about during the press conference. But I just can't figure the *right temp* out. Maybe the next wave of computers will have temperature-controlled circuit switches that Hinnom will require manufacturers to install and these will be activated by RF signals. Unless they are heated to the right temp, like a thermometer, the computers won't work. Sounds far-fetched . . ."

"*Shalom, shalom.* Yeah, it's far-fetched."

Everyone turned.

It was Dan. "Hi. I'm here because I have some news."

"Dan," objected Motke, "this is a secure place. You cannot be here. How did you come in?"

"Just flashed my *Itonayee* press card and the old geezer with the antique rifle let me in," he explained. Turning to the old woman on a stool, he asked in Yiddish for a glass of tea, and sat himself down. Pleased that he spoke Yiddish—no one did any more—she eagerly shuffled to the teapot.

"How did you even find this place?" asked Motke, turning to Park, wondering if she violated security.

"Forget that," scoffed Dan. "Years ago, before this was Derek's office, my answering service was right downstairs. "Where's Dr. K? He should hear this too."

"I am here," said the voice of Kuebitz over the speakerphone.

"Nice touch," commented Dan. "Can I share my news? I think you will all want to know."

"Proceed," said the voice of Kuebitz.

Motke demurred and settled back.

"None of you have a clue about the *right temp*," he began, "and I should have known it from the get-go. But I only figured the whole thing out myself this morning." He paused to get everyone's attention and tapped next to his right ear. "It's up here."

"It's giving you a headache?" joked Motke.

"Close," Dan shot back. He turned to Park, "For years I published what magazine?"

Park listed a few: "*Wingtip* . . . *Chicago Monthly* . . . *Highstyle* . . ."

"Brain Journal," Dan monotoned dramatically. "The bastard. The *right temp* refers to the right temporal lobe, the spiritual center of the brain: recognition of tones, images, faces, perception, and analysis of speech. Short circuits in the right temp are not a good thing." In his best lecture style, he recited the implications: "Lesions and/or manipulation can manifest bizarre behavioral and personality conditions, including persistence in statements even when shown conclusively to be wrong, *déjà vu,* inappropriate amusement, impaired recognition of visual and auditory cues. Control the right temp and you can create a man with no independent will, or turn a God-fearing small town high school boy into a satanic serial killer.

"I didn't believe my own right temp on any of this," Dan conceded, "so I checked some right temporal lobe research on the web, and lo and behold some far-reaching RF mind control projects were done for the military through DARPA–"

"The Pentagon's secret technology agency, the same one that helped establish the Internet itself?" Park broke in.

"The one . . . Very innocuous name designed to draw no attention. 'Defense Advance Research Projects Agency.' DARPA had a series of projects known collectively as *Influence Technology.* That's the *I.T.* I tried to corner Hinnom on during the press conference. I.T. equals *Influence Technology.* I did a search and found an academic paper on the web authored by a half-dozen Canadian researchers entitled *New Generation RF Mind Weapons.* Bingo."

He turned to Sal, "You found a guy called Max from the so-called I.T. Department sending email to Hinnom about the *right temp* and making reference to his initial projects in Canada." Turning back to the others, "Well . . . Maxwell Glennin was one of the junior researchers on this paper *New Generation RF Mind Weapons.* The paper analyzes the feasibility and desirability of the military subduing an entire population by sending RF manipulations via cellular phones, handheld radios, CD players, and, of course, computers. Correct. Computers.

"Skip over the fact that the university disbanded the project after it lost funding. And let's gloss over minor details like Maxwell Glennin's arrest for the equivalent of vehicular homicide in British Columbia. Strange, I couldn't find any disposition for the case. In fact, charges appear to have been dropped. Why, I don't know. Glennin was no longer listed in the phone book in Canada anywhere so I couldn't ask him. Just as a long shot, I call Seattle directory assistance. The phone book is a reporter's best friend. Maxwell Glennin? 'Sorry he has an unpublished number.' Bingo again.

"So again I pick up the phone," Dan smiled, "and call the Hinnom Computing switchboard and ask for Maxwell Glennin. Operator says all his calls are screened, name please? I click the receiver a few times, bad connection, and hang up. Gentlemen," he turned to Park, "and lady . . . I think Bad Ben actually thinks he can perfect what Madison Avenue and your average department store security has been doing crudely for decades—subliminal suggestion. But on a far grander, far more sinister scale. This is not about controlling the marketplace. This is about controlling the mental place." Dan jabbed his index finger against the right side of his head.

"It's all about the *temple*," Dan emphasized forcefully. "What does *temple* mean?" he went on in lecture mode. "It means a couple of things. Roman prophets used to look for a sign or a presence within a space. That's *tueor* in Latin. The Greeks say *theos* and the Romans say *deus*. But they both come from the use of this common root, *tueor*, 'the presence in the space.' The place where God made his presence known was the Temple. We all know that, right?" Dan emphatically slapped his palms above his ears. "The temple is right HERE. The right temporal lobe, the place where God makes himself known." His face reddened with rage, Dan exclaimed, "I'm telling you, we must stop this sonofabitch Hinnom before he destroys mankind."

The group erupted, some with anger, some disbelief.

"This is unbelievable," Motke shouted over the others. "RF to control the mind? Mind control!"

"Mind control," repeated Dan, adding, "No . . . it's more than mind control. That's too easy. We're not talking just about dictating who buys the next box of corn flakes. It's the battle to control man's soul, his essence, his sense of right and wrong, his will, his spirit. When the millennium turns, it's more than just a computer glitch at stake. It's him or us. We must destroy this guy."

Park added slowly, almost fearfully, "*If any man defiles the Temple of God, him God shall destroy; for the Temple of God is holy, the temple is in you.* That's First Corinthians 3:16."

"Never read it," retorted Motke.

"Do not deceive yourselves," she continued, *"If you think that you are wise in this age, you should become fools so that you may really become wise,"* she added. "That's the next verse. I guess we can have as many computers as we dare, and still we don't understand the big mysteries."

Motke shrugged.

Dan did not react.

No one in the room had ever looked at a New Testament. And only a few knew that First Corinthians referred to a book of the New Testament.

Detecting the disinterest, she said, "Try this one: Leviticus 20:3: *I will set my face against the one who defiles my temple."*

"That one I know," professed Motke, "but I don't like your translation." He pulled a palm-sized green leatherette Bible from his knapsack, moistened his finger two or three times flipping through pages and finally located the passage. "It says like this," he read. "Leviticus—just as you said: *And I will set my face against that man, and will cut him off from among his people because he has given of his seed unto Molech, to defile my sanctuary. Sanctuary* can also be *Temple.* So it's not quite what you said, because it refers to Molech. Which is funny. Because Molech is the evil one who was worshipped in Gei Ben Hinnom."

"Gei Ben Hinnom?" asked Dan.

"Down the street," Motke replied.

"What's Gei Ben Hinnom?" responded Dan.

Motke laughed with embarrassment. "The way you talk, the president of Hinnom Computing is connected to Gei Ben Hinnom down the street."

The other Israelis suppressed smirks and giggles.

"What . . . Motkele . . . is *Gei Ben Hinnom?"* Dan pointedly asked again.

"You would call it Hell," Motke replied professorially. "The Arabs call it *Gehennem—"*

"Hell," cut in Dan, "like where I told the bomber on the *midrekhov* he was gonna go. *Gehennem* is Arabic for Hell. I know that."

"Well, it's Arabic for Hell," replied Motke, taking the opportunity to be the expert, "and Hebrew for Hell, and your English equivalent is *Gehenna.* And it all comes from a shortened form of Gei Ben Hinnom, or more precisely, the Valley of the Sons of Hinnom. *Gei* is valley, *Ben* is son or sons, and *Hinnom* is the name of the owner of that piece of land. It is not a Hebrew family name, so Hinnom is alien and of course a pagan worshipper of Molech."

"Where exactly?" asked Dan.

"Valley of Hinnom is actually the big ravine running alongside the walls of the Old City," answered Motke. "In fact the Dan Pearl is on the upper end of it. My favorite movie theater, Cinematheque, with their wonderful restaurant on the balcony, is just over it. By the Sultan's Pool. The ravine starts shallow up by Jaffa Gate but becomes very deep as it goes south. It is filled with caves and extends down down down until it reaches its filthiest spot, below the Arab village of Silwan. No one goes there. Too dangerous because of problems with Silwan. The Jews stay up at the north end. So that's why you have nice hotels, an outdoor theater, restaurants, and a Cinematheque up here, but there is no Israeli investment down at the end by Silwan. And we're—let's face it—a little superstitious. There's too many dead bodies buried there. So Gei Ben Hinnom remains more or less the same dirty and untouchable place it has been for hundreds, I guess thousands, of years. Like I said, no one frankly wants to go there. It's damned land."

"Damned?" asked Park

"In the ancient days," Motke continued lecturing, "Hinnom was the valley of the unclean, of idolatry, of death and destruction, of child sacrifice. Children alive and screaming were killed on burning altars of terrible fire—the Tophet, the furnace—in front of their own parents. The Essenes drained their sewage from the Temple area right there. Later, it became a city dump. Fires were always burning either from sacrifice or trash. So whenever the men of the Bible—especially the second Bible—not that I ever read it—talk about Hell or hell fire—Gehenna or *Gehennem*—they are, in fact, specifically talking about this ravine. Many say this is the Valley of Death of Psalm 23."

"My favorite," Park commented. *"Even though I walk through the valley of the shadow of death, I will fear no evil, for You are with me."*

Dan could not hide his incredulity. "You're telling me that Hell is just a few blocks down the street?"

"No big thing," one programmer chimed in. "Gei Ben Hinnom is the place of Hell mentioned in the Bible as Motke says. Every schoolboy in Israel knows it. I imagine every Bible scholar in the world knows it."

"I know the Christian world thinks that this Hell is a place of eternal burning torment," Motke murmured in a mock odious tone, "for very bad people after you die. But this is Israel. Here, among the Jews, Hell is just a place with a terrible reputation located in a stinking ravine outside the Old City."

"And it's just a tremendous coincidence," blurted Dan in disbelief, "that the richest and most evil man in the world is," he spelled it dramatically, "B-E-N space H-I-N-N-O-M and no one thought to mention it to me or anyone."

"It's a name, Dan" Motke retorted. "Don't get excited about it. No one cares. We have Levis and Cohens everywhere and no one thinks they are high priests. There are thousands of people here named Moshe, but no one thinks these are the same guy who led the Israelites out of Egypt."

"But Ben Hinnom . . ." argued Dan.

"Joseph Heller wrote *Catch-22*," countered Motke. "He is not from Hell. You have the mayonnaise–Hellman's. So what? We have the famous Wingate Institute and no one connects it to Windgazer 99. They are just names. We should concentrate on what is real, the RF method you mention from Windgazer 99–assuming it's real."

"Real?" sneered Dan, perceiving some doubt. "It's real. It's as real as a man with the name from Hell giving us the software from Hell."

Everyone paused a moment as the woman shuffled in with her tea. Oblivious to the debate, she gently laid a steaming glass in front of Dan.

"Todah," Dan graciously thanked. He sipped a bit. No one spoke. Everyone looked at each other. He sipped a second bit audibly.

Motke tapped the table as he sorted out the implications. "Maybe it's a point. Maybe Hinnom is working with RF to control people's minds. So then we must find a way to stop Windgazer 99.9. But it would take a miracle."

"Sal, please pick up," said the voice of Kuebitz.

Sal did so, listened intently for several moments, looked at Dan, then at Motke and Park. "Yes, yes, yes," Sal abruptly blurted out to the surprise of the Derek team. He hung up the phone, terminating the call.

"Dr. Kuebitz said some things," Sal related haltingly at first, but with more confidence as the words proceeded. The group could not help but notice Sal's sudden verbalizing. "First," Sal said, "Dr. Kuebitz wants us to remember we still don't know the answer to the Y2K crisis yet, or even the form the answer will take. Second, he actually agrees it will take a miracle. But the greatest miracle will be *understanding* the answer, recognizing it. We need to be open to receive this miracle. Third, he says we need to all go home now, plus take tomorrow as a day off and just think about the implications of everything."

"A day off?" challenged Motke.

Sal retreated from his spoken words and grabbed his arm defensively. He nodded toward the phone.

"You're sure?" Motke double-checked.

Sal moved away an additional half turn and almost spoke but could not.

"He's sure," said Park to relieve the tension.

As the group was breaking up, Sal approached Dan, Park, and Motke. "We have the day off tomorrow to think," said Sal. "Could we take a trip?"

"Beach at Tel Aviv?" asked Dan.

"There's better beaches north a few miles, maybe Netanya," added Motke.

"I want to go to a place not far from here," said Sal quietly.

"Called?" asked Dan.

"Called Qumran," Sal answered with uncertainty.

Dan observed a strange and intense determination on Sal's face. His request seemed almost urgent.

Motke shrugged in agreement.

Dan answered back, "Qumran? Okay. Qumran, it is."

ON THE CRAGGY shore of the lowest point on earth, the Dead Sea, where bizarre barometric phenomena combine with salt, sulphur, and naturally pacifying bromides in the air and then reblend with blinding sun and parching heat, in this Biblical furnace that smelts souls and distills the mind, there is a mystic place of entombed secrets guarded by caves, cliffs, and wadis. That place is Qumran, the communal camp of the Essenes, the Judaic cult that lived and prepared all their days for one destiny: to right-eously oversee the triumph of the Sons of Light over the Sons of Darkness. Believing their bodies to be the holy implements of God, the Essenes bathed often, excreted at a distance, observed their own lunar calendar, and obeyed the literal dictates of both Mosaic Law and their own voluminous teachings—all in preparation for the final battle: the End of Days.

The 2000-year-old message of the Essenes only recently reappeared. In 1947, just before the State of Israel was founded, a Bedouin shepherd stumbled into the first of Qumran's precious caves. Inside, he found ancient Essene scrolls encased in jars wrapped in linen. Since then, hundreds of additional scrolls have been discovered, reconstructed, translated, studied, debated, and trembled over. The term "Dead Sea Scrolls" is misunderstood by many to mainly describe the six holy writings displayed in Jerusalem's Shrine of the Book; those six are the Manual of Discipline, Nahum's Commentary, the Temple Scroll, the Psalms Scroll, the Great Isaiah Scroll, and the so-called War Scroll. But, in fact, the Essenes created hundreds of scrolls and other holy writings detailing the panorama of their communal existence: psalms, liturgies, predictions, philosophies, prayers, sermons, visions, chronologies, administrative records, wisdoms, and secret revelations.

Discovery spawned fearsome questions. Are the Dead Sea Scrolls merely the fascinating accumulation of one sect's knowledge? Do they document or undermine the genesis of Judaism or Christianity? Are their messages divinely inspired or mortal? Who is endowed with the right to possess, control, interpret, display, and access the fragile scrolls? All these questions form the thorny center of a war among theologians, academicians, archeologists, and the faithful. Acrimonious interpretations, bitter scholarship feuds, charges of racial bigotry, accusations of dark conspiracy and cover-up, media smears and outrages, theological alarm, and even copyright infringement lawsuits over translation rights swirl around these ancient writings. Just confronting the knowledge of the Essenes of Qumran has proved that man fears nothing more than his own idea about God.

Now, while scholars squabble bitterly in libraries and museums, and archeologists continue periodic excavations amidst the jagged sun-bleached ruins, tourists swarm into Qumran's air-conditioned welcome center, adjacent to the dig. There, they can buy high-gloss pictorials, gaudy T-shirts, mass-produced souvenir relics, and carved camels before enjoying an exquisite buffet of tangy Moroccan meats and sauces, finished with ice creams and fudge. After the surfeit, they can step outside into the searing heat and discover for themselves a completely unguarded, unsupervised site of unparalleled biblical archaeology.

Anyone can wander among the ruins, often in solitude, beneath towering mountainsides that continually toy with light, under dozens of summoning caves dug into the heights, across from alluvial fans resembling great paws, within sight of the bluest blue water of the Dead Sea, and surrounded by spectacularly steep drop-offs overlooking deep canyons. All who step here cannot help but step into the history and psyche of this first-century sanctuary. Breathe this air. The burning in your lungs is more than desert heat. It is ancient spirit.

Park, Sal, Dan, and Motke arrived early, before the sun climbed too high. Contented from the welcome center's breakfast of spicy *shakshouka*, three types of yogurt, and an assortment of grapefruits, oranges, and pomegranates completed with a ritual turkish coffee, or two, and laden down with an assortment of glossy brochures and guide booklets, the group set out to explore the magnificent complex of high stone and mud walls, semicircular kilns, portals, stairways, subterranean cisterns, water troughs, and humble living quarters that comprise Qumran. Active dig zones were separated from public paths by mere plastic ropes, so everyone could walk at will in the steps of the Essenes, touch their walls, peer through their windows, absorb their isolation, sense their mission. The Essenes chose this desolate outpost of vigilance to communicate with God's presence. In a way, it was their Temple, for they saw God's presence in every corner and in every space.

Motke, who had visited the site many times—it was about an hour's drive from Jerusalem—was doing his best to play tour guide to Park and Dan. They luxuriated in the exquisitely preserved formations. But as the group meandered from the Scriptorium where sacred Essene scrolls were meticulously lettered, to the ritual *mikveh* baths, to the oven-like weapons forge, Sal's attention became more and more transfixed. Several times, he left the group to return briefly to the Scriptorium where he seemed to listen to voices no one could hear and observe images no one could see.

"Sal," said Park. "We're walking to the graves. You coming with?"

Sal loitered and finally asked Motke, "What is the Copper Scroll?"

Motke smiled broadly, and replied, "You picked a good one to ask about." He dug into his knapsack, setting aside tour pamphlets on the Essene lifestyle, the Dead Sea spas, walking trails, and found a thin but oversized full-color Ministry of Tourism booklet entitled "Mysteries of the Copper Scroll."

"Where did you hear about the Copper Scroll?" asked Motke. "Almost no one ever discusses it because it is so . . . well, so strange."

Sal winced slightly but did not reply.

Not waiting for a response, Motke laid the large booklet on the dusty floor of the Scriptorium. Dan and Park squatted for a close view.

Sal continued standing.

Motke asked him, "You can see this?" Sal, peering intently, indicated he could.

"Most scholars agree that of hundreds of scrolls they found in these caves," explained Motke in true tour-guide style, "maybe the strangest, most mysterious one is the Copper Scroll—a list of sixty-five buried Essene treasures. Silver, gold, oils, garments, many good things. Other scrolls, they were written on leather and stored in big jars. This one, the Copper Scroll, is quite different, written, or shall we say carved, into a thin sheet of purest copper."

Checking the description in the brochure, Motke continued, "The copper sheet was 2.4 meters long—about eight feet, I should say. They found it all rolled up in Cave 3 up there," he pointed at the mountain, and they all searched the landscape until they fixed on the point. "It was 1952," he continued. "A French archeologist was the one. Jordan owned the Copper Scroll at the time. But they couldn't figure out a way to unroll it for years. Later, someone at the University of Manchester in England invented a machine to slice the copper into panels, then piece it back together flat. They did it and translated the text." He pointed to the color photos.

"That's when they discovered that the Copper Scroll was the strangest scroll of all," asserted Motke. "Very little scholarship exists on the object because it is exactly what I said, a list of buried treasure—nothing more. They worry about treasure hunters and hidden religious messages. Is the man Jesus in it? Is the end of the world predicted? Maybe yes, maybe no?" Motke flipped a look at the heavens with open hands in a traditional Israeli gesture meaning "who the heck knows?"

Sensing his captive audience, Motke went on, "People have charged conspiracy of silence, accused a translator maybe he deliberately switched some letters around to hide the true meaning. Big big *balagon*. For Park," Motke pointed out, "*balagon* in Hebrew is messy problem you don't really need. This much is known: all these secret hiding places hold together a mass of silver and gold—worth maybe millions of dollars. It's like a mystery movie filled with secret puzzles and codes."

Dan studied some of the booklet. "Listen to this. It's unbelievable," said Dan, reciting some of the secret caches listed:

> *The third hiding place: a big cistern in the courtyard near the outer columns—containing 900 talents of silver coins . . . The sixth hiding place: in the salt pit located under the steps—containing 41 talents of silver coins . . . The twenty-eighth hiding place: In the cave of the pillar with two openings facing east, the northern opening, dig down three cubits and under the urn—containing thirty-two talents of silver . . . The thirty-fifth hiding place: at the mouth of the spring of Kohziba, dig down three cubits, to the row of stones—containing 80 talents of silver coins plus two talents of gold coins . . . The sixtieth hiding place: under the black stone—containing oil vessels.*

Dan spoke with incredulity: "It's under steps, between boulders, beneath a knife, in a grave, near a grave, by a wall, wedged in a pipe. Like a buried treasure map in a bad pirate movie."

"Many have tried to find these treasures," related Motke. "Some discoveries were made right here in Qumran. There was an unrelated underground vessel of silver coins. But none of the specific treasures listed in the Copper Scroll has ever been located."

"It's fabulous," said a disbelieving Park. "Nothing found with all the archeological digging they do in Israel?"

"All the clues are using terms and names with references only these Essene people knew 2000 years ago," answered Motke. "In the courtyard. Under the wall. Under the knife. But what courtyard? What wall? What knife? Here? In Jerusalem? In Galilee? Down in the wadi? Where? That's why a few of the scholars wonder if this whole list is not a fake. Many also believe it is *not* a fake, that this list was the accumulated wealth the Essenes tithed—I said it right, *tithed*—for God. But if these locations are real, they seem to be phrased like reminders or nicknames that the Copper Scroll's scribe only himself personally knew. Plus, no one knows what the secret Greek letters in various places mean," said Motke, pointing to the letters on the brochure photo of the Copper Scroll. "I read once that these compare to no known Greek abbreviation or meaning. So it's a mystery still—top to bottom."

"The Greek letters, that's a code," said Sal.

"Yes," replied Motke, "but we need the Second Copper Scroll to know."

"A second scroll?" asked Park.

"The final treasure," Motke read from the booklet, *"hiding place number 65 in the dry well north of Kehlit, with an opening on the north near graves, there lies a copy of this inventory plus explanations, measurements, and full details for each and every hidden item."*

Dan was still in disbelief. "Let me see that." He read the lines aloud, flipped over the booklet to verify the Ministry of Tourism logo, and exclaimed, "You're right. You can't decode the secrets of the first scroll without the second one. What a story."

"Like an API," said Sal.

"The computer mind," chuckled Motke.

"So where is Kehlit?" asked Dan. "Let's find that bad boy, the second scroll."

"It won't happen," scoffed Motke. "Okay. First, there are no vowels in Hebrew, and the Copper Scroll mixes in Aramaic, so all these translations are big guesses, especially for names of places. Kehlit is really four Hebrew letters *Kaf-Het-Lamed-Taf.* You would say KHLT. *Kehlit,* maybe Kahlt, maybe Khlot. We lack the oral tradition, the pronunciation."

Dan cut in, "I get it. Like in Illinois the town C-A-I-R-O is pronounced KAY-ro, and in Egypt it's KY-ro."

Motke didn't comprehend the linguistics, and just glossed over the interruption, "No one has ever found this Kehlit—and they have looked, believe me. Every cave and every hole has been checked and checked and rechecked by the Bedouin looking for the smallest piece of anything because they know there is money if they find something. Whatever was here to find, has already been found. Whatever has not been found already, will not be found. Sorry.

"Anyway," continued Motke, "the Second Copper Scroll, it says, is *'by the graves'*—and as you see there are graves everywhere. No one is allowed to touch them. All these spots with the rocks piled up. There are ancient bodies lying under them. Not to be disturbed."

"Like over there," said Sal, looking through a tinted blue polarizing lens he found on the ground, dropped by some recent tourist.

"Over where?" asked Motke.

"There's a small pile of rocks next to the man over there," replied Sal. "Near the canyon edge."

Motke shielded his eyes from the sun and looked toward the canyon edge where Sal had motioned. "No guy there. Where?" asked Motke.

Dan and Park looked to where Sal was pointing. They shielded their eyes from the sun. They saw the rock heap. But no man.

"*That* man standing next to that pile of rocks," repeated Sal pointing toward the precipice. "Look now. Like he's floating."

"Desert mirage," laughed Dan. "Drive up and down the Dead Sea highway. All the cars in the distance float. They're floatmobiles. It's the physics of optical distortion."

"But I don't see him at all," commented Park. "Over where?"

Sal grinned a bit. "Am I the only one who sees this man?"

"Drink more water," nudged Park, as she handed Sal her small plastic Neviot bottle.

"Mom, I don't need water," resisted Sal. He began walking toward the precipice graves. After carefully packing up the Copper Scroll booklet, the others followed, but no one could see the man next to the rock heap Sal had pointed out. Suddenly, Sal began half running toward the floating man's image, his arms flopping out of sync with his shoulders.

Park, Motke and Dan quickened their pace after him.

Sal stopped running some yards from the edge. The man had vanished from his eyes. The group caught up. "Where?" asked Dan.

"Now he's not here," Sal dejectedly conceded. "You're right. Optical distortion caused by heat." He glanced up at the sun and then surveyed the land. He began thinking out loud, an unlikely moment of exposure for Sal who performed all his calculations silently.

"See how the land slopes," Sal pointed. "Just up there, above, is a tiny cave in the rock. That's *north near graves.*"

"That's a hole, not a cave," said Motke.

"I'll call it an *opening,*" corrected Dan. "What did the booklet description say?"

" *'In the dry well north of Kehlit, with an opening on the north near graves'* is the Second Copper Scroll," reiterated Motke.

"Qumran is loaded with bizarre water tunnels," said Dan. He scrambled up the escarpment a few feet to the small opening Sal had pinpointed. It was just big enough to insert an arm, and he reached in. "This is certainly *an opening on the north near the graves,*" Dan grunted while stretching in.

"Before you stick your hand in a desert hole," warned Motke, "know what's inside. Scorpions are tiny animals. They love hands."

A startled expression appeared in Dan's face. "Hold it," he said slowly, lugging a heavy earthen pottery lid out of the hole.

"Congratulations," said Motke, "you have now found another piece of pottery to add to several thousand other pieces of pottery which have been found here and now instantly become the property of the State of Israel Antiquities Department. I hope you have your passport. There will be a lot of paperwork."

Park gently fingered the dirt-caked surface. "It's beautiful," she observed. "This was used for what? To cover a scroll in a jar?"

"No, no," said Motke, pointing to the bulging flat bottom. "Jar lids for scrolls are common, but such a lid would need a cone shape to fit atop a scroll. Concave. This one . . . this one is flat and extends down–to plug up a water vessel."

"A channel. . ." Sal said to himself, then loudly for the others: "Maybe there's a water channel from that opening to a dry well somewhere. Waterways were common through the Qumran settlement, the book said. Read us the hiding place again, please."

Motke pulled out the booklet and again quoted: *"In the dry well north of Kehlit, with an opening on the north near graves, there lies a copy of this inventory plus explanations, measurements and full details for each and every hidden item."*

With a boyish grin, Dan pointed to a row of bushes. "Hey, if you want to be crazy about it . . ." he pointed up and down the escarpment, ". . . we could have a typical Qumran water system thing from the little opening up there . . . to a lower level and . . ." he walked and waved toward some bushes along the cliff edge, ". . . you see this line of shrubs. Look, desert scrub in a neat row along there."

"It trails off the side of the cliff," said Sal, as he leaned over to see.

"Whoa! Careful," cautioned Dan.

Too late. Suddenly, Sal lost his footing on the crumbling edge of the cliff. Too many stones gave way. He slid off, even as he instinctively turned his body toward the mountainside, flinging to grapple anything.

"Sal!" shrieked Park.

"Stay calm," Dan told Park. "He's stable."

Petrified, Sal hung onto a slim rock ledge with his fingers. He tried not to look down the steep ravine. Hundreds of feet below, at the bottom of the canyon, a dry rocky river bed curved around the mountain base.

"Sal," Dan called out. "There's a little outcropping, a sheep path, just below your feet. Don't look down at it. Just trust me, it's a few feet, maybe just one foot below you. I just need you to slide down on your belly and chest until you reach it."

Sal's gripping fingers slipped off the rock ledge. He furiously grabbed the short trunk of a scrub bush just inches below that, digging his knees into the dusty mountainside.

"I'm running for help," yelled Park, racing off.

"No, no," protested Dan. "There is no one to help. Get back here. Motke, get her back. I'm gonna get Sal. You two guys hang onto my shirt."

Eyes tightly shut, Sal desperately pressed his cheek into the earth. Periodically some gravel noisily launched beneath his dangling feet, only heightening his terror. Afraid to add additional force to any surface, Sal remained motionless.

"Sal, I just need you to lower yourself some inches," Dan cried. "Hug the side. Hug the side. Get yourself a touch lower to that spot. You'll feel it." There was no reply from Sal.

By now, Dan had crawled on his belly head first out over the cliff's edge and toward Sal positioned less than a yard below. "You guys hold my ass," Dan instructed. Park and Motke wedged themselves against small outcroppings at the cliff's edge and grabbed onto the pockets of Dan's cutoff jeans. Sal was still beyond Dan's grasp. "Get me a little lower," Dan cried. "Lower down—a touch more."

The desert scrub Sal was gripping started to give way, its roots steadily pulling from the vertical cliff face. Small stones continued slipping down the ravine.

"Okay, grab me from my ankle . . . my ankles . . . and get me down more," Dan called up. Motke and Park yelled out for Sal to stay calm and then adjusted their grasp on Dan's backside . . . lower . . . lower . . . until their grasp was firm against the tops of Dan's hiking shoes. They lowered him further head first. Inch by inch, the sage bush holding Sal continued rotating perilously out of the ground.

Some Arab boys could be seen hundreds of feet below herding goats. They stopped to stare and pointed up. Lizards darted out across the stones. Desert flies figure-eighted noisomely above.

"The bush is coming loose," moaned Sal. "I'm moving down."

Dan's upside-down body slithered over the edge . . . a little further . . . until only his shins remained atop the cliff. He finally reached Sal's sage bush, and grabbed the top branch, counterforcing its rotation out of the ground. Sal's hands were now just inches from Dan's hanging arms. "Sal . . . Sal . . . hug the damn rock and lower yourself," Dan coaxed. "You can do it, guy."

It cracked. Park shuddered and suddenly remembered Sal as an infant in Kansas, then on his tricycle, at his seventh birthday party, no friends to invite, it doesn't matter, later at the science fair, the joy in his eye as his first computer flickered, all in a visually-cacophonous second dissolving into the terror on his face.

The scrub trunk partially snapped. Sal uncontrollably jolted lower, and more rocks went flying to the depth below.

"Hold on, Sal!" Dan shouted, extending his arms as far as he could. "I'm gonna grab your fingers. Intertwine with me. Open your eyes and look at me. Intertwine."

"I can't!" whimpered Sal. "Why is this happening?"

"I didn't bring you here to die at Qumran, kiddo!" blared Dan.

Abruptly, the scrub bush gave way completely. Sal's weight had ripped it, root structure and all, right out of the ground. But hugging the rocks, Sal slid straight down . . . only an extra few inches . . . until his feet came to rest safely on the level spot Dan had hoped he would reach. Sal was now upright and steady on both feet.

"Good!" exclaimed Dan. "Good guy!"

Motke and Park could barely see Sal's landing, but could discern he was safe. They exhaled.

"Hold on, Sal," pleaded Park. She and Motke, digging their heels in, lowered Dan upside down even lower until only his ankles remained above the top. Each one of them tensely held onto one of Dan's hiking boots. As Dan's beet red face inched past the spot where the scrub had broken free of the ground, he observed a slight texture from within the recess.

"Wait!" Dan yelled up. "Sal, can you hang tough a minute more?" Dan reached into the opening the sage bush had formerly covered. It was a dry well. He felt a pottery shard, and then metal. "Dear Lord. People, I found something." He loudly whispered, "Tell me this is *the dry well.*"

Dislodging obstructions carefully with his fingertips, he slowly saw the rim of a cylinder-like object. It was the size of one very wide page, slightly curled. "Sal, catch this sucker if it falls your way." Tugging, Dan was able to see a fuller outline. "I see it. I see it all." He yanked and the short semicircular copper scroll tumbled out of its hiding place, and slipped straight down. The rounded engraving landed snugly against Sal's chest. "Can you grab that?" asked Dan.

Sal was able to fit one arm through it, as a warrior would don a fore-arm bracer. Then, reaching as far as he could, and a bit further, Sal touched and then fully intertwined hands with Dan, first his right hand and then the left. Slowly Motke and Park hauled Dan back over the edge, pulling Sal's squirming form along. When Sal was finally safely back at the surface, Park draped herself around him, checking for scratches and bruises from the thorns and rocks. His forehead was bleeding from a cir-cle of tiny gashes, but Park was ecstatic in her relief.

While Park was tending to her son, Motke and Dan were staring in dis-belief at what they now believed was the Second Copper Scroll. Dan spit on its surface, smearing away dust and dirt debris. Looking over their shoulder to see if they were observed, they continued cleaning up the relic. Dan sprinkled some Neviot water and washed more caking away until the shallowly engraved inscription was entirely visible on the green patina of the metal page.

"We're dead if we don't turn this in immediately," cautioned Motke. "I mean prosecution."

"Can you read any of this?" asked Dan.

Motke nervously looked over his shoulder, then silently examined the letters, and finally took out the booklet and in some ways used it as a Rosetta Stone to compare translated phrases.

"It is places," reported Motke excitedly, "names of places . . . they are numbered . . . completing, I imagine, the secret sites of the first Copper Scroll. I see Bet Shean marked here. I see Jerusalem. I see Gamla in the Golan. Here is Qumran. Again Qumran. Masada once. Jerusalem again. Let me check for hiding place 65, which is this piece. Okay . . ." he read silently, then out loud.

"*Let the Sons of Darkness look . . .*"began Motke and then correcting him-self, "maybe it's *seek* or *search* not *look,* maybe . . . okay, try this . . . *Let the Sons of Darkness seek throughout the land for the treasure,*" he translated with uncertainty. "*They will find* "I can't decipher it." he complained. "Maybe it's they will *search* . . . I can't . . . wait, here's a part I can read."

Motke mumbled the translation slowly, *"They who seek silver and gold are misled from our greatest treasure, the final salvation, the C Scroll."* He stopped to explain, "There is no C in the Hebrew language. So I'm guessing it is like an English C. Actually it reads, *Sameh Yod,* two letters pushed together by the ancient scribe in an unusual way. I figure that is C. Maybe it stands for Caesar, or something else with the sound of C?"

Motke studied the writing, adding, "Here's more. It's says something like . . . *From the Scriptorium, seek the Lion's Right Eye.* Next to this statement," he added, "are two more Greek letters I don't understand." Chilled, Motke shivered a bit. Goosebumps needled his arms.

Dan studied the two Greek characters. "Alpha and Omega," he noted, commenting, "Means nothing to me."

"It means something to me," Park said quietly.

Convinced none among them was really hurt, the group reenergized. They began hiking to the Scriptorium to search for the Lion's Right Eye. *En route,* the sole site attendant, who had seen the rescue from afar, approached and asked in Hebrew if everyone was okay. Motke, who had deftly slipped the Second Copper Scroll into his knapsack, answered that he had to save a stupid American tourist but not to worry, the tumult was over. The attendant barked an obligatory warning and returned grumbling to his post inside the ticket booth.

The experience over the precipice hardened Sal, who having stared down the cliffside of death, now seemed to walk with more confidence, head straight up, shoulders level, eyes sharpened for anything in front of him. This was a new Sal, a toughened Sal, returning self-aware from the brink. His jaw seemed more square. It was almost as though his form had changed, bulked, transmogrified into a more substantial presence. Park was the first to notice the difference, but soon the others did too. Sal now walked with measured and deliberate steps, bouncing up stone steps and no longer shrinking from the ancient walls brushing against his side.

Dan and Motke kept visualizing and repeating: *Lion's* Right Eye . . . *Lion's* Right Eye. C Scroll. Lion's Right Eye. C Scroll. But as they hiked back, they remembered the Scriptorium was empty. No inscriptions or illustrations remained anywhere. No Lions of Judah. No eyes of lions.

Finally, the group arrived back at the main ruin. Quickly, they reentered the half-walled roofless area known as the Scriptorium. They gazed around at the mountains in the distance, the lifeless but exquisitely azure

Dead Sea, some clouds far off, birds flying overhead.

"C Scroll?" asked Dan. "No C Scroll here."

"It will reveal itself," said Sal rather staunchly, surprising the group. He panned the scenery and then suddenly jerked his head back. Pointing up at the cliffs directly across the expanse, atop the valley wall, he gestured demonstratively. "I see a lion's head," declared Sal. "Anyone can see it. That long runway-type ramp of a flattened cliff, maybe it's a slide area—that's the snout. The wrinkles and openings underneath are the mouth and nostrils; see, it all stretches upward . . . to those two caves on either side of the bridge of the snout. Eyes."

"Yes, yes. I can see it," agreed Park. Swiftly the others became electric as the image became distinct to them as well. "The Lion's Right Eye is the right cave over there," Park whispered loudly, afraid some tourists nearby would overhear.

Several minutes later, after finishing the jumbo bottle of Neviot, stopping at the bathroom, cleaning up with moist towelettes, gulping down a few Elite candy bars for energy, and questioning their own sanity, the group began their march to the Lion's Right Eye.

"Okay, the Lion's Right Eye," repeated Dan, breathing out in exhaustion. "The climb up, methinks, is a little longer than I thought. We could just take a picture for reference and come back another day."

"Fine. But we don't have a camera," deadpanned Motke.

"I'm for doing this," asserted Sal, again to the surprise of the group. "I'm not tired in the least."

"You need to slide into a life-threatening ravine more often," quipped Dan.

The group trekked down a steep path past rubble heaps of pottery shards thus far ignored by Israel Antiquities. Soon they were in the midst of the long expanse following the main water trough leading in a distinct line to the mountain ridge and the caves—to the Lion's Right Eye. Sal hiked with silent determination, as did Park, while Motke and Dan jabbered away.

"So what's the story?" Motke asked. "You hacked in on Ben Hinnom's global teleconference. That's very naughty. I'm surprised you're around to walk upright. He's looking for you, no?"

"He's looking for me, yes. For them too, that's for sure," confirmed Dan, a bit too cocky. "He's looking all over the world."

Park and Sal could not help but hide their smirks. Motke pressed him.

"I think he's looking for me in Arizona . . . and Peru . . . and maybe the Himalayas, and I think the middle of the ocean—unless he finally catches me driving through Nicaragua." Dan laughed, and took a swig of bottled water.

"You're everywhere?" asked Motke.

"I booked some trips—all simultaneously," continued Dan with a wry smile. "The 21-day combined mule train and Grand Canyon river running raft experience. . . the 18-day Pacific Ports of Call cruise out of San Diego . . . the 14-day Andes llama expedition—llamas are cooler than camels, you know . . . a 16-day Nepal mountain trek, yetis no extra charge . . . and the five week Pan-American Highway bus extravaganza including the side trip to the Falkland Islands. I left that whole tour list on my answering machine—as an informative advisory to my travel editors, but of course. So I think Ben and his asshole buddy Linzer are looking—everywhere but here."

"I wouldn't be so sure," cautioned Park. "It's only a matter of time."

"Babe, that's what this whole adventure is about," replied Dan. "Time. Everyone's watching the clock."

"Don't call me babe—unless you think I'm a baseball player," she said in a singsong.

By now the group had reached the ridge above the cave, where a flimsy protective wire fence stopped them. They nimbly stepped around it. By following a steep rivulet path, the four managed to descend down the cliff face several yards, up and around a boulder, then across to the cave mouth—the Lion's Right Eye. The cave itself was a small one, featuring a flat, slanted dirt floor. Large enough to stand in only at the center, the cave tapered as the roof sloped towards the edges. Sunlight illuminated most of the ten foot depth. Motke reached into his knapsack and pulled out two pocket flashlights.

"Anything you *don't* have in the knapsack?" asked Dan.

"It's the desert. I travel prepared," Motke proudly replied.

Flashlights shining, they methodically examined the cave, its upper corners, innermost depressions and potential hiding places. Balls of ram defecation. Streams of insects scattering. Brilliantly hued beetles. A typical cone-shaped sand hornet's nest pasted into the wall. Some water seepage. A feather. But nothing man-made.

"It's empty," said Motke. "Unless you want to dig, but we have no shovel. It's the only thing not in my knapsack."

After exchanging glances of agreement, they began scraping the ground with their hands. Quickly, they encountered rock. As they moved toward one corner, several wasps flew out of their hive and buzzed around their heads.

"Ram dung and wasp nests," said Motke. "All these caves have the same interior decorator."

They dug some more, until their knuckles were bruised and skinned. Dan poked and rubbed his finger into tiny fissures and crevices but detected nothing. One cut was long and sleek. "Give me the flashlight," he asked. He peered into the illuminated crack. Nothing. "Let me try," said Park, rubbing her eyes and then peering in once again.

"We have enough—the Second Copper Scroll," said Dan. "Let's skedaddle. I'm beat." The others finally relented as well.

"It's here," said Sal. "It just hasn't revealed itself."

Nonetheless, they moved out of the Lion's Right Eye, and back onto the path. Just then a sand wasp began buzzing Sal's ear. He swatted it repeatedly and finally ducked three or four times to evade it. The wasp, however, stayed with him. All at once, Sal stood motionless. He inexplicably closed his eyes for a moment as the wasp buzzed fervently, emitting a sound, not unlike a transformer's pulse, around his right temple. Sal inhaled deeply, then peacefully returned to the cave. Knowing he was allergic to stings, Park tried in vain to stop him. But from her position up the trail, she could not.

They all scrambled up after Sal and could only watch mystified as he serenely stepped to the cave wall, his face just inches from the sand wasp nest. In a furor, the militant wasps launched and circled. They buzzed, but did not light. Eventually, a dozen or more flew around his right ear until he lifted his index finger and then inserted it directly into the mouth of the conical nest. The wasps swarmed out of the cave right past the heads of Motke, Park, and Dan who nervously ducked.

With a slight shove of his finger, Sal crumbled the entire nest structure. As it disintegrated around his hand, a cloudy blue-green glass vial was revealed. One pointed end was wedged into a minuscule shaft. A linen fragment plugged the exposed end. Sal pulled the vial out slowly and held it up to the light. Moistening his fingers on his tongue, he washed the caked glass surface, rich in air bubbles and granular material but completely opaque. As Sal held the vial, Park delicately pulled the linen plug. Sal rotated the vial down, and a tiny inscribed leather scroll was seen protruding. Park extracted it.

"We are in so much trouble," mumbled Motke. "Antiquities will kill us. No dig permit, no nothing."

Park flattened the rolled document in Sal's palm, holding it down with two fingers, so Motke could scrutinize. Motke craned his head to within inches from the inscription. "*Sameh Yod*–pushed together," acknowledged Motke breathlessly. "The C Scroll."

"Give us a few words," said a stunned Dan.

Motke peered, shook his head to start again, peered once more, cleared his eyes with demonstrative blinks, and continued to stare. "There are no words," Motke finally declared. "Well, there are, but I don't recognize any of them. It's letters and some of them are larger than others. Words–but not words."

Sal lowered his head for a closer look. Scanning the characters, his eyeballs rolled and flitted almost involuntarily. He listened. He seemed to hear–with his right ear . . . something. Sal's face became pacific and white. He smiled through tears euphorically spilling out of his eyes, and announced, "This is a code. Mom, it's me. It's for me." He lifted his head as though in a trance and dramatically laid three fingers of his right hand onto the scroll. "Check it."

Motke gazed at the letters under Sal's three fingers, astonished by the three characters revealed: "Sameh–S . . . Aleph–A . . . Lamed–L . . ." Still facing up, Sal's trancelike expression became something more powerful, more joyful, as he repeated, "It's me."

Linzer beat his fist onto a desk in his Seattle office and growled. Dan's father spoke: "You know, you just don't know that you know." Park became fearful for an instant, she almost touched her son but stopped short with a gasp. Dr. Kuebitz called an Israeli Army general who marveled at what he was told. Raymond's mother dialed the phone to book a flight.

Children were dancing. All around they were dancing and the Shabbos Rebbe was dancing with them.

14

FORMAT C:

Secrets everywhere. All of them hiding.

Embedded within the cobblestone alleys, whispering from the trees and gardens, floating along the streams, and reflected in the eyes of birds flying above, secrets dwell throughout the city. Their essence wafts through the surrounding mountains as an intoxicating fragrance. This is Tsfat, an ancient fortress of Jewish mystics and magic, carved defiantly into a northern Israel summit. Originally a medieval refuge of Kabbalistic knowledge, concealed wisdom is still a way of life. Deep within the gnarled alleys and time-battered buildings of Tsfat's old city, rabbinical centers and synagogues exist not merely to worship and obey, but to study mysteries, examine codes, interpret visions, espouse predictions, generate magic, and take delight in numerological truths. Here they believe, and they wait for the Chosen One.

So it was to the city of Tsfat that Dan, Park, Motke and Sal traveled Friday morning with their two treasures in a tote bag, the Second Copper Scroll and the C Scroll. They drove up the one serpentine mountain road leading into Tsfat, passing through layered fog and low-hanging clouds, in search of answers.

"I hate this van," grumbled Dan as he squeezed the oversized white vehicle through Tsfat's slender thoroughfares. Despite several efforts to get a small auto, the rental agency insisted only the van was available for long-term lease. For Dan, driving it was an indignity.

After waiting for the city center's clogged streets to clear, they parked at the Rimon Hotel, the spectacular stone lodging hung from a cliff, not far from the old city. It was but a ten-minute walk through the artist district where sculptors, microcalligraphers, carvers, metalsmiths, and scribes display their wares, sometimes in elegant overpriced galleries chilling champagne in buckets at the door, sometimes in cluttered kiosks, and not infrequently on a cardboard box teetering on a stand. Just beyond, lay the maze-like Kabbalist quarter.

The four travelers waited for two o'clock when, on schedule, a caravan of massive tour buses ferrying noisome, souvenir-hunting American students retreated down the hairpin mountain road and back to kibbutz guesthouses in the valley. Such weekday incursions were tolerated by the Kabbalist community for the sake of dollars dropped into omnipresent donation boxes and the worthless earrings and overpriced candles tourists purchased. During the overpopulated week, the scholars seemed to disappear. Now with the orange disk setting on the horizon below, and the holy sabbath approaching, the streets of Tsfat's mystic quarter briefly resumed their empty and echoing allure. A moment of peace without tourists was all Tsfat's authentic Kabbalists needed to again reveal themselves. They filled the walkways, scurrying to finish affairs before sundown.

Motke knew Meir, a scholar of Jewish mysticism. The directions to his room were unchanged: from the plaza, down the steps to the Y along the right fork, through a small passageway to another lower walkway with a brief commanding view of the valley, over to a squat corner building, up a broken ladder, and finally traversing the sky blue painted roof to a weathered wooden door. Meir lived there.

Motke beat on the door. "Meir, open up!"

The screeching sound of moving furniture was heard as the door creaked open. The view within was dim. Inside, one wall was completely draped by a thick black velvet curtain. In another corner stood a gas cooktop surrounded by several half-empty Elite coffee cans. All other wall space was devoted to books stacked both vertically and horizontally on flimsy brown stained shelves, and, of course, piled onto chairs.

Meir stuck his head out. He was a slender dark-skinned scholar, whose baggy food-stained white shirt was neatly buttoned at the collar but only partially tucked into nondescript black pants topped by *tzitzit* fringe. His square-rimmed skullcap bore a gaudily embroidered palm tree and camel motif. Drawn cheeks hung below tired bespectacled eyes peering beneath expressive bushy eyebrows. Long *payess* locks were deftly folded out of sight behind his ears.

He greeted his old friend Motke and welcomed the group congenially. "Please come in," he said. Sal, Dan, and Motke stepped over the high threshold and into the room, but Meir stopped Park at the door. "Sorry not you," he said quite politely. "Women to stay outside."

Park was accustomed to—and now impatient with—annoying religious customs regarding women. But preferring not to offend, she simply waited for Motke and Dan to intercede. Motke attempted to justify her entry, but Meir remained uncomfortable and unyielding. Finally Motke gestured, "But she has the bag."

Park, careful to see if anyone was about, unzipped the tote bag, reached in, and exposed the top half of the Second Copper Scroll. Meir's eyes widened as he beckoned, "Come in, come in, come in." Checking for nosy neighbors, Meir shut the door, shoving a small bureau a few inches so that it blocked the hinge. He pulled a frayed gray rope and the huge black velvet drape gathered to one side, revealing a large window which illuminated the rooms and provided a majestic panorama of the valley below. Checking his wristwatch, he assured, "We have time until sundown. Show me *this*," he said, twirling his fingers fervidly in the direction of the tote bag.

Park gingerly brought out the Second Copper Scroll, wrapped in a towel from the Dan Pearl, handing it to Motke as Meir visually consumed the object. Then she handed Dan a slender cocoon of bubblewrap. He carefully unrolled the blue-green vial containing the C Scroll. Meir fidgeted uncomfortably as Sal silently pulled the linen plug and extracted the leather document. As the ancient document came fully into view, Meir audibly gasped.

"This is what?" asked Meir aloofly.

"Both found at Qumran, in the caves," replied Motke in a dramatic monotone, adding "Here is the *Second . . .*" he paused, ". . . Cooper Scroll—the one identified in hiding place number 65 of the original Copper Scroll. You can easily see all the burial places of the original are itemized in these columns," Motke pointed with a folded corner of the towel. "There's even one not far from Tsfat. The Second Copper led us to the C

Scroll, which is beyond me."

Meir pulled a large rectangular magnifying glass from atop some books and hovered over the two relics, examining the smallest details of the inscriptions. As he scrutinized the C Scroll, he paused at one spot.

"Good. Delightful," said Meir. "So?"

"We were hoping you could explain a few of the meanings to us," Dan volunteered.

"To you?" asked Meir. "Please don't take offense, but what I know and what others up and down the street know, these are not things we share, especially with someone, no offense please, like yourself. Are you a Jew?"

"You talking to me?" asked Dan with a Chicago street-kid tone.

"Please take no offense," Meir said as though slicing quickly through an apple. "Just because you have a cut *pisher* does not make you a Jew. Just because you maybe got a bar mitzvah from some illegal rabbi in America does not make you a Jew. A real Jew is one who understands his place in the universe and relationship to the Holy One, one who studies the concepts and teachings that have been handed down. Do you read Hebrew? I think no. Have you studied the Kabbala? I think no. Did you ever read the Book of Secrecy, the Book of Brightness, the Gates of Holiness, Book Temunah, Book Bahir, the Zohar? Ever heard of them? Do you understand the concept of Emanations, of numbers, of fire and light? I think no. So what I possess is divine information and it is meant to be taught slowly and skillfully over a long, unrushed time to a qualified recipient . . . Do you want some coffee?"

Dan politely nodded no.

The others also nodded no.

"So I would feel uncomfortable," Meir elaborated, "about sharing these secrets even with Motkele; he's a good guy and I know him. Maybe he and I could talk a little–a few sentences. But *you*? You don't strike me as worthy of this knowledge because knowledge itself is power and we must be careful who and under what circumstances we give power, just as you would in offering a weapon. These other two," said Meir, dismissively pointing to Sal and Park, "are out of the question."

Dan withheld his Chicago street-kid reaction for a moment as the others nervously eyed him. After a moment, he smiled. "Who appointed you," he asked quietly, "to be God's gatekeeper of knowledge?"

"I'm no gatekeeper," replied Meir testily. "But a little knowledge can be a dangerous thing. You've heard that. Imagine if you had spent your entire life in a dark room without windows and you had never been outside. But outside your room there are busy streets, beautiful hills and valleys, wondrous mountains, the skies and the seas, and all the flowers and the animals. Would you be ready to suddenly understand any of it? Imagine being completely ignorant and illiterate and being brought into the greatest library on earth. What could you do? Please no offense but do you understand? So unless you can tell me why I should help, I can't help you. Why should I?"

Dan said nothing.

Meir repeated, *"Why?"*

For just an instant, Dan squinted and made a fist. His mother asked the question over and over until the echo hurt Dan's ears.

PEOPLE WERE EVERYWHERE pushing carts, wheelbarrows, buggies—all of them piled high with the rags and remnants that would become tomorrow for survivors. The War was over. The victims were emerging. Some walked. Some limped. Some shuffled. Many merely wandered. A few wore placards around their necks seeking lost family members. Each hoped to find a direction home or a road to a new life. Where were they? Where were they going? Stranded somewhere between the distant smoke and their own footsteps, the haggard faces of the refugees promised one thing: they would never be the same. Nor would the world. Nor would they let it.

Moishe and Rivke stepped along their road pulling a splintered wooden wagon loaded down with their duffel bags and some foraged objects. Hungry, uncertain, exhausted, they fell in behind a long line of others going where no one could predict from a place no one could imagine. Rivke was wearing heavy riding boots, bartered, perhaps purloined, from the village. She stood out since many had no shoes at all. Moishe's gun with a chambered round, still on safety, hid wedged under his coat where he could reach it quickly. The War was over, but he still nervously examined every tree and bush, every refugee and passing Russian soldier.

They had been walking all morning hoping to find something to eat. The Russian Army had requisitioned everything. Not far from a crossroads, several meters into the clearing, two men fished at a bend in the stream. The two were staring strangely at Rivke and Moishe. Next to the two men was a bucket of hooked fish that caught Moishe's eye.

"Watch the wagon," said Moishe. "Maybe I can get us a fish for tonight." He walked off, calling back to her, "I have you in sight. Stay close to the wagon."

Both men were smoking German cigarettes and seemed almost carefree as they gazed at their fishlines and only occasionally glanced at the people trudging along the road. When they sensed a fish bite, they seemed delighted, as though it were an outing. It had been a long time since Moishe saw anyone fish for enjoyment.

"German cigarettes," observed Moishe. "Where did you get those?" he asked of the taller one, trying to strike up a friendly exchange.

"Oh, those," the taller one answered. "Not hard. They're around."

"You're from where?" asked Moishe.

"I've been everywhere," the tall one answered. "Who knows where anyone is from with all this," he gestured to the road.

Moishe thought that was a strange reply. In this cruel War, everyone knew where they were from. "And your friend?"

"Austria," the other man answered without looking away from the pond.

"Vienna?" replied Moishe.

"Nein," the other man replied in German. "Linz."

"You have extra fish," said Moishe, glancing back to check on Rivke. "It's just me and my wife over there. We have nothing to offer you. But if you can spare a fish, one day I'll pay you back a kindness."

The taller one took a deep drag on his cigarette, looked Moishe in the eye and asked, "Promise?"

"Yes," assured Moishe. "We're heading back to the front, maybe a DP camp. We don't know but in this world, you meet people again."

"You're hungry, aren't you?" the tall man asked.

Everyone on the road was hungry, thought Moishe. "What else? Of course," Moishe answered, trying to make light, but at the same time edging his finger close to the gun under his coat, adding "We had very little last night, and it made us sick."

"And you really need some fish for food tonight?" the tall one asked again, seeming to derive pleasure from the question.

"I have nothing to offer you except a thank you. . ." said Moishe, becoming worried. "But I see you have extra. So you'll catch another in a minute."

"Okay, but remember I helped you," the tall one said almost menacingly. "Remember you had no food and I took fish from my own bucket and gave it to you and asked nothing in return except that one day you or your children return the kindness." Moishe nodded yes. "Okay, so it's a great story you tell your

children. Tell them how one day in the middle of all this craziness you got a fish at the side of a road."

"I'll tell, I'll tell," promised Moishe, by now thinking the tall one was a bit daft, as many were by war's end.

"Well," the tall one declared, "everything is written, you know. So I guess it was written that I would help you eat tonight with a fish. Everything with a reason, no? Nothing by accident." He motioned to the bucket. "Take any that you like."

Moishe quickly pulled a cloth from within his coat and wrapped a medium-sized fish. "Thank you," he said, watching carefully that neither man would change his mind. He retreated back toward the wagon at the road, keeping the two fishermen in sight. Just when Moishe turned his head back to the road, the tall one called out, "His name will be Daniel." The other fellow from Austria took notice and grinned.

Moishe turned back and called, "Who?"

The bucket and the fish poles were at the side of the stream. But the men were gone. Moishe didn't care. He raced back to Rivke.

"Everything with a purpose," Moishe told her. "We got lucky. God arranged for us to get fish. All we have to do is remember the story." As they resumed walking, Moishe repeated, "Nothing by accident."

Dan unsquinted and his fist disappeared. He needed Meir's cooperation. This was not a time to butt heads and end up with nothing. He used his best reporter-psych technique, filtering every statement through the logic set Meir himself had established.

"You speak excellent English," Dan started.

"I spent time with my uncle. Jersey," Meir replied.

"You believe everything is preordained, correct?" Dan asked Meir, who didn't seem to understand the word *preordained.* ". . . Laid out in advance by God?"

Meir agreed.

"So let me tell you a story." Dan talked about his parents, about his mother's miraculous escape from a boxcar *en route* to *Treblinka,* about her being pulled from a shallow grave by his father, about their two years of survival in the woods, about their decision to remain Jews even while believing themselves to be the last ones.

"Is that why God permitted them to survive?" asked Dan passionately.

"Is that why God directed us to the Second Copper Scroll and the C Scroll, hidden for 2000 years, and then—*bang*—brought us to your room to seek wisdom from you—and not from one hundred other people? So you could stand before God and disregard the destiny he has wrought?" Park glanced at Meir, then back at Dan. Motke and Sal held their breath waiting for Meir to respond.

"Very good," conceded Meir, "for someone who is not really a Jew."

"How did I get to be 'not really a Jew?'" Dan responded, again in Meir's own lexicon, "by seeking enlightenment, by looking up at the heavens and being directed to you? Those that God directs to your door suddenly lose their Jewishness? Is that it?"

"Very, very good," Meir acknowledged with a grin. "Well. I apologize to you, all of you and ask God's forgiveness. So I will explain a few things. Until God stops me. I am sure, by the way, that for every idea I explain, you will misunderstand a thousand, but the effort I will make."

Turning to the scrolls, Meir declared, "From what I see, you have wonderful revelations written here. I am not an expert on Essene thought. But the metal scroll is more than just a list of buried treasure. The cult members selected places that when read carry a hidden meaning. It would take me a long time to decode this. This small leather scroll," he pointed, "this one is very complex because the words are all fragments. They need to be put together—step one. Then we can examine the letters and detect the meaning. This much I can see, the twenty-first letter of the alphabet, the letter *shin,* also known as *sin,* looks important in the C Scroll."

Dan and Motke exchanged glances.

"Numerology?" asked Dan with a look of skepticism.

"God enshrines his messages in letters and words that transcend language," replied Meir staunchly. "Sit. Everybody sit, and I'll explain you something before I have to go for Shabbat."

"We can accompany you to synagogue," offered Dan.

"No thanks," declined Meir, trying to be polite. "I heard you talk, so let me speak now." Rapid-fire, Meir built his case: "Letters and words are magical. The word of God—that is, the Torah—preexisted the creation of the universe. Only through God's holy utterance did the world come into creation. After creation, the words became cloaked in a physical manifestation, and by this I mean the black and white letters of the Torah, the Five Books of Moses, whether you see them in a book or as a Torah scroll.

Understand so far?

"God is all powerful," Meir continued at a quickening clip, "His words are all powerful, and His power burns within the letters and words we see and hear, and how they are arranged. They give insights into the past, the future, and the mysteries of both. Letters and words are, as I said, the power of God, and they are energy. Energy cannot be destroyed. Scientists understand such things. Neither can God's letters. You know what a *serif* is? The little squiggle line on the edge of a letter—especially the older letter styles? It makes the letter artistic. A *seraph* is also a heavenly six-winged being that stands in the presence of God. And *saraph* means to burn. There is a famous story—that every boy who is a real Jew knows—told about the sage Rabbi Chanina who violated the Roman prohibition against teaching Torah. The Romans tortured him terribly, wrapped him in a Torah scroll, and then burned him alive in front of his students. While he was burning, his students asked what he saw. Rabbi Chanina called out in his agony, 'The parchments are consumed, and the letters fly up to heaven.' Dan, may I call you Dan, you can burn parchment, but you cannot burn the law of God.

"Now," continued Meir, "these indestructible letters, they are all symbolic and energized in their construction and usage. Look at the physical structure of Hebrew letters and how they combine to create words. Take the word for *truth,* which in Hebrew is *emet,*" explained Meir. "*Emet* is constructed of three Hebrew letters: *aleph, mem,* and *tav.* Those three letters are the first, approximately middle and last letters of the entire Hebrew alphabet. Genuine truth is completely true, in its beginning, its middle and the end. And," he pointed to the word printed large in a book title on the table, "that each of the three letters of *emet*—you will notice—each letter has two legs—you call them descenders—that stand solidly on the line—like truth stands solidly on the ground.

"Now take the letter *sin* which we see abundantly in the C Scroll you have discovered so nicely," said Meir. "As you can see a *sin* with an *s* sound, normally also called a *shin* with a *sh* sound, also looks like what you would call in English a *W,* but with three flames at the top of the ascenders. These three flames represent divine revelation. Also, you know that Hebrew letters each have a numerical valuation. We take a word and total up the numbers to help discover the meaning. For example, all the letters in the word *Arie,* which means "lion," total up and equal the numerical value of the word *Gvura,* which means "courage and strength," and which is one of God's names. Calculating total number values in every word, in every sentence, in every book is critical. Otherwise you are wasting your time. The *sin* or *shin,* for example, has a value of three hundred. In this C Scroll, I see repeated triplets of *sins,* or what you would consider three Ws. The scroll definitely contains a message. I have to study it more, but so far . . . well, that is what I see."

Dan tried to mask his disbelief. "Meir," he said carefully, "the whole thing about numerology, it's very difficult . . ."

Meir snapped with irritation. "You see, you are a nonbelieving, not even a Jew, an impossible person!" He checked his watch, and threatened, "I have to leave in a minute. You want I should continue or not?"

The group visibly demurred, and Meir resumed.

"Let me try to make a comparison you can comprehend," Meir offered. "You believe in notes, yes? Musical notes." He turned to Park, "Do you know what notes are?"

"Like *do, re, me?*" Park replied.

"Like those, yes," said Meir. "By themselves notes are just sounds. When you put them together, they make music. People get emotional, they get put in a mood, happy, dancing, sad, they feel like fighting. All from this combinations of notes. This I'm sure you accept. People debate the structure of notes. The Gregorian monks from history sang one note at a time without harmony—you see, I know things. And the monks feared certain intervals—that's the space between notes. They believed certain intervals and notes were Devil notes, and they avoided these. Maybe you didn't know this.

"People in your country and England too," he went on, "get all upset because musicians hide Devil messages in the rock music very quietly. Sometimes you can't even hear the Devil message unless you play the music backward. Agreed? Agreed. But—and please don't be offended if I am honest—do you think that all the power you acknowledge in a simple composer, in a little song, in the people who record music, in a musical note which is nothing more than a circle on a line . . . that all these same powers do not exist in God and God's word?

"Words—spoken or written, heard or seen—stimulate the body," Meir said, gesturing across his torso. "Words excite, they arouse, they bring tears. They create *emanations.* If I were a scientist I would call them radio waves. When you speak falsely, you also create emanations. Police measure those false emanations in lie detector tests and voice stress analysis, do they not?

"The secret to all these mysteries is not here . . ." Meir placed his hand on his heart. "The secret is up here . . ." Meir placed two fingers on his right temple, emphasizing, "The mind. That's why we wear *tefillen*–these little leather boxes with the word of God right up here on our foreheads. God sends his signals to man's mind with music, with images of beauty and violence, and most of all with words, letters and numbers–with every emanation in the universe."

"The right temporal lobe," said Dan quietly.

"That's the brain," returned Meir, adding, "We know the brain. The brain is the place where the mind is sitting. And that mind, as I told you, is affected by letters and words, and the secret code within letters and words, and the powerful connections they stimulate in the brain. I see you are trying to think. That's progress. My words are having an effect. So, let's talk codes. Speak Russian? I don't think so. Can you translate *Komitet Gosudarstvennoi Bezopasnosti?* I think no. But you know the code, don't you, you know the first initial of each word . . . *Komitet Gosudarstvennoi Bezopasnosti* is the KGB. And the CIA is Central Intelligence Agency, RCA is Radio Corporation of America. Now take the first three words of the first book of the Bible, known properly in Hebrew as *Bereishit*, but which has been Hellenized into *Genesis* for you. Those first three words in the first chapter are *bereishit bara elohim.* The last letters of each of those first three words combine to create *aleph mem tav*–once again *emet* the word for *truth*, which I explained earlier. Now go to the end of the first chapter. The last letters of the first three words of the last sentence of the last verse, those three also spell *emet*. It's no accident, Dan. These words and their codes are God's will."

Meir closed his eyes a moment, prayed briefly, and then continued, "Now what is the most powerful sound in the universe, and the most powerful code representing that sound? Of course you don't know. If you were a Jew you could answer immediately–please take no offense. You do not. But Motke standing over there knows. That sound is the unutterable name of God. A sound! A sound! Mortal man has nothing but a code for that sound which to you is YHWA, four letters that make up the *tetragramaton*. Now some people connect those letters, reverse some letters, place vowels in between–and they have their favorite pronunciations."

"I've heard *Jehovah,* and *Yahweh,* and even *Yahveh,*" said Park.

"Regardless," Meir resumed, "mankind prays to this code name. And everyone knows–or should know–that terrible things will occur when the real name should be uttered. Even Moses was not permitted to hear this sound.

"Remember what created the universe," asserted Meir, wagging his index fingers up. *"God SAID: Let there be Light.* Creation occurred not because God mixed some chemicals in a test tube. He *SAID* his magical words–comprised of 22 letters and 10 numbers which combine to create the 32 paths of wisdom–and those words were enough to create all the universe and everything in it. Words, Dan. And numbers. They are the same, Dan. They are," Meir said with a wave, "God's instruments."

Elaborating with great speed, Meir went on: "All Hebrew letters have a numerical value. It's the ABCs. *Aleph* is one, *bet* is two, *gimel* is three, *dalet* is four, and so on. The Romans, Chaldeans, many ancient peoples, they did likewise. Letters equal numbers. You do it in America too, you prioritize alphabetically. You have your A list, your B list. Alpha battalion, Bravo battalion. You get the message?"

Dan nodded.

Meir slowed his elucidation and lowered his voice, "And now we come to darkness and light." Meir looked to his left as if to spy whether an unwanted spirit was lurking in the room. "Light and dark are not two different things, they are separate parts of the one presence. When the Holy One created celestial light, darkness was part of it, interspersed. God separated the two into Day and Night. Please Dan, think. Light exists only because of darkness. Without darkness to compare it to, there is no light." Meir went to a darkened corner and lit a match. You see the light from this match. The light is divided into many intensities, each of which has a spiritual meaning I won't go into now–it would take hours. But taken as a whole, this light is completely surrounded by what?" Without waiting for a reply, Meir answered himself: "Darkness."

Dan pensively rested his chin on folded hands for a moment, and posited, "If there is no light without darkness, then there is no good without evil. Evil is required to define good."

Everyone in the room looked as though a flashlight had been shone in their eyes. Meir wrinkled his face with delight and gently shook his head,

his eyebrows twittering. "You see the power of words," said Meir proudly. "It didn't take me long to make a real Jew out of you. Sure they are
related. Light is the world of the righteous and the pious. Dark is the other
side where dwell the demons and evil doers, the evil Lilith and her mate
the arch-demon Samael."

"*I form the light and create darkness, I bring prosperity and create disaster, I the
Lord do all these things.* Isaiah 45:7," said Park, adding ". . . basic Bible."

Meir applauded with his eyebrows.

Limbering his body to get closer, Meir reexamined the C Scroll, moving the magnifying glass up and down, but finally back to the one spot he
scrutinized before. He quickly consulted another book, and then leafed
through a thin manuscript laying flat atop his refrigerator. After praying
silently for a moment, he took off his glasses and spoke slowly, "I think
. . . I *think* . . . Three *sins* in this scroll, the way they are arranged, represent all knowledge, perhaps the perversion, yes the perversion of all
knowledge. Just as light was perverted by darkness before it was expelled
during creation to become the abode of evil, just as Adam perverted his
garden by eating from the Tree of Knowledge of Good and Evil before
being expelled, so these three *sins* represent something perverted which
has the power to bring in the final reign of the arch-demon—he has many
names. But you know who I mean . . . *The Devil.*"

He motioned Dan to hold the C Scroll in better light. "This section,"
he said pointing with his pinky, "here is a reference to the *abomination of
desolation* which predicts the final struggle between good and evil when a
Satan will attempt to place his idol in the Temple. *Abomination of desolation,* means the final attempt to defile the precious presence of the Lord."

Park quoted again, *"Then he will set up the abomination that causes desolation. With flattery he will corrupt those who have violated the covenant but the
people who know their God will firmly resist him,"* adding, "That's straight
Daniel."

"You know your verses," complimented Meir, eyebrows twitching
approvingly. "And the chapter?"

"Eleven."

"Correct again," responded Meir, adding, "Now I see other numbers
here . . . but they make no sense. Or, they are beyond my understanding." He looked at the C Scroll again. "First, I see a three-letter word—not
really a word, more like a letter grouping, whose total is 13 . . . *gimel, hay,*

hay which is three plus five and five making 13; then I see another three-letter grouping slightly different, *vav, hay, hay* which is six plus five plus five, and that makes 16." Meir picked at the mucus in the corner of his eyes. "I don't know why 13 and 16. Maybe later I'll get it.

"I also see a reference," Meir observed, "maybe it is to the Chaldean alphabetical numbering system. That, of course, is the alphabet Daniel would have known since he was in Chaldean Babylon and the Book of Daniel was probably written shortly after the fall of Babylon in 539 BCE at the hands of the Lord acting in his wisdom through Cyrus the Great."

"What was their numbering system?" asked Sal.

"He speaks," a somewhat surprised Meir observed. "You multiply every letter by six. Roughly comparing the Chaldean alphabet to English, it would be A equals 6 to start. Then B equals 12. Then C equals 18, and it would keep adding up by sixes until Z equals 156 and so on."

Meir tapped his forehead and said, "I'm presuming that you . . . well, maybe I should not presume, but you do know the hills of Jerusalem are formed in the shape of a *shin* or a *sin,* that almost W shape." He pulled out a flat pencil with a thick lead point and drew a trident on a piece of paper. You see, the *W,* let's call it, has three lines which correspond to the three valleys of ancient Jerusalem." Then he grabbed a nearby book with a topographical map of Jerusalem, pointing across the page to trace how the three curving valleys divided the city.

"I'll tell it," Motke chimed in, again enjoying the chance to be the tour guide. "Meir means on the right of the *W* or *shin* is the Kidron Valley where you find the Mount of Olives and this valley represents good. On the left of the *W* or *shin* is the Valley of Ben Hinnom—your favorite valley, Dan. You already know that is a bad valley. And in the middle is what can be called the Tyropoeon valley, which is now covered by sites in the Old City—it isn't really a valley anymore. But these two outer valleys—Kidron and Hinnom—converge together at the bottom of the Tyropoeon and become what is known as the Unified Kidron Valley, which then travels all the way to the Dead Sea. Not far from Qumran. You can actually walk along the route from the Old City to the Dead Sea in just a few hours."

"That's the geography," Meir cut in. "But I emphasize, these two outside valleys—Hinnom and Kidron—are a struggle between good and evil and always have been. Listen because I know what I am saying."

He glanced out the window to see the sun was about to set. "Finished.

Shabbat," he blurted abruptly. "Who knows about these two scrolls? You can't just keep them," cautioned Meir.

As he rewrapped the artifacts, Motke pleaded with Meir to keep their secret until they made a decision on whom to surrender the scrolls to.

"Keep a secret? I'm an expert," Meir assured, shooing everybody out the door.

Just as they were leaving, Meir, like any good teacher, reminded them, "So now you have the three shins . . . plus, the 13 and the 16–I can't figure that one out. Maybe you have the Chaldean alphabet . . . and for sure you have Daniel's prophecy about the abomination of the temple. So . . ."

Meir waited awkwardly at the door. Finally he asked, "Nu?"

Dan caught on. "Of course . . . for the synagogue," he said, pulling out some Israeli currency for a donation.

"Dollars is better," said Meir.

Dan reached into his back pocket and brought out some folded U.S. money. "Here, a ten and another dollar, that's it. Thank you for all your help, especially before the Shabbat."

Meir stared briefly at the money, arched his eyebrows, and smiled broadly. "Remember what I said," Meir reiterated. "God speaks through letters and numbers. *Shabbat shalom.*"

ISRAEL'S MORNING SUN was still an hour from showing itself when a slovenly dressed customs man stepped on his still-lit cigarette and then sleepily unlocked the padlocks of a massive barbed-wire gate. A weather-warped sign declared in Hebrew, Arabic, and English: "No Entry. No Smoking. Secured Cargo." Inside the massive pen, rows of stacked shipping containers formed linear canyons. The thick security chain clanged as the slovenly dressed man pulled it through three fastening locks, thereby allowing the gate to swing loose. Over his shoulder endless lights of waiting cargo vessels twinkled throughout Haifa Harbor.

Walking slowly between the rows, the customs man compared the list on his clipboard to the stenciled numbers on the doors of the grimy steel shipping containers. One by one, he inspected and cleared containers, checkmarking them for release with green chalk. At the far end of the compound, he came to a strange one, irregularly sized and unusually tall.

He unlatched, lifted, and swiveled open the securing mechanism. Gripping the reinforced handle with one hand, he tugged. The door would not budge. He placed his clipboard on the ground and using two hands finally swung the rusty door open. Three rats scampered past his feet. He deftly sidestepped the rodents—not unusual in these containers—and then reached for the flashlight in his back pocket. One last rat darted out after its companions. The flashlight beam shone in but he didn't recognize the contours. He rolled a nearby utility light to the container's mouth for a better look. With a sizzle, the bright lights flashed on.

He was about to aim them inside when two gentlemen approached. The customs man turned his flashlight on the two and shouted in Hebrew, "Excuse me, excuse me. Authorized only."

Ben Hinnom raised his hand to shield his eyes from the flashlight.

Linzer showed the customs man some documentation.

"Ooops," said Hinnom, "looks like we *are* authorized." He snapped his fingers dramatically, and grinned. "Came to pick up our cargo."

The customs man examined the papers in triplicate, punched it twice, stamped it, signed his initials, dated it July 11, 1999, and waved the two in to the darkened container's interior. "Stand clear," sang out Hinnom from within.

The man stepped aside.

A growl. Dense black smoke. The sound of gears grinding. Full speed ahead. A yellow school bus, license *June 66*, barged recklessly out of the container. The customs man had never seen such a vehicle in Israel. "That's a new one," he said to himself, watching the bus screech to a halt in the distance at the exit, yield the stamped papers to the guardhouse, and then peel rubber *en route* to the coastal highway heading south.

It was Sunday. On an isolated road midway between Haifa and Jerusalem, a mile from the closest intersection, in a lush tree-lined bottom stretch between tall hills, a kibbutz truck ferrying sheep to the slaughterhouse abruptly stopped. The driver turned to the hitchhiker riding next to him and asked, "You're sure. Here?"

The Shabbos Rebbe answered, "Here." He bounced down from the cab with his sign. As the truck pulled away, the Shabbos Rebbe could be seen in the rear view mirror sitting by the side of the road rhythmically praying over a small book.

Two hours later, the Shabbos Rebbe's attention was still riveted on his book. Suddenly, he listened. Ceremoniously, he slammed the book shut and placed it in his pocket.

A bird flew far overhead from left to right. The Rebbe waved serenely, and uttered another prayer.

There, at the top of the far hill, the yellow school bus appeared. The Shabbos Rebbe calmly picked up his sign from the grassy shoulder, held it with both hands high above his head, and positioned himself squarely in the middle of the road. The sign read:

In the name of the Lord,
blessed be His eternal word,
please drive no further.

Hinnom and Linzer saw the Shabbos Rebbe's far-off figure through the windshield. "Uh oh," said Hinnom. "Obstruction in the road."

The bus lumbered slowly down the hill toward the Rebbe's position.

The Shabbos Rebbe, his arms stiff against the wind, waved the sign left and then right.

"Step on it," ordered Hinnom coldly.

Linzer's foot pressed the accelerator to the floor. The motor howled and sputtered dense exhaust as the bus picked up speed.

"Faster," Hinnom whined as the Shabbos Rebbe stood his ground just ahead.

"*Shma Yisrael, Adonai Elohaynu, Adonoi Ehad!*" called out the Rebbe loudly.

Again. Loudly. "*Shma Yisrael, Adonai Elohaynu, Adonoi Ehad!*"

Again. "*Shma Yisrael, Adonai Elohaynu, Adonoi Ehad!*"

The final incantation was just escaping his lips when Hinnom's speeding school bus impacted his body, crushing it to death instantly with a hideous thump. As the bus continued barreling south, Hinnom scurried to the rear window to see the Shabbos Rebbe's lifeless body. Expressionless, he called over to Linzer: "Next stop: Jerusalem."

DAN, PARK, MOTKE, and Sal had set out for Jerusalem from Tsfat Sunday morning. Their oversized white van continued to annoy Dan, but at least it was powerful enough to handle the steep hills on the highway to Jerusalem. By 10 A.M., they were just a half-hour away. Sal was passionately punching away at his Windy, exploring permutations of the numerological wisdom imparted by Meir. Motke was reading sections of his Bible. Park replayed the profound spiritual concepts of good and evil, light and darkness. Dan was furiously debating in his mind whether they would have dinner at Ema's traditional Armenian restaurant or one of the trendy new seafood cafes south of town.

Suddenly, as the van reached Sha'ar Hagai area approaching Jerusalem, it began decelerating dramatically. "Cripe!" exclaimed Dan as the vehicle crept to a stop. He maneuvered to the side of the highway and pulled the emergency brake hard to prevent rolling downhill. Shaking his head in disgust, Dan helplessly turned the motor on and off several times trying to restart the engine. "Fuel pump, I'll betcha anything," muttered Dan.

He jumped out, checked under the hood, and declared in disgust, "I hate this van."

Dan climbed back in and tried to call the rental agency on his cell phone.

It beeped and displayed "Battery Low."

Park and Sal tried theirs as well. Batteries needed recharging on all three.

"We're just a few minutes away," Dan huffed. Motke tried to flag down a car, but every car, taxi, bus, and truck was speeding up the hill.

"No one will pull over," assured Motke. "They drive like maniacs this time of day."

"They drive like maniacs every time of day," replied Dan. "We'll have to hoof it in."

Just then, along the grassy shoulder, a small Arab boy, hissing at his donkey, came by. He slapped the donkey lightly on the snout with a branch and hissed again bringing the animal to an obedient halt. The young boy from a nearby village, maybe ten years of age, dressed in torn pants, a Coca Cola T-shirt and blue plastic shoes, crassly enjoyed asking in Arabic, "Want a ride?" He added quickly in perfect English, "Give me money."

With amusement, Dan deferred to Motke who, like most Israelis, spoke a smattering of Arabic. "On what, your donkey?" replied Motke in

Arabic. The little boy nodded no, giggled, and pointed up the hill to his friend who was standing next to a dilapidated moped.

"Take that into Jerusalem on this highway," laughed Motke, still in Arabic. "We'll be dead in two minutes." He turned to the others and said in English, "He wants to kill some Jews without shooting. We should drive that!" he joked, motioning above to the moped.

The boy waved and whistled. His partner on the hill hopped on his motorbike and slowly putt-putted down a zigzag of sheep paths and dirt bike trails until he came to the drainage ravine alongside the road. He turned the motor off and walked the bike up to the drainage ravine edge and onto the highway shoulder next to the disabled van.

"Give me money," repeated the Arab boy with the donkey.

Dan chuckled as he examined the moped, toying with the key and revving the handles. "This is cool," said Dan. The others reacted with uproar and disbelief.

"On the Jerusalem highway!" objected Motke, as the constant flow of speeding cars whooshed by. "Forget it."

"Hey," Dan boasted. "I once drove through Chicago's entire south side at sixty miles an hour, dodging debris all the way, on a skinny construction shoulder of the Dan Ryan Expressway in rush hour to make an interview for *Playboy*. That was in a real car. So this is a moped."

After a few minutes of complete craziness in which Park and Motke demanded Dan abandon the idea as suicidal bravado, even as Motke simultaneously bargained with the Arab boy, they agreed on a price. Ten dollars. Dan would drive the moped up the last hill into Jerusalem and call for towing. He would wait for the two Arab boys who would meet up shortly with their donkey to reclaim the bike. The others would remain in the van until the rental car tow truck arrived. Dan was about to power up the rickety scooter when Sal jumped out of the van.

"Can I do it?" he asked.

"The new and improved adventurous Sal," deadpanned Dan as Park immediately forbade the idea. Dan disagreed, suggesting that Sal be allowed to show some spunk, and anyway, it would just be along the shoulder. He began giving Sal instructions on how to get to the gas station near the entrance to the city.

An irked Park stopped Dan mid-sentence, telling him flatly, "Spunk is not suicide."

They were still arguing when Sal flashed an "okay" handsign to the Arab boy. The boy winked.

Sal suddenly hopped on the moped to gain a wobbly start, and took off up the highway. Park gave up chasing the bike after a few yards. Furious, she turned to Dan, "If something happens it's on your head, mister!"

Dan frowned.

Sal, however, was a smile in motion. Cars whizzed by like bullets, fanning his sun-heated form, but Sal calmly steered a steady course along the shoulder. Occasionally, he would cough and choke as a big, exhaust-belching Mercedes truck roared by in a deafening downshift. None of that mattered. This was fun. It got better. Passengers waved as they zoomed past. And then a kibbutz tractor appeared, pulling in on the shoulder behind Sal. Sal half turned and waved as the farmer waved back and tipped his Jewish-star-emblazoned kibbutz hat.

"Where are you going?" yelled out the farmer.

"To Jerusalem," Sal called back, pointing straight ahead.

The farmer returned the gesture with an encouraging wave of his fist. Now there were two.

In a moment more, a small shuttle bus of Catholic nuns pulled in behind them on the shoulder. The chattering nuns, just driving in from the Ben-Gurion airport, delighted at Sal on his sputtering moped. They reached out the windows, swinging their hands as though accompanying music. Now there were three.

The group passed a sweat-drenched marathon cyclist, struggling up the last hill toward Jerusalem in low gear. He waved his water bottle in camaraderie and Sal waved back.

"Jerusalem?" called the cyclist.

Sal called back with exhilaration, "Yes!"

The cyclist sped up and pulled in behind them. Now it was a caravan.

At the entrance to Jerusalem, Sal U-turned into the gas station, the one opposite where the Shabbos Rebbe normally sat. Sal jumped from the motorbike, waving good-bye as the others drove on. He looked toward the office for a pay phone to call the rental agency. There was none. But when he looked back he was surrounded. He couldn't move.

Dancing around him were little children, the same children who reveled with the Shabbos Rebbe in Mea Shearim. Singing songs and tugging on Sal's shirt and pants, they frolicked in pure joy as only children could.

Round and round they danced. Faster. Faster, until Sal became dizzy just watching them.

"I love you all," said a joyful Sal, "Just I can't speak Hebrew. I can't understand you." But the children did not stop and the dancing continued for some time until Sal finally broke away to find a pay phone. The children did not follow and disbursed as suddenly as they appeared. Except for one girl. Just before rounding the corner out of sight, she stopped, turned, called out in Hebrew, and threw Sal a kiss.

"Sorry," Sal yelled back. "I don't speak Hebrew."

~

Logon: Sal M.
Password: * * * * * * *
Verify Password: * * * * * * *

At 11 P.M., long after Motke went home, while Dan and Park were enjoying their final cappuccino at a trendy cafe in the German Colony section on the road to the south, Sal was still at Derek Institute working with his Windy, seeking answers, walking through the precepts Meir had taught.

Sal brought up a new powerful worldwide multilingual search engine he had just discovered. It asked: "What would you like to search?"

He entered: *13 + 16 = 29.*

After several moments the screen displayed: "No results. Next request?"

He entered: *16 + 13 = 29.*

After several moments the screen again displayed: "No results. Next request?"

He entered: *13 x 16.*

"No results. Next request?"

He entered: *13 x 16 = 208.*

"No results. Next request?"

In frustration, he cracked his knuckles, and jokingly entered: How about a revelation?

A list came up. "KJ, NIV, ASV, NRSV, RSV."

He chose NIV and Revelation appeared on the screen: "What Chapter and Verse?"

He typed: Chapter 13 Verse 16.

The verse appeared:

He forced everyone small and great, rich and poor, free and lave, to receive a mark on his right hand or on his forehead . . .

He clicked: Next Verse.

. . . so that no one could buy or sell unless he had the mark, which is the name of the beast or the number of his name.

He clicked: Next Verse.

This calls for wisdom. If anyone has insight, let him calculate the number of the beast, for it is a man's number. His number is 666.

Sal typed: *Hebrew Chaldean Alphabet + Numerical Values.*

The Hebrew Chaldean Alphabet appeared with numbers along side it.

He typed:

Hebrew Chaldean Alphabet as English Equivalents + Numerical Equivalents.

The Hebrew Chaldean Alphabet appeared. Next to it appeared English letters and multiples of 6 beginning with A and ending with 156 for Z.

Sal clipboarded into memory the alphabetical equivalents. He left the search engine and opened a second window, brought up a database, and typed each of the equivalents in a query field.

A = 6
B = 12
C = 18
D = 24
E = 30
F = 36

When he finished, he went back to the search engine in the first window and typed: *English Dictionary.*

On screen appeared 51 different types of general and specialized dictionaries offering word counts from 60,000 to 119,000. Sal clicked 119,000. He downloaded the dictionary and imported it into the database with the Chaldean Alphabet equivalents.

He typed: *Find word equivalents totalling 666.*

Results: *Display?*
He typed: *Yes*
One of the words caught his eye.

C = 18
O = 90
M = 78
P = 96
U = 126
T = 120
E = 30
R = 108
   666 Total

Sal wrote "666" on a piece of paper. He turned it upside down and saw "999." He added a period after the second 9 and then wrote a name in front of it.

Windgazer 99.9

Sal wrote in Hebrew as best he could *sin, sin, sin,* which resembled three *Ws.* He wrote www with a dash and a question mark.

Then he wrote: "World Wide Web."

Quickly, Sal turned to the computer, and went to the web. But his fingers mistyped when they touched the Windy's miniature keypad. Before he could retype a valid address he had logged on to some site. He could not see the address because it suddenly pixilated. The site began loading.

All at once, Sal felt sick. First, his head ached, then he became very warm, so warm that his palms sweated and throbbed. His armpits tightened in a horrific pain, almost like a seizure. His feet swelled so massively that the eyelets on his shoes cut in. He winced in pain. As the excruciation in his armpits increased, so did pressure in his chest. He could hardly breathe. And now his mouth was dry . . . very very . . . very . . . dry . . .

The site finished loading.

Whiteness filled a dot in the middle of the screen. Quickly it grew larger. Very large. Eventually the large white dot reached the limits of the screen edge. But it would not stop there. Now the powerful luminescence extended its glow and engulfed Sal in its strange, spreading radiance. Soon, much of the room was filled with a blinding, pulsing whiteness. At first, he shielded his eyes, but then dropped his hands and looked directly into the screen. He could not move.

The whiteness transfixed Sal. It swept him, transported him, entranced him, amazed him, and transmogrified him until he felt he was no longer in the room. It was as though he had departed, journeyed somewhere else, to the essence preceding the enshrined fire of words and letters, to the unfathomable mind of God. Perfection ripped and contorted his body until he shrieked: "Stop! Why won't you stop!"

The aura fizzled into a swirling white vortex that became smaller and denser until it receded into a disappearing white dot. A standard disconnect message appeared on the screen: "Server site down. Try again later."

Sal awoke weak, draped over a chair with his chest flat on the seat and his still throbbing arms hanging down, touching the floor.

"Are you all right, Sal?"

Sal turned his head slowly until an old man came blurrily into sight.

"Working late?" the old man asked.

Focus returned in a few moments and Sal could see the man more clearly. He wore a long, heavy coat even though it was indoors and a hot summer night. The man's hands were tucked into the pockets. Only his face was visible.

"I have the answer," moaned Sal, as he stared at his aching hands. Sharper now, he repeated, "I have the answer!"

"What is the answer?" the old man asked.

"Format C:," Sal replied wearily, continuing, "Everyone must reformat. Just that command. Format C: . . . I don't understand," he sighed, his head trembling. "Format C: is the command to wipe out people's hard drives. But that was the message—I heard it, I saw it, felt it. Unmistakable. And Windgazer 99.9 . . . Windgazer 99.9 is not the answer to the Millennium Bug. It will ruin everything. Everything! . . . Destroy everything!"

Sal peered back into his recollection, back into the whiteness, met the eyes of the old man, and declared, "Windgazer 99.9 will be an *abomination.*"

Sal tried to stand. He questioned his own statements. "But Format C:," said Sal, "will wipe out the world's hard drives. People will be left with nothing. Absolutely nothing if they type that command. Format C: can't help—it will ruin everything."

"Have faith, maybe it won't," the old man replied confidently. "So now you'll tell the world, correct?"

"No one would believe this, not over Ben Hinnom," replied Sal. "I am no match for him—the most powerful man in the world. He has everything. Publicity, promotion, money, advertising—big everything."

"They will believe you," the old man assured. "I will help you. Derek will help you. The world will believe you. December 31, it's either you or Hinnom." He smiled, "I hope they will pick you."

Sal asked, "Who are you?"

The old man seemed to glow, then replied, "Kuebitz. Dr. Kuebitz. And I always knew you would find the answer. I always knew it."

PART THREE

FORMAT C:

15

THE CHOICE

*W*hen Jerusalem officials realized the richest man in the world, Ben Hinnom, had unexpectedly arrived in their city, they mobilized. The possibilities were limitless: purchasing Israeli bonds, donating a small city park, funding a chair at Hebrew University, investing in a high-tech venture, transferring some of his billions to Israeli banks, using his prestige to further the peace process. No possibility could be overlooked.

A liaison from the mayor's office was assigned. Special parking privileges were afforded outside the King David Hotel for Hinnom's yellow school bus; the gas station next door scrubbed the goat splatter off the front grille, restoring its original luster. A letter of introduction from the mayor's office was conveyed requesting anyone in the city–public or private–to facilitate Hinnom's visit. Security briefings on the Golan, courtesy meetings with the prime minister, an audience with both chief rabbis, private tours of archaeological digs, lavish feasts at the best restaurants in both East and West Jerusalem, invitations to the most exclusive parties–the offers began to flow in.

Rumors burned from phone to phone speculating as to why Ben Hinnom had unexpectedly arrived. Did he discover previously unknown Jewish roots? Was he on a mission with a message from the American president, would he take one back? Where would he visit? Would he invest? Outside Hinnom's sixth-floor Presidential Suite, fruit baskets and floral arrangements began to pile up. The head of housekeeping was called back from vacation to supervise maid service. Complimentary amenities to the room were scheduled for delivery throughout the day: chilled mangos and papaya with Carmel champagne in the morning, a cheeseboard in the afternoon, and for night, strawberries dipped in chocolate.

Hinnom, however, had very few requests. These were to be verbalized by Linzer in a brief exchange with Magda, the mayoral liaison. Understandably, Magda chose to meet Linzer not in her cramped lifeless municipal building office but within the illustrious confines of the King David.

The King David was Israel's most magnificent hotel, antique and stately, from its oriental carpets to its handtooled gilded ceiling. Its supremely gracious staff, comprised of both Arab and Jewish Jerusalemites, catered with demure aplomb to the powerful and the pretentious without acknowledging they intrinsically knew the one from the other. Imbued with the veritable history of the State itself, this was the hotel that housed the British when it was bombed by a Jewish terrorist who later became prime minister. Once reconstructed, the King David became the meeting ground for diplomatic missions, philanthropists, the captains of industry, and their widows. The doorman was on a first-name basis with security chiefs from a dozen countries. On occasion, management would ask dozens of regular guests to vacate grand suites to make room for unexpected visits by kings and presidents. Jewish guests always graciously complied out of patriotic duty. Never an objection. Indeed, management cleared the entire hotel of its normal guests to make way for attendees of the Yitzhak Rabin funeral. That weekend, the building so overflowed with heads of state, they jostled each other on the stairwells trying to beat the overburdened elevators.

When short, stocky Magda arrived in her gray linen suit already drenched with perspiration down the back, dragging a heavy briefcase stuffed with color guidebooks, master plans and prospectuses, she wisely selected the most genteel setting in the entire hotel: the magnificent rear patio, which enjoyed an unobstructed view of the Old City and overlooked the Valley of Ben Hinnom itself. As afternoon tea was served, even before the dainty cookies and carefully crafted fruit tarts were wheeled in, Linzer tersely outlined the Hinnom agenda.

"For now," Linzer curtly told Magda, "Mr. Hinnom is making no investment decisions. This is a fact-finding trip. But everything—*everything*, is open for future discussion. He does think there might be something spectacular, however, about hosting the global download of Windgazer 99.9 from Jerusalem. Center of things, if you will. Rock bands, dancers, fireworks, live satellite hookups for a worldwide countdown as we usher in the new millennium. Get the idea?"

Magda was thrilled. "This is a magnificent idea indeed," she said, making notes in Hebrew on a powder blue King David notepad.

"Interestingly enough," Linzer added, "Mr. Hinnom has become intrigued with the name of the valley outside the Old City which very ironically bears an ironically similar name. Right down there." He pointed beyond the patio toward Gei Ben Hinnom. "Cute coincidence, *Ben Hinnom*. He thinks that location might be a fitting site for the Windgazer 99.9 festivities."

"Wonderful," Magda responded, as she adjusted her thick glasses, made additional notes and spooned a dollop of clotted cream into her Wedgewood china teacup. "Wonderful, yes. Concerts and art showings in the valley are held in the Amphitheater all the time. We have much experience with such things."

"Yes, but these events are mainly held on the restored northern side of the ravine," said Linzer, completely ignoring the waiter standing beside him. "We'd like to position our activities someplace new . . . further south, down at the edge of the valley, down below Silwan. This way it will be the first event of its kind in modern times from that location. Historic, wouldn't you say?"

"Down next to Silwan?" asked Magda, assuming there was a misunderstanding she could correct. "It's filthy there, burial caves everywhere, and bad legends about the sacrifice of children. Archaeologic problems . . ." She emphasized, "Access is very limited. It would take a great deal of time to get it ready, maybe a year. And even if we could, there are security problems."

Linzer was unfazed.

Magda didn't hold back, but spoke quietly to avoid being overheard by the staff. "Arabs," she reminded. "It's East Jerusalem—dangerous, you know. They throw stones. That's why there has been no development in that godforsaken place."

"Leave all that to us," assured Linzer. "All we want is the permit. We'll hire the contractors, arrange for seating, build a stage, we'll haul in the electronics, lights and mobile broadcast facilities. We recognize that December 31 is quite soon, less than six months away. But our people can finish on our schedule. No question. Mr. Hinnom will supervise it personally. As will I."

The initially enthusiastic Magda became visibly hesitant.

"Naturally," Linzer assured her. "Hinnom Computing will be happy to pay the city's expenses–any and all. Just tell us to whom the check should be written."

Magda, trying to be polite, said she would inquire–but could promise nothing. She tried one more time, "Can I convince you to move the event just a few hundred yards north to the area under Cinematheque? We can put on a very beautiful show from there."

"For us," Linzer replied, "being the first is part of the attraction. Mr. Hinnom has made his decision."

Magda was working out the ramifications in her head when Linzer mentioned almost as an afterthought, "By the way, the suite is quite suitable here at the King David. Very plush. But when Mr. Hinnom puts his mind to a project, he becomes rather intense. As soon as the permit for Gei Ben Hinnom is issued–"

Magda testily interrupted, "I can't promise such a permit can be obtained–"

"–as soon as the permit is issued," Linzer continued with determination, "Mr. Hinnom wants to set up his own private tent on site. He'll work from there. Take his meals and even sleep there."

"In Gei Ben Hinnom, right underneath Silwan?" Magda asked incredulously.

"Precisely," said Linzer, ignoring the waiter for the third time. "Sooner the better. And of course we can write a check to cover all those expenses as well."

"All expenses?" she inquired, not meaning it to sound the way it did.

"Everything."

Magda scribbled more notes on the notepad. "Let me call some people and see whether such a thing is possible. You are sure this is where you want the festival? Absolutely determined?"

"Hell-bent," Linzer responded in a confident tone that gave way to a subdued chuckle.

"What is funny?" Magda asked, wondering if she had missed some idiomatic humor.

"Nothing," replied Linzer. "Why? Was I laughing?"

∽

"HE'S HERE!" DAN shouted, slamming the suite door and holding up a copy of the *Jerusalem Post*. The headline read: "Ben Hinnom on Surprise Visit."

Stunned, Park and Sal could not believe the news.

"Go around the corner," said Dan excitedly. "There's a yellow school bus parked outside the King David! Look for yourself." He paced back and forth, grabbing some mint candies from the counter as Park studied the *Post* article. Dan always noshed under pressure.

"He knows we're here," Dan said nervously, but then reasoned, "Maybe he doesn't know we're here. On the other hand, what if we are here? A)–he can't do squat; I'm a journalist. Let him try. B)–even if he could do squat, why does he need to come here to do the squatting? He has his own squatters."

"It's not you," said Sal with quiet resignation. "It's me. It's Format C:. He knows. Somehow, he knows . . . that I have accessed . . . accessed what I accessed. It's going to be a battle for the will of the world–whether anyone knows it yet or not."

"Sal, I'm still finding my way on this whole Format C: matter," Park began, trying not to sound as if she was doubting.

Nonetheless, Sal's expression turned inward and impatient.

"Now, please," she appealed. "Since fixed disk PCs hit the market, we know that the command 'Format C:' means wipe out the hard drive and everything on it. It's like erasing paper. The paper remains and you start fresh with nothing on it."

"It's a very dangerous command," Dan agreed. "The scariest command in computing. And," he added to Sal with a tinge of good-natured sarcasm, "somehow little ole you has learned that this command is suddenly the opposite of what everyone knows. It's like we see a handle on the door in the airplane. DO NOT OPEN. You want us to open it. And then jump out."

Sal, the new Sal, squared off. "The Point Nine Update will not, repeat, will not–" he fanned the air in frustration, "will *not* correct the millennium clock. It's worse than the current version of Windgazer. Install the Update and Windgazer will require a new fix every week, maybe every day. Maybe all day every day. Eventually, Hinnom will be able to dictate what everyone does. What if he says, 'Don't buy Fords,' and the overnight refresh simply cuts off Ford Motor Company, or people who drive Fords? What if he says 'triple my annual registration fee,' or 'give me a tenth of everything.' Who will be able to resist him?"

"What if Hinnom doesn't bother *saying* any of that?" Dan added to the fray. "What if he just uses RF to control everybody's right temporal lobe? Bang. Suddenly people will just wake up one morning and simply do as instructed. No more Fords and no more discussion about Fords. You will literally have no choice because no one can afford to break away from their computers."

"No one will *want* to break away," Park asserted. "That's the point. It will be a trade-off that people will get sucked into. They'll never shake it. Personal productivity for everyone in exchange for . . . in exchange for . . ."

"A deal with the devil?" said Sal, completing the thought.

"Well . . ." Park replied with uncertainty.

"Well?" Dan cut in. "Is that it?"

"Yes," said Sal. "That's it."

"Sal, this has gone far beyond just ruthless business in your mind," said Dan. "Am I right?"

"That's right," Sal answered slowly. "Hinnom is evil. Evil for the sake of being evil. Just evil."

"Okay, we accept Windgazer 99.9 as a real bad thing," Dan posited. "But how does typing Format C:–the command that destroys all your data, your applications, the whole operating system–how does that make the world better?"

"None of what you said will happen," Sal countered. "Format C: has always meant what you know it to mean: wipe the drive clean and start all over. That would be as bad as the Millennium Bug. Agreed. But that won't happen on December 31." Dan tried to be sympathetic but he remained unconvinced.

"You already know that Windgazer 99 programmers deleted the traditional Format command," Sal explained. "Essentially, the user never gets that option anymore. The way it's rigged now, you simply hit the Reformat icon on the Windgazer screen and you sorta wipe everything clean—but the Windgazer operating system *remains.* In other words, you can't ever get Windgazer off your system, even if you try. But when Derek Labs was working on the original Zoom, they embedded a new version of the command Format C: as an undocumented command in the micro-kernel of the code. It becomes operational only at the key moment, midnight, December 31, 1999. Last year, when Zoom was absorbed into Windgazer, the command just stayed there, buried and forgotten. Now no one can delete it. Not even Hinnom. It's too deep."

Dan looked confused. "Micro*what?*"

"Microkernel," Park explained. "The lowest, most basic level of the code. The ground floor of the whole software structure if you will."

"Okay, I'm a little less confused," said Dan.

"You build an operating system—from the ground up," outlined Park. "The microkernel is at the very bottom—very basic commands—and it can control everything above it." She turned to Sal, "You're saying Derek Labs dropped this little completely undocumented command into the Zoom microkernel, like burying secret treasure in the floorboard, and that floorboard was then used to build the structure of the entire Windgazer 99 operating system?"

"Gotcha," Dan chimed in. "It's this way: after Hector was murdered, Zoom got sucked into Hinnom's Windgazer development. Format C: naturally went with it. Derek built the basics of Zoom in the first place and then transferred the same microwhatever into Ohr 2000. I can understand that. So the essence of Derek's Ohr 2000 actually exists buried deep within Windgazer."

"*Ohr* in Hebrew means. . ." asked Park.

"Light," answered Dan.

"So it's as Meir said," responded Park. "The light is hidden—hidden inside the darkness."

"Typing Format C:," Sal declared passionately, "that is the only way back. December 31, 1999. Do that and Format C: will load the essence of Ohr 2000 and delete Windgazer 99. Permanently. But only if people get smart and make the right choice. Download the Point Nine Update," insisted Sal, "and Hinnom controls your mind and soul—you submit to Hinnom. Type Format C:, you break free. Start the new millennium fresh."

"And you know all this *how?*" asked a skeptical Dan.

Sal did not answer.

"Not that it's far-fetched," Park intervened sympathetically, trying to reason with her son. "Well, it is. But . . . but to type a command as powerful as Format C: and reliably get the complete opposite result . . . I'm sure you latched onto some devastating documentation. But where? Did all this just *appear* to you?"

Sal folded his arms, bruised by their resistance. Clearly he wanted to answer. But for a protracted period he made no sound. The others did not even move, doing nothing to inhibit his eventual response. Finally he summoned the stamina and spoke: "I hit a site late one night at Derek." Trembling as he recounted the experience, "It was terrible. Images . . . images that took me somewhere . . . that cut into me . . . Piercing, piercing images. And then Dr. Kuebitz explained what it all meant."

"Kuebitz?" replied an astonished Park. "You met Kuebitz personally? At Derek? What does Kuebitz look like?"

"Just looks like anyone," replied Sal, not understanding the question. "Just a guy. But Kuebitz believes everything I have said just now. He told me all of it, and made me realize that I have to warn the world. Someone has to do it. I made the discovery. So it's me. And maybe you'll help," he said, glancing around for their reactions.

Dan paced and popped another mint. "How about you?" he asked Park. "Do you believe all this? It's a nice story. Very nice. But can anyone back this up about Format C:? Can we get a statement on the record from Derek? Some corroboration from Bluestar. Maybe commission an independent examination of the code."

"It's not a matter of statements and verifications," Sal exploded. "It's a matter of faith. What do people have now? Hinnom's promises. Every one of them turns out to be a lie. Yet people continue believing him. They're hooked on his lies. Give us more lies. We know they're lies, but give us more lies."

"Alternative?" asked Dan.

"Faith—that Format C: is the better way," replied Sal.

"Just faith?"

"Faith," repeated Sal.

"A leap of faith," Dan replied.

"Not a leap, not a crawl," Sal persisted. "Just faith. If even the faithless have faith in Ben Hinnom, why is the opposite idea so preposterous?"

"Faith . . . So it's in you, or faith in him," Dan summed up, popping a final mint in his mouth.

Sal fixed on Dan and remarked, "You have said it."

Park moved next to her son. "I know what faith is." She placed her arm around his shoulders. "I'm with my son. Dan, maybe you don't have anything to place faith in. Very few people do. I thought at least you believed in what you remembered: *nothing by accident . . . everything with a purpose.* You've been let down by life and by history and by the world. I see the scars. I know you bleed. Everyone bleeds. We all walk in our own blood just to get through the day. Maybe you are like everyone else, you just can't trust in anything anymore. So you prefer nothing."

Dan moved close to Park and Sal. He comically pointed Sal toward the window.

Sal turned around completely and looked away.

Dan kissed Park's shoulder as his hand softly embraced hers. Her fingers floated into his. Tears almost came to Dan's eyes as he tried to verbalize. His voice was smitten until finally, lips quavering, the words released. "Faith. I'll have faith."

AFTER TWO VERY intense weeks, Sal completed construction of a series of Internet pages to be posted at Derek's web site. *The Format C: Faith Page,* as he called it, was created to warn the world that downloading Hinnom's Point Nine Update would doom all information systems from then on. Hinnom was perfecting Influence Technology derived from mind control experiments seeking mastery of the right temporal lobe so that no one could buy, sell, or trade without Windgazer 99.9. Quickly, Hinnom would literally license and exercise dominion over every automated detail of human existence.

The *Format C: Faith Page* also detailed Sal's discovery of the undocumented microkernel command lurking within Windgazer 99. At midnight on December 31—and only then—the command could be activated, he explained. Upon typing the command Format C:, the system would ask: "Are you Sure?" After hitting *Y* for Yes, the system would reboot and the embedded Zoom-Ohr 2000 code would simply return the user's computer to its original state prior to Windgazer. The Millennium Bug would be defeated.

Sal's assault on Windgazer 99.9 would be easy for Hinnom haters everywhere to rally behind. Prone to Hinnom conspiracy theories and preoccupied with his ruthlessness, Hinnom haters would immediately spread the word. But Format C: as an alternative? Few would accept this. Sal anticipated disbelief.

"Believing that Windgazer 99.9 will save your systems and our society is a concept taken on faith," wrote Sal. "And on faith from where? From a man and a company with a dark record of lies, deception, manipulation, bugs, fixes that wreak even greater system destruction, and the hyping of vaporware. For the sake of enriching his coffers and consolidating his grip on all our lives, Hinnom has subjugated virtually every computer in the world to his will and his whim. Yet we take on faith his promise of a Deliverer in the form of the Point Nine Update, even though it goes against everything we know of this man.

"Admittedly, typing Format C: on December 31, 1999 will also take an act of faith," Sal wrote, "and will also require you to reverse your thought processes. Do that. Type Format C: on faith; have faith in one who has seen the light struggling to escape from Bad Ben's dark plans. On New Year's Eve, it is indeed a choice. Make the right one and save yourself. Make the wrong one, you belong to Hinnom."

While Sal was constructing his web pages, Dan prepared a special investigative article entitled "The Millennium Choice." He labored to make the 1,500-word, six-page story as non-alarmist and journalistically credible as possible. The report objectively cited Sal's discovery of irrepressible viruses and bugs within the Point Nine Update that would not only fail to cure the Y2K problem, but would also make all users continuously dependent upon Hinnom updates. More than just computer chaos, Dan's report warned, dangerous code from unrelated military mind control projects had been incorporated into the Point Nine Update. As such, there was no way to predict whether new radio frequency technology would create what he termed "an epidemic of irrational acts."

Dan wrote: "The cell phone scare has still not been resolved in the minds of many who fear cancerous microwaving. But Windgazer 99.9 is potentially far more catastrophic if loaded into your machine. A simple RF command by Windgazer emitted from your monitor, and perhaps from additional hardware mandated for future PCs, could alter how we perceive reality and even our understanding of that perception."

The report went on to cite an unlikely alternative solution buried deep within the Windgazer code. "According to programmers familiar with the innermost workings of Windgazer as well as Zoom, and its successor, Ohr 2000, a viable alternative exists. Typing and confirming *Format C:* at the stroke of midnight December 31 will cleanly delete Windgazer, reboot your system and cure Y2K. Format C: proponents worry, though, that this simple command will not be typed because it would require abandoning the old understandings about Format C: and adopting this new one."

Dan's bylined article would be released not through traditional newspapers, but through the new breed of journalistic endeavor: the Internet e-zine. Nineteen well-established venues had been lined up throughout the world, from *Pro Computing Minute* served from Chicago, to *Runamuck Times* served from Amsterdam, to *NipEzine* in Tokyo. The Internet in turn fed the print and TV journalists of the world. Dan and Sal would post simultaneously on August 7.

The postings would not be discovered incrementally. Sal and Dan were both prepared to broadcast their pages *en masse* as email attachments to hundreds of anti-Hinnom groups worldwide. These groups would in turn forward the pages to their own distribution lists—creating the online chain reaction the Internet had become famous for. Within minutes, *The Format C: Faith Page* would be circulated globally, reaching millions. The Information Age of green bar and fluorescent screens had yielded to the Instant Information Age of cyberspace and mass messaging. The empire Hinnom had helped automate might now set in motion his own decline.

BELOW THE OLD City walls, there is a ravine that begins as a gentle, grassy separation between hills, but then quickly descends south into the rocky earth until it becomes a steep and craggy depth scarred on the far side by shallow caves and pits which odiously vaunt hollowed-out chambers which lead to lightless passageways coursing into narrow crypts which drop into sharp chasms which empty into a strata of evil beyond the comprehension of man. Everywhere you see the scorches and bloodstains of human sacrifice, the smolder of trash fires, rivulets of urine trickling down from open sewers above watering thorn bushes, weeds and unexpected clumps of grass among the outcroppings. You smell the stench of decaying offal, the congealed stink of putrefied garbage, and the absorbed reek of incinerated human flesh seared into the rock face. Crows circle low. Worms and maggots slither throughout. Listen. And you cannot help but hear the tormented screams of babies being burned alive, the macabre incantations of the idolatrous in gruesome celebration, the agonized cries of helpless victims, and every other echo of death and disconsolation that dwells here so pervasively that not even the centuries can silence them.

This is Hell. The real Hell. Those who walked through the Valley of the Shadow of Death walked here. Images of torture and fire as a nadir of evil originate in this hideous reality. The prophets always understood that Hell existed, not as a hidden, allegorical place deep beneath the ground maintained as a fable of fear. Hell is on Earth, always lurking around the bend, just a short walk from righteousness.

The Valley of the Sons of Hinnom was named for an alien non-Semitic family, the Hinnom clan, that predated the First Temple period and immediately established the locale as a place of abomination. *Gei Ben Hinnom* became Valley of Hinnom or *Ge Hinnom* and eventually *Gehenna* or *Gehennem*. Early Bible scholars mistranslated the term *Sheol*, the shallow grave sometimes imbued with afterlife, and the name of "Hell" mistakenly emerged.

Perhaps it is fitting that the path to Hell begins delightfully. Gei Ben Hinnom first appears as a shallow depth west of the Old City where its pitch is hardly discernible beneath the streets of modern Jerusalem. As the ravine courses south, past the Old City, its steep sides become distinctive. In recent years, the northern and unoffensive length of the valley has become a zone of chic gentrification: exquisite townhomes, landscaped parks, a concert bowl at the Sultan's Pool, and movie theaters.

But, as the ravine carves deeper and deeper between the rocky hills, and as it rounds the corners of Mt. Zion into East Jerusalem *en route* to Silwan below which it conjoins with the Valley of the Kidron, in a stretch of depth that defies political peace, a place that Arabs cannot improve and that Jews dare not, the ancient Tophet comes into view. This is where the babies were burned alive.

Nothing has changed for thousands of years. Still visible are the origi-

nal deep angular cuts into flat scorched stone seating the Tophet, the burning altars so named for the noisy drum that devotees of Molech would
beat to drown out the ghastly cries of children immolated in sacrifice
before their own willing parents. The Molech idol was equipped with outstretched cantilevered arms that extended a small platform upon which
the innocent baby was tied. Slowly the platform swiveled toward the con-
suming flames as the baby shrieked in helpless agony. In the black rapture of their misguided faith, the mothers and fathers not only witnessed
the sacrifice, but glorified the act. Beneath the Tophet altars, foreboding
square entryways can be seen, barely big enough for a human torso to
squeeze through. Within their darkness lay a complex of carved-out
tombs, chambers and crypts devoted to corpses, ritual preparation, and
numberless unthinkable acts in honor of the evil god Molech.

No wonder this most hideous place has repeatedly been the focus of
Biblical wrath:

> He defiled Tophet, which is in the Valley of Ben Hinnom, so that no
> one would make a son or a daughter pass through fire as an offering to
> Molech." II. Kings 23:10.
>
> Therefore the days are surely coming, says the Lord, when this place
> shall no more be called Tophet, or the Valley of the Sons of Hinnom,
> but the Valley of Slaughter. Jeremiah 19:16.

Here where the blood of babies watered the desires of evil, where dark
stains of murder are still seen pressed upon the ledges, where the ancient
world's most sinister devotions became an abomination, where every
soot-scorched corner and crevice echoes the terror and pain of those desolate days, in this place, Ben Hinnom trembled with awareness and gleefully turned to Linzer, declaring, "My, what a cool place to have a party."

Hinnom's planning team, including event planners and publicists,
descended upon the Valley of Ben Hinnom beginning at the so-called
Flank of Hinnom, a cluster of immolation sites and burial caves. The
event planners, ignorant of the Tophet's nefarious history, enthusiastically sketched their plans, visualized the stage, portable power generators,
the lasers, a towering screen, dancers and revellers—an unprecedented
global moment to welcome the year 2000. Once again, men would worship at the Tophet in the Valley of Ben Hinnom.

While the planners were busy at the Flank, Linzer and Hinnom
descended even deeper into the Valley, to its lowest corner, where a great

cave loomed, its arched entrance guarded by six-foot-high thorn bushes. Urine from the unsewered toilet in the convent above trickled down the escarpment and over the cave's entrance. Feces from man and beast lay everywhere as a threshold. Rodents and snakes haughtily congregated about. And hanging from spikes nailed into the rock, one on either side of the cave entrance, were strangled jackals, their angry snarls frozen in death.

Hinnom scrutinized the ground fervidly, asking Linzer, "Have you checked?"

"The stone is not here," Linzer assured. "I checked before we got here. I'll check everyday. But they don't have it."

"Hah! They don't have the stone," Hinnom smirked as he walked right through the center of the cave opening. The thorns pierced his uncovered forearms but he did not react. A breeze blew briefly and the dripping urine droplets momentarily shifted a few inches, missing his head, as he placidly passed within. Arms spread in excitement, Hinnom observed the shelves chiseled into the cave wall like so many tables in a morgue, fingered the human bones still scattered about, and inhaled the foul mist of fecal remnants, decayed animals, and ancient remains strewn everywhere.

Finally, he folded his hands and turned to Linzer. "Yes, this will be fine. My tent . . . put my tent right out in front. And, my friend, it's time for security to finally show their face."

"The Anakim are just about ready," replied Linzer. "Ishbi can be here tomorrow. We are still looking for his brother." He took out his cell phone and made a call.

∾

ON AUGUST 7, 1999, 8:30 P.M., the sun had set. Sal and Dan, both weary, were in the Dan Pearl suite tweaking the final versions of their documents. Finally, Dan transferred the finished draft of his article into Sal's Windy for transmission to the newspapers. The web pages were also ready to upload. Israel TV would meet them in front of Derek Institute at 9 P.M. Park and Motke were already there preparing.

"Head over there," Dan told Sal. "I'll just check my voice mail at home and catch up."

Sal took his Windy and inserted it snugly in his back pants pocket, flopping his T-shirt over it. He left the suite.

The walk to Derek was short and downhill. As he often did, Sal took Dan's favorite, albeit longer, route through the park and the old cemetery. It was dark, but he knew the way. Usually, the park was crowded at this time of night, but tonight no one was about. As he walked past a bench, a man serenely looked up and plaintively asked, "I need some directions. Can you help me?"

Sal stopped to listen.

"I need to find something," the man continued. Coming very close to Sal's face, he asked, "Can you direct me to a small handheld computer, called a Windy? We've lost one of the three we had and we need it back . . . *now.*" It was Linzer.

Sal froze. His peripheral vision searched for some help. There was none.

"You are the bastard son of Park McGuire, are you not?" Linzer questioned abrasively.

Sal's nervous vibration was visible. Several very tall figures appeared at the top of the footpath. It was the Anakim, each with six fingers, standing amid their own long shadows, just waiting.

"Now then," repeated Linzer, "I think you know where our Windy is?"

He noticed a bulge beneath Sal's shirt. When Linzer tried to reach for it, Sal jerked back a step. Some tourists on their way to the *midrekhov* passed innocuously. As they did, Linzer stayed his reach.

"Now please hand it over," insisted Linzer. "What's ours is ours."

Sal began to slowly retreat in the direction of the Dan Pearl. Linzer followed. The Anakim security men at the bottom of the footpath moved forward as well. Sal quickened his pace, pulling the Windy out from his back pocket and wedging it under his belt buckle. When Linzer saw the device briefly appear, his eyes glowed. Sal darted off in his ungainly way up the path back toward the hotel, with Linzer in pursuit.

Dan appeared at the top on his way to Derek. When he saw Sal running, he raced toward him. In a moment more, Sal pulled up behind Dan.

Linzer stopped short just a few feet from Dan, and waved, keeping the Anakim security men at a distance.

"Mr. Levin, again," said Linzer feigning politeness. "Still abetting the theft of our proprietary equipment?"

"Not really," said Dan in a stern, formal tone. "But I would welcome a structured interview with Ben Hinnom so we can discuss serious charges that have come to the fore regarding Windgazer 99.9."

"Give us back our property and we can discuss the possibility," Linzer replied coldly.

"Who are your tall buddies yonder?" asked Dan motioning. "Members of the Hinnom corporate basketball team?"

"Don't you mind the Anakim," retorted Linzer. "But I do mind your theft of Hinnom Computing property, tortious interference, industrial espionage, and violation of trade secrets. Please. The Windy," he held out his palm.

"Sal," said Dan, "bring out the Windy."

Sal hesitated.

"It's fine. Bring out the Windy," Dan repeated.

Sal withdrew the device from under his shirt.

"Here is what we know," Dan told Linzer. "We know your corporation has perfected radio-frequency mind control through stimulation of the right temporal lobe, courtesy of your Influence Technology department under the auspicious direction of your buddy Max. By the way, lucky guy—his driver's license was reinstated after killing that girl? We also know that the Point Nine Update is just another fraud. We know it will not cure the Millennium Bug. It will just lead to a cascade of additional mandatory updates, refreshes and bug fixes, each more messed up than the one before. And then, fundamentally, Ben Hinnom will just control the world."

Linzer was expressionless as Dan continued, "Moreover, we believe there is a better way."

"Better way?" asked Linzer. "There is no better way. Nothing exists except the Point Nine Update. It is the best hope for humanity and will allow mankind to flourish as never before, obtaining productivity and powers never before granted to mortals. That is what Mr. Hinnom has been striving for. Hinnom is the great enabler. What better way could possibly exist? The clock is ticking. You have no better way."

Sal spoke up. "Format C:," called out Sal. "The command activates at midnight December 31. It's in the microkernel and cannot be deleted. The Derek people embedded it before they withdrew from Zoom. Users type Format C:. But it doesn't reformat the disk, it un-installs Windgazer, fixes Y2K, and restores systems to their prior condition."

Linzer's face contorted. "And who knows this besides you two fools?"

"Just me and some friends right now," replied Sal.

"But in a few moments the entire planet will know," Dan cut in, "because Sal is uploading a few pages of explanation to the Internet, and I'm granting an interview to some TV stations, and publishing an article or two on the topic."

Speaking directly to Sal without turning, Dan instructed, "Kid, upload the documents now."

Sal unfolded the computer and began furiously punching the keypad.

Linzer stretched out his hand in sudden desperation. "Don't do that, Sal. Don't listen to *him*. He is a troubled man, misguiding you. Mr. Hinnom can make it very bad for you and your mother. You will never have a life when we are finished with you. Neither will Mr. Levin. Do not, Sal, do *not* transmit those pages."

"FTP connection made," reported Sal as the Windy went through its paces. "Loading the pages for file transfer to the Derek web site."

Linzer lunged at Sal, trying to grab at the Windy. Dan blocked his arm. The Anakim came running up the hill. As Dan restrained Linzer's ice-cold hand, Dan felt a shiver, both hot and cold, jolt through him.

"Loading files," continued Sal, urging the Windy on with body language. "There's a bunch of 'em. Damn graphics. They take forever."

By now the scene had attracted attention. A crowd surrounded Linzer, Dan and Sal. A green jeep of the Mishmar Hagvul security forces drove up along the nearby street shouting for everyone to desist. "Stop now, all!" the Druze commander screamed as his squad jumped the fence between the park and the street.

"It's loaded," shouted Sal.

"Fire," yelled Dan.

"Don't touch the Enter button," screamed Linzer. "Don't hit Enter!"

Sal depressed the key. The screen graphic showed the files arcing to their target at the Derek web site.

20% transferred.

Linzer struggled even more violently as Dan held fast.

35% transferred.

"Stop!" bellowed Linzer.

100% transferred. FTP Complete. Try Another?

Sal typed N for no, and logged off, just as the Mishmar Hagvul arrived. The Anakim stopped short and dispersed toward the far side of the park. Security took Linzer, Dan and Sal into custody, even as Dan was flashing his press card and yelling he had to meet Israel TV. After carefully making sure it was not a bomb, the antiterrorist guards confiscated the Windy until everything could be sorted out.

But cyberspace was already buzzing. When Sal's files hit the site, the pages were automatically mass-emailed to thousands of anti-Hinnom sites around the world. Dan's special report was emailed to the e-zines as well. Within moments, the choice had been presented to the world. The debate would begin.

THE POLICE STATION in the Russian Compound was a dim gray place. Everywhere electrical wires and phone cables stapled to walls testified to the building's incongruity with modern times. Dan and Sal were held in an interview room instead of the dark, foreboding detention center beyond the green steel door. Linzer was held in a reception area. Hinnom attorneys were forcefully demanding Linzer's immediate release and the return of the Windy. They waved the letter from the Mayor's office asking for cooperation. They threatened complaints, suits, appeals to members of Knesset, and the Prime Minister. They even threatened to call the fundraisers at the Jewish Agency.

Through the doorway, Sal and Dan could see the commander staring in their direction while he talked on the telephone. He picked up the Windy from the desk, turned it a few times in a cursory once-over, and continued talking. Muffling the phone, he called out to an assistant, who came into the interview room and asked to see Sal's passport. Sal offered it. The assistant turned to the page with the Ben Gurion Airport entry stamp. Under it, customs had written in ink "Machshev Katan," Hebrew for "little computer." The assistant underlined the entry with his finger, and showing it to Sal, asked, "This means the little computer you were fighting about?"

Dan answered, "He doesn't read Hebrew. Yes, that's the Windy, the little computer."

"Okay, so you wait please," the assistant said.

A few moments later, the commander came in carrying the Windy. Speaking first to Dan, "You are the crazy American, the journalist, who last year talked to the bomber on the *midrekhov?*" Dan nodded confidently.

Turning to Sal, "You are working with Derek Institute and with Dr. Kuebitz of the military?"

Flustered, Sal didn't know what to say.

"Yes he is," answered Dan for him.

"Then okay," the commander said, adding in sometimes broken English, "Kuebitz called from Hakirya–Israel's Pentagon, you would say. This matter is something to do with national security that I was not really informed about. But I received a call because you are here. First, this small computer is listed in your passport, the serial number matches. Take it back," he returned the Windy to Sal.

Sal gripped it tightly with both hands.

"You are free to go, but please to stay in touch with Derek right away says Dr. Kuebitz. I merely pass a message."

To Dan, the commander complained, "And you. Please try not to make so many troubles. We know who this is over there," pointing over his shoulder to Linzer. "Very rich people from Hinnom Computing. So why do you make me a headache? They are screaming. Kuebitz is telling me another thing. The Government Press Office is upset."

Dan mumbled sheepishly, "Sorry, *chaver.*"

"Don't be sorry," the commander urged. "Be more quiet in Israel. I have enough problems." He added, "You are also free to go, but I was requested from Kuebitz that he also wants to talk to you at Derek. That is it. I am not delivering more messages. Another problem with you, and it will not turn out so nice."

Linzer and his crew were led out one door. Dan and Sal were escorted out another. Just before Dan stepped outside, the commander called out one last time. "You will behave?"

Dan looked back and replied, "If God wills it."

16

THE REVELATION ACCORDING TO BEN HINNOM

FROM: Ben Hinnom, Hinnom Computing Co., Inc.
TO: All of Humanity
DATE: Christmas Eve 1999
SUBJECT: The Next Millennium, Year 2000, etc.
CC: To File

First, I would like to say SHIT ON YOU! <delete> Greetings and
Merry Christmas.

I am writing first and foremost to invite you to the most spectacular
event of the millennium--the landmark release of Windgazer 99.9 as
it is simultaneously downloaded to more than 300 million computers
worldwide. As you know, we will be throwing Year 2000 parties in
sixty cities, worldwide cosponsored by our business partners and
Windgazer user groups everywhere around the planet to celebrate
this unique happening. You are all invited.

Some of the larger gatherings will be in New York, Chicago, Austin,
London, Beijing, Tokyo, and of course we'll have a big one in Seattle.
But the main stage will be right here in the beautiful Valley of Ben
Hinnom in ancient Jerusalem. I know, I know. The name is the same.
So this place was a natural. If we were Grand Canyon Software, I
assure you, we would have chosen the Grand Canyon. But beyond

the quaint name, this is a truly wondrous setting for our main launch. We at Hinnom Computing are very excited and thankful.

You may be wondering how you got this email. YOU'RE TOO STU-PID TO UNDERSTAND! <delete> Good question. Everyone received one--even if you don't have email. Now that all of humanity is connected to Windgazer Central, we can upload a message to you anytime we want whether or not you have email. You in turn can send us a message. Companies like to say "we listen." At Hinnom Computing, we are always listening. Via this email to the world, which Windgazer will translate into whatever language you happen to speak, I can personally answer everyone's question about the Point Nine Update, all at once--and with the personal touch.

Because we at Hinnom Computing are listening, we have heard the protests currently being conducted by the so-called Format C: Movement. We are sensitive to what people are saying. Actually, that movement was started right here in Jerusalem by the son of a dis-gruntled employee working in league with some people, including a journalist DAN DIES! <delete>, who stole Hinnom proprietary equipment and hacked into our sensitive commercial development labs. Our attorneys and law enforcement both in the United States and Israel are working on that issue. But the wheels of justice some-times turn very slowly ESPECIALLY WHEN A JEW REPORTER IS INVOLVED <delete>. As a result, these people have been free to tell lies and get many users all riled up about the Point Nine Update which will ship midnight December 31, 1999, just in time to correct any lingering problem with the Y2K crisis and usher in the new Millennium.

Most people have encountered or read about the paranoia that has swept the world the past few months. The theory, according to them, is that if you accept our simple update, you will be dooming your sys-tem, and I guess your own mind and soul, to Hinnom control. Hysteria can always attract followers and we have taken due notice of the protest marches in front of our offices, the sit-ins at the FTC in Washington, the gezillions of anti-Windgazer web sites, the Internet petitions, the boycott attempts, the recent cover stories in *Time* and *Newsweek*. Even some reputable computer publications have discred-

ited themselves by covering this silliness WATCH THEIR ADVER-
TISING COLLAPSE <delete>.

Don't think we aren't aware of every little thing. Bonfires of burning
Windgazer CDs in Milan--we saw that; the candlelight vigil in Kiev--
we saw that too; and those adorable HATE THEM <delete> little
children in Dallas frightfully misled by badly informed parents who
make them wear T-shirts with nasty slogans against our company--by
the way, we have already sent them Windgazer 99.9 T-shirts as a gesture. All of this is just a great, big diversion. What is truly important
is innovation, personal productivity, and technological advancement.

Protests and other unhappy things have always had a negative effect
on our dedicated employees I PAY YOU, SHUT UP <delete>. So
this message is also aimed at them, reminding our staff that they are
leading the good crusade. One day they will be remembered for what
they have done for the world. I know the daily chanting bothers you.
Sometimes it bothers me too. But we have a mission that rises above
chanting.

To clarify the above, many people know, but for those who do not,
there is some chanting going on. The main culprits are the two or
three hundred people who gather at the World Trade Center every
day at noon and chant out: "Format C: Reboot, Reboot, Reboot."
Okay, it's a free society. Anyone can chant. But chanting such nonsense isn't very productive. We get the message after one or two days.
There is no need to continue this week after week. To these people I
have some advice: get some lunch. I would note that this chanting
thing was tried in many other cities and hasn't gotten very far. Reboot
chanting in Los Angeles, Madrid, and Oslo only lasted a period of
days--and in one case about three weeks--before people lost interest.
Nor will this type of activity last in the many other cities where it has
sprung up. Why?

PEOPLE ARE STUPID AND LOSE INTEREST <delete> Because
the supposed alternative is preposterous and not advisable. If you
enter Format C: at a C prompt, you will as surely wipe out your hard
drive as if the Y2K bug gobbled up your data in one swallow. Yet that
is what is proposed. Crazy, isn't it?

So I guess it comes down to whether you believe the technologic expertise of Hinnom Computing--that's me--or the silly rantings of a confused little tongue-tied boy, who, by the way, has some stolen equipment we would like returned.

Actually, I welcome this opportunity to address these issues, recognizing that I and my firm have been much maligned in the past for our efforts to innovate quality products and advance the information age. I can take a good joke every now and then RIP YOUR THROATS OUT <delete>. But sometimes it goes too far. So let me say a few words on my own behalf.

First: Who is Ben Hinnom and what does he represent? Of course, I am your friend. But beyond that, I represent one thing and only one thing: *the power of knowledge.* Who among us understands knowledge and its relationship to the forces in the universe itself? Very darn few. That's the problem. Backward people would equate knowledge with original sin. They would claim that all mankind's trouble began when Adam violated God's only prohibition. He ate an apple from the Tree of Knowledge of Good and Bad. Big deal! you might say.

See, that just goes to show that the acquisition of knowledge has always been controversial from the first bite THAT'S WHY WE CALL IT BYTE <delete>. Such backward thinking would have you believe that by chewing on the apple, Adam would have gained enough knowledge to become like God himself, or herself, if you want to be politically correct GET IT, PC <delete>. The old book itself says "Behold Man has become like the Unique One among us, knowing good and bad. Pretty damn soon he's going to eat from the Tree of Life and live forever." Now mark that sentence; we'll return to that "live forever" reference lower down in this memo.

See, there's always somebody to get jealous when you try to improve yourself. That's why innovation has a price. But given the choice, man has always gone for the risk, always chosen to when the apple is part rotten. It's in his nature. That's just human.

But as a result, man has learned. What he has learned most is that man can be his own God. He can fly through the clouds like a bird, swim through the oceans like a fish, tunnel through the earth like a mole, and touch the stars like an angel. If anyone worried that man *might* maybe eat from the Tree of Life and become everlasting, think again. Friends, we have seen the Tree, we have grasped its fruit, and we have swallowed its savory meat. I say an apple a day . . .

That's right. Man has finally conquered the mystery of life. You want miracles? The computer is the magic wand that creates man's miracles, miracles that man himself can control, and control without asking permission from the gods or giving thanks either. See the previously referenced sentence above ending "live forever." Look what my computers have given you. With computer technology, man can clone life, whether it is salamanders, sheep, or fresh new babies. You want to make the blind see? I give you computer chips as optic implants that replace the retina. You want the deaf to hear? I give you computer-perfected auditory stimulators. You want the crippled to walk? I give you high-tech myoelectric prosthetic legs and Functional Electric Stimulation to make disconnected nerves work again. We're even regenerating spinal tissue.

You want the dead to rise? I give you defibrillators that reach into death five, ten, and even twenty minutes after the sojourn to the other side begins. These days, we bring 'em back all the time. One day we'll be able to reanimate hours, even days, after so-called death. Now, scientists are talking seriously about genuine eternal life—transferring that three-pound bundle of chemo-electrical impulses called the brain from a withered useless body to a brand-new one. Surgeons call this a "head transplant"--nerves, blood vessels and connective tissue, all of it going from one aging body to another younger body in perpetuity. I say, why waste a good head when you can just switch the stuff from the neck down?

Right about now you can see why there is so much jealousy and upset about knowledge and computers EMEVIGROFREHTAFYMLLIW-NEHW <delete>. A man tries to get a little knowledge, better his condition, maybe live forever, and the next thing you know it's a flood wiping everybody out, setting new limits, 120 and out. But technology beat that one back.

Computers unlock the secrets of eternal life, eternal death, and they organize all your files for later retrieval.

This is where I, Ben Hinnom, come in. I have devoted all my existence and all my resources to innovating the wizardry--be it software or hardware--that enables all these miracles. This preoccupation has allowed me to connect with my customers in very special ways. Many people have unique powers to get into other's heads. I have always enjoyed that too. Unfortunately, not being a God or anything, I can only do it one person at a time--and I must really concentrate even for that. Sometimes it works out great, sometimes not so great. It depends. I don't discriminate though. There were some great ones in Germany, even better than Rome, even better than Uganda. When I have something to say, I just get into someone's head and communicate. Being a busy executive, you might expect me to confine my efforts to important places like Berlin or Manhattan. But how about Pearl, Mississippi? Or Jonesboro, Arkansas? THEY WERE EASY <delete> I went into action there just to prove that all people everywhere have potential that can be tapped. Like I have earlier indicated, the rub is doing it one mind at a time--not very efficient.

Now here is where exercising the best of intentions, I have given some of the Hinnom haters something to distort NO STONE, NO WORRIES <delete>. It's true that I care about my customers. It is true that I love to communicate person-to-person, mind-to-mind. It is true that I can only touch one mind at a time. But Windgazer 99.9 does have a feature that will magnify my efforts and help the world in the process. By using radio frequency, I can communicate with millions of people at once--get into everybody's head.

Yes, yes, yes, it is the right temporal lobe. So what?

None of this is new. What is radio? What is television? What is the Internet? What is broadcast email? What is mass media? All of it offers the ability to get into everybody's head all at once. Millions can be inspired, helped, guided, directed, restrained when necessary, made to understand. I'm just innovating another in a long list of communication modalities, pursuing a time honored tradition. Progress marches on.

Of course, I want Windgazer 99.9 to be perfect. Perfect knowledge bothers some people. But like I say, you have to expect that kind of resistance since the dawn of history. Going back to Adam, if you believe in fairy tales.

Remember, computers are the great equalizers. They are not bound by prejudicial feelings, twisted codes of ethics, or antiquated rules. Anyone can push the Enter key and make anything happen. Look what the Internet has done. You can find anything in cyberspace. Who's to say what's right and wrong? The computer removes the obstacles. Fire burns. Fire illuminates. Fire destroys. Water sustains. Water drowns. Let everyone decide for themselves. That's true democracy.

Another point to remember, computers accept you--no matter who you are. You can be poor in spirit, you can be in mourning, you can be meek. But with Windgazer 99.9, it is you who shall inherit the world's data. Hunger and thirst for information, you'll get it. And if people persecute you because you believe in Hinnom or our fine products, or if this false Format C: Movement currently in vogue bugs you, so what? Be happy because all the prophets of technology have been persecuted before you.

Moreover, Hinnom Computing will be with you every byte of the way. First, everyone will get a mouse with a distinctive Windgazer 99.9 logo you can actually feel. It is ergonomically designed to fit every hand. For now we only have a right-handed mouse, so no left hands, sorry. But now computing will really be fun. You'll always feel the raised logo in the palm of your right hand--and know Hinnom Computing is near you. Second, everyone gets a real nifty headband with a Windgazer 99.9 logo. Now, this is really *kewl,* a little relay is woven into the headband that helps all our remote computing circuitry and helps meld the computer to your individualized desires YOU ARE MINE <delete>.

Please take note, once Windgazer 99.9 is installed, your systems will not be able to work without these proprietary features. So please remember, your computers can organize your life, extend your reach, provide entertainment and boundless information, connect you by words, images, and messages, help you manage your finances, and allow you to buy and sell anywhere--but only when you use our mouse and our headband. So use them with pride.

And now in the spirit of the new millennium here's how you should compute for maximum productivity. Try a little chant of your own. You talk to plants and to dogs, don't you? Try talking to your computer. Before you log on, try this:

My computer, connected to the great body of knowledge in the universe, you are the Greatest! Hinnom, what a logo! All data will come, your will be done in the enterprise as it is on my desktop. Give me data everyday, one timeslice after another. Pardon my error messages just as I would pardon those of others. Don't tempt me with anything you cannot deliver. Serve me and I will serve You--You and only You.

I like it BOW TO MY DOMINION <delete>. Maybe it could use some editing. Feel free to customize.

Anyway, I hope I have outlined a few points demonstrating that the only viable choice on December 31 is to download Windgazer 99.9 and reject the Format C: Movement.

Okay, bye everybody. See you in a few days at the midnight between the millennia. I promise you the biggest show of all time.

<Word Count: 2550>

<Spellcheck: no errors>

<delete entire message>

<restore entire message>

<load, ready to transmit>

<Enter>

17

THE VALLEY OF DEATH

*G*eneral Amnon Natan walked out of a small Hakirya hut and up the steps to a parking lot enclosed by barbed wire. Seeing no one could overhear, he telephoned a counterpart.

"I'll be ready," Amnon reported. During the next few minutes, he answered questions from his counterpart with a sequence of curt yes and no monotones. Until the last question. Suddenly Amnon's face reddened. After glancing around, he asked, "Is your phone secure?" Hearing that it was, he replied, "I know nothing of 'the stone.' I only know the man says we will have it soon. I don't know how. Somehow."

He strode across the parking lot to one of the many shacks comprising the extended Hakirya military complex. Inside the shack were Dan, Sal, Motke, and Park. They had been summoned for a security briefing. Although nothing had been explained in advance, they understood implicitly that this arose out of their activism against Windgazer 99.9.

Amnon locked the door, routinely peered out the window for a moment, and introduced himself. Addressing Dan, Amnon remarked, "You. I hear they call you the 'Crazy American.'"

Dan offered a salute in jest.

To Sal, Amnon respectfully declared, "The State of Israel is honored to have you here. And I am honored to work with you. It's quite a discovery you came up with."

Amnon offered coffee. "All I have is instant. It's okay?"

Only Dan and Motke accepted.

As he stirred in the bitter Elite coffee powder, Amnon casually explained that he was in charge of a special operation, highly classified, "perhaps the most classified in our history."

Pulling down a plate of stale cookies wrapped in cellophane from a cupboard to accompany the coffee, Amnon first set the ground rules. "Sal, you and your mother, and also Motke here, are employees of Derek, which is a government of Israel defense contractor. Under Israeli law, if you are disclosed certain security matters, you are covered under the security regulations. You, Dan, your press card covers you under the Censor's security regulations. Israel, as you know, is still technically in a state of emergency, so wartime rules apply. But I want to go a little further and make you a temporary consultant to Derek. That will cover you not only for things you will learn but also for certain special actions that you are about to become involved in that I will provide more details on soon. Sorry to be vague. But that is a must. Everyone clear?"

Motke balked. "Not clear. Not clear. Maybe these people don't know what this means. But I'm an Israeli and I think this is trouble. Are we being drafted into Mossad? Or what? Because I'm not ready for this."

"There is no trouble. No trouble," calmed Amnon. "Forget names, Mossad, IDF. *Drafted* is not the term. *Recruited,* I would say. But recruited, invited, requested, the word is not important. We need your help and I think you will give it. What you do now—in this meeting and for the rest of this week—is very important. So . . . before I can proceed, everyone is now clear?"

One by one, the group slowly answered yes.

"Now, let me bring up the speakerphone." He depressed the button on the desk phone. "Dr. Kuebitz," explained Amnon, "is our special technical adviser on all these matters which are now being disclosed to you in accordance with security regulations."

"He's usually here in Hakirya," observed Dan. "So where is he?"

"Today, I am not there, I am here," said the voice of Kuebitz.

Sal grinned when he heard the words.

Amnon began his briefing: "In many countries, such as the United States, Russia, England, and other places, they investigate special phenomena. The CIA had their Operation Stargate with psychics who could *remote view,* and they only disbanded it a few years ago. The Russians were way ahead on this subject. Mind control, *influence technology* is the new phrase—there are many areas with overlapping names. We in Israel also look into phenomena and I hope you will not be surprised if the Jewish people pay close attention to the Bible and the many holy writings that we have here that go in addition to the Bible. We have the Dead Sea Scrolls, these are very ancient, the Mishna, the Talmud, a whole collection of Kabbala too much to list, the Amarna Letters, scrolls and tablets from the Akkadians, Egyptians, we have Sumerian texts. Much of it is beyond me, but believe it, we spend a lot of money on good archaeology."

"We have a friend in Tsfat named Meir," interjected Motke. "We could use him here."

Disregarding Motke's suggestion, Amnon continued, "Remember, all that is written in the Bible, and in the other archaeologic materials, is generally within a few hours' drive of this office. I don't have to tell you. So for us, these are not dead writings. We are living and working within the midst of the Biblical land. I'm just a regular Israeli—not religious. But even me personally, I never know if the events we witness every day, every year, are just accidents of history or written in advance. Maybe it is both—which is okay by me. But we have many people here who take it all very seriously. They believe everything is laid out and planned by God himself. They say *nothing by accident*. To hear them, the struggle between Moses and the Pharaoh was all written in the heavens and acted out just to make a point."

"Well, think about it," commented Park. "The plagues came to Egypt not so much because Pharaoh refused Moses as much as because God *'hardened his heart'* and wanted Pharaoh to resist and receive the plagues. God made an example of Pharaoh just to prove a point."

"She's good with the Bible," interjected Dan.

"Very good with the Bible. So let us come to the present because the hour is short. Mr. Hinnom, we believe, is trouble. We think he has the power to destroy the world because he controls the world's computers. And we think he could do it with a snap of his fingers," said Amnon, snapping sharply. "That is, until the moment comes in four days when the world makes a big choice: to take the Update he calls Windgazer 99.9 or to take the advice of our young man here, Sal, and go with Format C:. For our part, we in the Israeli government of course have complete confidence in Format C: because we know Derek and Derek put the Format command inside. So it is our mission—all of us—to make sure the world makes the right decision.

"Now Hinnom," Amnon continued, "Hinnom is right now sitting down in his valley getting ready for his big midnight masterpiece. Fine. Let him. From our point, we prefer to have his big party held here under our nose and our eyes. Better here than in a place where we can't see him. We wish Sal to keep doing what he is doing with the reboot campaign because the more people who believe in this alternative, the better in our eyes."

"Why don't you just close Hinnom down right now?" asked Dan. "Stop his transmissions on December 31. Dump his party. End of story."

"Almost all the computers in Israel are also on Windgazer," replied Amnon, "just like the rest of the world. It is a little like the bomber you saw on the *midrekhov*. Hinnom has his finger on a detonator, if I can use that comparison. Every two or three days, he makes the overnight refreshes and without these, no one can function. Yes, we can shut him down in five minutes. But then what? No one can make a move against this man until this Friday when his system, with the help of God, is permanently replaced.

"At some point before that, however," Amnon warned, "we believe Hinnom will lose patience with Sal over here. Probably very soon. Sal is the big enemy now. He is the only one standing between Windgazer and the world. So, we want to move you, Sal, to a safer place. In the North."

"Where?" asked Park.

"A small place, not far from here," replied Amnon. "A kibbutz."

". . . named?" asked Dan.

"Megiddo," Amnon answered with hesitation.

Sal looked nervously at the speakerphone. "Do not worry, you will be safe there," said the voice of Kuebitz.

"I am leading a chanting rally against Hinnom tomorrow," said Sal, "right in Gei Ben Hinnom. It's too late to cancel. A lot of people are coming and they expect me."

Amnon nodded negatively, and was about to overrule the idea when Sal added, "It's too important. The movement needs me there."

"Then make your rally, do your chanting," Amnon relented. "But that's it. After that, we want you packed up and gone. Okay?"

Sal nodded and Park concurred.

"On December 31," said Amnon, "we are hoping that the people everywhere from the world–at least a majority–will make the right choice. And we have some special operations planned to coincide. These details, however, cannot be disclosed at this moment."

"So," asked Dan, "where do I come in, besides getting the exclusive on the whole affair which I place on the wires in a copyrighted story on January 1, which will be a full twenty-four hours before any details are released to the general media, including Israel TV and Army Radio, and in which I get in-depth color details from senior government officials for my book?"

"Your exclusive, your books and your news reports do not concern me, if you don't mind," Amnon retorted. "Talk to the Government Press Office about all that request. I'm trying to save a very, very bad situation. So please, for now, you can help us all by making sure Sal here doesn't get into trouble. And Dan, no more digging please without a permit, not at Qumran or anywhere."

"We turned in the two scrolls," defended Dan. "We just held onto them for a few days until we could find the right office at Antiquities. We're not digging."

"But no more," said Amnon. "Just take care of Sal."

"And me?" asked Motke.

"Take care of Dan," Amnon responded. "Here's a Jew in Israel who doesn't read or write Hebrew. And you Ms. McGuire, stay close to your son, he will need you."

"So," concluded Amnon, "does anyone require anything? Anything at all, because I must be elsewhere soon."

"Anything?" Dan responded.

"Anything in our power," said the voice of Kuebitz.

Dan scribbled a short list on a pad of paper and slid it across the table toward Amnon. "Just these three things?" asked Amnon, looking up at three clocks displaying foreign time zones. "Okay. We'll try."

"If God wills it, it will be done," joked Dan.

"If He does, it shall," said the voice of Kuebitz.

TWENTY BUSES WAITED in a long line at Jaffa Gate. One by one, as their doors whooshed open, the passengers playfully jumped to the street eager to discover everything. They radiated pure smiles as they touched the ancient stones and gazed up in wonderment at the awesome ramparts. Each wore a light blue baseball cap embroidered with the words "21st Century." Their T-shirts proudly declared the slogans they lived by. "Just a Little Extra," said one. Others stated: "Smile—I do," "Chromosome 21," or "Light of Your Life." But most boasted the words, "Up Syndrome."

More than a thousand Down Syndrome men and women representing varying degrees of function had organized their millennial celebration in Israel. Perhaps none in the group was more elated to be in Jerusalem than Raymond, who was given leave from his duties as janitor in the first-floor Senate bathroom to make the trip. No matter who Raymond passed, he gleefully volunteered, "I love you," adding to anyone else standing near, "And you, and you, and you." His mother silently observed the habit with affection and respect. Occasionally, Raymond would stop his random declarations of affection to swivel and almost secretively point both hands toward the sky, confessing, "And I love God too." His Down friends would nod energetically in agreement, and ask if they could join in. "No problem," Raymond would answer zealously. "God wants the whole group!"

~

DECEMBER 29, 1999. Noon. Hinnom event planners were finishing preparations for their colossal happening. A fifty-foot-tall TV screen with twin Sony projectors had been erected near the Tophet. Next to the TV screen rose a circular stage, the front half of which would be used by dancers, acrobats and rock musicians. Promotional flags had been posted everywhere around the concert grounds with one great WINDGAZER 99.9 banner strung the entire distance across the ravine. Light towers equipped with shape focusing lasers and smoke machines to texturize the illumination would create an eerie effect from any vantage point.

A commercial dirigible, emblazoned with the Windgazer 99.9 logo, circled above. Beginning at nightfall on the 31st, its powerful beacons, lasers and messaging lights would bathe the entire area in a spectacular light show. Airborne cameras would broadcast the scene below to a worldwide viewing audience. The dirigible had another purpose. At midnight on the 31st, unbeknownst to Israeli officials, the show would culminate with the Windgazer 99.9 logo being projected from the airship onto the Wailing Wall itself. The music to accompany this projection promised to be a throbbing sequence of unearthly cues unlike any ever heard. Composed by Hinnom himself, the opus was entitled "The Beast."

To create the mesmerizing sounds of "The Beast," Hinnom integrated the most sophisticated array of synthesizers ever assembled, capable of recreating any imaginable combination of acoustic, electronic, or choral music—from subtle tenor monodies and mind-boggling rasps to angelic harmonizing and syncopated orchestral swells. It could all be blended with any sound effect known to man, and perhaps some never heard before. Yet all this extraordinary music was to be generated by just four hired musicians, handpicked by Hinnom, playing an assemblage of racked keyboards. Six digital keyboards included a MemoryMoog, a Yamaha VL1 and GX-1, an Oberheim XPander, and a Korg Prophecy, as well as a Roland JD-800 and JP-8000. Three analog synthesizers would also be used: a Moog 10, a Roland System 100, and a Korg Polyfusion. All synthesizing would be mixed by a battery of Yamaha O2Rs and a ProMix Zero amplified, controlled, and synchronized by a Penny and Giles MM16 Midi Machine Controller, a pair of Opcode Studio 5LXs and Midi Time Piece IIs, as well as a Brainstorm SR-15+ Distripalyzer/Time Code Analyzer.

Bizarre, never before heard, *museffex* that Hinnom said "would penetrate the very soul of all who heard it," would be constructed sonic layer upon sonic layer by a host of sound samplers including an Emulator E-IVx Turbo, a Kurzweil K2500r, a Roland S-760, and a Akai S1100 + Expander working in tandem with a Roland SPH-323 for phase shifting, a SBF-325 stereo flanger, a Moog Three-Band Parametric Equalizer, several of Lexicon's most advanced PCM-80s, 300s and 480Ls, working with a Roland SRV-330 for dimensional space reverberation coupled to a Roland SDE-330. Added to all those devices were specially configured Yamaha SPX-990s for multi-effects, teamed with an AMX Rmx16 Digital Reverb, the Yamaha REV-1 Digital Reverb, and finally, three linked Denney Electronics Spatializers.

Nothing like it had ever been brought together in any outdoor setting. More than music for the New Age, "The Beast" would inaugurate what

Hinnom termed "New Millennial" music. Hinnom promised listeners would experience the most compelling concert in human history—one that would launch a new epoch of rhythmic rapture. Its captivating performance would be heard simultaneously by the largest live concert audience ever—more than a billion people in sixty nations.

Musical pyrotechnics and ethereal light shows were just the beginning for the last night of the millennium. Waves of Mexican, Cossack, Scottish, Zulu, and Thai native dancers, each wearing their own native festival attire, were scheduled to begin the event. Chinese acrobats would follow, yielding to a small army of gymnasts selected from universities around the world who would create an eight-tier human pyramid during the big finale.

Wondrous fireworks to be fired from special platforms ensconced throughout the Judean Hills, would commence at 11:30 P.M. on December 31, and continue until the Millennial Moment. These would explode, spray, fizzle, sparkle and splash across the skies, painting the heavens as no one had ever dared.

Just before midnight, Ben Hinnom himself would make the final televised global appeal for users everywhere to simply type the words "Windgazer 99.9" from their C prompts. That command would initialize the Point Nine Update. Everything else would be automatic. But, Hinnom insisted, each person had to make the decision for himself. Nothing by accident, Hinnom insisted. "The world must choose."

Opposing this lavish extravaganza were rebooters throughout the world who also considered Jerusalem their epicenter. As such, more than forty thousand protesters gathered along the Valley of Ben Hinnom that day, December 29. Carrying placards marked, "No Upload," and "Reboot," Windgazer logos with Xs drawn through them, and even signs that decried Hinnom as the Devil himself, the rejectionists filled the rocky slopes as far as police would permit; they stretched north to Yemin Moshe opposite Jaffa Gate. When the valley's capacity was exceeded, more protesters lined the streets above, draping bedsheets and flags down walls lining the ravine, urging the world not to initialize.

Police erected barricades just yards from the main Windgazer stage at the far southern end of the valley. Riot squads, augmented by horse-mounted crowd control policemen, were deployed in a protective phalanx. Armed with rubber bullets, pepper spray and batons, the police hoped violence could be averted.

Scanning protesters from behind the barricades, officers with binoculars looked for troublemakers. "Look there," remarked one to another. In his earpiece, he heard confirmation from police helicopters overhead reporting that the crowd was dividing from the rear.

The crowd was indeed parting. It was for Sal, slowly advancing through the throng. Dan, Motke, and Park were behind him. Gradually, Sal and the group made their way to the very front, stopping only at the barricades.

The police commander recognized Sal as the leader of the movement. Facing off across the barricade, the commander told him, "You may express yourself as you wish, so long as it is peaceful. Chanting is good. Just chanting. Please cooperate and do not incite this crowd. You see how many people are here." The commander steeled his expression and announced, "We are granting you one hour. Sixty minutes . . . starting ten minutes ago."

Sal answered serenely, "I'm only here to ask the world to open its eyes to what Ben Hinnom is doing." With that he began to softly chant: "Format C: . . . Reboot, Reboot, Reboot." Quickly the nearby crowd joined him: "Format C: . . . Reboot, Reboot, Reboot." Before long the entire valley was shouting in unison.

Format C: . . . Reboot, Reboot, Reboot.

Format C: . . . Reboot, Reboot, Reboot.

Format C: . . . Reboot, Reboot, Reboot.

The thunderous sound reverberated throughout the caves and crevices of the valley, and directly into Hinnom's tent. At first, Hinnom tried to ignore the chanting. He continued fastidiously programing for the midnight event. However, his concentration soon broke. He started to fidget, then to pace, first within the tent, then to and from the adjacent cave, dodging urine trickles from above as he shifted about. Linzer tried to approach, but Hinnom was getting angrier and angrier as the crowd chanted louder and louder and the echoes became more and more punishing and the roar of rejection drove him to a corner where he gripped his ears and then the aching right side of his head.

Meanwhile, at the barricades, the crowd surged forward. The police assumed a defensive posture, deploying batons horizontally and lowering their protective visors. Although protesters were agitating themselves into a frenzy, Sal continued to chant serenely, almost motionlessly. Then, all at once, his passive mode dissolved. He began to throb in cadence with the chanting. Just as suddenly, Sal became strangely silent. He turned to face the multitude and held up his arms to hush them. His wish spread among the protesters until all the chanting dissipated. The enormous throng quieted completely. Police took note of the change in mood. They stood down as well, lowering their batons, taking a collective breath, and waited anxiously to see what would happen next.

Unexpectedly, Sal raised one arm high for all to see and staunchly pointed at all the computer towers networked throughout the stage. He shouted at the top of his voice: "Man should control the computer–not the other way around." Sal jumped the barricade, and raced wildly toward the servers.

The police line returned to riot readiness, batons raised to contain the crowd.

"Sal!" Park cried, trying to run after him. But she could not break through the phalanx.

Two or three policemen chased Sal as he ungracefully scrambled up the stage, overturning computer towers here, now there, and over there. The crowd roared as Sal toppled one server after another. Finally, the police jumped him. Dan winced as he saw Sal wrestled to the floor, then a policeman's knee shoved into his back. Finally, Sal was handcuffed.

Park shrieked, unable to help her son. Dan tried to console her.

Motke shook his head.

Hinnom and Linzer came running from the rear to see the commotion. Linzer held his palms up to Ishbi and the other lurking Anakim to stay put in the tent. As Hinnom rounded the stage, he saw the servers laying prone, their cables pulled, monitors cracked and sparking. He growled to the policemen: "I want that man arrested. Arrested!" He lowered his voice as he saw nearby onlookers, but repeated his demand: "Arrested. I want that little fatherless bastard arrested."

The police were hauling Sal away when Hinnom shouted after them, "And if you find my little computer on his body, seize that. It belongs to *me*."

Using loudspeakers, the police up and down the valley began asking protesters to disperse. "You have made your point. The hour is up. Please go home."

As the crowd thinned, Hinnom stomped into his tent, closing the exterior flaps for privacy. He waved the Anakim and Linzer to gather round.

"I want that fatherless sonofabitch destroyed," he seethed, struggling to keep his voice down. "Shoot him, hang him, burn him. Do what you want, but I want him dead before midnight Friday. Long before Friday midnight." He stared up at towering Ishbi, ten feet tall. "Take these two colleagues of yours," hissed Hinnom, "and get your brother and cousins out of their dark hole. Then finish that boy off."

Turning to Linzer, Hinnom commanded, "Call the police. Call 'em, call 'em, call 'em. Tell them we aren't pressing charges. No real damage. The computers are repaired, restored, replaced, whatever you want," he yelled. "Just get the fatherless sonofabitch released. Then . . . finish him."

PARK, DAN, AND Motke were anxiously waiting in the Dan Pearl's lobby bar. Twice in fifteen minutes, Dan pointed to the lobby bar phone, reminding the front desk, "If I get a call, I'm not in the room. Transfer it over there."

Motke and Dan had each telephoned as many people as they knew to discover Sal's whereabouts and obtain his release. He was not at the Russian Compound police station. Police headquarters knew nothing. The riot squad said he had been transferred, they knew not where. Kuebitz' line at Derek was on voice mail only. The Government Press Office police liaison was networking on Dan's urgent request, but his main contact was getting ready for a trip overseas and her youthful and very helpful stand-in didn't have a clue.

General Amnon Natan could not be reached; everyone in the defense establishment knew who Natan was, but no one knew his phone number. Or his number had been changed. Or he shared it with someone else who was not answering. Like many in Israel, the general's antiquated office phone did not work well. Only his cellular was reliable.

Park was trying to stay calm but was now pacing and mumbling dark thoughts. Maybe Hinnom's henchmen have caught up to Sal. Maybe the anti-terror squad placed him in six-month administrative detention without charge and with no access to lawyers. Maybe Sal did something unpredictable and was injured.

"Maybe he's just having a glass of tea with marmalade in a reception room somewhere waiting for a rubber stamp at the bottom of a piece of paper," interjected Dan, trying to calm her. "Why theorize?" The waiter had served the most recent round of turkish when Amnon strode into the lobby.

"I called your room two times," said the general. "There was no answer."

"I told the desk to transfer my calls," complained Dan, slapping his knee and glancing unhappily at the front desk, "We have been right here . . . What do you know about Sal?"

"Sal is fine, he is not in a big problem," Amnon told an overwrought Park. "In the location of Gei Ben Hinnom where he was taken into custody, that was technically East Jerusalem. So they transferred him to the lockup there."

Park gasped.

"Don't be so worried," assured Amnon. "No one made a touch on him. He was not put in a cell or hurt." Amnon gestured no to the waiter's offer of a drink. "Your son is just waiting paperwork to be released. But it is not easy from East Jerusalem. We just needed to find the right person to authorize it. However, now it is arranged—or will be—and Sal will be delivered here in about three hours. Maybe four. We thought it would be easier to just wait until the shift change at the police station. The commander of the afternoon shift was in my unit in the army and he'll do what I tell him."

Park thanked Amnon repeatedly. Dan and Motke joined in thanking him.

"I said no more after this," stressed Amnon. "Now it is time to pack up and go to Megiddo. We will make arrangements. Until then, please, stay away from Ben Hinnom." After exchanging cell phone numbers with Dan to make sure they could stay in touch, Amnon hustled out of the lobby.

An hour later, while waiting in the suite, the phone did not stop ringing. All the people Motke and Dan had called were now calling back to say they knew nothing about Sal's whereabouts. Dan was expecting more of the same when the phone rang for the tenth time. But it was Meir. He was downstairs in the lobby.

"Meir? Yes, come on up," said Dan.

Meir declined. "Is the woman up there, Sal's mother?"

Dan said yes.

"Then I prefer to talk down here in a public place. Please come down." Meir explained, "Everyone in Israel knows what is happening with Hinnom. After you left my room in Tsfat, something came to me from the C Scroll."

Dan interjected. "Antiquities took a high-res photo. They gave me a copy."

"Then please come down," asked Meir, "because I didn't put two and two together until I heard about Hinnom and asked some people. Bring the photo."

Motke, Dan, and Park flew out of the room to the elevator. Dan ran back in, grabbed the slightly curled copy of the C Scroll print, and headed down with them.

Meir appeared as though he had never changed clothing. He was wearing the identical attire as the last time they met in Tsfat. His white food-stained shirt was still buttoned at the top, barely tucked in at the bottom. Motke tried to greet him first, but Meir's attention went right to Dan.

"You have the print?" Meir asked, twirling his fingers in anticipation.

Dan spread it out on the lobby bar table, using an ashtray and a sugar bowl to weigh down the corners.

Meir pulled out a small rectangular magnifying glass and a thick, thumb-sized, plastic-bound book. He referred back and forth between the two, occasionally turning pages and pointing to words or phrases, his eyebrows arching up and down like irregular heartbeats.

"What's this book?" asked Dan.

"It's a book," replied Meir without looking up.

After more checking back and forth, and after Motke, Dan, and Park exchanged glances repeatedly, and after attempts to peer over Meir's hunched form failed, Dan finally demanded, "So?"

"This is the wrong book," said Meir nonchalantly.

The three deflated for a moment until Meir added, "but I think that is good. The answer is not in this book. I hoped it wasn't. Instead, I think the answer is something a rebbe suggested to me in Tsfat. So please to listen."

They leaned forward. "We put the evil of this *mamzer* Hinnom together with the triple shin, and a few sacred writings that a brand-new Jew like you don't need to worry yourself about."

Dan let the remark pass.

"What we said about Daniel still stands," Meir added.

Park repeated the quote, *"Then he will set up the abomination that causes desolation. With flattery he will corrupt those who have violated the covenant but the people who know their God will firmly resist him."*

Meir looked at Dan. "You should learn from her. She would make a Jew faster than you could."

"Pleeeease," moaned Dan. "Stop *kvetching* and get on with it. We have come a long way to still have patience."

"Hinnom," explained Meir, "will attempt to cause the abomination of desolation, as it said in Daniel. The answer to stopping him is inside the *shin,* or *sin,* actually. You will find it *there.*"

The group looked askance at Meir and then at each other.

Seeing their lack of understanding, Meir drew a three-pronged *shin* on a cocktail napkin, then took a coffee stirrer from the table and pointed along the *shin's* left ascender, and finally circled it several times for emphasis.

Dan breathed out in exasperation. "Meir," he said curtly, "how do we get into the left ascender of this letter. Use a bigger magnifying glass?"

Meir dropped his shoulders in disappointment. "Start at the top of the flame. Get to the bottom," he answered. No response. "I said the *shin* represents the three valleys of Jerusalem. The left part," outlining with the coffee stirrer, "is Gei Ben Hinnom."

"Okay . . ." said Dan with uncertainty.

"And at the bottom is where Ben Hinnom himself is sitting, at the deepest part of the Gei–the valley."

"Yes . . ."

"So we go close to the bottom through the left part of the *shin* itself, into the valley," continued Meir, "and I don't mean in *through* the valley with a protest march like I saw on TV."

Even though still confused, Dan added yet another but more tentative, *"Okaaaay . . ."*

"We go into the earth itself. Descend to where he is through the earth."

Dan shook his head negatively, "Not okay . . . not okay . . ."

"The Convent of St. Onuphrius!" replied Meir, as though everyone should have known.

Puzzlement showed on all their faces.

"This convent," Meir explained in rapid clip fashion, "Greek Orthodox–started as a monastery and now a convent. It is sitting directly on top of his cave. You will go in there and find an answer. From there you can go right down."

Dan was silent.

Meir went on, "They have bones. From dead people." He asked Motke to translate some Hebrew so he could complete the phrase.

Motke chimed in, "Ah! Burial places from the dead."

"Crypts?" asked Park.

Motke agreed, but had a hard time pronouncing the word.

Then it finally dawned on Dan. "Okay, I get it!" He spread sugar bags on the table and grabbed his own coffee stirrer. "There are ancient crypts in this convent up here on top of the ravine." He turned a sugar bag crossways, "and the crypts go down, like straight down." He lined several up vertically. "And because they are, we can get right next to Ben Hinnom's cave deep in the valley." He moved a small bowl of brown sugar cubes to represent Hinnom's cave. "Okay. Then what?"

"Then you find an answer," said Meir pleasurably with a big smile, his eyebrows twitching in satisfaction.

"So let's go," said Dan enthusiastically, tugging at Meir's shirt sleeve.

Meir drew a long face, even longer than usual. "Not me," he declared standoffishly. "I don't go to a convent. You can go. Please don't be offended if I am honest, but a not-quite-Jew like you is better for a place like that than me."

Motke and Dan exchanged one of those expressions, the look that settles dismally on your face just after discovering that your very swift and powerful computer does not have a modem and can't communicate. They smiled at each other and Park smiled with them.

"Meir . . ." Dan began.

"Yes?" Meir replied.

Dan thought better of his reaction and just politely said, "Thanks. We'll see ya after."

Meir closed his eyes, and muttered a quiet prayer. A moment later, he opened his eyes wide and declared, "I change my mind. It's okay. I will go."

"To a convent?" asked Dan, who then waved his comment away,

replacing it with, "Good. Great. You know, we need a *real Jew* to help us out."

"Nothing by accident," Meir chimed back, adding, "everything with a purpose."

They went out to Jaffa Street and hailed an Arab taxi.

THE TAXI DRIVER dropped Dan, Park, Motke, and Meir at a point along the road above Gei Ben Hinnom. The group scrambled down the ravine slope. "Not long," Park kept nervously reminding them. "I want to be back at the hotel when Sal is released."

After the third reminder, Dan assured, "We'll be back in an hour, two at the most. The worst, he lets himself into the room and has some M&Ms unattended."

Abruptly, the St. Onuphrius Convent came into view. A slender dirt road cut into the side of the ravine was the abbey's only access. Built in the style of other Greek Orthodox mountaintop monasteries, but much smaller, the rotunda of St. Onuphrius' basilica crowned a sand-colored perimeter of sheer fortress-style walls that belied the compound's complicated interior. It stood directly atop Hinnom's personal grotto at the farthest end of the valley. Sewage and waste water from the structure trickled almost continuously over a nearby cliff and into the cave mouth below.

The group marched up the long, steep path that eventually ended at an ornate black metal portal topped by short twisted spikes. No one was about. After repeatedly calling out for an attendant with no result, Dan gave the others a glance.

Motke put his foot down immediately. "We cannot enter a convent without permission," he declared. "Let us come back when someone is home."

"We'll go a smidgen—just inside the gate," countered Dan, "and properly seek out someone to authorize us in. The monks are way in there, they can't hear."

Motke again declined, but by that time, Dan had gently leaned on the handle and the gate creaked open. "Look," Dan grinned, "someone left it open."

Park rolled her eyes briefly to acknowledge how unsurprised she was. They peeked in to survey a complex of stone and timber stairwells, bricked courtyards, and narrow passageways. Mysterious doorways were everywhere, some half-submerged beneath the terrace, some elevated accessible by narrow sets of steps, and in some cases only by ladder. Tiny opaque windows covered with heavy iron bars were all about. Like most Holy Land convents and monasteries, the premises included a dormitory, dining room, chapels, a library, some offices, cellars, workspaces, and any number of general rooms. But unlike most convents and monasteries, which are known for their drab, austere sightlines, St. Onuphrius was bedecked in colorful flowers. Azaleas, roses, lilies, and even sweeping birds of paradise added unexpected brightness to the otherwise colorless confines. Flowerpots were affixed to every railing, arrangements were planted in narrow soil patches along passageways, and bouquets bloomed in earthen pots atop window sills.

They were taken by surprise when a heavyset nun, wearing a combination of common clothes and a habit, appeared along a second-story walk toting a plastic bucket, some detergent bottles, wet towels, and a small step ladder. She looked down, wiped her brow and called, "Was that you at the gate?" She was Irish, and spoke with a typical Dubliner's lilt.

Dan immediately engaged her in conversation, and within moments she was happily imparting everything she knew about the St. Onuphrius.

Her name was Sister Nan, the third in her Greek Orthodox family to serve the Church. She had been at St. Onuphrius only twenty months, and there was still plenty of cleaning up to be done. For Sister Nan, cleaning was her on-ramp to heaven. She loved to sweep the dusty mantles and grimy corners, scrub the tiles and trim, and polish the ironwork and brass. It was she who planted flowers, probably the first color and brightness the monastery had known in nearly 1800 years.

"Yes," Sister Nan remarked, "St. Onuphrius is listed in almost none of the church directories or guidebooks. But it does exist—you are standing on it. The place has actually been here in one form or another since shortly after the Crucifixion."

She was happy for some visitors—the only visitors she had seen at the convent since she arrived in early 1998. And so long as the few supervising monks were all away for the afternoon attending to business in Jerusalem, she would happily show the group around.

"The story went," Sister Nan related, "that Judas' thirty pieces of silver were used to purchase the land from the then-landowners, probably descendents of Hinnom. They say the original deed can still be examined in the records room of the Greek Orthodox convent in the Old City. Most of the buildings you see are relatively recent. Some go all the way back."

Sister Nan escorted the group into a long narrow meeting room everywhere adorned with wisping gold censers and tall burning candles. "The Apostles came here after Jesus was arrested." She pointed out a removable covering in the floor. "Under the floorboards is some sort of water source," she explained. "No one knows where it comes from or where it goes. Only that it is not still or standing water. It does move. Drop an apple slice in and it flows away. Yet during heavy rains, the level never goes up. During dry spells, the level never goes down." She took a glass from a shelf, laid prostrate on the floor, removed the covering, reached in to her shoulder and brought out a glass of the clear fluid. "None of the sisters drink the stuff," she mused, "but some of the men certainly do." She poured the fluid back into the hole.

She was about to lead the group to the kitchen where fresh, fragrant bread was baking, when Dan stopped the tour to ask, "How about the charnel?"

"That's below," she answered. Sure enough, three flights down a sunken courtyard, there were two grottoes, sealed up by an ancient barricade-like door hung into a rough timber frame. Next to either doorpost was a small skull. Charnelhouses of decorously collected skulls were common in ancient Greek Orthodox monasteries. When monks died, their honored skulls were preserved and displayed in a macabre rite of sanctification.

"So the charnel is here," said Dan, motioning to the right doorway. "And the burial crypts—are they different?"

"Well, of course," Sister Nan replied, pointing to the left door. "The crypts would be down that way. Would you like a look? I can get the key," she volunteered, completely excited that anyone was interested.

Suppressing his unexpected delight, Dan shrugged nonchalantly, "I guess it would be okay. Why not?"

Park, Meir, and Motke just exchanged glances at the good fortune.

When Sister Nan went to retrieve the key, Dan looked off in pseudo-humility.

"This kind of thing happens to him all the time," Park dryly remarked to Motke.

Moments later, Sister Nan returned with a large rusted iron key distinguished by three jagged teeth. "We'll just need to be done before the monks return," she cautioned. "They might not approve." The rear of the grotto was dark, until she carried in a utility light, offering a few feet of illumination. After stepping over the high threshold and into the grotto, the musty, stale bone dust hit their nostrils. Coughing and squinting subsided in just a moment, but when it did, they beheld floor-to-ceiling internment shelves chiseled into the walls. Laid out neatly in each was a complete skeleton, every bone perfectly aligned, hollowed eyes looking straight up, hands serenely folded. The scene was too much for Park. She stepped back outside, trying not to gag.

Dan examined the corpses up close, as Sister Nan blew a fly away from one body's rib cage.

"These are the bones of pious travelers to the Holy Land," she explained, "Generally I would say from about 200 to 300 A.D. Some a little later. I dust these once every two or three months," she added proudly.

At the far end of the cave was a large archway leading to a lower chamber. "Mind the step down," warned Sister Nan, reaching for the flashlight stationed next to the opening. She went first, swinging her leg over the high bottom and onto steps leading down.

After making sure Park would be all right waiting outside, Dan, Motke, and Meir followed Sister Nan.

The second chamber was almost a perfect cube. Once everyone was standing upright, Sister Nan shone the flashlight on the kerosene lantern in the corner, which she lit. Like a tour guide, she began explaining that the bones in this chamber were of people with less money to pay for interment. The difference showed. Some of the ossuaries held more than one set of remains and the bodies were often cramped up against each other. "I try to keep these clean as well, but I can't do it all with no help," said Nan, somewhat defensively, noting the condition of the bodies.

At the far end of the second chamber floor, Dan spied another hole, this one much smaller. "And down there?" he asked.

"Seen it from up here, but I never go down there," she replied, adding with a blush. "Some of the smaller monks do, but I just can't fit through that little hole."

"Nor I," agreed Motke.

Sister Nan offered Dan and Meir her flashlight and lowered a narrow, crudely constructed wooden ladder down through the hole. "Please," she invited. "They use this." The men slowly descended below the chamber floor.

Once down, Dan rotated the flashlight to illuminate the third chamber. It was tall and narrow. The ossuaries were not linear but boxlike. Instead of full bodies, they mostly held skulls atop partially disjointed skeletons.

"Those are probably the poorest," commented Sister Nan from the hole above, as she peered down.

Midway up one corner, there was another opening, no bigger than the size of a small man's girth. Unlike the other portals, this hole was not smooth and finished. It was craggy, almost as though someone had broken through a thin cavern wall.

Dan shouted up asking where that opening led.

"Haven't a clue," replied Sister Nan. "I can't get down there. Too narrow for me."

Meir tried to insert the ladder through the opening. It wouldn't fit.

So Dan stuck his head in, flashlight first. "It's a chute," he called back, "going straight down." He leaned in further . . . a little further . . . until he felt something. "No problem," he reported, "we can slip down a knotted rope. I feel it hooked into the wall."

Motke protested from above, "This is too far, Dan. You will hurt yourself." He issued a more argumentative warning in Hebrew to Meir.

But both Meir and Dan ignored the warnings. Dan led. He squeezed through the small opening, feet first, and shimmied down. "Uh, my clothes are getting dirty," he groaned as the grimy surface smeared into his shirt and pants. After descending the third rope knot, Dan could feel nothing more. Wedging himself against the cavern chute for stability, he called up for Meir, "What do you see. How far is it down?" Meir shone the flashlight, but could not illuminate past Dan's wedged body. He dropped the flashlight down to Dan, who maneuvered to view the bottom. "No problem," called Dan. "It's not even two feet below . . . I'm going to drop."

Meir hesitated, "Maybe not. How will we come back up?" Dan insisted that if both of them descended, they could help each other back up to the knotted rope. Meir, against his better judgment, shouted up the word to Motke and Sister Nan above.

Dan shoved the flashlight into his belt, and then free-fell the few feet to the bottom of the fourth chamber. On landing, his flattened palms slammed into the ground, squishing some worms. Wiping his hands dry against his pants, Dan stood up to discover a slender, irregularly shaped chasm. Meir followed, landing with a truncated yelp, for which he added, "Excuse me."

Unlike the other three chambers which were dry and dusty, this chasm was suffocating for its moist, vile air. Putrefaction and dense mold forced their faces into painful wrinkles almost immediately. They pulled their shirts up to cover their mouths, but the pungent air remained unbearable.

Sometimes holding his nose, Dan scanned the walls with the flashlight. Shallow holes and oblong troughs carved into the wall became visible. Clearly, the fourth chamber was the most neglected crypt of all. Each space was filled with a jumble of human mortality: femurs, skulls, tibia, clavicles, spines–all in disheveled heaps as though unceremoniously dumped. Dozens of people were interred here, and obviously in a hurry. Unlike the other chambers, the chasm had no smooth walls or rounded edges. These confines were rough. Less than a crypt, it seemed like a lair. It was almost as though the lair and the burial chambers were separate structures created independently and at separate times, but connected when ancient monks broke through to the chute.

Dan shone the flashlight onto some of the skulls, and then the spinal columns. Recalling his days covering the Chicago morgue, he recognized evidence of great violence: fissures, cracks, large missing occipital fragments. The deceased included mature adults–both men and women, as well as children. "These people did not die in their sleep," remarked Dan, coughing. Some of the bones were snapped. "Looks like they were torn limb from limb," he observed in disgust. "This is no burial crypt of honor. This is the trophy room of killers."

Cave seepage covered the walls, dripping through growths of ancient fungus and onto the lower bone troughs where the moisture collected into pools surrounding the murdered remains. In some cases, the slant of the trough caused the grisly fluid to spill over the rim. That spillage gathered into runlets that coursed into a shallow angular blood gutter emptying down a long, narrow crevice. They peered down the dark crevice and saw blackness– except at the very end where a sliver of light was visible. "This drains into a lighted cave below," said Dan. "I wouldn't be surprised if it is Ben Hinnom's cave. Maybe he's using this filthy fluid to make turkish," he sneered.

"Shine by here," said Meir, running his hand over the cracks and angles of a wall closer to the chute. Dan directed the flashlight toward Meir. It was an inscription cut into the rock. No, actually a series of inscriptions. As they moved the flashlight more carefully, inscriptions could be seen etched everywhere.

"Meir. Read this stuff," Dan asked. Aiming the flashlight more carefully, Meir brought his face to just inches away from the writing. After studying the letters for several minutes of sustained silence, during which Dan tried to suppress even his coughing, Meir finally spoke.

"You know, a few years ago two very little silver scrolls were found in another cave just yards from here, close to the Tophet," he began, adding, "The scrolls say: *The Lord bless you and keep you. The Lord make His face to shine upon you.* And the rest of that blessing. Maybe you know it. Those two scrolls are twenty-six hundred years old, the oldest archaeologic reference to the Bible. Very nice. But *these,*" he waved dramatically across the inscriptions, "from this wall, are much older. Much, much, much. They go back I think, based on the letterforms, to King David's time.

"Okay, I can tell you," Meir started. "This one up by here says 'Slaughtered by the Sons of Anak.' The one below it says, 'Killed by Ishbi.' Over here, 'We defile the Ark of the Israelites.'" Meir stopped to mumble a prayer. He continued illuminating and reading the inscriptions across the wall. "You see," he declared, circling words with the flashlight beam, "It is obvious that everyone here was killed by the sons of Anak, by the Anakim."

Dan spoke slowly at first, as he made the mental connection, "Uh, Linzer . . . Linzer referred–" then all at once he completed the thought. "Linzer in the park, when he was hassling Sal, trying to grab his little computer, called these big gargantuan buddies of his lurking in the background . . . he called them . . . Anakim . . . Anakim!"

"Very good," said Meir. "So you are making progress. And the Anakim were . . ." Meir asked, waiting like a teacher for an answer.

Dan stammered a try but then gave up, "Meir. How do I know who were the Anakim? Who were they?"

"Please don't be offended," Meir retorted, "but this is why I have the problem. A Jew should know about the Anakim. They were all giants."

An exasperated Dan looked down and pinched his nose at the narrow between his eyes, trying to restrain himself.

Directing the flashlight vertically between the two, casting strange shadows up both their faces, Meir at last began reciting the history. "When God created the world and also mankind," Meir said, "a race of his celestial beings–a race of giant warriors, fell from the Holy One's favor. These giant warriors were called Nephilim, which in Hebrew, you should be aware, means 'The Fallen Ones' because they fell from God's domain. Kicked out of the heavens, they fell to earth. The Nephilim married beautiful women on earth and they could live forever. This angered the Holy One. Remember, Adam ate from the Tree of Knowledge to become like God and now come the Nephilim.

"The Bible mentions Nephilim twice," Meir detailed, "once very early in the book you call Genesis–Chapter 6, verse 4–you should know, very close to the creation account itself. It is written, *The Nephilim were on the earth in those days–and also afterward–when the sons of God went into the daughters of humans, who gave them children. These were the heroes of old, the men of renown.* Then again in Numbers, chapter 13, verse 33, it is written, *There we saw the Nephilim–the Anakim come from the Nephilim–and to ourselves we seemed like grasshoppers, and so we seemed to them.* Nephilim are also mentioned in many other Kabbalistic writings, which you need not concern yourself with.

"Now, God grew weary of man's evil ways," continued Meir, "especially because now with the Nephilim, man could live forever. So God wiped out mankind and the Nephilim with the flood–remember Noah– and started over. But this time he decreed that man would not live more than one hundred and twenty years. Even Moses only lived one hundred and twenty years after that."

"And that's why to this day, Jews toast 'to one hundred and twenty years,'" added Dan.

Ignoring Dan's contribution, Meir returned to his discourse. "The flood as we all know did *not* wipe out *all* of mankind. Some descendents of the Nephilim survived. Those descendents are the Anakim, the sons of Anak."

"And what is the meaning of *this?*" asked Dan, pointing to a small niche–maybe six to ten inches square, carved into the wall. Inside was a smooth, polished, gleaming white, elliptical stone. Meir shone the flashlight on the recess and the object within. He stared at it for a long time, muttered to himself, and then asked Dan, "Please, you hold the flashlight." Dan held it steady on the stone. The reflection lit up the entire niche. Meir gazed at the stone for several more moments, mumbled again, glanced back at one of the inscriptions on the wall, walked over to the crevice leading to the grotto below and peered in for a moment, stepped back toward the niche and then scrutinized the stone one final time.

"Maybe this stone is important," said Meir in a low, serious voice. "We should take it please for further study," he said, demonstratively clasping his hands behind his back. "You," he told Dan, "you take it."

"What do you mean? Why me?"

Again Meir insisted, "I will not touch it, but please, you can take it."

"Sure," said Dan, slightly confused. He lifted the stone, noting it was much heavier than it appeared, and casually deposited it in his pocket. As he did, Meir's eyebrows arched in amazement, perhaps even shock.

Meir began to choke in the foul air, and said, "But I cannot breathe here anymore. Please. Let us finish upstairs in the better air."

Dan agreed, coughing. They surveyed their exit route up. Meir boosted Dan to the knotted rope. Dan shimmied up and then climbed from the chute into the third chamber, scrambling and crawling the last few feet on his belly. As he did, he could sense the pocketed stone scraping between his body and the cave wall.

Meir, who stood taller, was able to balance on a small rock, and jump-reach for the rope. He slipped back several times, but with encouragement from Dan, he finally hoisted himself into the chute and then wedged himself up. Dan pulled him through the hole to the third chamber. The two then ascended up the ladder to the second chamber, where the waiting Motke and Sister Nan helped them in, pulling the ladder after them. All of them then continued up the short steps to the main crypt, and exited the grotto to find an irritated Park impatiently waiting in the bottom courtyard.

"It's been an hour! I didn't know what to think," she complained. "Nobody came out. I called in. Nobody answered. I called three times."

Dan, breathless and covered with black grime, apologized for her alarm, and explained the system of descending crypts. Seeing the tour was over, and sensing some dissent at hand, Sister Nan excused herself, suggesting with a smile that the group might conclude their discussion quickly and leave the convent as the supervising monks would soon return. They began walking toward the gate.

But once out of the gates, Dan stopped the group to report the Davidic-era inscriptions on the chasm wall and the references to the giant Nephilim. Motke and Park both knew of the intriguing Biblical references to the Nephilim but did not know their lineage continued.

"Yes," Meir assured, glancing nervously at Dan's pocket. "The descendents of the Nephilim were the Anakim. Please look at Numbers 13."

Motke pulled out a small Bible from his bag and verified the citation.

"Satisfied?" asked Meir, adding, "Okay, the Anakim were killed later on—everywhere except in Gath, and a few places. Check please Joshua 11:22."

Motke read the verse aloud: *"None of the Anakim was left in the land of the Israelites; some remained only in Gaza, Gath, and in Ashdod."*

"But Gath was the main place for the Anakim," Meir went on. "Throughout Deuteronomy chapters one and two and also nine, the children of Israel fear the offspring of the Anakim giants. Among the high and mighty of Gath was a very evil woman named Orpah, very bad person, who had four sons. All giants. One of these giants was Ishbi, and one of them was Goliath. As you know, David slew Goliath of Gath.

"Actually, to kill Goliath was not the end of the story," Meir emphasized. "If you check Second Samuel 21, you see Ishbi, the brother of Goliath, tried to make revenge on David, and that eventually four giants from Gath were killed by David and his servants. But there were many giants from Gath after Goliath. There was Sippai and Saph and many, many more mentioned throughout the Bible and Kabbala too."

"Now," Meir went on, "the Anakim continued for many generations, and some of them even had six fingers on each hand. Motkele, go please in your book to Second Samuel 21:20. Be good enough to read."

Motke tuned to Second Samuel, and read: *"There was again war at Gath, where there was a man of great size, who had six fingers on each hand, and six toes on each foot—twenty-four in number; he too was descended from the giants."*

Meir told him to check a similar passage in First Chronicles 20:6. Motke did, confirming, "Yes, it is verified there a second time."

"The point is?" asked Dan.

Meir folded his arms, took a deep breath and replied slowly, "The Anakim have always been the soldiers of evil. They hide, they come back. They hide again, they come back. The Evil One calls them when he needs them. They are the descendents of the Nephilim, the sons of evil."

"Sounds to me, like the Sons of Darkness from the Qumran writings," said Dan.

"Oh yes," responded Meir. "Adam had two sides–pure good and pure evil. David had two sides–good and evil. And even *Moschiach* knows evil and temptation–and must overcome them. Adam–mankind–will be redeemed by *Moschiach,* what you Park, and your friend Dan, call Messiah. I told you about letters and words. The letters for Adam are *aleph dalet mem.*"

Motke interrupted for clarity, "That corresponds to A-D-M, because there are no vowels in Hebrew."

"Yes, exactly," continued Meir. "Use the English. A-D-M . . . Adam David Messiah. That is the triple connection."

No one spoke. Dan's face lost its animation as he looked at Park for an instant, and then in a low monotone asked Meir, "And Ben Hinnom?"

"The abomination that is desolation," Meir replied. "I believe he will cause an abomination of the temple as the triumph of man's dark side challenging God. Maybe he will come to the Temple Mount, or his image will. I can't imagine such a thing. But he shall defile the Temple. And I believe it will be done on the final Shabbat of the millennium. This coming Friday. Again, the final desecration of God's will."

"Leading to?" asked Dan.

"The final battle between the Sons of Darkness and the Sons of Light," Meir replied.

"Who are?" asked Dan.

"The Sons of Darkness are the Anakim giants–are you listening–following their leader, the Evil One himself," Meir responded.

"And the Sons of Light?" Dan continued.

"The Sons of Light fight for goodness and for God," Meir answered. "But only one of purest purest goodness will be able to defeat the one of purest purest evil. And that cannot be done without the one weapon the Anakim fear and I'm glad they fear it.

"So now let me tell you something," Meir continued. "The stone that

David used to slay Goliath, was not just any rock laying on the ground. It was the most powerful stone in the world, and chosen by God to do his work. It is the very same stone that Abraham used to drive away Satan. So it is written in the Midrash, in Kabbala, in many writings. It has been debated for centuries. Some claim the stone was five stones representing God, Abraham, Isaac, Jacob and Aaron, and it miraculously turned into one representing all heavenly power. The Moslem people also write about the power of this stone. Remember, it is the only stone that carries the power of God Himself and the power to kill Satan."

Meir eyed Dan's pocket, as he said, "The big problem. No one has that stone. Many have looked. There have been many frauds. But no one has been able to find it anywhere in Israel, the one stone shaking with the power of God . . . So far."

Dan pulled the smooth elliptical stone out of his pocket. If it seemed to gleam when illuminated by just a flashlight in the dark chambers below, now in the brilliant sun, the stone's tiny crystal fragments were almost luminescent. "I got this down there," said Dan sheepishly.

"Amnon told us no more digging," said Motke.

"I didn't dig. It was already dug," answered Dan.

"But also, I am not good with fairy tales," Motke laughed. "How do we know this stone is not like five million other stones in Israel? I prefer a magic wand."

Meir answered, "Down there in the cave, one of the inscriptions read, 'Who can defeat the Anakim without the stone?' This stone was near to that spot."

"What's the difference?" said Dan. "Maybe it's a powerful stone, maybe it's just a rock like any other that's been pissed on by sheep . . . The Ten Commandments were written on two pieces of stone. People worship it. The Wailing Wall is just stone. People pray to it. The outcropping inside the Dome of the Rock doubles as the spot where Abraham was going to sacrifice Isaac and where Mohammed ascended to Heaven— if you want to buy in to either of those. People die for it. A stone is what you make of it. I can toss it or I can take it. I agree, it's a fairy tale, who gives a crap, so let me toss it."

Dan cocked his arm back and prepared to throw it into oblivion over the walls. As he did, Meir shrieked, and Park and Motke grabbed Dan's shirt sleeve in alarm. "No, no, no!"

"Just in case," Motke said. "Who knows? Don't make a problem with the stone. Keep it, keep it."

Dan playfully tossed the stone in his right hand.

"Stop, you're making us crazy!" said Park.

"You are making sacrileges on God," protested Meir.

"Okay, then," said Dan. He smugly popped the stone back into his pocket.

The group hurriedly left the convent grounds. Meir went to the intercity taxi stand to commence his long journey back to Tsfat. By the time Dan and Park arrived back at the Dan Pearl, they found Sal in the room happily munching on Elite chocolate. As the buses carrying the Down Syndrome convention began traveling north, Raymond gleefully pointed out the windows at people, everywhere singing and pointing, "I love them. I only love them. And them, and them and them." General Amnon began inspecting racks of shofarot. He turned to his colleague and said, "The special weapons are coming slow. Manufacturing is very difficult. But I promise they will be done on time—we will make the deadline. We must." Kuebitz walked unseen down a corridor of Hakirya.

Dan, looking deadly serious, asked Sal to send Hinnom an email, Windy to Windy. Sal unfolded the device and brought up an empty form. "The message?" asked Sal.

Dan answered, "Just tell him this: *'Cancel the Upload.'*"

Sal looked bewildered.

"Do it," Dan insisted.

Sal typed the three-word message and sent.

Five minutes later a reply came directly from Hinnom.

It was also only three words, simply: *"Why should I?"*

Upon reading it, Dan asked Sal, "Good. Now send him the following reply: *"Because we have the stone."*

18

DECEMBER 31, 1999

*B*en Hinnom's grotto was its usual self. Vile, brown droplets periodically dribbled from the high crevice at the ceiling into a tall earthen cask.
Snakes slithered lazily between computers like so many cables linking a
network. Rodents nibbled at animal flesh torn from a decaying carcass.
Flies and red ants swarmed over a mound of rotted food. Worms gathered
in a burrow beneath a laser printer stand. The six-fingered Anakim
snored on cots surrounded by cracked sunflower seed shells, date pits,
and nearly empty bottles of cloudy white Arak liquor. Hinnom sat at a
platform atop two saw horses that functioned as his desk and read reports
streaming in from his international organization. Just moments before,
Hinnom had arrogantly rebuffed Sal's email demanding that the Point
Nine upload be canceled. Sal's reply had just dinged onto the Windy
screen. Hinnom saw the email arrive, but purposely ignored it, choosing
any number of distractions.

He sent personal requests to Windgazer user groups around the world
urging them to begin their own chanting demonstration to counter the
rebooters. He suggested: "99.9–Make it Mine." Linzer had just reentered
the grotto, so Hinnom asked him, "How does it sound '99.9–Make it
Mine' as a chant all day tomorrow leading up to the show? For the user
groups." Linzer shrugged a vague approval.

"Then we'll do it," said Hinnom.

After selecting his worldwide user group broadcast option, which included home and office emails of the 1.6 million users in 14 countries that comprised the Windgazer World Users Movement, Hinnom pointed his finger down and characteristically dropped it atop the Enter key, dispatching his message. A smile of pride flashed as he savored the thought of reaching so many people by simply pressing one button.

As an afterthought, he sent instructions to Windgazer Central to program twenty or thirty million Windgazer screen buddies to sport Point Nine Update logos and remind users, "Be sure to initialize Friday at midnight." By Hinnom's plan, it would begin when midnight came to Jerusalem and proceed around the world as each time zone clicked in the new millennium. Asian computer clocks across the International Date Line were reset to accommodate the sequence.

Then Hinnom asked Linzer to instruct the dirigible pilot to double-check his projection equipment, making sure the planned Windgazer logo illumination on the Western Wall would proceed flawlessly and on time. When that brief exchange was over, Hinnom played an anagram game. Then he adjusted the Windy's color palette. Then he doodled. Finally, he clicked on the reply from Sal.

In response to Hinnom's comment, "Why should I?" Sal wrote: "Because we have the stone."

Hinnom's visage froze. His head dropped slightly even as his eyes remained fixed on the message. Slowly, Hinnom's arms folded, his hands tensed into fists, his nostrils flared and now his entire face appeared as though it were going to explode, eyes first. He forwarded the message to Linzer, dropping his outstretched finger vertically onto the Enter key.

Simultaneously, he scowled at Linzer standing just feet away. "Check your mail! Check it, check it!" adding with infuriation, "You said no one. No-oooooo one! Check it, check that email."

A panicked Linzer unfolded his Windy, checked for mail, and also discovered Sal's words. Linzer raised his eyes to see an enraged Hinnom. Sensing a meltdown, he spread his arms wide and tried to speak.

"Say not a word," snarled Hinnom, stopping Linzer in mid-breath. He ran over to the Anakim, kicking their cots, barking. "Wake up, you. Rise! Rise!" Ishbi and his partners shook from their slumber as Hinnom paced around maniacally, ranting to Linzer, "You said you checked. You said *no one*. No one has the stone." He violently toppled a file cabinet with so startling a crash, the rodents and snakes scattered. Face to face with Linzer now, he blared, "You! You told *me!* You told me no one had the stone."

Trying to restore some calm, Linzer clasped his hands peaceably in front of his chest and spoke softly, like a parent reassuring a child just awakened hysterical from a nightmare: "There is no stone. It's a fairy tale. Just something we have talked about forever. But it doesn't exist."

"You!" Hinnom screamed, pointing his finger almost in Linzer's eye. "For years, you've been telling me: *Beware the stone. Beware the stone.* Now all of a sudden it is a fairy tale?"

Linzer kept his voice modulated, "It was just something we talked about. It's a legend written down over the centuries by wishful mystics in worthless books because they are powerless pukes. And now this father-less puke Sal has gotten wind of it, and he is using this silliness to antagonize you. Look at it. In forty-eight hours, our every plan will be realized. Sal and his whore mother and her vile Jew boyfriend and a few measly million idiot rebooters around the world will be completely forgotten. The globe will initialize and we *will* upload the Point Nine Update."

"I asked you to finish him off," seethed Hinnom. "And instead, I have to receive emails from this geek . . . and on property stolen from me. Why does he have my Windy and why is he walking this earth alive and well? Didn't I make a request?"

"I tried to find the puke," replied Linzer, "and this bureaucratic night-mare of a country sent me running from place to place—and nobody's phone worked. I could not locate him. But I did try. I tried for hours. For all I know he sent that email from a prison cell in a police station."

"Or maybe it was from that fancy suite at the hotel," growled Hinnom. "Can we buy that hotel and evict him and his pathetic group? I want that."

"Yes, we can buy it," Linzer replied calmly, "but not before Friday. So that isn't going to help the present situation. I think we should ignore this Sal and his baseless fairy tale email about a stone. Even if he had the stone, he wouldn't know what to do with it. It's no good in his hands."

Pause. "You just said the stone was a fairy tale," yelled Hinnom.

"It is!" Linzer replied, raising his voice to be heard, "but even if it were not a fairy tale, even if every slimy syllable of this Kabbalistic crap is gen-uine, authentic, verified mumbo jumbo, none of Sal's people could use the stone. So relax." He again spread his arms to calm Hinnom, who now allowed him to approach, and eventually to embrace and comfort him.

"We have *them*," Linzer said, pointing to Ishbi and the Anakim. "We have Windgazer 99. We have a very, very good party planned. And we have a world to conquer. *They* have nothing. Relax."

Hinnom pulled away from Linzer's embrace, stepped up to Ishbi, and thundered, "You are here for a reason. Now prove you deserve to wear the name of your illustrious if nearly forgotten ancestor. Go get your brother and your cousins out of the hole, and for the last time," now turning to Linzer, "all of you . . . destroy this boy." Hinnom became sarcastic and readdressed Ishbi, ". . . That is, unless perhaps *you* fear the stone. That would be understandable. Do you fear the stone?"

Linzer objected, "Don't fill his mind with silly fairy tales."

Ishbi bent his ten-foot form down to pick up a drained bottle of Arak. Spying a rat scurrying on a ledge, he hurled the bottle at the rodent. The creature fell dead to the grotto floor, its crushed head bloodied, its teeth bared from the death blow.

"Let them come to me!" roared Ishbi. "Let them send their champion, a hundred champions. I fear no one." He pointed up through the chasm. "Look up there. Who do I fear?" He drew a swordlike knife from his belt. Wrapping all six fingers of his right hand around the hilt, he carved an upside down *shin* into the cave wall. Then he and the other two Anakim ceremoniously spit at it. "We will finish."

"Okay, that's a very good thing," Hinnom observed, clearly impressed with the ferocious response. "Keep that thought."

Linzer's cell phone rang. He listened intently and finally told the caller, "Very good. That is quite helpful . . . We'd like to clear up the problem and settle things . . . You did the right thing." He listened some more. "Oh yes, you'll receive a little something for your trouble . . . It's a gift from Mr. Hinnom personally."

Linzer reported matter-of-factly, "That was a policeman in the Jerusalem police intelligence unit—a man with whom I have cultivated a very good friendship. This man has located the puke Sal McGuire, and he has been good enough to inform us of his whereabouts. All he asked for in return was a few shiny CDs and I found that request most reasonable.

"Now then," Linzer continued, "for your information, the puke was released some time ago to the custody of his mother. But the government wants him out of the way, out of Jerusalem. So, my friend tells me, they are moving him out of town. That means Sal McGuire is gone from here and that's all that counts. Forget about him." Linzer looked at the clock. It was after midnight. "It is very, very late. Let's go to sleep and resume our work tomorrow."

"This Sal person has my Windy," shouted Hinnom. "It doesn't matter that he is not here. He'll find a way wherever he is to interfere with the event. Maybe he can stop it. He could jam something, send a virus into our system, make some extraordinary last-minute sap-witted appeal to the world. So. I want him dead. Eliminated. There is–" He stopped, and looked Linzer in the eye. "They moved him out of town? Let me guess. He's up *there?*"

Linzer conceded the fact, "Yes, he's on his way to Megiddo. They're hiding him there. But they barely–"

Hinnom held up his palm, hushing Linzer. "What do they say?" Hinnom asked. "We always seem compelled to select the dangerous choice. Or is it that everything is all just figured out in advance: who will slice whom to ribbons, when, and where? Predestination is such a nice game if you know the rules."

Hinnom turned to the Anakim to declare brusquely, "That rat lying dead on the ground was there for a reason, and Ishbi has already figured that one out."

Whirling back to Linzer, he cried, "This fatherless scum, with or without his fairy-tale rock . . . we will kill him there. *At Megiddo,*" he enunciated with exaggerated tremolo, "just to prove a point. Just to prove that I," stamping his right fist into his left palm, "cannot be challenged, will not be challenged. I will kill him up there–*and* we will proceed with the show down here. We will do it all."

Linzer exhaled with exasperation. The Anakim sat down on their cots. Hinnom walked over to a small fridge, pulled out a vial, downed it in one swig, shivered briefly from the drink's pungency, and spoke plainly: "Okay. Everyone get a good night's sleep. Tomorrow we go north."

DECEMBER 30, 1999. 4:45 P.M. An Arab peasant was walking his brightly festooned camel to the village along a small neglected hill road leading north from Jerusalem. It was a shortcut fewer and fewer Israelis preferred these days. So traffic was sparse, even late in the afternoon. The Arab had just come to the top of a rise, when a yellow school bus came into view rippling above the surface in the distant heat. He halted his camel with a hiss and waited patiently as the bus sped past him with a whoosh and a flurry of road gravel. Resuming his trek into the village, he wondered who could have such a vehicle in Israel.

Linzer was at the wheel. Ben Hinnom and the Anakim were slouched in the back, sharing exhilarating swigs from a vial and chasing them with shots of Arak. They were on their way to Megiddo where they would first fetch Ishbi's brother and cousins from the hole and then attend to Sal and company. The mood was one any warrior feels before combat: tension mediated by mindless distraction. An array of photos of Sal, Park, and Dan flashed on Hinnom's Windy for the Anakim to review so they could know their enemy. They barely paid attention. Sections of Hinnom's composition, "The Beast"–part lamentation, part squeal, part rock canta-ta–played on the stereo system. The Anakim thought the music noisome. Once in a while Hinnom would punctuate the tempo by toying with Ishbi's swordlike knife, an act which caught the eye of the other two and eventually caused Ishbi to move away lest he be provoked. All the Anakim wanted was to arrive at their battle. Periodically the bus would hit a bump or a pothole in the old, unmaintained road and Hinnom would exclaim, "Ooopsy."

At the same time, an oversized white van driven by Dan pulled into the tiny S'de Dov military-civilian airport north of Tel Aviv. Park, Sal, and Motke were seated within, as was General Amnon Natan, who gave direc-tions. A just-landed Hercules C-130 was taxiing to the hangar. Amnon instructed Dan to drive across the tarmac and pull up to a designated ser-vice area near the hangar. Dan struggled to navigate the van through a narrow gate, muttering, "I *hate* this van."

"Okay, everyone can go out," said Amnon. Motioning toward the pro-pellers, he added, "and stand over there because it is a little safer." After the C-130 cut its engines, and the ground crew blocked its wheels, the plane's tail ramp whirred down, meeting the concrete with a clang. Amnon called Dan over.

"You asked for three things," began Amnon.

Dan looked puzzled.

"At Hakirya, I asked you what you needed, you wrote down three things."

"Yeah, well . . ." replied Dan, a bit confused.

"So don't say the government of Israel did not try to make you a special favor," Amnon said, as he walked Dan into the C-130 cargo hold.

The sound of cargo belts unfastening could be heard, then a restraint chain being released, then some clicks, a slam, and finally an engine purred on. In a moment more Dan zipped out of the cargo hold driving his beloved red Del Sol. The top was down. He gunned the motor, pulling up to the group in a spurt of bravado.

They were all amazed.

"Now I *know* this is Mossad," asserted Motke. "The military doesn't have this power."

Park was essentially speechless but finally managed to say, "How are we all going to fit in that?"

The chattering continued as Dan showcased for Motke and Amnon the special custom features of the vehicle, demonstrating the detachable roof, the removable CD player, and quiet engine. They ran their fingers along the brilliant red finish, and played with the power windows, as Park looked on with ambivalence turning to boredom. Sal almost smiled.

Grabbing the general affectionately by the forearms, Dan exclaimed, "Amnon, *habibi,* how did you manage this?"

"It's not so much a problem," explained Amnon. "Hundreds of cars are brought into Israel by diplomats and journalists every year. Usually, it is by ship through Haifa. But we have our friends in America, maybe you know a man—Udi—who runs a restaurant in Washington. Udi helped us go to your address in Chicago where your car was easy to find behind your house. We just boxed it. This car is tiny, not much bigger than a refrigerator. El Al cargo did the rest, so you owe them the real thank you."

Never satisfied, Dan asked, "And my other two requests?" Amnon directed him to open the storage compartment behind the driver's seat. In it was a bottle of Laphroaig. Motke and Amnon couldn't wait as Dan unwrapped the green foil seal, poured a dram into the cap and passed it around first for a ritual sniff, and then an elaborate, well-narrated taste of the fabled scotch. As Motke and Amnon expressed breathy delight and complained bitterly about Israel's old import restrictions, Park rolled her eyes and looked away in disconnection.

"And . . ." said Dan, as he checked in the CD player, then under the seat and in the back compartments.

"Two of the three," replied Amnon. "No one knew of the Gypsies."

"Gipsy Kings," corrected Dan.

"Not Kings, and not Queens," replied Amnon. "But you're in Israel now, so I'm giving you something even better. From me. He reached into his bag and brought out a copy of Ofra Haza, one of Israel's most popular singers. The CD was "Shaday," her most rhythmic and captivating.

Dan accepted the CD with thanks.

"Now, I'm just a regular Israeli," said Amnon, "so I don't mind driving an ugly vehicle like this one," he said, kicking the large white van's tire. "I will drive the others up to Megiddo. You take your friend in your red car."

Park moved to step into the car, when Dan said, "Him," pointing to Sal. A wild smile appeared on Sal's face, reminiscent of his moped moment. He hopped in without opening the passenger door. Dan nodded in approval.

Park ran up, asking, "Where are you two going?"

Dan gunned the motor, answering, "We'll meet you at Megiddo, at the kibbutz office." He floored the accelerator, raced across the tarmac, stopping ever so briefly at the gate.

Within ten minutes Dan and Sal were cruising north on the coastal road that hugs the Mediterranean Sea. The salt-laced wind lapped at their faces and sometimes they could actually feel the foam of the waves crashing at the shore. To the right, the modern Israel, beautiful shapes constructed from concrete and glass. To the left, the ancient dunes, the clumps of inexplicable grass, the smell of sea, the sparkle of ocean and breezes to scintillate the soul. "Like it?" Dan asked Sal. Sal nodded an enthusiastic yes.

Ofra Haza. Blasted.

⤳

FOR SIX THOUSAND years, great battles have been fought on a small rocky hill in north central Israel and the once swampy now, verdant valley it overlooks. This place is called Megiddo. For millennia, this small but mighty fortress city on the Via Maris, the route from the sea, commanded the ancient crossroads between the empires of Mesopotamia and Egypt, and beyond to Rome. Megiddo's nearly impregnable stone fortifi-

cations housed magnificent palaces, massive cisterns, fabulous storehous-
es of gold and grain, vast stables, and an amazing complex of secret chambers and tunnels. Great forces of charioteers, bowmen, and foot soldiers
ably defended the height, controlling who could travel safely along the
trade routes below.

From its high ground, the roads surrounding Megiddo were all clearly
visible for miles, making any attack a terrible choice. Yet it was a choice
continuously selected by invaders from Egypt, Rome, Persia, Syria, and
Israel. Some twenty-two times the choice was made—and always at great
cost. When, in about 1468 BC, the Egyptian Pharaoh Thutmose III took
Megiddo, the battle report extolled the capture as equal to the conquest
of a thousand cities. One siege lasted eight months. King David conquered Megiddo, making it an outpost of Israelite military strength. Later,
the city was fortified with hundreds of horsemen and charioteers, probably by King Solomon.

Those who triumphed at Megiddo brought their gods with them. Here
the altars of the victor were always built atop the altars of the vanquished
in an endless cycle of domination and ritual defilement. How many
nameless thousands fell here as monarchs and chieftains sought to control
this strategic hill? Blood has run here, and often.

It is no wonder that even after Megiddo faded as a killing ground of
antiquity, it was remembered as a good place to fight wars. In this century, Britain defeated the Turks at Megiddo in World War I. Axis forces
planned but never launched a pincer action through the corridor in World
War II. And Jewish soldiers fought the Arab Legion bitterly to capture and
hold the junction, thus including the territory in the new state of Israel.

Today, Megiddo seems like little more than a historic intersection in
north central Israel, at the juncture of Highways 66 and 65. On one side
of the road is a small kibbutz named Megiddo, the only settlement here.
Across the junction is Prison Megiddo where Israel houses high-security
inmates. Between the prison and the kibbutz are the ruins of ancient Tel
Megiddo, preserved in a continuing dig and celebrated by one of Israel's
best archaeological welcome centers, one known for its sumptuous buf-
fets, designer T-shirts, and easy public access to the fallen ramparts and
other unearthed structures of the fabled site.

But in truth Megiddo is far more than just the intersection of a kibbutz,
a prison, and an ancient ruin. The Hebrew word for mountain or hill is

Har. The name *Har Megiddo* over the years became westernized. It evolved into the word we know today, Armageddon.

It was to Megiddo that in the early evening of December 30, 1999, Dan drove to sequester Sal as Amnon had directed. Entering Megiddo intersection from the east, Dan turned left and into the long, narrow kibbutz access road. It terminated at a high-security gate, manned by an old-timer. A heavy-duty roadblocking security gate was nothing unusual for a defense-minded kibbutz on guard from terrorists during years gone by, but this was one of the few such gates in north central Israel still in operation. Dan offered a friendly wave to the sentry, indicating he was due at the guesthouse. The old-timer nodded back as he retracted the motorized red gate just long enough for Dan and Sal to pass.

Dan drove his Del Sol onto the unlighted curving dirt road and within a few moments reached the guesthouse office. There he and Sal met Yaacov.

Yaacov was a kindly old man, offering a warm, wrinkled face atop a short, once muscular body. Gentle, white hairs curled distinctively out of an unbuttoned shirt that revealed a chest long tanned from daily labors in the field. His visage declared a man completely at peace with the world.

The easygoing Yaacov explained that the kibbutz barely had room for Dan and his group. Most kibbutzim operated rudimentary bed and breakfast guesthouses, and Megiddo's was a popular one with both Israelis and American Jewish groups touring the north. As Dan could see, tour buses were parked everywhere. Only after Amnon's urgent telephone call did kibbutz management agree to provide two rooms—one for Park and Sal, a second for Motke and Dan—in the old unused guestroom building still under renovation. As he filled out registration forms, Yaacov made sure Dan and the others did not mind the absence of air conditioning or TV.

But Dan was not interested in the amenities. He immediately recognized Yaacov as a Holocaust survivor, as only children of survivors can. "Fuhn vannit kumst dere?" asked Dan in Yiddish. He always asked survivors where they came from in Yiddish. Few in Israel still spoke Yiddish, and it was the tip-off to survivors that Dan could communicate in the language of their European upbringing.

Soon, Yaacov and Dan were conversing energetically in an amalgam of broken Yiddish, English, Hebrew, and even a little French thrown in, with constant give and take to find mutually understandable words. This was a common solution to communication in Israel, one that often made the simplest of dialogues a fascinating linguistic challenge. Sal could comprehend none of the exchange, so Dan translated everything for him. Because it was Sal's first meeting with an actual survivor, he found every phrase a revelation and hung on every word, even though it was the dark imprecise telling of history, not the bright clarity of mathematics. Sal simultaneously enjoyed the recollection and his own self-observed willingness to enjoy it.

Yaacov explained that he was from Poland, a survivor of ghetto resistance. Dan knew there were basically three types of Holocaust survivors: concentration camp victims, ghetto resisters, and forest fighters. Dan's parents had been forest fighters, but they had much in common with those who resisted in the close confines of Europe's ghettos. Dan wanted to know the history of Kibbutz Megiddo, and why Yaacov had come here of all places.

"Why? Our whole group came here," replied Yaacov, not really understanding the question. "There were forty of us—all teenage survivors from various ghettos and some from the forest. We shared one thing in common. We all fought to stay alive. When death tried to take us, we escaped in miraculous ways," he continued quietly and proudly, enunciating his words like a storyteller reciting an oral history.

Unlike many survivors who display pain at wartime recollection, Yaacov smiled as he spoke. "Some crawled away from killing pits, from under the bodies of friends and family shot next to them. Others were shot but they did not die. Some, the bullet went right through. I know a girl who looked a Nazi in the eye and for no reason he pulled her out of one line and put her in another, saving her life. Yes, such things happened. One man lived under a floor for two weeks waiting for the moment to escape."

"And your story," asked Dan.

Yaacov smiled beneath crinkled eyes, assuring, "I have my story too. Not tonight. I'll tell you another day. There are many stories here."

"So the whole kibbutz was settled by survivors? That's unusual."

"We all wanted to go to Palestine," Yaacov responded, "and met the Jewish Agency boat in Italy. We arrived in Eretz and they took us right to here to fight. We were all good fighters, afraid of nothing. After Independence, the Jewish Agency told us we would be starting a kibbutz here. So we did. We had no home. This became our home. Most of the people wanted to name the kibbutz after Kaplan, a ghetto fighter we knew. But the kibbutz would sit on the old site of Megiddo, which is mentioned in the Bible. After a big, big debate, it was decided that the old history of Israel was more important than when we were in ghetto. This way we do not live in a name connected to victim times, but instead to Israelite kings." Yaacov tilted his head as though serving a cup of coffee, pleased with his discourse.

Sal asked, "So there was nothing here before you came?"

"There was not a town," Yaacov replied to Sal, looking at him sweetly in the eyes, "but a few Arab houses in a place called Lejune. They ran away during the fighting and the houses are all gone except for a piece of the mufti's mosque by the field on the other side. No one from Lejune ever came back."

Night had come and the headlights of the white van could be seen approaching in the distance. It parked in front of the office. Park and Motke jumped out first, followed by Amnon, who exchanged niceties with Yaacov in Hebrew before signing paperwork to bill the government for the rooms. The kibbutz had arranged for Amnon himself to sleep as a guest in a kibbutz member's home, a courtesy extended because Amnon grew up on a similar kibbutz near Rosh Pina. Tomorrow morning he would drive at dawn to attend a military briefing in nearby Afula, so he didn't need breakfast.

A worried Park immediately sought out Sal, making sure he was well, and quizzing him on Dan's driving. Motke only wanted to know if it was too late to eat or whether they would have to drive to Afula for a meal. Fortunately, some leftover cold cuts were in the kibbutz snack bar.

Once room keys were distributed, the group munched on thin slices of salami, washing it down with cans of cold Schweppes from the small office cooler, all served graciously by Yaacov as if it was a grand dinner.

With translation assistance by Motke and Dan, Park with great anticipation asked Yaacov, "This is supposed to be Armageddon, right? It's Har Megiddo?"

The old man just smiled.

She was expecting a reaction. Dan too was a bit surprised at Yaacov's lack of interest.

"Revelation 16:16," Park explained, adding a short summary of the legendary final battle between good and evil.

The old man shrugged. "People sometimes mention this," he finally replied out of courtesy. "Groups from America who stay here talk about it. And the one and only time the Pope visited Israel, he did not go to Jerusalem or Tel Aviv, he came here to meet with the president of Israel. They discussed something of great importance I heard. No one knows what. It was many years ago. There's a photo in the Tel Megiddo museum. The Pope mentioned that thing you said. But no one here knows what it means."

Neither Yaacov nor any of the kibbutz founders had ever read a New Testament or knew what Revelation was. Neither did Motke or Amnon, who confessed they were unacquainted with "the new Bible." Even Dan, although he understood the common meaning of Armageddon from movies and pop culture, only vaguely knew the reference to Revelation.

Trying to add an insight for helpfulness, Yaacov did say, "I remember reading Zechariah when I was a boy in Poland. I liked Zechariah, and I used to read it. He said that when the big battle of the final finish comes, there will be great weeping in Jerusalem like on the plain of Megiddo. That's all I know. But then, we don't have a copy of any Bible here."

Dan took notice, "No Bible?"

"There is no rabbi, no religion, no synagogue, and no politics on this kibbutz," Yaacov said proudly. "On Shabbat, we all just stop working, but no praying."

Dan found this hard to believe, but Motke thought it was a good idea and not so unusual for a kibbutz.

"Our kibbutz was founded by Holocaust survivors," explained Yaacov, "but now we have volunteers from all over the world. Chinese, South American, from Milwaukee, Nigeria, Finland–all lands. So there is no religion here. Just farmers. Why not? And all people here live in peace. We farm, we make jewelry in the factory, good milk from the cows, we rest on Shabbat. Nothing more. It's a good life. How bad could it be? Zechariah also says that when peace comes to the world, there will be no priests, just farmers."

Dan and Park looked through the windows into an adjacent room where a kibbutz committee meeting was underway. As Yaacov said, the committee room was filled with people from all races. Everyone was smiling, talking agreeably. "If I didn't know human nature better," observed

Park, "I'd say the people on Kibbutz Megiddo indeed are . . . well, living in harmony."

Dan and the others walked outside into the chilled Megiddo night, perfumed with wildflowers, the smell of red earth, and the potential for rain. As they undertook the short trek up the hill to the guest rooms, they were struck with the tranquility surrounding them. Some of it was the atmosphere in any kibbutz. But most of it was this special kibbutz, this historic high ground where serenity and simplicity ultimately replaced sixty centuries of war and devastation. Peace was the final conqueror of Megiddo.

The quiescence could be sensed in every direction. Children played and giggled at the swimming pool. An old man in shorts slowly pedaled his old-fashioned bicycle along the walking paths that crisscrossed the gardens. A Chinese girl and an old Jewish woman waved good night at the door of the African couple they had just visited. The stars were out. The night was clear.

Park turned to Dan and said, "This is a wonderful place."

He kissed her on the cheek, and bid her good night.

Amnon assured everyone that they could sleep safe.

Three Down Syndrome men were walking toward one of the tourist buses parked nearby. "I forgot my hat in the bus. I am going to get it now," said Raymond. As Dan and his group passed, Raymond smiled under the stars and demonstratively declared with his index finger: "I love you—and you and you and you and you." Dan's group waved politely, not knowing what to say. Raymond added with uncluttered joy, "And God loves you too."

DECEMBER 31, 1999. The Final Sunrise of the Millennium.

Cucumbers. Tomatoes. Green peppers.

Every morning for decades Yaacov has repeated the kibbutz breakfast ritual. Pass through the line, place the cucumbers, tomatoes and green peppers in a bowl, take them to the table, slice or dice them, mix it all into a salad. Add some salt and pepper. Eat. This has always been breakfast on the kibbutz. Today, as he has for the past half century, Yaacov found it very satisfying.

Dan and Motke had both spent time on a kibbutz in their youth and enjoyed their ritual vegetable cutting as well. Motke commented that Dan diced very well. Dan returned the compliment. Park and Sal weren't prepared for the exercise, but quickly got into the spirit, cubing and salting to taste.

With slicing out of the way, Dan bubbled with more questions about Megiddo. For example, why—of all places—was there a prison across the road?

"From what I know," Yaacov replied, "there has always been a prison of some type there. Israel inherited the prison from the British, who operated it since the First World War and in Mandate times too. The British took it over from the Turks when Allenby drove through Megiddo in the First World War; that battle made it possible to finish off the Ottoman Empire. The Turks operated the prison from the 1500s. And actually it goes back and back to Roman times when the Sixth Roman Legion was there, the Iron Legion known as *Ferata*. A Legion stockade was there."

Motke queried, "The old Arab encampment, *Lejune*—that's not an Arab name, is it?"

"That's right," said Yaacov. "They named it after the Legion . . . *Lejune*. I checked the history when I wrote the Kibbutz pamphlet. It's very interesting. Maybe the prison goes back even further than the Romans."

"Any Anakim up this way?" Dan asked abruptly, triggering chagrined glances from the others.

Yaacov was confused. "Anakim? You mean giants—from the Bible?" He shrugged, "I don't know what you mean. There are no giants here. Hitler tried to make giants, but nothing here."

Dan perked up, "Hitler?"

"Of course," Yaacov explained. "Hitler wanted to perfect the master race, the blond, blue-eyed, very muscular, very tall people, what he called 'pure Aryans.' Hitler said Aryans were the true Germans—or the true German he wanted to create. On farms and in special nurseries, Hitler tried to breed these very big people. But he did not finish the plan." Yaacov turned the tables. "Let me ask *you* a question. How did you get to Megiddo?"

Dan pursed his lips, sliced some more, and conceded, "I don't know. Let me think about it," he laughed.

After fifteen more minutes aimlessly discussing the kibbutz dairy, its jewelry workshop, the plastic folder fabricating enterprise, pool hours, and the kibbutz library and archives which Yaacov managed, Dan found the right time to excuse himself from the group.

As he was leaving the breakfast hall, Yaacov asked again, "So do you know how you ended up here in Megiddo—or not?"

Dan's mind was on other things and he just shrugged. Yaacov smiled warmly, and dismissed the topic with an offhand remark: "Maybe you know. But you just don't know that you know."

Nearly out the door, Dan stopped and returned to Yaacov's table. "You said what?"

At first, Yaacov did not understand the question, but after Dan prompted him about the specific remark, Yaacov casually replied, "Oh, it's just an expression. Doesn't mean anything."

"It just struck me," explained Dan "because my father used to say that to me."

"It's an expression," Yaacov responded. "I first heard it years ago from one of our group in Poland, during the War."

Dan pressed him for more details.

"This is from my own story," recounted Yaacov with a peaceful smile. "It was just after the War and no one knew where anyone was going. Except the fighters in our group. We were going to Palestine. I was going to meet with some of them and get to the boat. On my way, I got very hungry. I was on a road, and I met two young people. Very brave, they survived in the woods somewhere. I had no food and I was so hungry I could not even walk. I was weak, sitting. These two people had a fish—not so big, that they just got from someone on the road. They were hungry too. The woman was sick from eating *dreck* in the woods. But maybe I was sicker because I couldn't even move. I was just sitting on the side, dizzy, with a pain in my body from hunger. In the ghetto, we were used to no food. Always hungry. But somehow, on this day, I could not go on anymore. These two people took from their mouth and gave to me. The boy made a small fire, cooked the fish, and we all ate together. It saved me. So, they joined up with my whole group and were supposed to come to Palestine. If they did, they would be here on this kibbutz now, because our whole group came here."

Dan asked, "But they didn't come?"

"No. At the last minute they left our group. Him, the boy, would say, 'Something is telling me to go to America. Many are going to America. I keep hearing in my mind, *Go to America.*' So he never went on the Jewish Agency ship, and instead went to a Displaced Persons camp–not too far from where we were. And that was it. These two people never came to Megiddo. But if it weren't for this nice boy–very brave, then I think I would be dead and buried by now. I wouldn't be here talking to you."

Dan was consumed by the account and saw the similarities to his own parents' story. They had often referred to an episode when they were hungry just as the War was ending, when a bizarre person on the side of the road gave them a fish on condition only that they remember the story to their children.

Yaacov took no notice of Dan's rapidly changing demeanor and simply continued, becoming fascinated with his own recollection. "Before these two left for the DP camp, our whole group and the Jewish Agency people tried to talk them out of it. We said, why? What is in America? Come to Palestine. Can you explain why you changed your mind? This boy said to me the last time when I asked him why, he said, 'Maybe we know, we just don't know that we know.' It's a funny comment, no? That's where I picked up the expression. Nu?"

"Yaacov," asked Dan almost entirely in Yiddish, "maybe you remember the name of these two Polish kids?"

Yaacov smiled warmly as he answered, "Oh. So many years ago. Who could remember? Names. Who can remember? He didn't finish with the group. So I don't know."

Motke and Park, seeing Dan was still a bit emotional, gently pulled him. "Come on to the pool," said Motke. "They'll give us trunks to swim."

Dan acquiesced and the group headed off to the pool.

They had walked halfway there when Yaacov came after Dan, calling, "I remember now. Maybe. It was . . ." he looked up, searching his memory again, 'it was . . . the boy was Mendel." A disappointed Dan dismissed the possibility of a connection, a connection survivors and their children are always searching for. He was thanking Yaacov for the effort when Yaacov interrupted, "Wait. Not Mendel. Moishe. He was Moishe and she was . . . she was . . . Rivkele. Now I remember better."

Suddenly moist-eyed, Dan rubbed Yaacov's palm along his face, almost overcome with the story. Not quite understanding yet, Yaacov simply soothed Dan, as a father would seeing a child in heartache.

"Yaacov, I think that was my parents that you met," Dan declared, shaking with excitement. "My dad was Moishe, my mom Rivke, both forest fighters in Poland, and a few times they talked to me about getting a fish on the road one day that saved them from hunger. They never mentioned you or sharing the fish, or even the possibility of Palestine. But they mentioned the silly fish. It's so crazy, that they would mention this one story. They had a thousand stories they wouldn't tell. But this is one they liked to talk about."

Yaacov, grasping the significance at last, tugged affectionately on Dan's cheek, saying, "It's very possible. There are so many stories on this kibbutz. So we will talk after the work. Now I have to go to the cows. This is my job."

Dan wasn't prepared for Yaacov's unexpected departure. He tried to get more, but the old man graciously ended the exchange by repeating, "Now the cows." He walked off.

Motke and Sal faded away so Park could step up and comfort Dan who was still aquiver from the exchange. For no real reason other than his own emotional distress, he rebuffed her touch. She tried again, and he yanked his head from her kiss.

"I'm here—God knows how," began Park, showing her hurt at being shut out. "I met you . . . it was just a parking space in Chicago. Now I'm standing with you at Armageddon of all places. I'm willing to be with you, to care about you, share in your culture and experience. Put my life on the line. My son's too. But you won't let me in."

Dan tensed at the air, looked at Park, then away, and then back again.

She continued, "You have had a crappy deal—yes. So have others. So have I. I lost parents. I lost loved ones. I have pain. But you live your pain. In fact, it lives you. It's a scab that won't fall off. You are so locked into the past, the door to the future, the door to today, it's shut. You won't open it. And when others try, you push them away."

Tears came to her eyes at last, "What do I have to do to get let in? What do I have to do for you to open the door? And if I come in, will you show me you care or will you pull away like always?"

Dan exploded as only a man in pain speaking to a lover can. "You want me to forget things! You want me to act like I didn't lose a family twice, my parents when I was young and my wife and son in front of my eyes? I should be just fine?" He pulled his shirt open, beating his exposed chest. "Look," he broke down as he rasped the words, "It hurts." Park took his head to hers.

"Don't forget. Feel your pain. But share," she pleaded. "Let me in." She saw no response. "Let me in, or not only will I have no place in your life, you'll have no place in mine."

Dan wanted to react, but was unable to.

"Let me in or let me out," she demanded.

"I can't," said Dan weakly. "Talk to me another day. Not today."

Park turned and walked down the hill to the rooms intending to pack up and find her way to the airport, and take Sal with her, come what might. Dan watched her walk off, squinted, made a fist, and then began beating his own head. Smoke and fire singed his eyes. Jenny lighted two slender white Shabbat candles. Simon fell off his bike. A jet plane roared through his head. His mother offered him a glass of juice. He took it but it was empty. Jenny refilled it. *Seig Heil.* The boxcar clanging on cold steel rails, sliced his body in half as it rolled across him. His mother and father grabbed one half, Jenny lugged the other half, Simon helped. They all tried to put his dismembered torso back together. He watched his body from above. "You know," his father chided, "You just don't know that you know."

Dan unsquinted and ran up the hill. Park, out of earshot, could not hear him calling her name. She turned the corner and climbed the stairs to her room. In the corner of her eye, Park noticed him chasing toward the building; she paused at her door long enough for him to catch up.

"And?" she asked.

"And, okay . . ." he replied, panting from his run.

"Okay, what?" she asked again.

"What you said," he came back, having difficulty saying the necessary words. "Okay . . . what you said."

"This is your way of saying, you're going to let me in," she demanded, "and show me that you care?"

"Yes," acknowledged a breathless Dan. "Like that."

"You'll show me that you care?" she asked again.

He nodded yes.

She swept her soft hand under his chin, locked into his eyes and steadfastly said, "Then show me."

Dan calmed himself, and came close, holding her hand in his and finding her lips with his own needing kiss. He boldly pulled her from her door to his. She stopped him and repeated, "You'll show me." Dan promised. They went into Dan's room. He kept his promise.

SHORTLY AFTER THE last dawn of the millennium, Amnon arrived at a small auxiliary military base on the outskirts of Afula. Driving Dan's large white van, he maneuvered past several Egged tourist buses on military charter as well as trucks, vans and command cars, plus one large dump truck. He parked in front of the detached briefing room for special operations. Three assistants were waiting to escort him to the front. Canisters of reconstituted apple and orange juice, as well as hot coffee, along with small plastic cups were set up on a long table at the rear. But few bothered. Everyone was focused on the mysterious mission.

Waiting inside were one hundred specially selected fighters, the strangest collection of commandos ever assembled in the history of Israel. They could not help but view each other with a bizarre combination of comradeship and contempt. Leading the ranks were Israel's toughest, shaved-head Yami commandos and Sayeret Matkal special paratroopers, all hardened from secret operations in Lebanon, each wearing serrated combat knives strapped to their legs, and straddling unloaded Uzis beneath their feet. These men were accustomed to extraordinary tactics often in missions of doubtful return. They were Israel's finest and bravest.

Next to them were several dozen senior officers ready for retirement, all greying veterans of the miraculous lightning victories in the Sinai and the last-minute breakthrough in the Yom Kippur War. All served with or under General Moshe Dayan. They were unarmed except for briefcases and cell phones.

A third contingent was comprised of forty Holocaust survivors, all forest fighters and ghetto resisters, many were also veterans of the War of Independence. They wore berets and armbands. Some clutched their vintage Czech bolt action rifles. Each reflected extraordinary peace and pride on their weathered face, and felt privileged to be called. Completing the force were twelve rabbis from the Israel Defense Forces chaplaincy.

Amnon had just called the group to order when one of the Yami commandos rose to challenge the assemblage. "What mission needs these guys?" he asked, pointing at the old-timers and provoking barely suppressed laughter from his squad mates.

"Sit down," instructed Amnon. "Today, we are going to have discipline. More discipline than you have ever shown. We do have a very special mission, and you have been selected for a reason. The rabbis have already been briefed. So now listen to what I say.

"First, you are members of the Israeli military, or the reserve. We did not invent our military yesterday, or even in 1948. We are the descendents of the fighters who took Canaan, who made the covenant. You can read about victories and defeats throughout the Bible." He stopped and turned to one smirking Yami commando. "If you will make jokes or smile, you will forever be remembered as a man who was thrown out of the briefing of our nation's most important mission. I will call the newspapers personally. Then you will be court-martialed." The Yami commando settled down immediately. The older generations continued listening with riveted interest.

"The rabbis have already been briefed," Amnon reminded, as he beckoned the chaplains to come to the front. "As I was saying, this is the Land of Israel, and you are its warriors. The military as you know has always been guided by a belief in God, and we watch events, we pray for miracles. We have seen many miracles. We routinely call them miracles." He turned to the rabbis. "And some think they actually *are* miracles. The establishment of the state attacked from six sides, the capture of the Sinai in '54 in one hundred hours, and the Six Day War. Entebbe. These were miracles. Yom Kippur was a disaster. I lost a son like many lost sons. But we avoided even greater disaster when we broke through and surrounded the Egyptian Third Army. That was a miracle."

He continued with an example the younger soldiers could relate to. "Iraqi Scuds," Amnon recounted, "came down on Ramat Gan like messengers from Satan. They could have done terrible damage. They could have been outfitted with VX gas or anthrax. But Iraq was defeated in a great lightning victory. Our generals went on TV and called it a miracle. The Scuds were stopped. You think there was no divine intervention? Many who study this believe there was." Amnon paused to wipe the sweat from his brow. "I don't study it . . . but even I think there was."

An old-timer stood up. "These young ones don't know," he cried. "The Nazis came and killed my whole town like nothing. The ones that escaped—me and three others—we fought with our hands and God at our side. You want weapons? In the ghetto we had bullets with no guns and guns with no bullets. What was our weapon then?" The chaplains all muttered short blessings for emphasis.

"What that man says is what we never want to admit," Amnon lectured. "We prefer to think we are superhuman, we can do it all alone with superior training, technology, money, logistical support, guts. Yet every unit prays for help from the Almighty on every mission. I knew Ben Gurion, I knew Golda, I knew Moshe Dayan. They all believed it was God that helped us conquer our enemies. Hakirya is spending millions to convert the Torah into numerical formulas looking for answers. Who am I to differ?"

The smart aleck Yami commando stood and declared, "General, I apologize to you, to my comrades, and to the men in my unit. I will observe discipline. And so will my men. Totally."

Amnon accepted the apology, and then startled the entire group by explaining that their mission was related to a computer date crisis virtually none of them understood, as well as the grandiose Hinnom festivities taking place later that day in Gei Ben Hinnom which they had heard about but which they also did not understand. Their mission, however, would not be in Jerusalem, it would be at nearby Megiddo.

He then distributed envelopes marked TOP SECRET to each commando. Inside was a stapled briefing with the title page: "Mission Briefing and Excerpts from the War Scroll."

One of the army chaplains, a stocky full-bearded man, then stepped to the center to continue the presentation. "Dozens, actually hundreds, of Dead Sea Scrolls have been found at Qumran," the rabbi began. "Among the first seven discovered by the Bedouin boy in 1947 was the War Scroll. It is one of the most studied and some of you have seen parts of it in the Israel Museum when you were students. For those who don't remember, the War Scroll describes in extreme detail the deployment of forces in what is called the final battle between good and evil, the final battle between the Sons of Darkness and the Sons of Light."

"Which ones are we?" asked the Yami commando.

Before Amnon could react, the commando apologized again, and theatrically hushed himself.

The rabbi continued, "There have been many interpretations of the War Scroll, and now we have additional writings that have guided us.

Read the text in your briefing papers. There are many specific directives in this ancient writing but only some of them are to be followed and we have cited them in the paper. We think the Essenes of Qumran worried that if an enemy discovered the scroll, he would have the whole attack plan. So they hid their meaning in codes and other phrases. For example, one we shall obey reads: *There shall be seven forward rows to each battle line, arranged in order—one man behind another.* The general will give you orders to follow this instruction. There is another interesting phrase: *Goliath the Gittite, a mighty man of valor, You delivered into the hand of David because he trusted in Your great name and not in sword and spear.* And it adds: *You have rescued us many times, not because of our good deeds but in spite of wickedness.'* Men. Please, please, please, use this moment to believe in your heart in what we are doing. Believe like never before. Go back. Go deep and go back to your Jewish soul. Remember who you are and from where you came. Believe this day. Believe."

The rabbi, eyeing his copy of the briefing papers, added, "Plus, there are many things we don't understand, but, with God's help, will understand before the day is done. There is one phrase we have all been studying. In the middle of the attack instructions the scroll suddenly declares: *A heart that melts shall be as a door of hope.* We don't even have a theory of what this means.

"But . . . learn with us. Read it all, including a description from the Rabbinate of our very strange enemy, and this historic God-commanded opportunity," said the rabbi, twirling his beard nervously. "Then we will answer whatever questions we can answer. As I said, there is a great deal we don't know."

The rabbi nodded to Amnon who directed his assistant to bring in several cardboard boxes. With thuds, the bulging off-kilter boxes were stacked on the floor. Each was filled with brown leather pouches fastened to straps.

"Now you one hundred," Amnon announced, "will all be provided with special weapons—more or less developed, you could say, for this engagement. They will be distributed to you later and the briefing paper will give you full explanation on the use and deployment of this weapon."

One commando asked, "Are we expected to fulfill a same-day mission against an undescribed enemy, with an untested weapon, with no dry run, and no to-scale training?"

Amnon replied, "We have had over two thousand years to rehearse this operation. We're ready now."

As the men read the briefing paper, the room became silent. Their eyes widened. The rabbis began a quiet chant and several of the old-timers stopped to pray. The men turned the pages noisily in anticipation, rubbed their heads in amazement as the words flowed to them. Some of the old-timers could not help but weep, and some clasped their hands in wonderment. Even the Yami commando pressed his fingers to his eyes to keep them dry. He turned to one of the ghetto fighters and locked palms. The commando spoke for all of them when suddenly he rose, his slovenly untucked shirt flowing from the window breeze as though it were a desert wind, and bellowed, "*Hevre*, we shall smite them, hip and thigh!"

ALTHOUGH INMATES AT Prison Megiddo were mainly Arab political risks and terrorists, they were maintained in a combination of medium- and high-security zones. Because it was a security prison, Megiddo was actually operated jointly by the Israeli Prison Authority and the Army Military Police. Although fortified in places, it resembled an armed camp more than a prison.

Low turrets manned by army machine-gunners marked the corners of the facility's tree-obscured perimeters. Two stood watch in every turret, one man surveilling the approach and another the facility. Even still, the main yard was out of their view, as was the main entrance.

Chartered buses, and sometimes specially permitted taxis, carrying families bearing food and clothing, regularly parked in a large adjacent lot accessed by a special entrance around the corner from the prison's main entrance. The twelve-foot-tall iron bar main gate was manned by a small guardhouse connected to the rest of the facility by an old rotary phone. Generally, three young military policemen hailing from northern kibbutzim were on duty to search authorized visitors and scrutinize packages. There had never been a security breach, so procedures were more bureaucratic than strict.

However, on the last Shabbat of the millennium, most of the supervisors were off, staff was minimal, and there was only one young soldier on gate duty, a young part-time guard named Gal. He was amazed when a yellow American-style school bus pulled up. He had never seen one in Israel. There were no Arab markings on it. And instead of stopping in the parking lot where it was supposed to, it drove close to the main gate. Too close. That was a violation of security that could force him to write a report and explain. Vehicles were not allowed to approach that close for fear of ramming.

Gal came out of the booth, his unloaded M-16 swung over his shoulder. Flailing his arms in rebuke, but still behind the locked gates, he waved the bus back, cussing that they should know the regulations.

"You want your permit pulled?" he chided.

The bus lurched forward to within feet of the gate and then made stalled engine noises.

Gal gestured angrily that now this yellow bus must simply move back. While Gal was protesting to Linzer through the windshield, the Anakim crawled out the back door and onto the bus roof, slithering toward the front. The lead Anak raised his shoulders slightly. Ishbi stood up and ran forward, using his partner's shoulders to catapult over the gate. Gal saw them hurl over. Within a moment, all three Anakim were over the gate.

Gal was racing into the cubicle to get a clip of bullets when two of the Anakim grabbed him, one at his arms, another at his feet. As though wielding a rag doll, they slammed his back against a flag pole, snapping Gal's spine in half. Then the two held Gal's already demolished body down as Ishbi jumped atop the soldier's skull, crushing it. Ishbi wiped his boot on the ground, and dragged Gal's limp form into the sentry station.

Hinnom and Linzer emerged from the bus, casually slipping through the iron bars of the still-locked gate. In the cubicle, Linzer took the phone off the hook, then demonstrated to Ishbi how to load and fire an M-16. Ishbi waved the gun as though it were a spear while Linzer explained its effectiveness.

Hinnom aimed his Windy at the administration building up the road and complained, "Can't get in. It's not me," he added defensively. "It's their cheap hardware."

Linzer squeezed back through the bars, reentered the bus, and backed it into the regular parking area. At that point, the bus was again in view of the turret guards who watched his every move. Walking casually as any visitor would, Linzer waved them a meaningless written message, pointing to his wrist watch and making a writing motion. The turret guards probably thought Linzer was just trying to get his paperwork straight. Once out of their view, Linzer again passed through the main gate and then directed the waiting Anakim up the long tree-lined road toward the administration building. As they ran past the last pines and briefly into the clear, the top of the minimum security compound came into view sloping off to the left and ringed by a twenty-four-foot-high picket and barbed wire fence. Most of the Arab detainees within were resting in pup tents or gathered around a fire grilling kebabs brought earlier by relatives. Guards in three elevated army green booths were facing not the administration building, but the prisoners in the compound.

The invaders simply slipped into the administration building unnoticed.

Hinnom walked in first at the ground-level reception foyer and found it empty. He sent a jamming signal to the surveillance camera, frying its circuitry. As the Anakim entered after him, they surprised a female soldier just returning from the bathroom. Maintaining absolute silence, two Anakim grabbed her, and, as though she were a battering ram, forcefully drove her into the wall head-first, killing her instantly. They scooped up her Uzi and clips. Then Ishbi took his knife and in one vicious move sliced off her ear, popping the ghastly trophy into his pocket. Linzer was impressed, and nodded approval.

Hinnom punched up his Windy. The schematics for the prison appeared on the screen. "Got it!" he sang. "The roof," he said. "That's where all the computers are."

They dashed up the stairwell four flights to the roof. Once past the heavy metal door, they encountered the two unarmed soldiers who normally operated the prison network. The unarmed men tried to react, but Ishbi and his fellows silently dispatched them with knife thrusts to the neck. Their bodies were stuffed into empty oil drums, and then crushed down by the lids.

At the edge of the roof was a simple military tent. Inside that tent lay the prison's entire computer-driven security system, including surveillance camera controls which relayed images to the main console as well as the four observation turrets along the perimeter.

"At least they're using the product," mumbled Hinnom, recognizing Windgazer 99 software. He punched into the files and found the prized location they were seeking. "It's in the basement of the admin wing," he reported. "They just call it, 'Old Bloc.'"

Then he hit control-alt-delete, forcing the prison server into a long reboot that would require periodic real-time passwords, meaning that the system would not return online. The five raced back down the stairs, moving stealthily past some third-floor office workers to the reception area. They stepped over the body of the mutilated female soldier. Hinnom pointed to the corpse and Ishbi pulled it out of view into the women's bathroom.

"This way," Linzer pointed down a corridor. Swiftly, they walked toward the end, past the men's toilets, past the small kitchen used for coffee and tea, past where the modern British-era plaster and bricks stopped and the ancient stone blocks began. The corridor led to a dark interior passage. At the end was a rough-hewn stone archway with the Latin word *Ferata* chiseled at the top. A makeshift handwritten sign in Hebrew, hung from masking tape, warned, "No Entry Except Authorized Rabbinate."

Modern lighting was installed into the ancient archway. Flipping the switch revealed an auger-like stone staircase spiralling down three turns. A string of naked bulbs loosely laced down the steps illuminating the descent.

"So this is where the rabbis have been keeping you," Hinnom sneered.

The Anakim scrambled down the timeworn Roman stones until they reached a large dank chamber constructed of large, rectangular stone blocks. An amalgam of restraints, from modern handcuffs to ancient spiked leg irons, hung from crudely forged pegs. Disused iron torch standards protruded from the walls. A small stone platform was in one corner. Philistine and Israelite coins were decorously nailed into the wall like so many notches in a pistol. Two large teeth hung by leather straps beneath one of the coins.

A gravel-rasping roar echoed through the chamber. Ishbi bellowed back. They looked down and saw a bronze and timber dungeon door in the floor. Slits between the timbers allowed in air, foodstuffs and fluid, and shafts of light.

Bracing the dungeon lid tight were two long crossbars stretched across its circumference. The two locking bars crisscrossed through grooves over a midlength center hole. A spike wedged inside the center hole fully immobilized the two crossbars, making the dungeon inescapable. Ishbi pulled on the rusted spike but it would not budge. The others quickly and

violently grabbed the heaviest of the ancient leg irons and began whip-
ping at it. Still rusted solid in place. Twice more. Still rusted solid. Again.
It budged slightly. Using one of the ancient cuffs as a hammer, Ishbi
pounded the spike until it completely dislodged. That loosened the crossbars, which were then slid out of their grooves. Four side fasteners along
the rim were flipped open. The Anakim then together lifted the weighty
lid, dragging it a few feet and letting it drop with a loud reverberating
crash.

They all stared at the hole, the Anakim with anticipation and Linzer
and Hinnom in awe. A few moments passed. Finally, a six-fingered Anak
warrior stuck his head up through the hole, his lengthy beard curled into
points and his mangy hair rising wildly from his head. He sprang from the
pit, naked and smeared with his own feces. Ishbi immediately spoke to
him in a language only the Anakim could understand. The released warrior looked at Hinnom and Linzer with a contemptuous grin, withdrew
that and then brought his towering form next to Hinnom in what seemed
like a threatening move.

"You must be Nekrish, descendent of Goliath," chimed Hinnom flippantly as though talking to a new intern. He waved the giant close so he
could whisper. Nekrish brought his ear to Hinnom, who spoke softly for
nearly a minute as the Anak's facial expression contorted and grimaced.
After hearing it all, Nekrish roared approval, and wiped saliva off his
lower lip. Nekrish seized one of the iron crossbars, stood above the dungeon, narrowed his form to hug the bar, and dropped back down the hole.
From the long tunnel below was heard an immense racket of rattled cells,
snapping chains and locks, burst doors, and the unending cheers and
howls of a barbaric horde. Linzer and Hinnom stood back. Ishbi eagerly
leaned over the hole. All at once, the noise hushed, replaced with muffled
growls and whispers.

Nekrish emerged a moment later. He directed Ishbi and the other
Anakim to station themselves along the stairwell. Hinnom and Linzer
went to the top and kept watch above at the archway. When ready,
Nekrish clapped his hands and whistled. Another Anak appeared from
the hole. Nekrish helped him out and positioned him on the other side of
the dungeon hole. Then, as if a machine, Nekrish and the other began
rhythmically lifting Anakim prisoners out of the hole. First five, then
twenty more, then another fifty. In all, one hundred naked Anakim mus-

tered, most of them six-fingered and about ten feet tall, some along the spiral stairway, but most crowded shoulder-to-shoulder in the main chamber. Many bore open wounds. All were unwashed and smelled of putridity. But unlike Nekrish's earlier unruly moment, they now exhibited alertness and discipline.

Linzer casually walked down the corridor to the main reception area. Still undiscovered. He nonchalantly nudged a wastebasket over a small pool of blood, and snapped his finger. Hinnom nodded and joined Linzer.

Nekrish came out first. He looked around, checking the rooms located off the corridor. In the women's bathroom he saw the murdered receptionist. He ripped off her pants, turning them into a loin cloth, tying the legs round his waist, so his genitals were covered while his buttocks remained exposed. Just then a small group of soldiers walked into the receptionist area. The Anakim crushed them. Nekrish gouged one man's eyes, and then, while maintaining his animal-like grip of his head, smashed the unfortunate solder into a side room.

Instructing the others to wait for him, Linzer walked out of the administration building and back down the road to the gate. Only twenty-eight minutes had passed. He unlatched the main gate, and strolled casually back to the yellow school bus and back into view of the turret machine-gunners. He waved a small piece of paper and shrugged innocently as if to say "bureaucracy." They nodded as if to say, "What can you do? That's life."

Very slowly Linzer drove the yellow school bus through the gate, then up the tree-lined road toward the administration building to pick up his legion. He pulled alongside the blood-splattered reception foyer. The distance from the entrance to the school bus door was just inches. The just liberated Anakim began silently piling into the bus, ten by ten, with Linzer constantly hushing them to move quickly and quietly, and checking the steps leading up to see if anyone was coming. Within a few minutes, all the seats and aisle space were stuffed with the released Anakim.

Linzer climbed into the driver's seat, maneuvered through the service driveway and then drove toward the gate. Slowly. Very slowly, so as not to arouse suspicion.

After clearing the gate, Linzer locked it. He drove off at a snail's pace beneath the inattentive eye of the machine-gunners, still completely unaware of the attack. From their perch, the guards could not see the

Anakim hunkered in their seats and along the aisle.

In a moment more, the bus exited the prison grounds and chugged down the road to a prepared hiding spot. As the Anakim reveled in their reunion and freedom, and Nekrish drank Arak, Hinnom coldly told Linzer, "Call the Israeli police. Report that my prized yellow school bus has been stolen. We think by Arab terrorists trying to disrupt tonight's festivities. Tell them I hope they find it soon."

THEY WERE RUNNING. They were jumping. They were touching. They were smiling smiles that radiated from deep within.

"I like it!" swooned Raymond as he rubbed the old stone fortifications of Tel Megiddo. "They are old, very old. Very old!" The others were discovering their own thrilling touchpoints to antiquity: the stables, fountains, doorways, and walkways of the tel. Irna, the English-speaking Israeli guide, could not keep up with the Down tourists as they jumped from step to step through the remnants of the ancient fortress' narrow main gate, climbed out precariously above the sunken altars, and walked in and out of palace ruins. Even when they were all in one place, it was delightfully daunting. Irna kept trying to recite her story of Megiddo's past, but the Downs constantly interrupted with impatient questions about who the warring kings were and why they were always fighting when instead they could play with each other. Sometimes, one would run up to her and volunteer, "I love you." Then another would affectionately chastise, "She knows that. You don't have to tell everyone all the time."

When Irna wasn't referring to her script or answering questions, she was calling out to the Downs to be careful . . . stay away from the edge . . . keep behind the ropes . . . don't step there, that's an active dig . . . okay, now come this way. Finally, she sat down near the entrance to a tunnel, blew her hair off her forehead, and simply marveled at the joy the Downs displayed. Raymond's mother joined her for a moment of respite.

"Goodness," said Irna, "they are wonderful. Who needs to explain? I think they can touch the rocks and understand everything."

Raymond's mother replied, "I think they understand a lot more than we think. They don't express themselves the same way. But they have deep sensibilities. Sometimes I think they are angels, sent on a special mission from God that we don't understand yet, and they can't quite explain to us."

Irna took her camera and snapped a picture of Raymond as he was pointing into the sky. "Your son, he has a heart that melts."

Raymond's mother responded gratefully, "All of them are the purest of the purest; not an evil thought has ever entered into their consciousness. We can only marvel at their completely incorruptible sense of goodness."

Irna looked at her watch. "You think we can gather them up? It's time for the pool."

Just then Raymond and some friends walked up and said, "What's next?"

"Oh there's a lot to do today," Raymond's mother answered.

"Okay, I'm ready for it all."

BRIDGES EVERYWHERE WERE filled with teeming Windgazer loyalists chanting "99.9–Make it Mine." Marching en masse, wearing Windgazer 99.9 golf shirts, sweaters, and baseball caps, waving demo diskettes, many with the 99.9 logo painted on their foreheads in black letters against a white backdrop, Hinnom's millions demonstrated across the bridges of the world symbolizing their journey to the 21st Century. The Golden Gate in San Francisco, the Nanpu in Shanghai, the Michigan Avenue in Chicago, the Westminister in London, the Brooklyn in New York, the Pont Royal in Paris, the 14th Street in Washington. In Moscow, Mexico City, Vancouver, and in dozens of other cities, bridges became the high places of Windgazer worship. Some municipalities granted emergency permits and shut their bridges to vehicular traffic. Others confined the swarming Windgazer advocates to pedestrian lanes. Either way, on December 31, 1999, the bridges of the world belonged to Hinnom.

Although the demonstrations had only been planned overnight by the worldwide Windgazer user groups responding to Hinnom's personal broadcast email, they seemed well organized. Supporters turned out on time at muster points. Logo-imprinted trinkets and trash were abundantly provided by local Hinnom officials. Candy bars and super-caffeinated sodas were delivered by Hinnom corporate caterers. In many cities, TV news helicopters were informed by Hinnom media managers just when and where to hover to capture the most dramatic scenes.

Music was part of every march, adding an air of jubilation and rhythm—rock music at some, ragas at others, downloaded snippets from The Beast, plenty of Doors, Pink Floyd, Van Halen, Smashing Pumpkins, Metallica, Marilyn Manson, and Prodigy, as well as *Ode to Joy*, *Born to be Wild* and *Sgt. Pepper's Lonely Hearts Club Band*. Some danced as they marched, others marched as they danced. It was a festive global appeal to Ben Hinnom to make their moment happen and deliver the destiny of the next millennium.

But in some cities, Windgazer devotees were met with opposition as Format C: chanters came out to meet them, and in a few cases ambush them. In Paris, eighteen rebooters met at the outdoor Terrace Cafe atop the Musée d'Orsay, just beneath the giant rooftop clocks, with an unobstructed view of Pont Royal and the Ferris wheel opposite the Louvre where scores of Windgazers were massing.

Reboot advocate François held postcard reproductions of paintings by Renoir, Monet, Toulouse-Lautrec, Gauguin, and Van Gogh, all of which were proudly displayed in the gallery below. "These men were Impressionists," said François. "They painted working men and empty rooms, ballerinas and turkeys, flower pots and bowls of fruit. Why? Because they dared to view the world differently—in form and substance." Holding the postcards high, he added. "The world these painters knew was controlled by church art, royal art, kings and queens and popes. All that. To see things differently and put their vision on canvas, Van Gogh and the others were ridiculed. Cast out. Rejected. Starved. But they helped change our world and how we see it."

Below, Windgazer supporters were inflating 99.9 balloons and unfurling banners.

"Now," said François, "you are the rejected, you are the nonconformists, you are the visionaries. But unless we show the world our vision, mankind will be forever locked in this craziness from Hinnom." He moved to the edge of the Terrace Cafe, steadied himself on one of the tall ornamental statues. "Look," he said pointing across the street. "We meet them now."

The eighteen rebooters dropped ten franc coins on their tables, sipped the last of their demitasses and hurried down the unadorned modern stairwells of the Musée d'Orsay, past the Monets, Van Goghs and Renoirs they loved, down to the main hall. They streamed through the exits and walked onto the wide plaza, past the rhino statue, along Quai d'Orsay, determined to meet the Windgazer proponents at the bridge and obstruct their passage. As they did, they donned white armbands, exquisitely painted in blue, red, violet, brown, and lime. They all read: "Format C:."

But nowhere was the confrontation greater than in Chicago. That December 31 was the warmest in memory, encouraging thousands of Windgazer revelers who massed in front of the *Chicago Tribune* waiting for their triumphant crossing over the Chicago River. But rebooters in several minivans pulled up at the lower bridge level on the south side of the river. Sporting signs demanding "Cancel the Upload," they scampered up the steep steel staircases and circular stone steps to the street level. They formed a cordon across the intersection of Wacker Boulevard and Michigan Avenue, chanting: "Format C: Reboot . . . Reboot . . . Reboot."

Upload advocates shouted: "We're marching into the next century!" and "Cross the bridge!" They proceeded at once, ignoring police orders to halt.

Rebooters passed the word among themselves: "Stop them here. Stop them everywhere." They sat down on the pavement.

Chicago police were unprepared for the Windgazer marchers, let alone any opposition showing. The watch commander at Loop Traffic had only minutes to assign just a half dozen officers to assist during the rush hour. When they detected the potential clash, they radioed for the riot squad. But there was no time.

"We're ordering you people sitting down to stand up and leave this area," a supervising Chicago policeman blared on his loudspeaker. "Leave this area and there will be no arrests." Rebooters sat firm. He then turned to the Windgazer supporters. "Your permission to march is now revoked. We order you to disband. Do not cross the bridge. Repeat: do not cross the bridge."

The Windgazer advocates walked slowly forward like a great lumbering animal. They egged each other on with the mantra of the moment: "Windgazer 99.9 . . . Make it Mine."

The police supervisor, from his position at the Wrigley Building called into his mike, "I need manpower down here now, south side of the bridge. We can't stop this. I have no one on the south side of the bridge. I need manpower!"

"Format C: . . . Reboot, Reboot, Reboot," they chanted from the ground.

"Windgazer 99.9 . . . Make it Mine," the marchers replied.

"Format C: . . . Reboot, Reboot, Reboot," they chanted from the ground.

"Windgazer 99.9 . . . Make it Mine" was the reply.

At the point where the bridge met the intersection, the Windgazer marchers encountered the sit-down protesters. For a moment, both sides stopped chanting. Looking down on the protesters, Windgazer advocates tried to understand why these people objected to their technologic advance. Looking up from the ground, the rebooters believed it had all gone too far and had to stop.

One teenaged girl sat among the first row of rebooters. She was a slender blond with wire-rim spectacles who looked as though her mother or grandmother protested against the Vietnam War, and she was dutifully carrying on the tradition. A tall heavyset man in front of her wore a Windgazer 99.9 golf shirt. His forehead was painted with the logo.

"Please stop," she called up to him. "Please don't."

The heavyset man asked, "Don't what?"

"Don't initialize tonight, and don't walk over us now," she replied peaceably, trying to appeal to his decency.

The man looked pained, as if he wanted to turn around. He asked: "Do I know you? You look familiar."

"My name is Sandy," she replied with a smile.

"Sandy," he asked, "why are you people doing this? It's our computers. We want them to work better. Hinnom Computing is not perfect but they have innovated the products that have made the computer what it is today. What's your problem?"

"I'm not a computer nerd," she replied, "just a person who cares about our world. I have a computer just like you–"

"Then, why can't–"

"–Let me finish," Sandy cut back in. "I use electricity. I don't want coal plants fouling our air. I drive a car. I want to breathe in a city without smog. Yeah, I use a computer. But I do not want our society placed under the effective control of one man and his multinational company. That is why we oppose the Point Nine Update. It's the final nail in the coffin of mankind's free will. What I can't understand is why you are so fanatically in favor."

"We're not fanatical," scowled the heavyset man. "We're a user group!"

Sandy could not understand the concept. Computer user groups often represent something far more charismatic than simple support circles. In the computer world, virtually all software enjoys its legions of ardent loyalists. Graphics programs, word processors, databases, programming languages, operating systems, even tools and utilities, although nothing more than an elongated assemblage of ones and zeros existing in an esoteric, electronic state, each bit of any software worth its salt and sectors generates its own cultic following. For reasons unclear, members of user groups identify personally and deeply with their software, advocating its proliferation, rising to its defense, beta testing its upgrades, organizing discussion groups, attending conventions and proudly labeling themselves as devotees. Frequently donning such monikers as *evangelists, zealots, gurus, bigots, fighter pilots* and *SWAT teams,* the software faithful inexplicably find self-worth and validation in software. Why?

Is it the isolation devoid of human eye contact in front of a monitor? Is it hypnotic? Is it the answer to disconnected loneliness, to brittle self-esteem? Or is it the unstoppable connection of the flickering image and the right temporal lobe? Some watch a screen—sometimes just once or twice—and become infatuated with movie stars. They form fan clubs. *Fan* is short for fanatic. Some watch a monitor for hours every day and become infatuated with the logo and how it performs. They form user groups. Hinnom screen buddies had now elevated that fascination to an intense new level.

Whatever the reason, for many in user groups, the phenomenon compares only with religion itself. The software becomes their Father, Son, and Holy Ghost, all configured into one inspirational and exhilarating 32-bit godhead espousing a theology and dogma of user manuals, service bulletins and related documentation, offering daily miracles of productivity and sleek graphics to regale and fascinate. Watch them appear before your very eyes right up on the monitor. Don't adjust the brightness. The connection to the right temporal lobe is fierce—often undefeatable. Hitler issued radios to every citizen. TV has become addicting. So has the web and email. The right temporal lobe always craves more—the need for gratification only increases. The software wants to become like the man. The man wants to become like the software. User groups see any challenge to their software as a profound personal affront, a declaration of Holy War.

Sandy appealed to the heavyset man. "It's just electrons," she pleaded. "Just fluttering images on a screen. It's not worth all this. It can't justify confrontation." She held hands with the people seated next to her. "We ask you to join us. Turn back now. Reboot tonight."

He blinked forcefully and responded breathlessly, "Can't help you today, Sandy." Turning to the other marchers he shrieked, "Initialize!"

He began to walk, as did hundreds more behind him. They waded over the sit-down protesters, stepping in between them, over them, atop their legs, and then their shoulders. Sandy was the first to be crushed, as her cracked glasses cut into her face and her bones fractured one after another. Some rebooters prostrated themselves, allowing Windgazer advocates to march over their bodies as though they were stepping stones to the next century.

The Chicago police supervisor, unable to restrain the Windgazer marchers, called into his mike, "What in God's name is happening? What in Holy God's name is happening!"

Similar clashes occurred in other cities. Each of them was graphically covered by television cameras which only encouraged others to emulate the scenes elsewhere in the world. Eventually, Format C: protesters did not bother to sit down. Like civil rights and Vietnam War protesters before them, they deliberately laid flat, faces to the pavement. In each case, Windgazer marchers gleefully walked over the opposition. In some cases, the police were able to avert confrontation by revoking permits or obstructing rebooters. But in most instances, the Point Nine Update forces proved they would not be stopped by peaceful protest.

Developments reached Hinnom and Linzer in real time as they accessed web news updates on their Windies. They had already pulled the yellow school bus into a shallow cave just a few miles from Megiddo junction, a hiding place Ishbi had located hours before the prison break. A tall farm trailer partially filled with kibbutz cotton masked the cave mouth. Israeli Army helicopters buzzed overhead and indeed throughout the country as security mobilized to find the terrorists who had attacked the prison. Antiterrorist units assumed the culprits were *en route* to Lebanon, Jordan or perhaps the West Bank, and had by now abandoned the bus. Although the government forces were searching throughout the country, they were unaware that the bus was parked just minutes from Megiddo.

From the comfort of the bus, Hinnom and Linzer communicated with their subordinates and team leaders in Gei Ben Hinnom, condemning the theft of the bus and its use in a terrorist incident, and informing them that, regrettably, Hinnom could not be present for the final midnight festivities, but would participate live via Windycam. It was not the first time Hinnom remotely appeared at a pivotal event. But he assured team leaders that he and he alone would personally enter the codes that would start the final initialization sequence. The Update would proceed as planned.

At about that time, Dan and the group were in the kibbutz dining hall, trying to understand how they fit into the midnight event. Amnon only wanted Sal to stay sequestered. Nothing more. "But that is not enough," argued Dan. "Sal needs to get out there and rally people–tonight of all nights."

"He has done enough," Park said. "There are protests all over the world. I just heard on BBC Radio that there have even been riots between rebooters and Windgazer crazies in America and across Europe."

"Okay," Dan told Sal excitedly. "Here's an idea. Send our buddy Hinnom another email. This will drive him nuts. There is no way out from this one."

The group waited and Dan finally explained.

"Tell him you–using your little Windy over there–have hacked into his deep, dark system. You corrupted one of his big initializing files, or attached a virus or whatever you want to say. Tell him that when people type Windgazer 99.9, it will not initialize the Update–but *destroy* it. He's cooked. He'll be afraid to go forward because he can't counter that kind of thing in so few hours. The whole shebang tonight will be canceled. He can just blame it on you."

"But that would be false," Sal responded, adding cautiously, "I haven't done that."

Park exchanged glances with Dan.

"Right," said Dan. "That part will be our little secret."

Sal relapsed for a moment into his traditional pauses, but then shook the feeling and replied confidently, "I agree. Hinnom would be paralyzed if I transmitted that message. I could get to work on developing such a virus, but I doubt I could do it by tonight. So we can't send that message."

"Because?" asked Dan.

"It's just not true."

"It's maybe the end of the world tonight."

"The world will be saved by a lie?" asked Sal.

"If it works, it's what people in my business call permissible deception," Dan replied.

"Translated into Hebrew," added Motke, 'that means 'little white lie.' Am I correct?"

"You got it, Motkele," said Dan, exchanging a slow-motion five with Motke.

"I have a better idea," said Sal. "Let me use my intelligence honestly." He opened the Windy and began typing an email. He pressed Enter before Dan or anyone else could read it.

A moment later Sal's message dinged onto Hinnom's machine. This time Hinnom opened the email immediately. His mouth dropped.

"I knew it! The puke sonofabitch has done it." He ran to the Anakim in the back of the bus. "He's just ten minutes from here. Written or not, we are going to destroy this asshole before midnight. I will *not* be challenged or dictated to!" He forwarded the email to Linzer, who read it aloud with disdain:

"Cancel the midnight Upload and it won't be necessary to launch a virus into your system at 11:55 tonight that will turn the Point Nine Update into a disk eater that will destroy every system in the world within minutes—including your own. It's your choice."

19

MIDNIGHT AT
MEGIDDO

*T*he End of the Current Millennium. The Beginning of a New One.

By 10:00 that night, Hinnom's global event had been grinding for hours. The fifty-foot screens at Gei Ben Hinnom were flashing a wild collage of scenes: babies being born, starving children in Africa, cannibals slicing off skulls to eat human brains, waterfalls, hummingbirds, traffic jams, sheep on a field, children delighting on carousels, birds killed by oil spills—all to the mesmerizing pulsations of "The Beast." Periodically, the montage would interrupt for a commercial of sorts: either a famous actor, basketball player, or singer, explaining why they were looking forward to initializing the Point Nine Update at midnight.

In a macabre presentation, a stunning sequence of well-known personages flickered rapidly on the screens with the words "Windgazer 99.9– Make it Mine" artificially dubbed onto their lips. Laurel and Hardy, Babe Ruth, Mahatma Gandhi, Albert Einstein, Mickey Mouse, Idi Amin, Bela Lugosi, George Washington, George Bernard Shaw, Napoleon Bonaparte, Frank Sinatra, Humphrey Bogart, Lenin, Harry Truman, Fidel Castro, Elvis Presley, Adolf Hitler, and finally a graphic of Christ on the cross. The Christ image repeatedly flipped left to right, and then ultimately upside down as the word "Windgazer 99.9–Make it Mine" kept appearing from his animated lips. Around the world, nearly a billion giggled and marveled at the visual pyrotechnics.

As the multimedia event unfolded, rebooters throughout the world continuously chanted "Format C:! . . . Format C:! . . . Format C:!" Millions of them were prepared to type that command, reboot, and pray they had made the right choice. In the meantime, the Windgazer celebration was punctuated with prerecorded derision of the Format C: movement. "Be forewarned," loudspeakers blared, "rebooters will be reviled for a thousand years."

Slouching in his school bus, peering into his Windy, Hinnom was able to monitor the entire Jerusalem telecast and reports from around the world. He watched quietly, shifting his glance every now and then to Nekrish and the other Anakim as they played with the safeties on their Uzis, occasionally staring down the barrels. Once in a while Nekrish would point his gun at Linzer, who would gingerly shove the muzzle aside with his pencil. Nekrish was completely unpredictable. From time to time, he would abruptly become irritated with his brethren, slapping them viciously until they cowered or crawled under others not being assailed. Then he would become subdued and grin congenially. Hinnom only smiled at the antics.

At 10:15 Dan burst into Park and Sal's room on the third floor of the guest building. Motke came in from next door.

"That's it. We're gone," said Dan. "Amnon just called on my cell. He says they suspect Hinnom and his Anakim buddies were connected to the massacre at the prison. If that is so—"

"The *killings* over there!" shrieked Park.

"Yes, the killings." Turning back to Sal, "Amnon wants me to get you out of here. The IDF has something planned. Haven't a damn clue what. But if the Anakim come looking for you, you ain't gonna be here."

Addressing Motke as a brother, Dan said, "Motkele, take Park to Yaacov and the survivors. Get guns from kibbutz defense if you have to." He tugged on Motke's sleeve, "Take care of her, *chaver.*"

He kissed Park deeply, holding both her hands in his own, fingers intertwined, arms raised high. For just a moment, he did not smell burning gasoline, did not hear screams of anguish, did not see forlorn images, but felt only soft, loving, invigorating lips. For just a moment, she sensed the bright morning of a clear Kansas day, the far-off grind of truck gears on the highway, the blurring wave of wheat when the wind agrees, and the joy of a young girl's innocence unlocked from its hardened shell deep within her memory.

"This is it," he said, pulling off. "I'll come back with your son. After midnight."

Park grabbed Sal, held his face in her hands, and cried, "I don't know what you have, or how you got it."

"I'll be okay," Sal replied, trying to extricate himself from his mother's embrace.

Dan pulled them apart. "You'll have a thousand years to hug each other," he said. "But not unless I get his ass out of here."

Dan embraced Motke for an instant. They exchanged five and hugged again.

Dan patted the stone in his pocket, the stone that had never left his side since the descent into St. Onuphrius.

"Want this?" he offered his friend.

"I prefer a rabbit's foot," joked Motke, "You need it more than me."

Dan flipped the stone in his palm and with a snap buried it back into his right pocket.

"Love you," Dan told Park, as he ran down the steps with Sal right behind him. Park saw her son and her lover descend. At the bottom, Sal waved with a shrug as though experimenting with a new gesture.

Dan called up to the third floor, "Love you!" He touched two fingertips to his lips and wafted her a kiss.

Park touched two fingertips to her lips and returned it.

Sal and Dan jumped into the red Del Sol. Dan reached into the back compartment and tippled a long swig of Laphroaig.

Sal asked, "Can I try?"

Dan, surprised only for a second, responded, "Sure." He extended Sal the bottle. As soon as the powerful fluid touched Sal's lips, Sal choked and spit it out.

"Stick to computers," chirped Dan, as he tasted once more and stowed the bottle in the back.

The Del Sol peeled out of the parking lot, and coursed the unlighted perimeter road to the iron gate. The old-timer on guard smiled, tapping his beige kibbutz hat in a friendly salute. He retracted the gate so the car could pass. Dan headed down the long road back to the highway. Visibility was low because a dense, fast-moving fog began floating through, first across the hill and then along the road itself.

Dan asked Sal, "You strapped in?"

Sal rapped the buckle showing he was.

Just then an image appeared faintly up ahead. It was the yellow school bus, headlights on high, blocking the road.

"Okay, hold on," said Dan.

He screeched to a halt in a cloud of dust that filled the foggy air, creating bizarre striations in the glare of the headlights. Dan slammed into reverse, and drove backward—"Hold on, dammit!" he yelled—until he came to a wide spot, then braked suddenly as he pulled the steering wheel sharply. The car J-turned. He floored it back to the kibbutz. The bus followed.

Beeping his horn as he approached, Dan waved and shouted for the old-timer to open up. *"Effen uff. Effen uff,"* he cried in Yiddish. Just then, Nekrish appeared in the guard booth with the old-timer's beige kibbutz hat clutched in his hand. The bus was fast approaching from behind. The Del Sol was trapped just a few feet from the iron gate.

"Out!" yelled Dan.

Sal and Dan toppled out.

An instant later, Hinnom's bus rammed the Del Sol into the iron gate, the Honda's open doors careening off from the impact. Linzer, at the wheel, backed up a few feet. Accelerator. He rammed the Del Sol a second time, crumpling the trunk and part of the engine compartment.

Linzer backed up again to a safe distance. The Del Sol gas tank exploded. Incendiary trails shot into the air and scorched red fragments flew away. Key kibbutzniks had already been briefed by Amnon on the phone that an attack was imminent. Now, the alarm sounded.

Dan and Sal scrambled down the side of the hill, around the guard booth, and back up to the perimeter road. Nekrish opened the gate for the bus, then ran after Dan and Sal. Linzer rammed the burning Del Sol, bulldozing it through the gate and out of the way, then turned left and sped down the perimeter road until he overtook Nekrish in pursuit. Linzer slammed on the brakes and opened the door. Nekrish jumped in. Linzer floored the accelerator.

As the alarm sounded, Yaacov told Park to hide in one of the many crude bomb shelters scattered across the kibbutz designed to protect kibbutzniks, especially the children, from either a terrorist invasion or mortar attack. This shelter was in the middle of playlot, all decorated with children's paintings and barely recognizable. Motke escorted her into the simple concrete bunker. The massive metal door was operated by a simple swivel lever handle. Once sealed, it could not be opened from the outside.

"Take the flashlight," said Motke as he examined the shelter. "Okay, it's a nice one. Here is water, and canned peaches if you get hungry. Try to find a can opener. If it's me, to knock, I will do like this . . ." He rapped thrice, then twice. He helped her bolt the door, tested it from the outside, and then rejoined Yaacov.

The perimeter road was long and circular. Dan and Sal had jumped off, running through the pines and thorn bushes on the hill, and directly up and across to the kibbutz.

"Go. Go!" yelled Dan as Sal struggled to keep up.

"I'm trying," said Sal, whose hands were bleeding from the rocks and thorns.

The kibbutz came into sight just over a ridge. They scaled the top and ran across the grounds. The yellow school bus was just pulling in. As it skidded to a dusty halt, its accordion door opened. Four Anakim jumped out, and began racing after Sal and Dan. The two disappeared into the shadows and more Anakim were dispatched to join the search. Linzer and Hinnom stepped out imperially to watch the drama, as they checked their wristwatches.

"We have time," assured Linzer. "Tonight, we do it all."

In Jerusalem, the hypnotic music of "The Beast" pounded throughout Gei Ben Hinnom. Syncopating lasers in many colors electrified the crowds. Hallucinogenic substances were chewed and sniffed. Enthralled revellers undulated with their laptops held high above their heads, each set to the command line: >*WINDGAZER 99.9.* Eagerly, almost erotically, they awaited midnight to complete their ecstasy and depress the Enter key.

But beyond the Valley of Death, time was running out. The globe had been engulfed in angry bodements that had been building for days and now seemed to be culminating in a day of universal shudder.

Engineers all over China readied for the Point Nine Update. But their country was in utter chaos. Sudden simultaneous flash flooding of both the Yangtze and Yellow Rivers was devastating the provinces. After just hours, thousands of villages had been swept away, 119,000 people had been killed. More than 90 million were homeless. And the numbers were growing. Chinese cities were now so threatened that officials began piercing rural dikes to divert waters, thereby sacrificing millions of acres in low-lying peasant lands.

In Malaysia, a killer wave came ashore, drowning six thousand, following a rare ocean quake. Villagers said there was absolutely no warning other than the watery rumble heard just before the massive swell crashed onto land. Virtually all the children living along the coast—an entire generation—were wiped away because they could not run fast enough.

Fierce storms off southern California cut into beach towns, unleashing murderous mud slides that buried helpless residents and their homes, and then swallowed them into the Pacific when the shoreline collapsed. In Greece, flooding rivers were ravaging valley towns. Three thousand were already counted dead. More than sixty thousand were unaccounted for. In France, the overflowing Rhone drove hundreds of thousands from their homes.

And there was great heat even in the midst of winter. In Texas, weeks of triple-digit temperatures and drought had culminated in a new record of 137 degrees. Air conditioners were failing and in many neighborhoods overtaxed power plants browned out, then blacked out altogether. People began dying in their own homes. Parched field rats forced into residential neighborhoods now swarmed into homes seeking water and cooler air. Many in Dallas reported their swimming pools were overwhelmed with thirsty rodents, which first drank to satisfaction and then turned to the kitchens for food. The Windgazer 99.9 party in Austin was canceled. Nonetheless, thousands of bare-chested technology executives camped out at their servers and PCs to make sure they were ready for the midnight moment. In many instances, mission-critical computers at Texas banks, insurance companies and military bases were manned by two and three LAN managers just in case the searing heat overcame any one man. Attempts to create macros that would automatically initialize Windgazer 99.9 at midnight were completely unsuccessful. The Upload required a real-time human acceptance. So the executives, ensconced with bottled water and battery-operated hand fans, held their vigil.

New Delhi was also battling record temperatures—151 degrees—causing throngs to crowd as never before into the Ganges River to wait for a cooler night to fall. In 124-degree Madrid, a national emergency was called as people began dropping on the street from heat exhaustion. In Venice, 119-degree heat drove some tourists into the polluted canals while many others with heat stroke were evacuated in long caravans to the mainland.

Meanwhile, wildfires blazed across much of rain-starved Mexico, Louisiana, and Florida. Massive clouds of smoke choked cities as far north as Memphis and St. Louis, turning day into a gray night of heat and haze. IS and IT managers donned face masks as they sat by their servers, ready to hit the Enter button at midnight. Some brought their wives and children ostensibly to witness the momentous occasion, but in truth to make sure the LAN managers themselves did not succumb under the stifling conditions.

Everywhere the world was suddenly suffering nature's wrath. The planet was never angrier. Nor would its spectacular anger subside.

Many locales were crippled first by massive snows, then by abrupt heat which produced floods, followed by destructive fire from the collapse of infrastructure. People were awed and humbled as they saw fire and ice, flood and hail all in a single town in a single hour. One Montana farmer and his family stood atop the roof of his home, just inches from the waters cascading through frozen river banks, watching gas mains in town spray flames into the air. The farmer's family all held hands and prayed. The little girl whispered, her eyes closed tight, "Dear Lord up in heaven, can you save the good ones? We have been good."

Then the volcanoes began exploding. First came Korovin in Alaska, then Pacaya in Guatemala, followed by Etna in Sicily and then Sakura-Jima in Japan. Finally, three of Indonesia's most active and dangerous volcanoes, Semeur, Merapi and Peuet Sague all erupted within ninety minutes, spewing a dark fiery dome over the entire Indian and Pacific Oceans. Each mountain exploded with the ferocity of hundreds of nuclear bombs, rocketing pillars of smoke and ash to the heavens. Their synchrony gave the impression as though hellfire itself had learned to punctuate. The devastation was unimaginable. Lava flows covered entire regions with ashen landscapes where nothing would live again for decades. Millions had been incinerated by the unexpected molten violence. Quickly, emergency services were overwhelmed. Each of the eruptions had been on the Top Ten Volcano Watch List but scientists believed all were years from reaching criticality. Volcanologists and emergency management everywhere downloaded unending satellite GIFs and burned email messages to each other trying to understand how a global volcanic chain reaction could have been triggered. One besieged monitor sent a final message before evacuating his post at Soufriére Hills, Montserrat, which was the next to blow. His message was brief: "On this mad volcanic day, the eruption here will be greater than anything we dreamed. I cannot get off the island in time. Tell my wife I love her. Tell humanity that God is speaking. We must listen. Offline now."

It was as though the world was coming to an end in one cataclysmic, surreal day. Horrors of biblical proportions pressed every corner of civilization. No place was safe from the tribulation. Everywhere there was death. Everywhere there was weeping. Tears and blood watered the lands.

Most 99.9 parties were canceled as the world tried to cope with its unprecedented chain of disasters and destruction. The news began streaming in to Gei Ben Hinnom. Upload devotees in Jerusalem could not help but pause from their jubilation and worry. Some panicked and began screaming, "We're making a mistake," and "Maybe we're making the wrong choice!" A few began chanting "Format C:," which enraged Windgazer stalwarts who demanded that the queasy amongst them stop ruining the festivities. Fights ensued. Event leaders were having little success reassuring the assembled. Reports of canceled Upload parties and frightened users were piling up in his Windy's inbox. Hinnom finally interceded.

Hinnom didn't care how many rallies were canceled in Melbourne, London, and San Francisco. He was determined that the one in Jerusalem finalize. Come what might. Crouching beside the damaged fender on the school bus parked in a corner of the Kibbutz Megiddo parking lot, he sent an email message to his lieutenants at the Jerusalem rally: "Prepare for a live feed from me in two minutes. I will address the crowd."

In the valley, organizers shut down the blasting music to announce a message would be coming from Ben Hinnom himself. The giant screen also flashed the news. All eyes turned to the main screen and smaller monitors set up throughout the ravine.

Moments later, a live picture of Ben Hinnom appeared to roars of applause. Via his Windy from Megiddo, Hinnom declared: "We have all heard the reports of bad weather coming in from around the world. Please do not become alarmed. It's El Niño. The little bugger is still angry. But you have nothing to worry about. Thanks to Hinnom Computing technology, emergency services around the globe are coping with these little blips. Using our software to communicate, track and forecast, they will deploy new and improved high-tech rescue efforts. Researchers are now investigating the cause of all this bad weather and the whole volcano thing. It could be profound sun spots, tidal effects, tectonic aberration. No one knows. But we will find out soon.

"Remember," he continued, trying to assuage the crowds, "on any given day in history, there will be thousands of severe storms. Volcanic eruptions of one magnitude or another occur every week. Wildfires–typically you can have hundreds burning. It happens. Floods–a day doesn't go by somewhere without them. Several. None of this is connected to our Point Nine Update or," he forced a transparent giggle, "any kind of year 2000 cataclysmic crisis. Come on!"

He smiled and raised a finger in emphasis. "In fact, the only connection any of this has to computers and Hinnom is that if it weren't for improved global communications, the rise of instant global knowledge on the Internet, all these natural phenomenon would have happened as freaks of nature but we would have heard the news only days and weeks later. Or not at all.

"The media loves to play up this stuff," Hinnom pressed on longer than he needed to, "because it plays on the fears of people concerned about Y2K. That's not fair–but that's the media! In a fascinating rebuke, I note, we have learned that brave system managers across our planet are standing by their computers–and probably sipping on more than a few cans of Jolt Cola," he joked, "waiting for the initializing moment. It all begins right here in Jerusalem. Within the hour. And then proceeds west across the time zones. I might add . . . as I said before . . . uh . . . uh . . . where was I?"

Hinnom was distracted as Anakim raced back and forth looking for Sal and Dan.

"Okay, we're okay." Hinnom resumed, trying to collect his thoughts. ". . . And to prove we're okay, I'm going to sign off now . . . Yes. And I'll ask our event coordinators to resume the music and performances . . . plenty of good entertainment . . . and hey–free beer and wine for everyone from now until midnight. And I want you all to look at the dirigible above you. Look up, look up. Come on, look up. You can't miss it. Can someone on staff inset a picture of the blimp please? Inset, please."

He waited. "Inset, please," he repeated with irritation.

A picture of the small, commercial dirigible dropped into a corner of Hinnom's image. At that moment, he sent an email to the pilot authorizing the Windgazer 99.9 logo to be projected onto the Wailing Wall as planned. A second inset window opened on the screens. It was the aerial camera's view of the Old City, panning and then zooming onto the Kotel.

"Here it is everybody!" cackled Hinnom. The Windgazer 99.9 logo was then beamed onto the great white stones of the Kotel. Not right side up—but upside down. Once or twice the image broadened to include the entire Temple Mount, including the Holy of Holies area, and then reduced back down to a concentrated projection on the Wailing Wall. When aimed at Islam's holy place, the Dome of the Rock, the logo was reflected toward the stars as if putting the heavens on notice.

"Wooooooeeee!" screamed an excited Hinnom, adding under his breath, "Well, at least I got *that* done."

Just then the earth shook. Three large mounds rose beyond Gei Ben Hinnom, not far from Mt. Zion, amid screams all around. As the hills appeared, gas lines cracked and caught flame, spewing great spires of fire into the air. Structures along the hill crests crashed to the ground crushing all within and below. Jerusalem was burning.

Viewing the reports on his Windy, Hinnom hurriedly blurted, "Hey, hey. Remember, Jerusalem lies on fault lines. Fault lines. It's *their* fault—ha! Earthquakes have been rattling this part of the world for centuries. Just routine." He began prattling, "Uh . . . well . . . I have to go now . . . have a meeting. See you soon. Uh, bye."

Blank screens.

At that moment, Linzer frantically summoned several Anakim over to the bus. "We're still looking for the little puke," he reported. "I had wanted to keep this a little quieter. But now, it looks like we'll have to get very high-profile."

Hinnom snarled back, "Kill everyone, destroy every living thing until they deliver him up. There's death and destruction the world round this night. Megiddo can share."

Linzer grabbed a megaphone from the bus and shouted out to the kibbutz. "This is a Hinnom Computing Company security task force working in cooperation with the Israeli Defense Forces. We understand the terrorists who committed the atrocity at the prison are on the premises. They are two Americans, Dan Levin and Sal McGuire, and possibly his mother and other accomplices.

"We need your cooperation," he blared. "Do not offer them shelter. Cooperate. There are no working phones on the kibbutz, no radio, and all cell phones have been jammed. So the kibbutz is completely isolated. A contingent of special forces–very fierce antiterrorist commandos–is backing me up. Anyone not cooperating will be deemed aiding and abetting the terrorists. You will be destroyed. I will not repeat this warning. We will begin our search . . ." He waited a moment, heard nothing and added, ". . . *now*."

Just then, from beyond the dining hall, a phalanx of survivors came walking out, sure and confident, unafraid, holding a variety of weapons, from late-model Uzis and Galils to relics from both World Wars. Motke was with them, shoulder to shoulder, swinging a Galil from a long patrol strap.

A squad of twelve Anakim, led by Ishbi, laughed and grabbed nearby oil drum lids. The old men held their ground just yards from the Anakim as Yaacov called out, "We know you. You are the ones. You did not die in Berlin, did you?" Yaacov looked at the other fighters who understood the same. Calling again, "Nazis! . . . Still trying to make big people, still trying to control the world."

Linzer answered, "Old man! You shouldn't even be here. You were just another disgusting bit of vermin about to die when you happened on the fish. Help us all now. Tell us where the two Americans are. We take them, we go away. I'll even give you another fish to fry tonight."

Yaacov's mind sped through those final days when all the fight had drained from his soul, when the last ounce of resistance had been spilled in some field as he hid face flat in the dirt, and when the prospect of living in the world he had survived was in some ways more frightful than the compulsion to survive in the world in which he lived. On that day, he met Moishe and Rivke by the side of the road. They did little, except show that human kindness had not died during the ultimate war against human kindness. But Yaacov understood that the War had not ended when the Berlin bunker smoldered. Nor had it begun in the *biergarten* with the rise of Hitler.

Yaacov looked at Linzer, locking on his eyes. He saw the square mustache appear and then fade from Linzer's clean-shaven face. Yaacov strained to look again. Now it formed and lingered. Linzer smirked and shook his head to the right, allowing his hair to fall to one side.

All the old men began trembling at the sight. One by one they raised their arms, outstretching their fingers, pointing.

"It is you!" cried Yaacov. "It is true. You did not die, not from all the armies and all the bombs. But you will—here on our little kibbutz. Right here and right now. So we can finally say: Never again."

From behind the Anakim, Hinnom sneered back loudly, "Ohhhh, yes! Yes, definitely again. Again and again. Again and again. Again and again." He liked the musicality of it and twiddled his fingers as though conducting himself. Then he stopped, and brazenly ordered Linzer, "Proceed."

Yaacov and the others steeled for the onslaught. They raised their weapons. The Anakim charged across the broad clearing. The survivors fired. Deflecting the bullets with oil can lids, the Anakim sprayed the survivors with Uzi fire, shooting wildly in unpracticed swinging motions. Bullets hit about half the defenders. Motke took a bullet in the side in the first volley. He grabbed his pain and squeezed it away with gritted teeth until he could see the blood pumping out of his side but could no longer feel the bullet's white-hot sting.

The Anakim, braving fire from the others survivors, descended upon the old men, swinging their Uzis like clubs and their oil can lids like shields, bashing heads and crushing bones. Motke, now on the ground, tried to get off another round, but Ishbi stomped his hand and shoved his knee into Motke's throat. Ishbi then swung at Yaacov. The old man ducked and poked his emptied Uzi into Ishbi's groin. The giant barely felt the blow, but grabbed Yaacov with one hand while another grabbed his legs and slammed him down to the ground like a carcass in a stockyard. They laid an oil can lid on his body and one Anak jumped on it, crushing Yaacov beneath. Then another jumped on for good measure.

Within a few moments more, all of the two dozen survivors lay dead or dying, their blood forming shallow bulging pools and rivulets. The Anakim moved to the residences, bursting into cottages behind the main hall looking for Sal and Dan.

Dan and Sal had witnessed the battle with the survivors from the jewelry workshop where they had hidden behind tall mirrors in the storage room. The mirrors were scheduled to be installed in renovated guestrooms and they were leaning upright, reflective surface to the wall to avoid scratching. From his vantage point crouched beneath, all Dan could see was his own image . . . and just around the edge and through the window, the scene of devastation.

When the Anakim ran out of sight, Dan and Sal squeezed out of their hiding spot, went to the window to check again, and then ran out to the decimated survivors. All twisted and bleeding, they were for Dan like the sculpture at Dachau, like the photos in Yad Vashem, like a scene in the forest near a Polish village in the snow after the A.K. had opened fire.

Dan and Sal went from body to body seeking signs of life. When they found one breathing, Dan could do nothing but say, "Help is coming. Amnon is bringing help. Hold on. Please hold on."

As he turned one body over, he saw Motke staring face up, his collarbone crushed, gasping and wheezing as though breathing through a whistle.

"Motkele!" cried Dan helplessly. "Motkele. Hold on *chaver*. The IDF is coming. Dammit where are they?" he whispered in agony, looking about for Anakim who by now were burning the homes they had ransacked.

"Where's my mother?" Sal asked Motke.

"Park," said Dan. "She in the room?"

Motke painfully blinked "no."

"The dairy?"

Motke blinked "no" again.

Motke's eyes shifted left to the bomb shelter disguised in the children's playlot.

Sal and Dan swiveled toward the shelter and understood.

"Okay," said a weeping Dan. "Hold on."

Motke spit up a large fibrous clump of blood. More followed in spurts. He gurgled involuntarily, and then finally gasped his last.

Dan placed his head on Motke's bloodied chest and began weeping uncontrollably, "I'm sorry . . . I don't know kaddish. I'm a Jew, damn me, and I don't even know kaddish." Dan thought and remembered. "Wait, it starts *Yiskadol viyiskadol* . . . uh . . ." but then he quit. "Damn me. I can't remember," he moaned. "I'll just see you, Motke . . . on the other side."

Keeping one eye on the bomb shelter, and glancing at the burning homes across the center gardens, hearing wails of pain and screaming women in the background, Dan continued checking bodies and now looked for an Uzi. He found one without a clip, and clips without any bullets. He lifted an oil can in the carnage. Underneath was Yaacov, his arms crushed above his head, almost forming a *shin*.

"Yaacov. Yaacov," Dan wept. "Come back to me. Dad, dad, come back."

Yaacov's eyes opened slowly. "I'm here . . . for a minute," he said in a barely audible voice. "I cannot move . . . But," he breathed painfully, ". . . I am here."

"Yaacov . . ." lamented Dan.

Yaacov attempted a smile that dissolved into coughing. Petroleum tanks began exploding in the distance as Yaacov shakily whispered words without betraying his gentle, affectionate inflections: "Dan. Your father and your mother . . . nice people . . . helped me . . ." He coughed and his eyes rolled away. "Now . . . I helped you . . ." He smiled as though finally understanding a great truth, "Dan . . . it didn't start in '33 . . . it didn't end . . . in '45 . . ."

"Why?" wailed Dan, muffling his anguished voice, "Why?"

Yaacov nodded several times. He smiled for the last time, "You know . . . you just . . ." Yaacov inhaled unexpectedly and gave out. He passed.

Dan slammed his hands against his head trying to make sense. He finally found clips and a second Uzi. He armed himself and then gave a loaded Uzi to Sal.

"I can't use this," said Sal. "It's a gun."

Dan grabbed Sal by the shirt and snapped, "It's just mass, velocity, and trajectory!"

"Okay," replied Sal. He surveyed the weapon, found the safety and flipped it off. "I can handle it."

Hearing the tumult in the main part of the kibbutz, Irna the guide, aided by kibbutz defense, urgently tried to evacuate the Down children into the buses to escape. "Come, come into the buses," she cried. "Terrorists!" The bus drivers, some still in their underwear, raced down to start their engines, and the Downs good-naturedly lined up to board.

Suddenly an old man with a long overcoat appeared. It was Kuebitz.

"There is nothing to worry about," Kuebitz told them calmly in a reassuring voice. "Don't be frightened." He turned to Irna. "These nice people need to follow me. They will be safe."

Walking down the hill, Kuebitz led hundreds of Down men and

women, all smiling and excited as though they were going to a special event. Irna brought up the rear, whisper-shouting, "Where are you taking them? Where?" Kuebitz just waved her off and kept walking, the Down people right behind him. First in line was Raymond, smiling and whistling playfully, holding Kuebitz' hand.

Skulking from shadow to shadow, Dan and Sal could see teams of Anakim fanning through the grounds, murdering and pillaging all in their sight. Now wearing as battle garb a motley collection of bedsheets, bathrobes, tablecloths, torn tarps, skirts and coats, the Anakim fashioned necklaces of eyeballs and ears, fastened by bits of string and leather, just as Croatian *Ustashe* militiamen had done during the Holocaust.

Nine Anakim were busy trying to break into one of the more obvious shelters where many of the young kibbutz volunteers and children were hiding. Using short lengths of irrigation pipes as battering rams, they repeatedly slammed into the door. Others climbed onto the protected room's reinforced roof, peering down the narrow caged air vent. Inside the children held hands and prayed as an older girl from Scotland spoke repetitively to the heavens: "Thy will be done. Thy will be done."

Dan and Sal finally crept over to the playlot where Park's shelter stood. They knocked on the door as quietly as possible, wincing at the noise. No answer.

"Mom, it's us," whispered Sal as Dan scanned the perimeter. The latch squealed open and Park's petrified face came into view. Just then the entire kibbutz began vibrating. Patches of earth began dividing, while others were upheaved into craggy prominences.

The ground rumbled and gave way beneath Sal and Dan just as they were climbing into the shelter. They dropped into a fissure ten or fifteen feet deep. Park was helping them climb out when Linzer appeared at the far end of the walkway, his flashlight slicing through the drifting fog.

"Got them. Got them . . . just down there," shouted Linzer.

Hinnom peeked out from his secure spot at the school bus to see.

A dozen Anakim came running with many more streaming out from the reserve in the bus.

The ground continued to quake. Just as Sal and Dan climbed to the top of the fissure, they slipped back down its slippery sides. Park screamed, and stretched her hand to help them back up and into the shelter.

Linzer and the Anakim were running toward her.

Finally, Sal's hand connected with Park's. She pulled.

Anakim from another direction appeared on the shelter roof and were about to pounce.

Just then, the ground groaned and divided more deeply, dragging Dan and Sal down, creating a narrow walled chasm twenty or thirty feet deep that began rapidly extending in both directions like a fast splintering in the earth. Park tumbled in when the ground beneath her disappeared. The Anakim jumped in after them, but landed at a much lower point in the elongating chasm. The giants scrambled up the subterranean incline even as Park, Sal, and Dan fled down the other downsloping track.

Running, sometimes stumbling when the ground unexpectedly sank beneath their feet, sliding on their sides and then running again, Dan, Park, and Sal struggled to escape their pursuers while the hill was acting out its conflagration.

The instant chasm continued tearing through the terra firma, cracking open as they ran, descending tortuously, ushering them toward the valley below. As lightning streaked from the sky, as uprooted trees crashed overhead, and more petroleum stores detonated in fiery blasts, the continuous upheaval of the earth began unleashing its ancient, bloody secrets.

Skeletons of slain warriors from forgotten millennia popped through the soft mud like so many hurdles and protrusions on an obstacle course that the fleeing threesome had to dodge and sidestep. Park shrieked as each gruesome bone vaulted toward her. The Anakim, racing through the chasm in pursuit, would sometimes round an edge and run right into a sharp, impaling femur or tibia. Or they would stumble and fall into sudden sinkholes disappearing into the bottomless depths. Still, the chase continued.

As Dan, Park, and Sal darted through the chasm, splattered by belching slime and mud eructations, bones showered onto their heads. So many skeletons rained into the fissure that soon the path ahead was strewn with bones. They were now actually running atop a bed of bones. Some cracked underfoot, others were fossilized rigid. Many were coated with slime. Others with thick, black worms that oozed a dense, oily fluid when squished.

Just when the Anakim seemed close enough to grab them, the chasm forked. The three coursed down the left fork, skidding down the steep muddy crag. As they did they saw a group of Anakim in the fissure below running up toward them. Everyone took a breath. Several Anakim were just yards behind as well.

Just then Ishbi appeared. He was up above. Dropping down from the surface, he landed almost on top of Dan. Ishbi's right hand and sharp fingernails sliced through Dan's shoulder, dragging him down. The two tumbled. Ishbi righted himself and shoved Dan into the earthen wall of the chasm. They were face to face for an instant. Ishbi's dark eyes were glassy and soulless, completely black, devoid of any shading between pupil and iris. He swung his knife and sliced into the edge of Dan's back. It felt as though a scraping hand had reached into his flesh.

Ishbi centered his knife and was about to plunge squarely into Dan's heart.

Sal raised his Uzi and fired.

The first bullets startled Ishbi more than they wounded him. The warrior snarled at Sal, who fired again, strafing Ishbi's body. Ishbi fell to the ground, bleeding and, at least for the moment, disabled.

Dan looked with amazement at Sal's shooting. Sal remarked, "Mass, velocity, and trajectory."

One of the small sinkholes opened nearby. Dan, Sal, and Park dropped through just before Anakim arrived from both sides. The sinkhole, too narrow for the giants, led to one of ancient Megiddo's man-made tunnels. Though dark where they entered, moonlight could be seen at the far end. The three sprinted toward it, Dan ignoring his painful and bleeding shoulder and back.

The tunnel emptied into a shallow natural cave which opened onto the Plain of Megiddo.

They wandered yards into the mist-engulfed valley clearing. A wind gust dispersed the fog somewhat, revealing a long linear structure. Now it came completely into view: the school bus. Hinnom regally stepped out of its accordion doors, waving his hand for the Anakim within to pause. Linzer stepped into sight as well. Nekrish moved to the front of a column of warriors that stopped behind Linzer. Ishbi staggered in, bleeding, with a length of fabric stuffed into the bullet wound in his leg even as other holes oozed grisly fluids. Dozens of regrouped Anakim had now formed a semicircle.

Dan, Park, and Sal were surrounded.

Suddenly motors could be heard off to the left. It was a squadron of

UH-60 Blackhawk helicopters ferrying Amnon's commandos. Their skid-ding black bellies righted to allow the soldiers to rappel. Army trucks sped in from the highway, screeching into positions not far from the landing zone. The older fighters, with cleanly pressed shirts, jumped out, their gun belts and D-rings jingling, occasionally adjusting their berets as they hit the ground. Searchlights and light batteries sizzled on, illuminating the entire area as though a new sun in new heavens had come to a new earth. The fearsome noise from the air and the land was the Army of God fore-told by the War Scroll.

Momentarily blinded as they looked directly into the searchlights, the Anakim rubbed their eyes and whirled about furiously. Some roared. Others waved threatening fists.

The commandos, wearing full flak attire, formed seven lines and faced the Anakim, just as the War Scroll required. The Anakim fired their Uzis, mainly spraying the air with wild fire. Very few of the commandos took bullets.

Amnon from the rear called out on loudspeaker: "Hold all fire. Not yet, no matter what." The Anakim tried to reload their Uzis but fumbled with the clips. Linzer grabbed one of the guns from Nekrish and tried to slam a clip in. It wouldn't go no matter how many times he tried.

The military rabbis, dressed not in their traditional uniforms, but in flowing white linens, jumped atop the hoods of the army trucks. They lift-ed their shofarot, each bearing a label, such as *The Rule of God, The Princes of God, The Called of God, The Tribes of God* and *The Army of God.* Each label was mandated by the War Scroll to be affixed to horns, shields, and weapons during the Final Battle.

The rabbis ritually raised their horns and blew long shattering blasts. The Anakim winced at the piercing *tekiahs,* which could be heard above the thunderous din of the helicopter engines. Sensing the coming battle, Hinnom and Linzer sought refuge in the school bus.

Amnon called out to his force: "Put aside your guns." The commandos, in crackling unison, as though they had drilled for weeks to become one fighting machine, swung their guns over their shoulders and onto their backs.

Amnon called out: "The pouches! *Hevre,* the pouches."

One hundred commandos in seven rows flipped open the leather cov-erings and pulled out slingshots. Each slingshot also bore the labels specified by the War Scroll: *The Rule of God, The Princes of God, The Called of God, The Tribes of God* and *The Army of God.*

Amnon called, "Stones." They inserted stones into their slingshots.

Amnon yelled, "Prepare." Synchronous fanning ensued, a whooping sound, like a mighty angel fluttering massive wings.

Amnon screamed, "Release!"

One hundred stones flew through the air, whistling as they soared. Dozens of thuds could be heard as the weights pelted the Anakim, breaking bones, bashing heads. The Yami commando, wounded and bleeding from a bullet in the leg, called out at the top of his voice, "Smite them hip and thigh!"

But only a handful of Anakim had fallen.

Amnon glanced furtively for less than a second, and then yelled, "Onnnnnce more!"

The commandos loaded a second set and waited for the signal. Old-timers began to chant the biblical plea, Judaism's most potent prayer: *Sh'ma Yisrael, Adonai Eloheynu, Adonai Ehad.*

Dan's eyes welled with tears as he clenched his fists and repeated in English. *Hear O' Israel, the Lord is our God, the Lord is One.* Park and Sal repeated the words silently, their lips trembling.

Amnon hollered, "Reeeee-lease!"

Another bombardment of stones whistled through the air. The second volley was more accurate. Every one hit a giant. Amid roars of rage and wounding, their bodies one by one crashed to the ground.

None were left standing save Nekrish and Ishbi. They staggered to the side of bus, reeling from their injuries. Slowly they lifted themselves upright. Nekrish wiped the blood away from his forehead and exchanged glances with Ishbi. Turning toward the bus, they saw Hinnom bring his fists together defiantly.

Without warning, Nekrish and Ishbi mustered new strength. Before any commandos could react, they leapt toward one of the rabbis atop an army truck hood. As Ishbi held him down, Nekrish seized the thin end of the chaplain's shofar, and dug it deep into the rabbi's chest. Withdrawing it, he broke the dripping horn in half, giving the other end to Ishbi. Yelling war cries, both of them then raced toward Dan, Sal, and Park.

The commandos loaded up another volley of stones.

Dan fingered the trigger guard on his Uzi.

Sal began calculating trajectory for his own weapon, lined up the targets in the sight, and mechanically shifted the muzzle an inch to the left, then once slight to the right. Park moved behind them.

As Nekrish and Ishbi drew closer, the angles became all wrong. The commandos could not launch their slings without hitting Dan, Park, and Sal. The huffing Anakim racing toward Dan seemed unstoppable.

"Bullets don't work on these guys," said Dan, anxiously pressing onto the trigger guard. "They only slow them down."

Amnon stepped laterally, pulling out a sling from his own pouch. He loaded two stones and began whirring. Faster. Faster. Until the whooshing became shrill. Amnon closed his eyes and released.

The stones flew horizontally, generating their own whistle, striking both Nekrish and Ishbi in the right temple. The giants broke their gallop, stumbled, then wobbled. Finally, in a final lurch, they fell dead in a dusty heap, yards from Dan.

Amnon walked cautiously to their bodies. They were motionless. He circled the corpses suspiciously once, lifted Nekrish's head by the hair, dropped the lifeless mass, and then did the same with Ishbi. "I believe in miracles," Amnon said quietly. Then he loudly proclaimed, "I believe in miracles."

Dan flipped the safety back on his Uzi. Sal saw Dan's move and did the same to demonstrate he understood the weapon. Both looked at their watches. 11:39 P.M.

Hinnom and Linzer emerged from the bus. Hinnom raised his hands high to show he was unarmed and addressed Amnon. "Whooops," he began almost comically. Stop. ". . . Things have . . ." Stop. Nothing was working in his mind. He started over two or three more times.

Finally he declared rather formally, "I am Ben Hinnom, founder and chairman of Hinnom Computing. As you probably know, I and my colleague have been taken hostage by these savage terrorists. The same people who stormed the prison. And . . . And," pointing to Sal, "those three over there are responsible. They control these Anakim killers.

"Now I have just a few minutes left to complete my work here," he sputtered. "In case you haven't noticed, everything will go *baaaang* unless I upload some codes at precisely midnight. Do you understand? Midnight!"

There was no reaction.

Linzer stepped forward, and announced, "Mr. Hinnom demands your response right now–this instant. World technology is depending upon it."

Amnon called out to his commandos, "Stones . . ." The men loaded another volley.

"Prepare . . ." The whooshing sounded like bursts of tornadic fury.

"Release!"

Scores of stones flew at Hinnom and Linzer, and their school bus. The bus windows shattered, the yellow exterior was punctured throughout and the gas tank was penetrated. Dozens of the projectiles pelted Hinnom and Linzer. A fireball burst from the bus. In another moment, the bus itself exploded into fragments, its tires spiralling off in spinning flames.

As the drifting fog passed, and the virulent smoke and flames blew to the side, the school bus was a destroyed, smoldering hulk. But standing erect were Hinnom and Linzer.

It was 11:49.

"The Upload," growled Linzer. Both men flipped open their Windies and began punching in code.

The ground trembled. It was about to swallow the helicopters and the trucks. Amnon herded his commandos aboard. One helicopter disappeared into an instant chasm, spraying blinding fuel explosions as it sank. The trucks dropped next, igniting in belches of flame. A number of old-timers fell into the flame as well. The younger commandos retreated to the other Blackhawks now hovering just feet above the rapidly crumbling ground. Frantically, they grabbed onto the wheels, runners, and drop ladders. When there was no more room on the runners and ladders, commandos grabbed for comrades already hanging. The helicopters pulled away, hauling dozens of fighters hanging onto each other's legs three and four men down.

Hinnom and Linzer were thrown by the tremorous earth into a nearby gully. Its bottom disintegrated into a muddy chute. The two slid down and were deposited in a lightless man-made tunnel under ancient Megiddo. Teeming with fat, oily worms and dripping with putrescence, the tunnel was part of a seemingly unfathomable maze.

"One never forgets the way," chirped Hinnom, as he and Linzer using small flashlights walked swiftly and directly fifteen paces to a triple fork. Right, then left, then back. They turned left once more and went nine paces, encountering steps precisely where they expected them, and then descended to what appeared to be a dead-end.

"It should be about here," said Linzer. He braced himself against the opposite wall and kicked. There was movement. Again. The large block began dislodging. Linzer and Hinnom both pushed until it fell away along with two other adjacent blocks. The opening was directly over the ancient altar to Baal at the very bottom of Tel Megiddo.

The altar, pieced together from stone and mud centuries ago, formed a perfectly round raised platform. It was built on the desecrated altars of countless other gods of the vanquished peoples of Megiddo. The structure lay at the bottom of a giant archeological excavation, in progress for years. Earthen walls surrounding it were at least fifty feet high, creating a massive pit, with the altar at its base.

Hinnom and Linzer squeezed through the kicked out opening and dropped six feet to the ground. As they landed, Hinnom could not help but run his fingers along the altar sides. Beveled spans, fluted edges, some chipped portions, crude in many places, but this was the place of so much of man's distracted devotion throughout the millennia. Jaunting up the crude steps to the altar top, Hinnom barked, "Okay, everything written. Nothing by accident!"

Now the densest fog of the night passed over the pit. Its surging clouds began seeping over down the sides and eventually swept onto the altar.

"Four minutes," said Linzer matter-of-factly through the mist, as Hinnom took a comfortable seat atop the altar.

"Four minutes," repeated back Hinnom. "I'm on it." Barely able to see, he continued punching his preliminary initializing protocol.

Just as suddenly, the fog subsided. Linzer looked up. His mouth dropped. Hinnom looked as well. Unbelieving and aghast, Hinnom said breathily, "It's not!"

Emerging from the dissipating clouds was Kuebitz, walking down the narrow, circular path from the surface above to the altar. The Downs were marching behind him. Softly he marshaled them: "Come along. It's good. Come along." All of the Downs wore T-shirts they had fingerpainted: "SONS OF LIGHT."

Hinnom froze, shook violently, and screamed, ". . . not . . . not . . . son-of-a-whoring-bitch bastards . . ." He was unable to utter anything further.

Kuebitz positioned some of the Downs on one flank and some along another. 'Everything will be fine," he reassured them. "Your place is here."

Linzer propped up his frozen master, pleading, "There is time. Three minutes. Three minutes!"

There was no response.

"Give me the code," yelled Linzer. "I'll do it. Let me do it."

Hinnom could not speak.

Kuebitz motioned the Downs to go closer. The frightened group approached, crying, "We can help. He is hurt. People are hurt."

Amnon appeared with several remaining commandos, including the chief Yami commando. The commando swiveled his Uzi and flipped the safety. Kuebitz held up his hand. Amnon acknowledged and the Yami commando stood down. The battle command had now clearly shifted from Amnon to Kuebitz.

"Very clever," yelled Linzer to Kuebitz. "These freaks are the only ones who can do your bidding. You know he is powerless around them."

Kuebitz answered, "Why, because they are completely incorruptible? Because they have absolutely no capacity for malice? Because they are the purest of the pure? Or is it that *A heart that melts shall be as a door of hope?* That's a door you can't get in."

"They're freaks, with their strange, twisted little 21st chromosome," Linzer bellowed.

Kuebitz replied, "You don't understand numbers."

Linzer roared back, "I don't understand your fascination for these decrepit ones."

"Whose image do you think they were made in?" Kuebitz replied. He then began a smile that started as an almost imperceptible movement of the lips and soon spread broadly across his visage, so broadly that his entire face seemed to become a smile. His eyes joined in the expression. So intense was Kuebitz' facial change that he almost seemed to transmogrify into a Down himself. Raymond noticed and glee burst across his countenance. "I love him," said Raymond. "He's like us."

Linzer tensed as his eyes opened wide in amazement, but shook it off, snapping, "I don't have time for this silliness." He grabbed Hinnom's Windy and started punching into files, trying to find the code. "What is the code!" he shouted at a speechless Hinnom. Linzer snarled at the Downs, "Get away." His voice reverberated as though echoing through a deep tunnel.

"You can come back," Linzer cried as he shook Hinnom.

Hinnom slowly formed words, "The code is . . ."

Linzer leaned closer, trying to hear.

"The code is . . ."

"Go ahead," yelled Linzer maniacally to the Downs, his arms spread wide. He laughed. "You can't kill him. Shoot some guns. Use your puny slingshots with your little white rocks. None of you has the *stone. The stone.*" Linzer turned to Kuebitz yelling, "You know that. You know nothing but *the stone* can harm him—and no one has it."

Just then Dan stepped forward with Sal and Park next to him. Their Uzis were gone. Still bleeding, standing off-kilter from the pain, Dan reached into his pocket, and held the object up high, "Would this one do?"

Linzer scowled and Hinnom's face seemed to melt into his bones.

But then Linzer's manner grew bizarrely calm. "Dan Levin, is it?" he began shakily. Fear had invaded Linzer's slick, corporate style. His voice lost its poise and at times wavered and cracked. Gone was the lordly tone. He sounded like a man on a precipice. "Dan, listen for just a little moment," Linzer said, trying to mask his shaking. "You, sir, owe me a lot and Mr. Hinnom as well. So I want you to put that stone down. You are right, that *is* a special stone, not just any old piece of camel-pissed rock. But you, Daniel Levin, *owe* us."

Dan did not reply, but the words struck him.

"Oh yes," said Linzer with extreme exaggeration. "We gave your dear old mom and dad a fish. You remember, when they were starving in the bad times. That's right, back in bad ole Poland. You were actually there, bouncing around as a few pathetic cells clumped together in the girl's womb. I see your memory is being jogged. Good. Good. You wouldn't be here, Dan Levin, if we didn't lend a hand. So now put the stone down."

Dan quivered with rage, but held the stone fast. Linzer tried a different approach. "Hey, Dan, how's Jenny and the boy? Sorry about the accident. Would you like them back? We can arrange that. Would you like them back? Put the stone down. We can talk about it."

Anguished, Dan looked up at Kuebitz. At first Dan saw nothing. Then, Kuebitz nodded whiteness. Dan's eyes blistered for a swirling moment as a streak of brilliance flashed directly before him and his hand felt heat. Tears bursting, he seemed to understand and managed the words, "Thank you."

Dan violently rushed Linzer and Hinnom with the precious stone in his palm. Linzer dropped Hinnom, grabbing Dan as he approached—one hand on Dan's throat, the other restraining the hand with the stone. Linzer squeezed Dan's hand until blood popped through the fingernails. Finally, Linzer reached into his back pocket, and pulled out a Derringer. Dan bashed the stone above Linzer's right ear, at the right temporal lobe. Linzer swooned, waving the gun. Dan hit him again. Harder, this time cracking Linzer's skull. Linzer pulled the trigger, shot Dan point-blank, and then fell to the ground.

Dan, contorting from the bullet in his chest, slumped to the ground.

Park went to him crying in anguish.

Linzer raised himself slightly, and aimed at Sal. Roaring, Linzer fell dead just as the gun was going off. The bullet struck Park instead. Her body toppled next to Dan's.

"Parrrrk," Dan shrieked, even as the life was spilling out of him.

Park held her burning midsection, and watched it seep through her fingers. Sal collapsed at her side trying to comfort her.

Kuebitz walked over to Dan and Park. Raymond was behind him. Anyone else using the stone would be merely acting out an act of human violence. But in the hands of a Down, the stone was a triumph of the innocent.

"Come, Raymond," said Kuebitz. "Pick up the stone."

Raymond smiled, "Can I help someone?"

"Hit 'em," gasped Dan. "Hit Hinnom—that guy there—in the head."

"I cannot do that. I love everybody," a confused Raymond answered back.

"Kill the bastard," Dan squealed back, looking at Park, and then back at Raymond. "He's bad. Bad. Very bad. Kill him!"

The time was 11:59. Hinnom now stirred. He moved his right hand over his Windy keypad to type in the initializing code.

Kuebitz stepped over to Raymond, and whispered.

Raymond cried, "I cannot. I love everyone."

Kuebitz whispered again. Forty seconds left. Hinnom typed a 6 . . .

. . . then another 6 . . .

. . . finally his finger dropped onto the 6 a third time to complete the code.

Hinnom then moved his pinky above the *Enter* button. His hand stalled as he tried to gather the strength to depress the key.

The evil one looked up and faced Kuebitz. Somehow Hinnom summoned the air to growl, "None of them deserve to exist. You know that."

Kuebitz responded, "No one destroys good grapes. You make wine."

Fading, Hinnom mustered one final question, "When will my father forgive *me*?"

Kuebitz turned his face from Hinnom and said, "What you have done is unforgivable."

Raymond uneasily moved closer to Hinnom, stone in hand. Not sure if he should smile or cry, Raymond lifted his arm and tried to bring the stone down on Linzer. But he couldn't. Dan raised himself, reeled over to the altar where Hinnom was, grabbed Raymond's hand and in one final burst of life, slammed Raymond's hand and the stone onto Hinnom's right temporal lobe. His head shattered like a smashed icicle into a dozen fragments. As it did, Hinnom's finger froze above the *Enter* key. He roared from within and fell limp.

No code was initialized.

Birds overhead swooped down over Linzer and Hinnom and began eating from their flesh as a steaming sulphurous pool bubbled up around them.

Dan, coughing fluids, squinted and saw his mother and father pass before him. He glanced at Kuebitz who said, "And now, Dan, you know. And you *know* that you know."

Sal shouted, "Midnight!" even as he tried to sooth his mother's pain.

"I tried," she said softly to Sal. "But I never understood. Maybe. . ." she moaned and gasped in pain, fading, ". . . maybe, uh . . . now I see . . . I see . . . you are a blessed boy." She tried to stroke her hand over Sal's head, but lacking the strength, her arm dropped back.

"Park," called out a weakened Dan, who now in his final moments faced her.

"It won't be here, Dan" she replied weakly. "Not here . . . There. Yes. We'll be together, but only *there*." A look of peace came upon her face as she breathily said, "Nothing by accident."

"Yes. There . . ." gasped Dan with his final breaths. "I love you, Park . . . here and now . . . and when we get *there* . . . Nothing by accident." Dan's voice trailed off as he expired.

Park saw his death, and gave in, joining him.

Sal rushed up to Kuebitz and demanded, as though talking to a parent, "I want them back."

Kuebitz nodded no.

"You can do it," shouted Sal. "You can do it. I was a cipher. A cipher— until they helped me break out of the dot of my existence. Mom gave me love even when I couldn't quantify it, didn't understand it. Bring her back. And bring back Dan. He was a wind—the only one I could face and fly with. Bring them back. You have the technology."

Kuebitz said, "You mean the *power.*"

"It's all the same," stammered Sal. "We both know that. Technology, power, divine force—it's all just a bunch of code words for one thing. Bring them back."

Kuebitz answered, "They can't come back. But you will be here. You can help man reach the stars, the furthest star, back to the pinpoint of creation. Take as much time as you need. Take a thousand years if you like."

Sal fell atop his mother and screamed to Kuebitz, "Bring them back. I can get the technology without you if you don't."

Kuebitz smiled, passed his finger atop Sal's head, and softly assured, "You won't. You know that. You're different from him," he said motioning to Hinnom's corpse beneath the feasting birds. Then Kuebitz walked off with the Downs majestically trailing behind him.

Sal wept, looked at his palms and touched them first to Park, and then Dan. But after a moment, he pulled away. They remained lifeless.

He looked around. Carnage and seething smoke plumes were visible in every direction. The afterstench of death and destruction stung his lungs. The flutter of birds and the lamentations of innocents in the distance rang in his ears. Sal slowly collected the two Windies from under Hinnom and Linzer and added them to his own.

In the distance, Kuebitz could be seen at the summit of the pit. He turned and waved. Sal watched in wonderment. From his perspective at the bottom near the altar, Sal saw Kuebitz' outstretched waving hand seem to touch the one star shining in the sky. It was just perspective, but as the star was momentarily obscured, Sal sensed a contact, a contact within. He stared up.

Rapidly the whiteness of the obscured star began to enlarge beyond Kuebitz' hand. Its brilliant sheen swirled furiously until throbbing whiteness reached across the entire dome of night. Soon black was no more over Megiddo. The powerful luminescence extended its glow and engulfed Sal in its strange, blinding radiance. This time–unlike the two prior times–Sal was not frozen. Running into the unfathomable layers of exquisite brilliance, he zigzagged and stumbled until he reached the steps leading up the pit surrounding the altar.

Frantically scrambling up the steps, using all fours as though blinded, feeling his way, hugging the interior wall, struggling and faltering, bumping his head repeatedly on stones he could not see but could only feel, Sal finally reached the top. Through the shine, only one object could be seen, the bright outline of Kuebitz at the top of a ridge.

From deep within the formless white, there came a sound. This time it was not some unidentifiable mystic noise of incalculable origin. It was Sal. Crying across the whiteness between himself and Kuebitz, arms outstretched and pleading, he beseeched one last time, "Bring them back! God, bring them back!"

Raymond, at Kuebitz' side, looked up and asked with a smile, "Were they good?"

Kuebitz stroked the smooth skin on Raymond's face and replied, "Yes, they were good."

"Then bring them back," chimed Raymond. "Bring them back." The other Downs became fascinated with the idea and they echoed the refrain. "Bring them back," they chanted delightfully. "Bring them back."

Sal, overcome and broken, collapsed to his knees, sank his head into the bloodied earth and repeated sorrowfully, "You have the technology. Bring them back."

When Sal raised his head and opened his eyes, he heard nothing. Kuebitz was gone. The Downs were gone. Sal was alone in the gleam. Then, as suddenly as it had exploded onto the sky, the whiteness receded back into the original star as though inhaled by an all-powerful breath.

Sal felt a hand on his shoulder and heard the words, "I need help."

It was Park. She dropped to the ground, holding her wounded torso. Sal tried to speak but his voice cracked in bewilderment and thanks. Finally, he exclaimed, "Mom!" He just kept jabbering "Mom" excitedly until he realized he needed to act.

He creaked open Hinnom's Windy. Its screen powered on with a startling flash. He brought up the email address book. Thousands and thousands of names loaded. He selected all the Israeli security and police addresses and broadcast a single message to them all. "Hinnom and Linzer are dead. The living need help. Come to Megiddo. Sal."

Sal turned to his mother who lay silently on the ground. His hands jittered in confusion, not knowing how to aid her. "Mom," Sal whimpered, "I emailed for help. Someone should be here. Someone should be here. Please hold on. Help is coming soon."

Just then a figure staggered across the dim landscape and weakly spoke. "I'll help."

Sal looked up speechless. It was Dan, his shirt wrapped tightly around his bloodstained chest, and a piece of reddened fabric over the bullet wound. Dan wilted next to Park, but in his weakened state lifted her head and spoke softly. Her eyes moved to meet his and a measure of peace came across her face. His lips touched hers not in a kiss, but in a commitment. Dan pressed down on her torso to help stem the bleeding.

"Someone pulled me up," said Dan. "I thought it was Yaacov . . . It couldn't be Yaacov." Park nodded and raised her finger in agreement. She had also thought she saw Yaacov.

"But it couldn't be Yaacov," said Dan in amazement.

"I'm hungry," Dan muttered weakly. "It couldn't have been Yaacov. I'm hungry."

Sal clenched his fist in hope, looked at the star and whispered to Kuebitz, "You have the technology. Thank you. For an eternity, thank you."

As they waited for help to arrive, Dan and Park spoke with their eyes and brought their fingers together.

∽

THAT NIGHT, AS expected, at exactly midnight, millions in the Jerusalem time zone initialized, typing Windgazer 99.9. But nothing happened. Without the code, the Point Nine Update was never initialized. All Windgazer systems crashed.

But one hundred thousand in the Jerusalem time zone did type *Format C:*. Their screens flashed a notice:

This will be a long install. Please be patient.
It will take longer than 24 hours.

As each time zone brought in the new millennium, the overwhelming majority of people, having heard of the Jerusalem events, typed *Format C:*. Those that did not saw their systems crash. But those that did all received the same message.

> **This will be a long install. Please be patient.**
> **It will take longer than 24 hours.**

Finally, after all time zones had had a chance to accept Format C:, the world saw a long licensing message flash upon all screens simultaneously. It read:

> **Derek welcomes you to the new Millennium. You have now installed the most powerful operating system ever created. Enjoy it. Use it wisely.**
>
> **Those who refused to reboot will have a second chance. The events of the past are completely forgotten.**
>
> **Please note: there will be a long refresh and diagnostic routine at sundown every Friday. It will take 24 hours. During this time, you will not be able to use your computer. Or any computer. Or any device which uses a computer. All computers in the world will refresh on Friday nights for 24 hours and be inoperable. Use that time to think, to slow down, to discover your families, and yourself.**
>
> **During the other six days, you may use your computers any time for any honest and kind purpose. The system will help you do anything you wish. Build houses and reside in them. Plant vineyards and enjoy the wine. Children will no longer die. You can live long like trees. One day you will even come to the furthest star, the unseen point at the very end of all sight and sound. You are welcome to do so.**
>
> **But do not misuse your system with lies or unkindness. Do not take or create life. Misuse will violate your license.**
>
> **If you agree to these terms, please press Enter.**

Throughout the world there was marvel and debate. Everyone who wanted their systems saved pressed the same key.

>Enter